TILL THE DAY GOES DOWN

Till the Day Goes Down

JUDITH LENNOX-SMITH

St. Martin's Press
New York

TILL THE DAY GOES DOWN. Copyright © 1991 by Judith Lennox-Smith. All rights
reserved. Printed in the United States of America. No part of this book may
be used or reproduced in any manner whatsoever without written permission
except in the case of brief quotations embodied in critical articles or reviews. For
information, address St. Martin's Press, 175 Fifth Avenue, New York, N.Y. 10010.

Library of Congress Cataloging-in-Publication Data

Lennox-Smith, Judith.
    Till the day goes down / Judith Lennox-Smith.
        p.   cm.
    ISBN 0-312-07096-9
    1. Great Britain—History—Elizabeth, 1558-1603—Fiction.
I. Title.
PR6062.E65T5   1992
823′.914—dc20   91-41551
                                                              CIP

First published in Great Britain by Hamish Hamilton Limited, a subsidiary of the
Penguin Group.

First U.S. Edition: April 1992
10 9 8 7 6 5 4 3 2 1

But will ye stay till the day goes down
Until the night comes o'er the ground
And I'll be the guide worth any twa
That may in Liddesdale be found.

Tho' dark the night as pick and tar
I'll lead you o'er yon hills full hie
And bring ye a' in safety back
If you'll be true and follow me.

(The Ballad of Hobie Noble – Anonymous)

THE estate of the Borders standing so tyckelye and daungerous as it nowe dothe, and of late there is great feudes and slawghters risen amonge the surnames of the Borders of Scotlande, which cawseth greate disobedience there.

(Sir John Forster to Sir Francis Walsingham – 3 May 1582)

TILL THE DAY GOES DOWN

Chapter One

'THEY'LL send us to Adderstone.'

Arbel Forster, seated on her mother's four-poster bed amid a tangle of clothing, keepsakes and letters, looked up as Christie entered the room.

Christie nodded, and shut the door behind her. 'To Northumberland. To your Aunt Margaret.' She walked to the window, watching the last of the guests straggle along the street, black cloaks and tall hats fighting the March wind. The Forsters' house, a tall, thin, half-timbered affair, leaned over the narrow street that wound around Salisbury's Poultry Cross. Christie straightened her own black gown. 'They've all gone now,' she said.

Arbel, pale hair falling over her face, let out a vast sigh of relief. 'Uncle Charles – I thought I would die. He *snorts* so. Even in church.'

'He has a rheum,' said Christie, knowledgeably, sitting on the edge of the bed beside Arbel.

Arbel frowned. 'I couldn't marry him, though, could I, Christie?'

There was, for the first time in a long, awful week, an echo of distress in Arbel's voice.

'Of course not,' said Christie, firmly.

The idea of lovely, delicate Arbel bedded with the gross Charles Webster was obscene.

There was a silence, broken only by the whine of the wind.

Anne Forster, Arbel's mother, had died four days previously, leaving the two girls and the servants alone in the house. The funeral, a feeble affair, had taken place that afternoon.

'Of course you couldn't marry Uncle Charles,' said Christie, beginning, like Arbel, to go through the pile of clutter on the bed. 'You'd have to go to church six times a week and never wear another bracelet or bangle. It wouldn't suit you at all, Arbel.'

Arbel giggled. 'And take canary wine with cousin Elinor . . . and bathe Uncle Charles's *feet* –'

'– in liquorice and honey,' said Christie, absently. 'Did you find anything, Arbel?'

Arbel's small hands lifted silks and beads, papers and samplers. 'Nothing. I found this, though.'

'This' was a lock of hair, once dark, now faded, tied with a red ribbon.

'My father's, do you think? Cut from his head as he lay bleeding on the threshold?'

The lock of hair was dropped carelessly to the floor.

Arbel, picking up the papers, crumpled them one by one and threw them in the direction of the fire.

'I was hoping for something –'

Christie found that she could not finish her sentence. I was hoping, she thought, miserably, for an explanation. An account. *In 1572 Christiane Girouard sailed to England on board the ship* – what was a suitable name for a ship? – the *Bonadventure*. Yes. *In 1572 Christiane Girouard sailed to England on board the ship* Bonadventure, *and lived happily with her adopted family in Salisbury for ten years. Her father's name was* . . .

But there was nothing to fill the gaps. The papers were bills, receipts, recipes, shopping lists. Arbel, sliding off the bed, dropped them one by one into the fire, watching the flames seize and devour the deckled edges of the paper. No explanations, then, only Adderstone, an immense unknown.

'Do you think your Aunt Margaret will mind?'

Arbel's grey eyes did not leave the fire. 'About you?' she said. 'Of course not. You must come with me, Christie. It wouldn't be the same without you. I remember mother saying that she was very fond of Aunt Margaret. Aunt Margaret's brother lives in a castle. Imagine!'

Aunt Margaret's brother was called Stephen Ridley. Aunt Margaret had once been a Ridley, but now she was a Forster, as Arbel's father had been, as Arbel herself was. Stephen

Ridley lived in a castle and the Forsters in a tower because of the proximity of Northumberland to the Scottish Border.

Arbel's small, perfect face was bright with excitement. 'They steal horses and sheep,' she said. 'From the Scots. Father died trying to get a horse back from Scotland.'

Christie, privately, thought it sounded silly and disorganized. She had always detested disorganization. It was she who had increasingly, as Anne's health had deteriorated, taken over the running of the Forster household. Not Arbel: Arbel was destined for something other than housekeeping.

'I'll come,' Christie said, watching Arbel. 'But I won't stay.'

Arbel turned at last. The fire was dying down and her eyes were unfocused and dreamy. 'Dear Christie,' she said, and dropped another piece of paper on to the flames.

IT had begun to rain by the evening: a cold, fine rain sucked from the grey North Sea.

Rain always seemed colder in Berwick. Berwick was perched on the easternmost edge of Northumberland, eyeing Scotland with an expression of unmistakable defiance. And Berwick had never been the cosiest of towns: alternately Scottish and English for centuries, the scene of burning, pillaging and massacres, it was, in 1582, Queen Elizabeth's strongest fortress, a necessary guard to the inconvenient postern gate to her kingdom that the Scottish border provided.

Towers and bastions guarded Berwick; so did the Queen's men: soldiers, over six hundred of them. Henry Carey, Lord Hunsdon, Warden of the English East March, was reputedly Queen Elizabeth's bastard cousin. Sir Henry Woodryngton, whose family had long known the Borders as a battleground, a treacherous board for a deadly, fascinating game, was Lord Hunsdon's deputy.

Sir Henry Woodryngton possessed his own players. One of them now endured the night in Berwick's busy harbour, his collar turned up in a futile attempt to keep water from trickling between doublet and shirt, his eyes fixed on the oily black plain of the sea. Malachi Ratsey was used to the cold and the wind and the rain. He had been, at various times in his forty-five

3

years, a baker, a dog-catcher, a pedlar, a pot-boy, and a cutpurse. For a variety of reasons he had been forced to abandon these employments: poor health, an unsuitable temperament, and a whipping through the streets had all made him think carefully about his future. He was small and quiet, not the sort of person to stand out in a crowd. The sort of person, in fact, who could melt into the stone walls of Berwick's quayside like lichen.

For Malachi Ratsey had found, at last, a role suited to both his attributes and his needs. Sir Henry Woodryngton, a percipient man, had realized that Malachi was determined and patient, that his hearing was as sharp as a hare's, and that his small dark eyes noticed everything. Malachi had a prodigious memory, so the fact that he could neither read nor write was rarely a hindrance.

Malachi enjoyed his work. He had haunted taverns and quays and back alleys in other lives, seeking out scraps of food, or a carelessly watched purse, or a fine silk handkerchief. Now he rooted out different kinds of leavings, leavings for which the gentleman his employer paid well. He had no need to cut purses or filch pies off window-sills, for he had money to spend at the ale-house or market-place. He could have bought himself a velvet cloak like any gentleman, but he kept to his broadcloth and his linen because he needed to be part of the shadows.

Malachi was at Berwick harbour because he had heard (a whisper in the darkness under the creaking, blistered sign of the Three Wheat Ears) about the merchant ship due in that night. The *Speedwell*'s master was a loyal and respected citizen, the *Speedwell*'s cargo nothing more than kegs of French wine, bales of Flanders cloth. But the whisper had mentioned that the master's son had gambling debts, and that the small galleon had taken an unconventional route along the French coast.

The *Speedwell* docked just after midnight. Malachi, chafing his hands in the shadow of the quayside, saw her masts and rigging like lace against the clouded moon. He drew back into the darkness as the ship approached the quay and the first rope was flung into outstretched, waiting hands.

You watched ten times, twenty times, and saw nothing. You

4

watched, and remembered every detail of everything you saw, because one day – weeks, months, years away – a single word or action might make sense of a larger pattern. You watched when you were cold and bored and hungry, because the reward was the squeeze of excitement in your stomach when you realized you had found something worth the waiting.

Tonight, Malachi could feel the excitement, like the rush of warmth after a glass of wine. The *Speedwell* was a sea-worthy, well-maintained vessel, newly painted and well armed, capable of making a man's fortune. The sort of vessel, in fact, that any man would be reluctant to part with. Malachi waited, his cold hands buried under the folds of his jacket, while they hauled the cloth and the wine on to the wharf. The harbour-master's man, yawning, counted barrels and bales, list in hand. The master and the pilot joked, their laughter almost dying before it reached the bulwark sheltering Malachi.

You watched ten times, twenty times, and saw nothing. As the men started to drift away to their wives or to the brothels in Berwick's back streets, Malachi began to feel cold. The lanterns bobbed along the quayside, doubling themselves in the glassy water, words and laughter ebbed away like meaningless seagull cries.

Still he watched.

Still there was (obstinately) the excitement in the pit of his stomach. Only his aching throat and cold feet told him that he had been wrong, that there was nothing for him here. The *Speedwell's* masts and furled sails were pasted against an uncompromising sky; Scotland, less than five miles distant, was lost in darkness. Malachi wiped the rain from his face with his hand, and then stopped, frozen into bas-relief by the sound of footsteps from the ship.

A flicker of movement in the blackness. Not all the sailors had left the *Speedwell*.

Malachi hoped he had made no sound. The gentle rain still muffled the rustle of his clothes and the scrape of boot on stone. He had almost made a mistake.

He saw the sailor cross the deck and jump the gunwale to the quayside.　　　*

IT also rained at Adderstone, fifteen miles from Berwick.

Adderstone Tower, perched like a carrion crow on a hill between Wooler and the coast, took the rain as steadfastly as it had taken Scots invaders, Scots and English raiders, and all the other adversities that a close proximity with a foreign (and frequently hostile) country might fling at it. Armies on their way to Otterburn, to Homildon Hill and to Flodden had marched past Adderstone. Adderstone's men, armed with swords and lances, bills and pitchforks, mustered for their sovereign when required, and fought for their country, harassing the enemy on small, neat-footed hill-ponies.

Adderstone manor house, built at the turn of the century, might have made some superficial concession to peacetime, but the adjoining tower's walls were fully six feet thick, its windows unwelcoming arrow-slits, its towerhead topped with the jagged, stubby fingers of crenellations. Elizabeth's England and James VI's Scotland might remain officially at peace, but try telling that to an Armstrong, an Elliot, a Scott, or a Kerr. Or to a Forster or to a Ridley, for that matter. The great riding surnames on both sides of the Border were the armies of occupation now, leaving their pele towers, their castles and their bastle houses at night to thieve someone else's sheep, cattle or horses.

There was a law of a sort – the law of hot trod and March treason – and government of a sort. The Lords Warden of the six Border Marches, three Scots and three English, were charged by their sovereigns with the uncomfortable task of keeping in check a people whose activities constantly bubbled only fractionally above the abyss of anarchy. The rest of England might know peace, albeit an increasingly uneasy peace, but the Borders nightly prepared themselves for war.

Now, in one of Adderstone's many draughty bedchambers, war of a different kind prevailed. Richard Forster and Janet, his bride of two months, were discussing the weather.

'Do you think I care if there was a tempest – or a whirlwind –' Janet's bony fingers curled purposefully round a pewter candlestick '– or an earthquake –'

'It was snowing a blizzard, Janet. You wouldn't expect me

to ride from Black Law to Adderstone when it was snowing a blizzard?'

'Oh, wouldn't I?' The candlestick soared through the air. Richard Forster ducked. 'I'd have expected you to ride through hell and damnation, Richie Forster, to save me from looking a fool in front of those twenty evil, clacking old biddies!'

Picking up pieces of candle and candlestick, Richie said soothingly, 'I'm sure Mother understood. And as for Mistress Selby and Susannah Grey – well, it was you they'd come to see, not me.'

Janet, five foot to her husband's six, her cheeks scarlet and her reddish hair escaping from its caul, folded her twitching hands in front of her, and said carefully, 'They'd been invited to congratulate the bride and groom, Richie. The bride *and groom*. Even if you'd not a civil word in your head to say to them, you could have passed them their biscuits and sack and canary wine. You could have stopped me having to repeat, *I expect he's been delayed*, until I felt like Susannah Grey's damned popinjay!'

Janet's small round black eyes sparkled. With anger, not with tears, thought Richie, ruefully. Janet was a Laidlaw of Liddesdale, and the Laidlaws and the Forsters had feuded intermittently for years, taking each others' beasts and belongings, spicing things, when they became dull, with the occasional murder or kidnapping. Richard Forster's marriage to Janet Laidlaw was an attempt by Richie's mother, Margaret, to heal the feud.

He tried again. 'I had business with Stephen. I thought I'd be back by the afternoon, but you know how it is when the weather turns –'

'You were seen in a tavern in Rothbury! Lettice Selby's servant saw you! With Rob –' Janet picked up the book that lay on the chest '– and some strumpet in pattens –'

'Nan was with Rob.' Richie moved hastily sideways. '*Not* the book, Janet – it was father's –'

Erasmus's *Colloquia* rebounded off Adderstone's stone walls and tumbled to the floor.

'And I've never been stared at so much in my entire life. I

swear Susannah Grey kept her eyes on my stomach the entire afternoon, the interfering old besom!'

Janet's stomach, under its layers of buckram and cramoisy, was as flat as her small boyish bust. Unwisely, Richie grinned.

'Well, we can soon do something about *that*, Janet,' he said, and glanced at the bed.

He forgot to duck, that time, and Janet's silver hairbrush struck him neatly on the temple.

Richie cursed.

Janet hissed, 'If you were at home more often, husband, then we might share a bed more often!'

Richie dabbed at his forehead with a handkerchief. 'I'd as soon share my bed with a –' he began, and then stopped as someone knocked at the door.

Rob, Richie's younger brother, opened the door. Rob was as dark as Richie, but his eyes were not Richie's grey, but true Ridley eyes, a dark indigo-blue fringed with black. All the Ridleys had dark blue eyes – except the bastard, of course.

'You've cut your forehead, Richie,' said Rob, innocently. And added, catching the expression on his brother's face, 'Mother wants to see you both. Now.'

Without waiting for his wife, Richie followed Rob out of the room.

MARGARET Forster had been a widow for five years. Unlike so many of his name, Richard Forster had died in his bed, cursing Laidlaws and Armstrongs to the end. The letter in Margaret's hand, which had taken a full month to travel the three hundred miles from Wiltshire to Northumberland, told of a more recent death. It would have been more sensible, thought Margaret impatiently, for some wretched Sibley to have delivered the news in person. Except there were, she reminded herself as she sat down in the parlour, no Sibleys left. Anne had been the last of her name.

Patience had been, for Margaret, a laboriously acquired attribute. Setting the letter aside, she picked up the sleeve she had been sewing and went back to work. The thin candlelight struggled to illuminate the plain linen cuff. Outside the wind might wreathe round the bare trees and unsown fields, but inside Adderstone's parlour there was only the roar of the fire and the gentle beating of the tapestries against the walls to show that it was still winter. Margaret threaded her needle and considered the follies of others.

She remembered her dead sister-in-law, Anne Forster, formerly Sibley. Anne had been foolish ever to come to the Borders. It would have been hard enough for any gentle southerner to accustom herself to Border life, but Anne's temperament had made it doubly difficult. Margaret had no doubt that the Borders had killed a part of Anne, just as they had also killed Anne's husband and Margaret's beloved elder brother, Davey Ridley. Just as they might, one day, kill any one of Margaret's three sons. Margaret had never permitted herself to watch for Richie, Rob or Mark, had never given in to the dangerous luxury of expressing her anxiety. Twelve years ago Anne had watched for hour after hour, her hands gripping the window's stone sill, her knuckles white. She had watched for her husband for a day and a night, long after any sensible woman would have known that something unspeakable had happened. Mark should never have married Anne Sibley, Margaret could have told him that, but she had not, because Mark was as pig-headed as all the Forsters, and would not have listened. And it had been every bit as unsuitable as Margaret had known it would be – five years, which had cost her both her husband and her looks, and Anne had returned to the Wiltshire she never should have left, with nothing but a fair-haired daisy of a daughter to show that she had once been a wife.

Margaret clicked her tongue in pity and disapproval, and pushed her needle into the cloth. When Anne had gone, taking her daughter Arbel with her, Margaret had been left at Adderstone with her own husband and three sons. She had never, like other women, longed for daughters. She had lost two daughters at birth, and mourned them, but had never missed the discussion of fashion and fripperies that some women seemed to find so important. She got on well enough with Janet, Richie's wife, seeing, perhaps, some poorly reflected echo of her younger self in Janet's small, stubborn frame. At the thought of Janet, and the sound of footsteps nearing the door, Margaret frowned, and pulled the thread more firmly. Adderstone's walls were not completely soundproof.

She noted, and ignored, the bruise on Richie's forehead, the red stain of anger on Janet's cheeks, the glint of amusement in Rob's eyes. Thankful that Mark, her youngest son, was asleep, Margaret Forster permitted herself the smallest of sighs, put aside her sewing, and picked up the letter.

'This arrived a half-hour past,' she said, when they had all sat down, Janet and Richie on opposite sides of the room, Rob in Adderstone's only box chair. 'Anne Forster died last month of the sweating sickness.' And seeing no comprehension on her eldest son's face, she added impatiently,

'Anne was your uncle Mark's wife, Richie – you remember.'

She had his attention at last. Richie frowned, his big hands pushing back untidy dark hair from his face.

'Father's brother . . .'

'I remember Anne,' said Rob, from the box chair. 'There was a daughter, wasn't there?'

Rob's face was hidden by the carved sides of the chair. In looks Rob reminded his mother of her elder brother Davey: in temperament he was his father's son. Not one of her sons, thought Margaret wistfully, was quite like Davey. Only Lucas, sometimes, unexpectedly recalled him in a fleeting expression or movement. Which was nonsense, of course, because Lucas and Davey shared none of the same blood.

'Anne had a daughter called Arbel,' said Margaret, firmly. 'For whom we must now make a home.'

Rob's face appeared round the side of the box chair: slightly slanting dark blue eyes, long mouth, narrow nose. Margaret's own features were built on sturdier lines: good looks, in the Ridleys, were the province only of the men.

'Here?' said Rob. 'Arbel is to come to Adderstone?'

'We have room enough for her. And we seem to be her only surviving relatives. This –' distastefully, Margaret glanced at the letter on her lap '– is from some brother-in-law of Anne's who plainly wants nothing to do with the child. She appears to have nowhere else to go.'

Richie, of an altogether easier disposition than his brother, had shaken off most of his bad humour.

'How old is Arbel now, mother?'

'She is seventeen.'

Margaret still retained a clear picture of Anne and Arbel as they had left for the south, so many years ago: the little girl laughing and wriggling, her nurse holding her hand; Anne distant and confused, giving poor answers to simple questions, inadequate responses to Margaret's well-meaning attempts at sisterly comfort.

'Of course she must come here,' said Richie. There was neither question nor resignation in his voice, and Margaret had not expected that there would be. He rose, and walked to the window, and Margaret touched his sleeve as he passed.

'There's something else, Richard. Anne brought up another girl with Arbel. To keep her company.'

'We're to provide a home for her as well?' Richie stopped in front of his mother, frowning. Even Janet's round bright eyes now studied Margaret instead of gazing straight-browed down at her bodice.

'She has nowhere else to go. She is illegitimate – of French origin, the letter says. Anne brought her up as a daughter – she has been given our name.' Unexpectedly, Margaret found that some of her irritation was directed at herself. 'I should have tried to keep in touch. Anne was my sister-in-law, after all.'

Richie took her hand. Unused to gestures of physical comfort, Margaret blinked and cleared her sight.

'I think we should take them both, Richie,' she said. 'They are of the same age, and it would be cruel to separate them after so long. Besides, this other child – Christie – would be a companion to Arbel. I really do not want a grown girl under my feet all day.'

'Let's have them both, Mother!' Rob rose from the chair to throw more logs on to the fire. 'After all, what house can hold too many seventeen-year-old girls?'

Margaret glanced at her second son sharply. There were rumours, all too credible, that dark-eyed babies wailed and puked in the villages and shielings. Just as they had when

Davey had been alive ... She set her mouth, a tall, imposing woman in crimson velvet, her greying hair contained in a complicated head-dress. Not beautiful as Anne Forster had once been beautiful, but with a dignity won by years of self-restraint.

Sending Janet to the kitchen for wine and biscuits, Margaret said, 'Stephen and Lucas must be told of Anne's death. One of you will ride to Black Law and Catcleugh tomorrow.'

'Lucas?' Rob again, staring wide-eyed across at her. 'Of what possible interest can Aunt Anne's death be to *Lucas*?'

Rob, the cleverest and most troublesome of Margaret's three sons, studied his mother with interest. Margaret's mouth set in an even thinner line.

'There is some sort of relationship, however distant. And it would not be right for Lucas to learn of Anne's death through common gossip.'

'Or through Stephen?'

Rob retreated back into the chair; Margaret's palm itched to strike him.

Janet returned with the wine. Margaret, refusing drink, turned her back on the three of them, and stared out of the window at the blackened sky.

And there, she thought, lay the greatest folly of them all: that Davey, who had sown his seed so liberally the entire length of the Marches, had not produced one legal heir. Not one son to bear his name, to inherit one whit of his charm. The grey stone of the windows blurred a little: how could she still miss her brother so much when he had been dead eight years? It was Anne's death that recalled it all, of course. All that was left of Margaret's family was Stephen Ridley, her other brother, at Black Law, and Lucas at Catcleugh, while Margaret struggled with the stupid, useless, deadening task of keeping the tatters of her husband's family in some sort of cohesion.

'Mother.' Richie, having finished the letter, touched her shoulder. 'Rob is right – Luke has no Ridley blood. And he has proved – surely – over and over again that he wants no more to do with your family. I dare say he'd use another name if he had one.'

'Lovell would do quite well, Richie, don't you think?' said Rob.

Margaret did not miss the answering flash of amusement in Richie's eyes. Not for the first time, she wished that they were still children, and that their father was alive, with a whip in his hand.

She tried again.

'Whatever name Lucas is or is not entitled to, he bears the name of Ridley. Davey brought him up, and Davey loved him as a son. I have no quarrel with Lucas, and I will not take part in someone else's quarrel. You will ride to Catcleugh tomorrow, Rob. No –' just in time, Margaret recalled the unholy alliance of earlier years '– *you* will go to Catcleugh, Richie, and tell Lucas of Anne Forster's death. You will also tell him that he will be welcome at Adderstone if he wishes to meet Arbel.'

'He won't be at Catcleugh.' Rob stretched out his long legs to the fire. 'He's terribly busy, is Luke.'

Margaret saw him glance at his brother again, and cried, exasperated, 'Even Lucas must employ a man to tend his horses, or a woman to cook his food!'

'To warm his bed, more like.' Both brothers laughed that time.

'You will ride to Catcleugh tomorrow evening, Richard.' Margaret's voice was like ice; even Rob shifted in his seat. 'I dare say Lucas possesses pen and paper, so you may *write* your message if he has no respectable servant for you to speak to. But you will go. And you, Rob –' rising, she addressed her younger son '– will go to Black Law.'

They did not argue with her then, any more than they had argued when they were children. But Margaret, leaving the room in a straight-backed whisper of velvet, felt unusually tired. Three sons, a new daughter-in-law, and a multitude of sheep, cattle and horses were enough for any woman, she thought. Soon, there would be two nieces as well.

THE rain had eased a little, allowing the swollen moon to show between the clouds. Malachi held back, hidden by a clump of trees, watching the man he had followed from the *Speedwell* tether his horse to one of the crumbling stone walls of the ruined tower. The building was roofless, the towerhead a rotting aureole of stone lit by the intermittent moonlight. But the lowest floor, although blackened by fire, looked intact, and a light showed in one of the undamaged windows.

They were in Scotland, now, somewhere in the fertile land of the Merse.

Malachi scrambled off his pony and looped the reins over a branch. There were at least two people in the ruined tower: the sailor (who was no sailor) and the man he had ridden to meet. The man who had lit a candle in the darkness, waited. But how many others also waited, perhaps in the open ground, perhaps inside the tower itself? Malachi shivered and hugged himself, and peered through the darkness, his rodent's eyes narrowed.

But he could hear nothing, see no one. The only movement was the wind in the grass, the trickle of rain on the black branches of the trees. Slowly, Malachi began to walk across the grass separating copse from tower, knowing that now he was at his most vulnerable. By the time he had reached safety, the muscles in the back of his neck had knotted with fear, and his breath was thick and hard. Clambering noiselessly up a pile of fallen masonry he looked through the window. The rain had blurred his sight: he had to rub his eyes before he could see anything through the gaping hole in the wooden floor. The floor had once divided the basement of the tower from the living quarters. The livestock would have sheltered in the basement when the tower was under attack from marauding English or unfriendly Scots. Now, the charred wood framed a candle. A rich cloak made a pool on the shattered remains of the stairs. There was a man there. Malachi knew he was a gentleman because the doublet he wore was of heavy quilted velvet, puffed and slashed at the sleeves. Fleetingly, he reminded Malachi of his master. He, too, wore fine clothes like that and sported a pointed beard like that. He, too, would be at ease in a hovel or a palace.

But the bearded gentleman was not, Malachi felt sure, the man he had followed from Berwick docks. He felt a pang of disappointment as he realized that his quarry was hidden under the shadow of the scorched wooden floor, and that, though he could hear his voice, he might never see his face. He could see the gentleman clearly: the single candle etched a beaked nose and hawk's profile against the darkness. But Malachi wanted to know whom he had followed through the wind and the rain from the quayside at Berwick. He wanted a face, if not a name, to take back to his master.

But even if he could not see, he could listen. The voices were funnelled up to him by the wind, clear sometimes, at other times almost drowned by the squally weather.

'These are – useful, my friend.' The gentleman held a package in his gloved hands. The seal was broken, the ribbon untied. Malachi could see writing on the paper, incomprehensible birds' footprints on new snow. What he would not have given to be able to read that writing ... what he would not have given to be able to present those papers to his master! He would have been a rich man, then.

The bearded gentleman added, 'You have done well, sir.'

A purse was tossed across the room.

'I hope you find the reward adequate. I trust we may continue to do business.'

'The master's name is Robert Dalgliesh and he makes frequent voyages to France. He has operated illegally already, so I'm sure he may be persuaded to do so again. If not, you could consider buying up his son's debts. I'm sure that would provide an incentive.'

The voice was light, pleasant, edged with amusement. Malachi, gripping the damp stone rim of the sill, wished more than ever he could see to whom it belonged.

There was a short pause, and then the bearded gentleman said, 'Do I take it that we will not meet again?'

'The experience has been most edifying, sir, but I do not think it would be of benefit to me to continue the relationship.'

The bearded gentleman wore a sword, a fine French sword. He smiled, but the smile did not touch his eyes. 'It might be of benefit to *me*, though. After all, such services as those you have provided are not easy to come by.'

'Oh, I doubt if you will have too much trouble. There are few honest trades in the Borders.'

The amusement had metamorphosed to scarcely concealed laughter. The gentleman rose, the candle's flame underlighting the bones of his face, the puffed silk of his doublet.

'But how can I be sure, sir,' he said, softly, 'that you will not sell me, just as you have sold others to me?'

Malachi heard a low chuckle in the darkness.

And then, in a tone of utmost reason, 'Well, you can't. You never could. But you have the letters, which appear to be genuine, and you are in Scotland. That is really all the security you can expect.'

'There are other kinds of security, my friend. I dare say it would be easy enough to fit a name to your face.'

'And what would you do with my name? Tell it to Sir Francis Walsingham?'

One of Malachi's boots slipped on the wet stone, and his heart hammered like a drum. When he had regained his breath and his equilibrium and edged the stone back into place with his toe, he heard the bearded man answer:

'Perhaps I would seek out its owner and ensure that he was no trouble to me in the future.'

A hand hovered round the hilt of the fine French sword, and the threat in the cultured voice was unmistakable. But the other, maddening voice was undisturbed:

'You're welcome to try. But assassins in the night are my trade. Your sword is no different from an Armstrong's or an Elliot's.'

'I would not soil my blade with your blood!' The gentleman rose, thrusting the papers inside his doublet. 'You deal with men of belief, yet you act solely from avarice. You would sell your Saviour for thirty pieces of silver!'

'And my mother for a serviceable horse. Doubtless. But I live quite well on the commissions of men of belief like yourself. And will continue to do so for some time, I expect. After all, you don't want to expose your beliefs to too much unpleasantness, do you?'

Malachi heard a sudden intake of breath, whistling up

through the gap in the floorboards. But the gentleman took his hand from his sword, and said,

'Then we have nothing more to say to each other. Good night, sir.'

Malachi watched as the gentleman left through the doorless gap on the far side of the tower.

Malachi could hear the sailor's horse cropping the wet grass. He did not have time to run for his own horse, but if he crouched low behind the pile of stones he should be unseen. He heard the second set of footsteps walking from the tower. He heard the horse trot across the grass. And he waited.

It was the shout that jerked him from his stillness. The '*Move*, you brute!', the thwack of a gloved palm on horse's hide, the sound of horse's hooves in the night.

His horse's hooves, *his* horse's hide.

Rob Forster was right. Lucas Ridley was not at Catcleugh.

The pele house perched on a long sloping summit of the Cheviots, about five miles to the south-west of Kirknewton. If you stood on the crest of the hill and let fly an arrow, it would like as not fall on the wrong side of the Border. Luke had always been rather good at firing arrows . . .

Catcleugh was straggling and stone-built, patches of moss crawling up its walls like shadows. Like many other pele-houses and bastle-houses, it was built to a simple pattern: a byre at ground level to shelter the stock, living quarters on the first floor, and a small, wooden-built platform overhead, to provide a little privacy at night.

Fleetingly, as he dismounted and looped his reins around a branch, Richie wondered what it had been like for Lucas, leaving somewhere like Black Law to live at Catcleugh. But empathy had never been Richie's strong suit, and besides, Luke didn't seem to mind. Anyway, there was no house big enough to hold both Luke and Stephen Ridley.

It was cold, a mist still hung over the streams and valleys, shading the ridged hills with grey. There was a silence about Catcleugh, the silence of the vast, difficult range of the Cheviots. A silence often broken, Richie knew, by the thud of horses' hooves in the night, the whirr of a lance through the damp air. Richie rode – all the Forsters rode – because their surname was one of the greatest on the English side of the Border. Luke rode because Luke liked to drink and wench and have a stableful of fine horses. And because, thought Richie, Luke enjoyed riding.

The house looked deserted, the two small windows blank and cold. The door was on the first floor, up a flight of stone steps. Richie hammered on the door with his fist, half expecting to hear nothing more than the distant cry of the kestrel, the gentle wind soughing through the scrubby grass. But there was a sound, a muffled voice, a shuffling step, and the door opened.

She was a black-haired slattern of eighteen or so, one dirty hand still rubbing the sleep from her eyes. A Jenny or a Peg or a Moll from the nearby village, thought Richie, trying not to look down to where her nicely rounded breasts swayed, barely covered. She wore a blue woollen skirt, and a man's shirt knotted carelessly around her waist. Luke's shirt, realized Richie, and he thought of Janet, who had bones where she should have had flesh. Momentarily, Richie envied Luke Ridley.

But he recalled his errand, and said, keeping his eyes fixed on her broad, sun-tanned face, 'Good-day, mistress. Is Luke in?'

The girl shook her head and moved away from Richie with a swirl of dirty blue cloth. 'Naw. He went out a wee while ago. To Rothbury – or Hexham. Or Berwick.'

'On his own?' asked Richie, delicately, and the girl turned, so that the thin sunlight washed all the planes of her body with gold.

'Aye. But the gypsy's still here, if you want him. Upstairs.'

Richie was silenced for a moment, considering all the fascinating, illicit possibilities conjured by the single word *upstairs*. Randal Lovell, *upstairs* (in Luke's bed?), this girl with Luke's shirt knotted round her bare breasts. And when Luke came home –?

'Snoring like an old sow,' the girl added. 'He's an idle devil. But I'll wake him if you want.'

'No.' Richie had no liking for Randal Lovell, who spoke too

18

little and smiled too much. 'No. But perhaps you could take a message for me, Mistress –?' He dragged his gaze upwards again, and smiled.

'Mariota. Aye, I'll give Luke a message for you.' She moved a little closer; Richie was sure he could see the tip of a rosy nipple beneath the white holland. 'Or you could wait for him.'

Mariota's dark eyes met Richie's grey ones. She had the same colouring as the gypsy, thought Richie, dazed. But her arms and breasts looked soft and yielding, dusted with a thousand tiny golden freckles, and her skin was the close, fine texture of satin. But there was Lovell upstairs, and Luke God-knows-where, and Janet at Adderstone. Duty overcame desire, and Richie, his mouth slightly dry, said,

'I'll leave a note.'

STEPHEN Ridley was in the withdrawing-room when Rob, having ridden the fifteen miles from Adderstone to Black Law, was announced. Black Law's withdrawing-room, with its painted ceiling and linenfold panelling, was the envy of many a lesser landowner. Rob, throwing cloak and gloves on to Stephen's smoothly polished table, noticed neither the Creation nor the swathes of pleated wood that framed it, but only grinned, and said,

'I'm here as a bearer of good tidings, Stephen. Adderstone is to be blessed with the arrival of two delightful seventeen-year-old girls.'

And when Stephen, raising one fair eyebrow, looked up, Rob added,

'Aunt Anne has died – Uncle Mark's widow. Thus the girls. And they will be delightful because all seventeen-year-old girls are delightful. Don't you agree, Stephen?'

Stephen put down the pen with which he had been writing, and permitted himself the smallest of frowns. Thirty-two years old, golden-haired and indigo-eyed, Stephen had owned Black Law and all its lands since his elder brother Davey had died eight years previously.

He said, 'Anne Forster had one daughter, Rob, not two.'

'Anne Forster,' said Rob, ecstatically, helping himself to

wine from the flask on the table, 'adopted a child as a companion to Arbel. Her name's Christie, and she's someone's by-blow. Nowhere else to go, so mother said she was to come to Adderstone too. She's French, I think – or Italian –' Rob perched on the edge of the table '– though she's used our name for years. So they're both Forsters.'

There was a small silence, and then Stephen picked up the pen again.

'I should make sure to keep it that way,' he said as he signed the letter and sprinkled sand over the paper. 'It will be better for her to bear your name. Illegitimacy is a slur in itself, but a foreign name would only make life more difficult for her. And remember' – Stephen leaned back in his chair – 'if she is French, then France is a country that has generally aligned with the Scots rather than the English. No, let the girl remain English, and a Forster. It will be easier for her.'

The light from Black Law's high mullioned windows spilled on to Stephen's golden hair, braiding the rich fabric of his doublet.

Rob shrugged. 'Very well. It is of no consequence.' He poured wine into a second glass. 'Richie and I have to meet the girls next month at Hexham.'

Stephen took the glass that Rob held out to him. 'Tell me when you go,' he said. 'I'll ride with you. I look forward to meeting Arbel Forster.'

'And I,' said Rob, happily. 'Aunt Anne was a beauty by all accounts. Let's hope her daugher takes after her.'

Rob's glass touched Stephen's. 'To Arbel,' he said.

'To Arbel,' said Stephen, and smiled at last.

THAT night, Sir Henry Woodryngton, the Deputy Governor of Berwick, wrote a letter to Sir Francis Walsingham, Queen Elizabeth's Secretary of State.

Sir, he began, *I have tonight received information which may be of interest to you* . . .

Chapter Two

*I*T was raining when Arbel and Christie Forster rode into Hexham three weeks later. Rain hazed Hexham Abbey to an amorphous grey blob, rain seized straw and vegetable peelings and small drowned creatures and dumped them in the gutters, damming the flow so that viscous puddles glazed the width of the streets. Rain misted the afternoon sky to twilight and trickled from the bare-branched trees, drowning the optimism of daffodil and crocus.

Christie Forster was unimpressed with Northumberland. She had been unimpressed with much of the England she had seen since Salisbury's broad chalk plain had faded into the past. Oxford, York, a myriad hamlets, villages and towns: Christie had seen and noted them all with sensible, dispassionate brown eyes, appreciating the mechanics of travel, if not the scenery. Post-horses, toll-gates, inns – some decent, others utterly dreadful – tumbledown bridges and ill-repaired roads, had taken Arbel and Christie, their uncle Charles, and a collection of cursing, complaining servants, delivering them, tired and wet, to the unknown, savage north. At least in Salisbury, thought Christie, as her horse stepped fastidiously through the flooded roadways of Hexham, the sun had sometimes shone, and the meandering valleys of Avon and Nadder had given shelter against the wind. Hexham gathered the wind and funnelled it through narrow streets, so that it pulled and tugged at cloaks and skirts. Rain streamed down the distant Cheviots and along the great swathes of the Roman Wall. Christie sneezed.

Not that Christie, who took what Fate allotted her with apparent acceptance, and meanwhile made her own plans behind Fate's back, intended to stay in Northumberland for long. Long enough to find Arbel a creditable husband, long enough to gather the means to travel again. Christie would stay and see Arbel happily settled, because Arbel lacked what Christie possessed in abundance: common sense. Arbel would take off with a tinker if he had blue eyes and a way with women, and only regret her decision when her shoes were holed and her belly was empty. Christie would help Arbel find a kind, gentle, wealthy man, who would love her for what she was, and not learn to hate her for what she was not. If there were kind, gentle, wealthy men in Northumberland, then they would want Arbel. Every man wanted Arbel.

Money, thought Christie with a sigh as a manservant stopped to ask for directions, would prove a far greater problem. Money always was a problem if you were illegitimate and landless. If you were foolish enough to have been born a girl as well, then the problem seemed almost insuperable. Girls became wealthy by marrying rich men or inheriting from their fathers. Lacking both a father and a dowry, Christie had long accepted the improbability of marrying a rich man. A man could win money at dice or cards, or with a fast horse: despite the rain, Christie smiled at the thought of herself, crouched in some dark tavern, winning a fortune at the turn of a card. Christie's fortune, Christie's dowry, consisted of a ring of her mother's, and a chain that had belonged to Anne Forster. She would not sell the ring because it was all she possessed of her own family, and the chain, Christie strongly suspected, was counterfeit. Glass, not rubies, in an ancient setting, a relic of Anne's own hard times.

They had found the inn, the Golden Fleece, its brightly painted sign reduced to clanking obscurity by the weather.

'They're here!' hissed Arbel, catching sight of a blue-liveried servant in the courtyard. Christie's stomach contracted a little.

The ostlers took the horses, and the servants began to unload the baggage. Christie, entering the tavern behind Charles Webster and Arbel, regretted briefly that she must appear for the first time in front of the Forsters looking like a half-drowned dog. Still, she thought philosophically, if, as planned, the two elder Forster brothers had come to meet them, then they would not look long at her. They would look at Arbel.

22

But there were, Christie found when the innkeeper opened the parlour door, three, not two, men rising to greet them. Two dark, one golden-haired.

THE Forsters were dark, their uncle Stephen Ridley golden-haired. Stephen Ridley was, Christie recalled, Margaret Forster's younger brother. Christie, lacking a family of her own, studied the families of others.

The elder Forster was called Richie, and the younger one was Rob. When Uncle Charles drew Arbel forward and she let fall the hood that covered her loose fair hair, Rob and Richie made the accustomed sudden transition from men of sense into gawping fools. Rain and exhaustion only improved Arbel, twisting her hair into delightful tendrils that framed her face, bestowing on her pale skin and grey eyes an expression of heartbreaking fragility. Arbel's skirts had somehow escaped the inches of mud that hemmed Christie's gown; black velvet did not dim Arbel's beauty, but merely transformed her into some ethereal mourning ghost, the unobtainable enchantress of a fairy tale.

Stephen Ridley was taller and older than the Forsters, fair-haired and good-looking, his clothes – dark blue doublet and hose, plumed hat – better than his nephews'.

There was a good deal of bowing and curtseying and, as everyone recovered the use of their tongues, polite expressions of greeting. Christie watched, enjoying it all, making in turn her own curtsey to the Forsters. Their welcome lay, she thought as she assessed both grey eyes and blue, in the category of indifference. A generous, friendly indifference, but indifference none the less.

'And this', said Arbel, seizing Christie's hand and presenting her to Stephen, 'is my dear, dear sister Christie.'

For the third time Christie curtseyed and bowed her head. But when, again, she looked up, it was as though the rain and the wind had begun anew, here, inside the Golden Fleece's warm parlour.

Not indifference, this time. Nor pretended affection, nor even puritanical assumption of inherited sin.

23

None of those. Just a cold, knowing hatred.

THERE were two taverns in Rothbury, twenty miles north of Hexham: the Angel and the Green Man.

No riotous taint of the pagan clung to the Green Man: quiet, proper, warm and welcoming, it took the travellers from the inadequate roads, fed them, warmed them, and bedded them, and sent them back on their journey with a suspicion that the north was not quite so bad, after all.

The Angel, on the other hand, was not for the angelic. The proprietor of the Angel, who went by the name of Clem the King, served strong ale and kept a knife in his belt and a cudgel close to hand. Clem was not averse to a fight: no, in the street or in the hills he'd be as happy as anyone to use his fists for what they were made for, and his guile to find a good fat sheep. But inside the Angel it was different: he'd had some glass put in the front windows, which had cost good money.

Clem expected a fight because Luke Ridley and his particular band of devils had ridden in from Catcleugh in the early evening with ale and women in mind. Clem, unlike some others, had no objection to Luke. It was the windows that worried him.

Just now, Luke was nowhere to be seen. The taproom was a haze of smoke from the badly draughted chimney, a seething, swimming, chanting collection of bodies. But Clem would have found Luke, had he been there, because Luke was always in the centre of things, even if he did no more than orchestrate the mayhem with a flicker of his light blue eyes. Dand's Jock was there, and Red Archie, and Willie Graham, all roaring for Mouse, the potboy, to refill their cups. And the gypsy, Randal Lovell, who rode a better horse than the Warden himself, and whose small clever hands could cut a heavy purse as easily as Clem could draw a quart of ale. Clem kept his money inside his leather shirt, but when the gypsy was there he would find that his hand often went to his purse, checking the weight against his sweating barrel chest. Some said that Luke Ridley and the gypsy were cousins, or even half-brothers, and Clem, who was anything but credulous, was inclined to believe them. Except

24

that Lovell's tangled curling hair was as black as sea-coal, and his eyes had the dark liquid depths of the most silent of murder holes.

You might have said that Randal Lovell was Luke's shadow, if the gypsy had not possessed a bearing and a pride which made him no man's shadow. But he was always there, small and silent, leaning against the Angel's dirty plaster wall, cards fluttering from one hand to the other in waterfall patterns. Clem kept one watchful eye on Randal as he drew more ale for the tankards on Mouse's tray. Randal was smiling: Clem distrusted Randal's smile just as much as he distrusted Luke's eyes.

He saw the gypsy stoop and whisper something in Willie Graham's ear. Willie Graham had sparse, frizzed clumps of dun-coloured hair, and the loudest mouth in Northumberland. Willie's watery grey eyes travelled once around the crowded room, and then he thumped his fist on the table, and bawled,

'Luke! Luke Ridley – where are you, you bastard?'

Which wasn't an epithet Clem would have necessarily chosen for Luke – unless he had wanted to provoke him, that is. Clem felt once for the knife in his belt, and once for the money in his shirt, and gave Mouse a shove to speed him on his way. Then he stood beside the barrels of ale, watching the front and back doors. And the windows, especially the windows.

Randal Lovell still leaned against the wall. Willie Graham gazed around the taproom in drunken discontent. His two huge fists crashed down on the table once more, and he howled like a she-wolf,

'Ridley! We had a wager, you bastard!'

Clem found that he had winced. And this time the rear door opened slowly, and there was Luke, blurred Beelzebub-like in blue smoke.

It was easy enough for Clem (or anyone else) to guess what Lucas Ridley had been doing. His shirt and his leather jack were unlaced, his silky fair hair untidy. A priest might not have approved, but Clem did not complain. It might have put him in a better frame of mind.

It might have, but Clem suspected it hadn't.

25

'You were shouting,' said Luke, still in the doorway. 'Were you shouting for me, Willie?'

The soft voice only just reached Clem, by the beer barrels. He saw Willie Graham adjust his huge frame, and redirect his gaze towards the doorway.

'Aye,' he said, in no softer tones than before. 'That's right. Bastard.'

Luke's smile, which Clem distrusted just as much as he distrusted Randal's, grew broader. In no hurry, Luke left the doorway and wound his way through the tables and benches, past the delighted, expectant faces of his own men, past the more doubtful faces of those who had come to the Angel just for a drink, or to pass a cold spring evening.

Clem had the cudgel in one hand and the knife in the other by the time Luke Ridley reached Willie Graham. Willie was taller than Luke, and a good ten years older. But Luke had lived on nothing at Catcleugh for five years now: no, not on nothing, on other peoples' sheep and cattle and horses. And calivers and gunpowder . . .

Graham was on his feet, one thick finger prodding Ridley's uncovered chest.

'We had a wager, Luke –'

Mouse had moved to a far corner of the room, his tray cluttered with empty tankards. Luke still smiled, but the smile had not reached his eyes. They were the colour of a clear sky on the coldest, most wintry of mornings.

'I remember the wager. But you called me something, Willie. What was it?'

Willie Graham was not a man to back down from a quarrel. Clem balanced the weight of the cudgel but did not yet move forward. The constable was a fool, and the Warden's men were in Hexham . . .

'Bastard.' Willie Graham's wind-burnt face split into a grin. 'I called you a bastard.'

Mouse, in the corner, quivered. You could hear only the sound of flames licking the logs, and see the light of the tallow candles, reflected as two bright dots in Luke Ridley's sky-blue eyes. Luke's hands moved towards Willie Graham.

'Bastard . . . Well, then, I can hardly find fault with that, can I, Willie?'

And he took the reddened, weather-beaten face between both his palms and kissed it audibly, once on each cheek.

Someone began to laugh, and the gypsy, splicing and shuffling the tarots in mid-air, spat into the rushes.

In the end, it was neither tarot nor primero they played. Luke had a better wager: a bottle of aqua vitae, matching each other gill for gill. Clem did not object, because he thought that one or both of them might drink themselves to insensibility. And besides, there was the money for the aqua vitae.

The tavern had emptied a little by the time they had almost drained the bottle dry. Rothbury's more sober citizens had gone home with a good story to tell their wives, and those that stayed clustered round one wooden table. Peggy, who had a missing front tooth and a bosom that spilled out of her buckram bodice, leaned over the table, one plump hand on her hip, the other on Luke Ridley's shoulder. Even Mouse had crept out of the corner, and stood next to Red Archie, his eyes bright with excitement.

It was Willie Graham's turn: he balanced the bottle and poured, but the liquid planed over the lip of the cup, trailing across the scuffed and scarred table, to fall, drip, drip, drip, on to the floor below.

'Damned stuff won't stay in the cup,' Willie said, belligerently. 'Clem's sold us damned poxy stuff that won't stay in the cup –'

'Then stick the bottle in your gob, and be done with it,' said Dand's Jock. He rammed the bottle between Willie's uneven teeth. 'God knows, it's big enough –'

Willie's eyes distended as he swallowed. Aqua vitae ran down his chin: he wiped it away with the back of his hand and set the bottle down, rather heavily, on the table. There was about an inch left, covering the thick dark base.

Luke took the bottle from the table.

'To our Queen – our country – and to many moonless nights,' he said and, leaning back on the bench, threw his head back, and drained the flask dry.

There was a roar of applause as he tossed the bottle in the air and someone caught it before it touched Clem's hard stone floor. Even Mouse joined in the shouting, his half-broken voice lost in the tumult. But Clem, who knew better, had the cudgel back in his hand, if not the knife.

Luke stood up. He was swaying only slightly. He gripped Willie Graham's broad shoulders, and hauled him to his feet.

'Another wager, Willie,' he said. 'On horseback, once round the town. Across the market-place, by the river and back down the High Street. Ending here, at our beloved Angel, with a tankard of ale for the winner.'

'Aye, to puke up on Clem's floor,' said some cynic. But Willie, pushed by Luke and cajoled by Peggy, had risen to his feet and was lumbering towards the door.

The gypsy had gone for the horses. Clem knew that because Lovell was no longer there, and the door banged open and shut, letting in the wind to stir up the smoke and scatter the rushes.

They erupted into the street: Luke's men, Mouse, Peggy (on Red Archie's arm) and Clem himself, with one last glance at the windows and one last reassuring touch to his purse. And Willie Graham and Luke Ridley, of course, Willie cursing the cold, crisp air, Luke's eyes bright in the torchlight.

The horses the gypsy led into the street were hobblers, small strong hackneys capable of taking the steep, stone-scattered Cheviots as well as Rothbury's slippery cobbles. Willie Graham had to be helped into the saddle. He slithered once to hang precariously over the other side, but they righted him so that he fell on the horse's neck, clutching the short mane with his fingers. The gypsy took the red scarf from his neck and held it high over his tangled head, so that the breeze caught and whirled it like a small scarlet banner. Candles had been lit in windows, faces peered out into the street, some disapproving, some amused.

The scarf fluttered for an instant, then plunged, drawn like a red feathered kestrel to the ground.

They were across the square and down the hill before Randal could knot the scarf round his neck and duck back into the crowd. The cold air had sobered them both a little, and besides, they had lived half their lives in the saddle. But the stones, still damp from the day's rain, and burdened with a haphazard collection of refuse and slops, were treacherous, and there was only the half-moon, nothing else, to pick out the potholes and the ruts.

Willie Graham had the edge of it to begin with. Level with Luke across the market-place, he elbowed his way first through the narrow alleyway. The stone walls of the houses crowded close; a careless move and an unprotected head would meet hard granite. The windows were dark and shuttered, and the cries of the market-place soon ebbed away to nothing. Here there was only the rough leather of the reins running through the palms of their hands, the white of the horses' eyes in the moonlight.

The alleyway spewed them out on to the riverbank, fringed with reeds, laced with streams and gullies. Willie Graham was shouting again: Luke could not make out what he said, though the word 'bastard' pounded through his head like a heartbeat. The trees were still unleaved, and the river thickened by heavy rain. The mist from the men's and the horses' mouths was like the smoke in Clem the King's taproom.

There was a place where the grassy bank shrank to only a few feet in width. Luke's eyes were narrowed, assessing the trail of mist, the flood of white moonlight on the water, the exact breadth of the riverbank. He was level with Willie before Willie, his head blurred by alcohol, realized what he intended to do. Luke's reins were in one hand, and the horses so close that their flanks almost touched. Then it was just a matter of leaning across, one arm at just the right angle, and toppling Willie Graham into the cold dark waters of the Coquet.

Luke heard the sound of Willie's large hands beating the water (but no shouting now) before he rode up the path towards the town. He had only the length of Rothbury's High Street to ride, and then he would be back at the Angel. He found that he was shaking slightly, and that he felt nauseated. It had been a complicated day.

But the complications were not yet over. As he turned into

the High Street Luke saw that the road was not, as he had expected, empty. A small band of travellers straddled across the cobbles, some servants, some women, all with the muddied, weary look of too long in the saddle. Oh, and Richard Forster of Adderstone.

And Stephen Ridley, Luke's cousin.

CHRISTIE could not see the horse, but she could hear unshod hooves on the cobbles. She could not see the rider until the moon and the rushlights outside the baker's shop illuminated him from the night.

He was hatless, jacketless, and very wet. She heard him say, 'Richie. And cousin Stephen. How delightful.'

Richie Forster did not look delighted. Richie, who was, Christie had decided, a fairly sensible man, inclined his head in the smallest of bows. 'Luke,' he said. And then, eventually, 'What brings you to Rothbury?'

'Business. Just business.' There was a loud hiccup, a burst of sound in the quiet night air.

Arbel, on Christie's other side, giggled.

The rider turned in the saddle so that the amber light of the flare caught his face, his head, the wet clinging folds of his shirt.

His fair hair lacked Stephen Ridley's gold, his eyes seemed to Christie to have no colour whatsoever. Shadows indented the cleft in his chin, the hollows under his cheekbones, the thin straight nose. He wore a short sword at his side, and a smile that slowly spread the width of his face.

'Cousin,' he said to Christie, and seized her hand and kissed it. And then, letting his gaze trail unsteadily to Arbel, 'No – *two* cousins. The Forsters are a prolific breed. Unlike the Ridleys.'

A swirl of a dark blue cloak, and Stephen Ridley had swung his horse round.

'Dear me, Lucas. I wouldn't have thought even you would attempt to claim cousinship with Miss Forster.'

Stephen's voice was as icy as the rain. Christie shivered – with exhaustion and cold, she told herself.

Luke hiccupped again. 'Miss Forster is my mother's cousin-in-law's husband's brother's child,' he said. 'Therefore we are cousins. Aren't we?' he added, looking again at Christie.

He swayed, and she thought for a moment he was going to kiss her hand a second time. But he contented himself with another glorious smile as Richie said wearily,

'Christie is not your cousin, Luke. Arbel is Mark's daughter.'

But Stephen Ridley's hand had already grasped Luke's shoulder, pulling him round so that he was almost unseated. Stephen's face was only a few inches from Luke's, but Christie could hear what he said. His words seemed to echo round the market-place, the town, the Cheviots themselves.

'Go back to your own kind, *cousin*. You stink of the tavern and the brothel.'

Lucas's hand did not reach, as Christie thought it might, for his sword. Instead he said, with obvious effort,

'Are you implying, Stephen, that I lack the address for company such as this?'

His words ran together, his wide, expansive gesture took in the Forsters, their servants, the mongrel hound rooting in the gutter.

Stephen said softly:

'Go back to Catcleugh, Lucas. *That* is your inheritance.'

Lucas's face, away from the flare, was paper-white, washed almost green by the moonlight. But when Stephen spurred his horse forward, his face a pattern of disgust, Christie realized it was not just the moon, and no longer only a hiccup.

She, too, put her heels to her horse's sides as Lucas Ridley vomited on to Rothbury's dark damp cobbles.

ARBEL began to laugh as they rode along Rothbury High Street: Christie saw her, trying to stifle her giggles, her head lost in the folds of her hood, only her shaking shoulders giving her away. For herself, Christie felt neither amusement nor revulsion, only a sting of annoyance. Lucas – and here even Christie could not sort out the ramifications of the relationship – had merely confirmed her initial impression of Northumberland: cold, wet, and decidedly unsubtle.

By the time they reached the tavern, Arbel had become calm again. Light lined the edge of the Green Man's shutters, and rimmed the wooden door. An ostler appeared to take the horses.

Arbel's hand crept into Christie's as they walked into the hallway. Arbel's face looked taut, the colour drained from her skin by the candles and rushlights.

In their chamber (clean, and with the fire already lit), Arbel's cloak tumbled to the floor and she spun round, her pale hair fanning out around her like a dove's tail.

'Did you see their faces, Christie?' Arbel's hands were clenched, her eyes bright. 'Richie's and Stephen's, I mean. I thought I would die!'

Christie stood in front of the fire. She felt grey with dirt, and her cold hands struggled to tidy her tangled hair. The flames of the fire formed pictures, faces, echoes. She heard Arbel say, 'But who *was* he, Christie? I thought Aunt Margaret's sons were my only cousins,' and Christie found that she recognized the tone of Arbel's voice. There had been the notary in Oxford, the carter's boy on the York road, the band of strolling players in Hexham . . . Little ever came of it.

Tonight she did not want to talk, to discuss Arbel's latest improbable fancy. For tomorrow there would be Adderstone, and Margaret Forster. Another temporary home, another borrowed family.

Kneeling on the floor, she pulled clean skirts for herself and Arbel from a bag. It was only, she thought, as she shook out woollen and velvet, that every step northwards took her further from where she wanted to be. It was only the tiredness and the cold and this damnable rain. Only Stephen Ridley's eyes and his cousin's awful manners. Tomorrow she would not feel sad, she would plan and save again, and the incident in Rothbury High Street would retreat to the insignificance it deserved.

Randal Lovell, dealing his tarots on a dirty stable floor, might have told her otherwise.

LOVELL was awake first, tending the horses, circling once round Rothbury before there was light in any window but the baker's and the midwife's. He had bread in one hand and ale in the other when his boot nudged the dark shape sprawled in the sticky straw.

The sun was only just beginning to show, silvering the puddles in the street, etching every branch of every tree against the sky. Randal had to apply a little more pressure with his boot, but then the shape rolled and groaned, moulting straw like some fantastical bird.

'I've brought you food.'

Luke Ridley's eyes opened, blue and pained, and focused on the bread and ale. 'A bucket of water for my head, if you please, Randal. Nothing more.'

The gypsy took a bucket and crossed the street to the well. Rothbury had begun to wake. Dogs barked in the alleys, shutters opened and slops were thrown into the street. In the stable, Luke upended a bucket of icy water over his head, and emerged, darkened hair streaming, with his faculties intact.

'Has anybody left?'

Lovell took the straw from his mouth. 'A pedlar, for Alnwick market. Your gentleman from the Angel, riding south. Willie Graham, damp, and in a temper.'

Luke was towelling his head with a horse blanket.

'Willie needed a bath.'

'And you need Willie. Or his kind.' There was no reproach in the gypsy's soft voice.

'There's no shortage of Willie Graham's kind in the hills.' Luke tied the laces of his shirt and leather jack. 'They come when I whistle. Like sleuth-dogs.'

Lovell sat on the upturned bucket near the stable-door and began to tear the loaf of bread in half.

'And two women, riding north with the Forsters' men. One was the fairest lassie you ever set eyes on.'

'Yellow hair and eyes to tempt priests from their vows?' Luke's voice, as he saddled his horse, was dismissive. 'They're all the same in the dark, you know, Randal. Fair, black, ginger . . . was my cousin with them?'

Lovell nodded. 'The tapster's boy said that Stephen Ridley rode with the Forsters from Hexham.'

They swung into the saddle and rode out into the courtyard. The sky was a clear light blue, the streets lit with sunlight, as though an alchemist had discovered the secret at last, and gilded Rothbury with an abundance of gold. The town had begun to rouse itself, painting people on to a bare canvas of stones and cobbles. They rode through the town centre, past the Angel, past the Green Man. Lovell glanced at Luke.

'Are you wanting to visit your cousin Margaret, then?'

'I don't think so.'

Luke's eyes, the blank and beautiful blue of the sky, met Randal's and, as usual, they told nothing.

THAT night, at Adderstone, they dined on capons and kid, goose and boiled mutton, syllabub and fromenty. The three Forster brothers, Christie and Arbel, Janet and Margaret Forster and Margaret's younger brother Stephen, gathered in Adderstone's Great Hall, a cavernous room with few concessions to comfort. Margaret directed servants and handed round vegetables, and waited for the cobwebs of twelve years' parting to drift away.

Rob was in love with Arbel already. He had seated himself next to her, and his eyes followed her. Arbel wore a dark gown, appropriate for one still mourning her mother, but nevertheless a suitably dramatic foil for her pale skin and silver-fair hair. Arbel reminded Margaret of Anne, who had been little more than Arbel's age when she had married. You could have picked tiny, fair-haired Anne from a room of a hundred just by looking to see where the men were. Now, even Mark, at barely fourteen, bestowed on his cousin the attention he had hitherto only devoted to a fast horse, or a good game of ball.

The girls had arrived at midday, having ridden from Rothbury in the early morning. Already Adderstone had begun to alter: Arbel's laughter, the rustle of Christie's gown, light footsteps echoing against walls more accustomed to heavy boots, the clink of steel against stone. Even the Hall seemed lighter, brighter, the candlelight catching and flowing on Arbel's long blonde hair.

34

Rob, glass in hand, was describing to Arbel the complicated rules of a trod.

'Within six days, cousin. You must follow within six days of the raid. If you ride immediately it's a hot trod, if you leave it until later it's cold. You can cross the Border –'

'– with a flaming peat on your lance,' interrupted Mark, leaning across the table. 'And horn and hounds –'

'– but you must announce your trod to the first person you meet after you've crossed the Border.'

'Who's then obliged to help you.'

'Exactly.' Rob speared himself a pigeon. 'Whether they be the Lord Warden himself or a band of marauding Elliots. More collops, cousin?'

Arbel shook her head. The hound sleeping by the fire beat its tail once, and then lay still.

'And when you catch up with the raiders?'

Rob grinned. 'Then you reclaim your cattle or sheep or horses, and take a few prisoners as well. For ransom, my dear.'

'Or the gallows.' Mark, bread in hand, drew an imaginary line across his throat. 'Sometimes they hang 'em on the spot. Sometimes –'

He subsided, having caught his mother's eye. Arbel's eyes had grown round and dark. Richie poured more wine into her glass.

'He's quite right, cousin Arbel, if a trifle crude. Justice can be a little summary. It all depends on which side you happen to be at the time. If it's Adderstone's sheep and horses, we don't mourn too much the lack of a trial.'

'Johnnie Collingwood lost a hundred head of sheep last week.' Stephen, on Arbel's other side, glanced up the table to Richie. 'Followed them across the Border, but lost them in the moss. Burns and Robsons, apparently.'

Richie ventured the opinion that Johnnie Collingwood couldn't find his way to his bedchamber if his wife didn't lead him there.

Rob said, 'Quite – but he's a good eye for a horse. They didn't take that mare of his, did they, Stephen?'

'No.' Stephen Ridley wore a black velvet doublet, the sleeves slashed and inset with gold. 'It is rumoured that a man with an arquebus sleeps with Johnnie Collingwood's mare. I don't expect Jackie Burns cared to discover whether there was truth in the rumour.'

'Better sleep with the mare than with Collingwood's wife,' said Rob, and Arbel giggled.

Margaret turned to Christie, at her side. 'More pie, my dear? Or pigeon?'

Christie shook her head.

Christie was as dark as Arbel was fair, with cool, sensible brown eyes, and chestnut hair of the unhelpful sort that neither curled nor lay truly straight. Margaret had breathed a small, private sigh of relief when she had first met Christie. Arbel was Anne all over again, but without the fear – for her child, her husband, herself – that had been Anne's only restraint. But Margaret had recognized a perspicacity similar to her own in Christie's clear brown eyes. You had to be both easy-going and adaptable if you were a nameless by-blow, because you went where the winds of fate blew you. Just as those same winds, ably assisted by Davey Ridley, had tossed Margaret to Adderstone and marriage with Richard Forster, almost thirty years before.

Stephen was speaking.

'To return to the Collingwoods. It's been a bad month. The Herons lost a dozen horses a fortnight ago – did you follow the trod, Richie? – and Tom Milburn's tower was razed to the ground. I should make sure your watches are wide awake, Margaret – someone's busy.'

The servants had cleared away the dishes, replacing them with syllabubs, pies and cakes.

'Luke?' said Rob, slyly.

Arbel's eyes flickered, darting from Rob to Stephen.

Stephen's face did not change at all, but he said, thoughtfully,

'I think that Lucas generally considers the other side of the Border to be Catcleugh's particular speciality. Although I wouldn't put it past him.'

'Lucas?' said Arbel to Stephen.

Stephen looked down at Arbel. 'Lucas Ridley. You were . . . *introduced* to him in Rothbury last night, Arbel, if you remember.'

Margaret's thin brows raised almost to the edge of her head-dress. 'Lucas called on you? In Rothbury?'

'Not quite.' Rob helped himself to a large piece of apple tart. 'Luke was as drunk as a lord and sick all over the road in front of us, mother dear.'

Margaret's brows threatened to disappear completely. 'Lucas can act the gentleman perfectly well when he chooses. One could wish he chose a little more often.'

There was a short, uncomfortable silence.

Then Arbel said, 'Who is he, Aunt Margaret?'

'Lucas?' Margaret pursed her lips. 'He's the son of my cousin's wife. She was called Catherine.'

'Note,' said Rob, his spoon pausing halfway to his mouth, 'my mother's careful choice of words. Luke is Catherine's son, but not Catherine's husband's son. Catherine's husband died a year before Luke was born.'

'*Oh!*' Arbel's mouth was as round as her eyes. 'Lucas is a bastard then, like Christie?'

Christie, Margaret was delighted to see, did not even blush.

Before Margaret could speak, Arbel went on, 'We think that Christie's mother must have been a beautiful courtesan. Beautiful courtesans must have a lot of bastard children, mustn't they? Was Lucas's mother beautiful?'

'Very.' Margaret seized a pudding-dish.

'And his father. Who was Lucas's father?'

That time, the silence lasted a little longer.

Then Rob leaned back in his chair, cradling his wine glass in his hands, and said,

'That is a matter of some debate, cousin. Personally I favour the theory put about in the taverns. That Luke's mother bestowed her favours on a passing gypsy – a Faa, a Heron, or a Lovell – who knows?'

Margaret spoke stiffly, signalling for the servants to begin to clear away, 'After his mother died, Lucas was brought up by my elder brother Davey. Davey treated him as he would his own son.'

37

'Which kindness Lucas repaid in his own inimitable way,' said Stephen, slowly. He turned to Arbel. 'Lucas lives in a tumbledown hovel in the hills, Arbel. Shall I tell you how he earns his bread? By stealing other people's livestock and selling them. By taking clothes and goods and food from his neighbours, the poorer and more defenceless the better. By blackmail and kidnapping. The little display of good breeding you witnessed in Rothbury last night is nothing out of the ordinary, I assure you. No doubt he's drunk when he rides, as well. Lucas will end his days strung up on some hastily erected gallows on the wrong side of the Border. You should not concern yourself with him.'

'He's had a good run, though, Stephen,' said Richie. He rose, and went to his mother's side. 'You must allow him that.'

The wind had picked up again, tossing golden sparks on to the hearth. 'I allow Lucas nothing,' said Stephen, calmly. 'Nothing at all.'

He stood up. The firelight spilled on to the rich scrollwork of his doublet and lit the ends of his feathered golden hair.

'A good run?' said Stephen, raising his glass. 'Even Lucas must run out of breath soon, don't you think?'

And drank, long and hard.

Chapter Three

*T*O the imprisoned Queen of Scots, immured in Sheffield Castle, summer was a band of sunlight, thick with dust-motes, through an old, closed window. Fifteen years previously, Mary Stuart had married her husband's murderer, suffered imprisonment at the hands of her own rebellious nobles, and finally thrown herself on the mercy of her dear cousin, Elizabeth of England. Fourteen years of disappointment, intrigue, tedium and hope had followed, during which time Mary's status had inexorably progressed from that of royal guest to prisoner. The hope was the worst, and somehow, even in the most disillusioned soul, summer always rekindled hope: hopes for a visit to Buxton, to take the waters, hopes for freedom. Hopes for a letter. Letters, letters . . . always letters – to France, to London, to Scotland. Some written and sent, by messenger, or by more hidden, secret means. Others scrawled constantly in her aching head, to be denied even the exorcism of pen on paper.

For Queen Elizabeth's court, summer meant an escape from London's heat-drenched, plague-infested streets, to progress at a suitably stately pace through the green and dappled countryside, stopping for a night, or several nights, at some gentleman's residence. Sometimes the fortunate gentleman wanted to house the entire court, with its ladies-in-waiting, its gentleman ushers, its chamberlains, its yeomen of the wardrobe, clerks, carvers, sewers, grooms, falconers, physicians, and apothecaries. Sometimes the gentleman saw his hard-earned gold crumble to dust in one glorious extravagant evening, or before his doors had even opened, in some tortuously complimentary jewel, presented to her Majesty on her arrival. But whether or not he sought the honour of entertaining his Queen and her huge, glittering, untidy entourage, he bowed and smiled, and flattered, and kept his worries for the small silent hours of the morning, when he could be by himself for just a little while.

And meanwhile, the business of government continued. The de Guise faction in France did not rest because it was summer, nor did Philip II, now King of both Portugal and Spain as well as the rebellious Netherlands, nor did the worrying English Catholics and their equally worrying counterparts in Scotland and at the Jesuit Colleges on the Continent. Rome, Lisbon, Edinburgh, London; the Jesuit Fathers' paths crossed like an ever more intricate cat's-cradle, weaving a net of intrigue and sedition around the crowns of Western Europe. And at the centre of the knot, always, the Queen of Scots.

More letters: from Douai in Northern France to the North of England, sent via a sympathetic (or impecunious) courier on a galleon bound for Gravesend. Other letters, some enciphered, bound for Sir Francis Walsingham, Queen Elizabeth's chief Secretary of State, at his house in Barnes, near London. Letters from Sir Henry Woodryngton, the Lord Marshal and Deputy Governor of Berwick, letters from Sir John Forster, Warden of the Middle Marches, Alnwick.

The Warden's men still rode the Border in summer. Sunlight speckled the hills, thawing the pock-marked remainder of the winter's snow-drifts. Three of Sir John Forster's men – Robert Snowdon, George Stevenson and Matthew Wilkinson – rode the hills and valleys in May. The valleys were a treacherous patchwork of bog and reed and heather, only a half-mile from the Scots Border.

Robert Snowdon, reining in his horse at the top of the hill overlooking the valley, grinned to himself. He could see a figure in the moss below, embattled with horse and cloak, black mud up to his knees. 'Daft beggar,' said Snowdon unsympathetically, and, clicking his teeth to his horse, rode down the incline, Matty Wilkinson and George Stevenson following.

Robert Snowdon knew this country as well as any man: indeed, before reason had suggested that he might earn a more reliable living in the pay of the Warden, he had ridden the Middle Marches to a different purpose. The grey-cloaked man did not notice their descent down the hills, and even if he had he would have been able to do little about it, for he had surrounded himself with water and reeds, and his horse was enveloped to the hocks in mud.

They hauled the horse our first because a horse was worth money, and then extended a hand to the man on the islet, bidding him follow them to firmer ground. It was only when the traveller had shaken the excess mud off his breeches and wiped the sides of his boots on the grass that Robbie Snowdon said,

'It's early to be about, Tell us your name, sir, and your destination?'

'My name is my own business.' The man had turned away to check the buckles of his saddle and bridle. 'I thank you for your trouble, gentlemen, but I must be on my way.'

Robbie's hand caught the rider's elbow before he was able to swing into the saddle. 'Your name and destination, sir. Please.'

The man swung round. The hood of his cloak fell back from his face, and Snowdon saw a long, thin jaw, and lined and hollowed features.

'I said my name is my own business. But, if you insist, my trade is that of a dentist. And I am on my way to visit Martin Croser of Bewcastle.'

'There are easier roads to Bewcastle,' said George Stevenson mildly.

The stranger shook his head. 'There's often a tooth wants pulling in one of the villages on the way. It isn't only townsfolk that are troubled with the toothache.'

Robert Snowdon's jaw had began to throb. Had the man been sensible and given his name, Snowdon might have found the courage to ask the fellow to draw that damned molar there and then, before he had time to think about it. It had troubled him for a year now, on and off, yet he had not quite been able to bring himself to attend the fair at Rothbury or at Alnwick and submit to the dentist's booth. He pushed the dentist aside and began to unbuckle his saddlebags.

There were noises of protest, but as Matthew had taken the dentist's knife and sword, no more.

'If you won't tell us your name,' said Snowdon, 'then you can tell it to Sir John Forster.'

'Are you arresting me?'

Snowdon took out a blanket, a shirt and a pair of gloves, and dropped them to the grass below. He opened the other saddlebag. 'We are. Unless –' and his hand touched something wrapped in leather at the bottom of the bag '– unless you have any better suggestion?'

Snowdon opened the leather roll before the dentist could reply. The sight of the metal instruments, some pointed, some bulbous, turned his stomach. They reminded him of a different sort of instrument, encountered in an oubliette or dungeon. There was a looking-glass in the roll as well, a fine looking-glass with a silver and tortoise-shell back, and a well-polished glass. No doubt the dentist would have his own terrible purpose for such a thing, but Snowdon thought of his own pretty wife, and how she had to peer into the still surface of a rain-barrel, or a hastily wiped piece of glass. And there was something else, too: a prayer-book, old and well used.

Robbie Snowdon repeated carefully, 'Unless you have any better suggestion?' and let his fingers run through the deckled pages of the book.

The sun had fully risen, and there was a smooth film of sweat on the dentist's forehead. Snowdon smiled, displaying all his uneven teeth, and not caring. He saw the dentist reach inside his doublet, and saw Matty Wilkinson's hand fold round the sword at his side. But the dentist brought out neither a dagger nor a pistol, but only, to Snowdon's delight, a purse.

'Look, gentlemen.' The man's hands shook as he loosened the draw-strings of the purse. 'I'm in a hurry, you see. I simply don't have time for delays – Mr Croser is expecting me –'

The purse was open. Snowdon could see shillings, angels, golden rials. He took the purse from the dentist's open hands and distributed the rials. Three each. He left the white money for the dentist. Robert Snowdon was a Christian.

'I'll ride with you a while,' he said, and mounted his horse.

The dentist clutched his own reins, but did not yet mount. His eyes were fixed on his bag, now slung across Robert Snowdon's saddlebow. 'My instruments – my looking-glass –' he said.

Snowdon grinned widely. 'What instruments? What looking-glass?'

The dentist's mouth opened and then closed. Then he swung himself into the saddle and clapped his heels against his horse's side, and was out of sight before Matty Wilkinson and George Stevenson could finish laughing and pick up the shirt, the blanket and the pair of gloves.

AT Catcleugh, that night, the noise of twenty men, bored, rattled the pele-house. They had eaten, they had drunk – though not to excess because Catcleugh was almost clean out of ale – and they had then found themselves with time, a long night, and an over-abundance of energy. There was a limit to what distraction even Mariota could provide, and besides, though she had abandoned Luke's shirt for a gown of spirited but dirty red, she was still Luke's. And Luke was quiet tonight: seated at the small trestle table upstairs he was, to the irritation of most, writing. Paper in front of him, a pen in one hand and a bottle of aqua vitae in the other, paying no attention whatsoever to the riot in his house.

The gypsy was upstairs, too: Randal Lovell had appeared halfway through the evening and, propping himself against the wall next to the table, had stuck there. Mariota, escaping someone's fumbling hands, received Lovell's smile as she scrambled up the ladder and sat down at the table. She did not smile back. Randal's had not been a nice smile.

Dipping her finger into the inkwell, she began to draw on a piece of Luke's good paper. An apple, a flower, a snake, sketched with a blackened fingertip. Mariota looked up at Luke, but he was still writing, his hand quickly covering the paper, his eyes lidded. Randal Lovell still smiled. Slowly, Mariota reached out her hand to tilt the inkwell.

Strong fingers curled round her wrist, and the inkwell remained upright.

'You may paint the walls if you wish, Mariota, or the floor, or even the horses in the Byre. But not my letter. If you find the night wearisome, then there are twenty downstairs who would be delighted to entertain you.'

Mariota scowled, and wiped her inky fingers on her gown. Someone was climbing the ladder.

Unexpectedly, the gypsy said, 'She's not the only one to find the night overlong, Luke.'

A fist battered on the trapdoor. Randal Lovell kicked open the latch. As Dand's Jock's balding head appeared through the hatchway, Luke Ridley applied a neat, fictitious signature to his letter, and sprinkled a little sand on the paper. The noise from below had gathered momentum: the unmistakable sound of a pistol shot sliced through the jeers and chanting and laughter.

'You think our friends lack entertainment?' said Luke. 'You think that my hospitality is not complete?'

'I think,' said Dand's Jock, perching on the edge of the hatchway, 'that Red Archie will boil Long Martin in his ane cooking-pot if ye find him naught better to do.'

Luke Ridley's sky-blue eyes widened perceptibly. 'And I should try to prevent that? Why?'

'Because it'll make an awful mess of yon nice floor.'

And Mariota, peering downstairs to the tangle of smoke and straw and upturned ale cups, forgot her bruised wrist and her sulks and giggled.

'Ah.' Luke folded and sealed the letter and placed it inside his shirt. He leaned back on the stool, his hands cushioning his head. 'I found them wine and women a while ago, Jock. What do my poor bairns need now?'

'We havena ridden for nigh on a month, Luke,' said Dand's Jock, dolefully. 'And if we dinna ride soon, it'll be too light.'

'And there's neither food nor drink.' Mariota's dark eyes coaxed, her fingers threaded through Luke's. 'I'm tired of black bread and oatcakes.'

Luke lifted her black-smudged palm to his mouth and licked it thoughtfully. 'The Trotters feast on honey-cakes and Rhenish wine, I'm told. And syllabubs and quince tarts and sack posset. And I've heart that Jamie Trotter has just acquired a rather fine new gelding. Shall we take a look at it, Randal?'

But Randal Lovell was already down the ladder.

*

THE Trotters infested the Scottish East March, beyond the cold, snaking line of the river Tweed. Trotter pele-houses and towers crouched in the shelter of the dark hills like toadstools, Trotter riders forded the Tweed at Wark or at Norham and stole what they could from the Herons, the Forsters, or the Collingwoods. Twenty men were perhaps too few to take a tower, but twenty men were easily enough to take a fine horse and maybe a dozen cattle from Jamie Trotter's decrepit pele-house.

Within ten minutes Luke's men were in the saddle and following a winding path to the Border. The noise and chaos of Catcleugh ceased: on horseback they were silent and well ordered, leaving no evidence of their route. A thick mist blanketed the valleys and shadows, blurring the outline of the riders ahead and behind, muffling the click of the horses and the small sounds of leather bridle and bit. The gibbous moon, rimmed with a smudged halo of silver, hardly touched the sudden stone precipices and the acid-green marshland.

The absence of moonlight did not perturb Dand's Jock, riding in Luke's wake, his steel bonnet already dewed with mist. Jock knew the hills – English or Scots – better than most men, and besides, he was following someone who knew every twist and turn, every patch of scree or bog. Aye, thought Dand's Jock with something near to a grin, every stone and blade of grass. Which was why, after all, they put up with the bastard, why they tolerated Luke's moods and absences and insanities. Dand's Jock might not have trusted Luke Ridley with his mother's honour, but he would have trusted him to find his way through the Cheviots in a snowstorm. A glimpse of fair hair under a steel morion, the small echo of Luke's hackney picking its way down the stoniest of hillsides, was enough. Dand's Jock might neither expect nor desire to feel safe; he did, however, need to feel a little optimism about his future. To know that there would be food on his plate and money in his pocket. To know that there would be a cup of ale and a warm bed at the Angel or at Molly Turner's whenever he felt in need of a little company. Dand's Jock had ridden with Luke Ridley for nigh on two years now, and he had gone neither hungry nor thirsty.

45

They crossed the Border at Coldstream, wading the horses through the thick icy waters of the Tweed, their eyes searching for beacons or the Warden's men on the opposite bank. But there was no sound except the run of water on stone, and no orange bale-fire to lighten the black sky. Dand's Jock felt no rush of patriotism on entering the country of his birth, only the hangman's rope tightening about his neck. England, Scotland, it made no difference, it was the skill of the men you rode with that preserved your life for another night. There had been an unfortunate incident a few years past – now, his wife and children lived on one side of the Border, Dand's Jock on the other. Outlawed in his own country, too long a stay in Scotland would offer him nothing more than a certain trip to the gallows.

Dand's Jock drew level with Luke as they rode within sight of Jamie Trotter's pele-house at Leitholm. The cold air had cleared his head. Jock studied the pele-house that stood squat in the jewelled grass, its contents a tempting prize. 'The fool's nae dogs and nae watch,' he said, softly.

Luke's eyes were bright; he nodded. Luke looked sober, but then Luke always looked sober until he threw up or collapsed. The gypsy was behind him, his black curly head turned towards the pele-house, his square hands gentling his pony. Randal Lovell never wore a helmet and rarely carried a hand-gun, only a short sword, and a wicked, narrow-bladed knife.

They had their orders within minutes, and even Long Martin had wit enough to appreciate the beauty of it. They spread themselves in the darkness as silently and easily as oil spreads on water. Dand's Jock watched Luke dismount, throw his reins to the gypsy, and stroll to the pele-house door. Dand's Jock flattened himself against Leitholm's crumbling stone wall, and he felt his stomach clench a little. There was only the filtered moonlight, and Luke's footsteps, soft on the dew-tipped grass. The house looked quiet enough, but you could never tell, and the Trotters were an old and familiar enemy. Who knows, Jamie Trotter might have begun to use his head at last.

He watched Luke climb the flight of steps to the door. He didn't look in the least bit worried, the cold bastard. Dand's

46

Jock heard, sudden and shocking in the darkness, the sound of a fist hammering on the door.

'Jamie! Jamie Trotter! The Scotts are on their way, and we need ye, man! There's a hundred of them coming – get out of the bed, Jamie Trotter!'

Dand's Jock bit his lip and edged a little closer to the steps. There was an echo of movement inside the pele-house as Luke thumped the door and shouted again, his voice almost breaking with urgency and exhaustion. Dand's Jock gripped his sword in one hand and his dagger in the other, and grinned to himself as he heard footsteps vibrating through the stone. Jamie Trotter was a fool and a sloven, and didn't deserve a nice horse.

It took, hilariously, a good ten seconds for Jamie Trotter's sleep-stewed brain to recognize that the face under the steel bonnet was not Martin Kerr's, in desperate need of assistance against the Scotts, but that damned Ridley's from across the Border. By then it was too late, of course, for a sword was poking at his ribs, grazing his skin through his shirt, and he was stumbling backwards into his own house, curses freezing on his lips. He had little time to call for his own men: black shapes were pushing past him, and he sat himself as requested at the bottom of the steps, Luke Ridley's sword balanced delicately against his throat.

Jamie found his voice when he heard the bolt being slipped in the byre below. He could have cried when he remembered the horse, but he confined himself to shouting at his wife as she peered down the ladder, her colourless hair tumbling about her face.

Dand's Jock soon discovered the cause of Jamie Trotter's stupidity: a case of Rhenish wine. The byre door creaked as it was swung open, and then there was the sound of horses' hooves on grass. Randal Lovell was returning the Trotters' fine gelding to England.

They were out again in no time, Luke having bid a fond, Kerr-accented farewell to Jamie Trotter. The remaining Trotter horses had already reached the woodland. The cattle had been thought to be of more trouble than they were worth, a half-starved handful, with rotting hooves and blistered mouths.

Back on the English bank of the Tweed, Luke reined in his horse and uncorked a bottle. The mist had cleared as the men finished hauling the last of Jamie Trotter's horses through the river. Dand's Jock shook his head in disgust.

'I've seen better beasts in the knacker's yard.'

Luke temporarily detached himself from the bottle. 'We'll sell them to the Greys. That should annoy the Trotters.' The clouds had cleared; Luke had taken off his steel bonnet, his hair and skin were bleached of colour by the moonlight. 'You can take them to Stob's Edge, Jock, until we know whether the Trotters intend to follow.'

Dand's Jock noted Luke's choice of pronoun. 'Will ye go back to Catcleugh?'

'Not yet.' Jamming the cork back in the bottle, Luke shoved it in his morion inside his saddlebag. 'I've a little more business tonight. In Wooler.'

Luke rode away into the darkness. Dand's Jock lifted one hand in salute, and then applied himself to the serious business of hiding the Trotter horses.

WOOLER was silent; only a dog, asleep in the gutter, whined as Luke passed. The windows of the houses were dark and shuttered, the litter in the market-place blown into small eddies by the breeze. Luke slid from his horse as he reached the churchyard, his feet a little unsteady on the overgrown path, the chinking of the bottles muffled inside his jack.

Tethering his horse in the graveyard, he went into the church, the half-finished bottle swinging from his left hand, his right hovering round the hilt of his sword. The church was dark and smelled of damp; clumps of grass sprouted from the uneven walls, birds nested in the patched roof. By the pulpit Luke knelt, but not in prayer. Removing both the letter and the bottle from his jack, his fingers searched in the gap in the pulpit's heavily sculptured oak. With a hiccup of triumph, he extracted a sealed and folded paper from the trumpeting angels and obese cherubims. 'Praise the Lord and all his saints,' said Luke Ridley, happily, and tucked the letter's twin into the gap.

Outside, perching on the edge of a gravestone, he broke the seal. The first bottle, empty now, slid to rest on the earthly remains of Martha Collingwood, spinster of this parish, its dregs trickling over the stones and mossy grass. Luke pulled the cork from the second bottle, and studied the letter. There was scarcely enough moonlight to whiten the page. Cursing, he went back inside the church for a candle.

The gravestone provided a good barrier against the breeze, and he had tinder in his pocket, in case the Trotters had proved particularly obdurate. Luke rested his back on the lichened stone, the candle jammed into the soft earth, the wine bottle, already emptying, to his side. There were figures on the paper he held, not letters. The numbers danced in the guttering candlelight, reforming themselves into different patterns. Luke drank conscientiously, his eyes only leaving the letter when there was the smallest noise. The candlelight had whitened the tips of his fair hair and reduced the colour of his eyes to two pinpoints of black. When the bottle was almost empty, he laughed suddenly, and held the paper to the candle so that it flared and glowed orange, shedding a red light on Martha Collingwood and her temporary cohabitor. Delighted with himself for the second time that night, Luke Ridley tossed the bottle into the air so that it landed with a dull thud in the spongy ground beneath the yews.

Lying on his back, his head cushioned by stone, he could see the clear imprint of the stars in the sky, and the pale moon that had lit his journey across the Border. Over there, between the town and the sea, was Adderstone. And today (yesterday?) was the tenth of May. Luke had an invitation to Adderstone for the tenth of May.

He shifted a little, the stones and earth suddenly less comfortable. He had not forgotten the invitation – to meet Margaret Forster's niece – because he forgot nothing. He knew why Margaret had issued the invitation, and he knew also why he had not taken it up, but had stayed at Catcleugh, composing devious letters, drinking, and letting his men do precisely what they wanted. Margaret had invited him to Adderstone because she still remembered her brother Davey, and Luke had not gone because Stephen would have been there. He had filled his mind with intrigue and noise and distraction rather than spend an afternoon with Stephen at Adderstone. Rather than let anyone have the pleasure of witnessing him spend an afternoon with Stephen at Adderstone.

A man of great discipline and exquisite self-control, that was cousin Stephen. Stephen's self-control was a consequence of his gentle upbringing by his brother and his brother's wife. And his legitimacy, of course. The son of an old, propertied Border family was likely to be a more respectable man than the son of a whore and her gypsy lover. After all, they had both shared the same upbringing, hadn't they? David Ridley, lacking legitimate sons of his own, had lavished equal money and education on both his younger brother and his cousin's widow's little mistake.

He could face Stephen now: he would have had the greatest delight in facing Stephen now. Luke hauled himself into a more upright position, regretting that he had not taken more of Jamie Trotter's Rhenish wine. He could fight one of those bastards for it, but that would mean returning to Catcleugh and drunken male self-congratulation. There was – and Luke smiled to himself again – wine a-plenty at Adderstone.

Luke hauled himself to his feet, using Martha Collingwood as a support, and looked across the churchyard through the tangle of yew trees and gorse. Somewhere out there was Adderstone, rising like a swordthrust from the hill, moonlight braiding its crenellations. Luke clicked his fingers to his horse, his eyes bright and narrow. If Margaret Forster had issued her damned invitation, then he was still at liberty to take it up. Adderstone, with its well-stocked cellars, was less than a half-hour's ride away. Stephen's voice saying, *I would not have thought even you would attempt to claim cousinship with Miss Forster* was still remarkably clear.

Luke raised an imaginary cup in the vague direction of Adderstone Tower. 'Cousin Arbel,' he said to the sleeping inhabitants of Wooler churchyard, and swung himself into the saddle.

Only the candle remained, a solitary will-o-the-wisp to brighten the darkness.

*

ADDERSTONE, having been raided itself only the previous night, was well prepared to meet its second intruder of the week. If Luke's ascent of the barmkin wall was unobtrusive enough, being just a matter of searching for foot and hand holds in the close-packed stone, then the descent was a rather inelegant affair, accompanied by curses and the clatter of falling masonry. Hushing himself, dusting the earth from his clothes, Luke heard the dogs and the rush of footsteps before he began to cross the courtyard. That he had his knife in his hand was purely instinctive; that he slipped to his knees and found himself faced with a length of sharp steel and the impatient grey eyes of Richie Forster, was a consequence of alcohol, and an overlong night.

The tip of Richie Forster's sword scratched against Luke's breastbone. Luke looked up and smiled.

'*Luke*,' said Richie. 'For God's sake, it's –'

'The tenth of May. I know.' Luke tried, and failed, to scramble to his feet. 'Do you think you could put up your sword, Richie –?'

'Sorry –' Richie's sword dropped, and was rammed hastily back into its scabbard. 'Thought you were one of those damned Craws.' Extending a hand, he hauled Luke upright.

'*Richie*.' Luke's eyes, blue and pained, fixed themselves on Richie Forster's apologetic face. 'If I were here for your sheep or your horses, you'd have heard nothing from me until I'd lit the brushwood to fire the Tower. Still –' his gaze unfocused again, wandered towards the Tower. 'Craws, you say? At Adderstone?'

'Last night. Some Dixons as well, I think.' Richie frowned. 'Got rid of the bastards, of course.'

'Did they take anything?'

'A couple of horses. Nothing good.' Richie pushed Luke towards the house. 'One of them found their way into Christie's bedchamber – you can imagine the commotion *that* caused –'

'Christie. . .?'

'*You* know. Cousin Arbel's sister.' Richie grinned and glanced at Luke. 'You met her in Rothbury.'

'Nice eyes,' said Luke, happily. 'Did she screech to defend

her honour, or grab a sword and fight the unfortunate Craw to the ground?'

'Neither.' Richie pushed open the heavy door. 'Arbel shrieked, Rob came running, and Christie stood well out of the way.' He looked at Luke, who had followed him inside and was leaning against the staircase. 'Why in hell are you here, then, Luke?'

'To meet cousin Arbel, of course. As requested.' Luke folded both hands round the newel-post. 'And I haven't seen Stephen since Rothbury –'

'Stephen,' said Richie, patiently, 'will be back at Black Law by now. And Arbel is in bed.'

'Oh good,' said Luke.

He started up the staircase, sword scraping against the stone steps. Outside, the dogs and the hens had quietened a little; inside, doors began to open, candles flared in the darkness. At the top of the staircase Margaret Forster waited. She was wearing a voluminous bedgown, and had a thick shawl over her shoulders. Luke repeated his errand to her, and from somewhere in the darkness he heard Rob Forster's snort of amusement.

'You're a bit late, Luke,' said Rob, moving to his mother's side.

'And you appear to be rather wet,' said Margaret.

'And there's blood all over your sleeve.'

'Lucas, my dear,' said Margaret, kindly, 'might I suggest a clean shirt and a bed for the night? You really are rather drunk.'

'Two bottles of Jamie Trotter's good wine, Margaret,' said Luke and tried, and failed, to find something to bind his hand, which was dripping redly all over the floor. 'A reward for a very busy night.'

He held out his hand, and let Margaret tie her own lawn handkerchief around it.

'Richie will find you some dry clothes, Lucas,' said Margaret. 'And you will stay the night and see Arbel and Christie in the morning. One day late does not signify at all.'

Luke was about to take her advice, submitting himself to the unaccustomed pleasure of taking someone else's orders, when the door at the end of the landing opened.

There was a window beside the door, and framed in the window was the silver disc of the moon. Arbel Forster had no candle; she simply stood long enough in front of the window for the moon to gild every strand of her long, pale hair, and outline every curve of her body beneath her thin muslin nightgown. She did not wear, like Margaret, a shawl, but let the moonlight draw her throat, her neck, her fragile, perfect face, and the deep hollow between her breasts.

There was a silence.

Then Margaret said sharply, 'There's no need to disturb yourself, Arbel. Go back to your room.'

'I thought there was a fire,' said Arbel. 'Oh!' Her hand covered her mouth, the picture of surprise. 'Mr Ridley.'

She moved away from the window, and walked towards Luke, her hand outstretched. He saw everything then: Margaret's impatience, Richie's confusion, Rob's resentment. Luke bowed superbly and raised Arbel Forster's small white hand to his lips.

It was only when he looked up to her face that it occurred to him that he might have made an error. He read faces as easily as he read ciphers, generally. But Arbel's lovely face was not clear to him, and what he did understand disturbed him.

ARBEL Forster liked Adderstone. There were Richie and Rob and Mark, all of whom liked Arbel and showed it, in their different ways. Richie had taken her to Alnwick fair, Rob had proposed marriage, and Mark had given her a puppy. She had enjoyed the fair, turned down Rob's proposal, and had kept the puppy, christening her Dowzabel. Dowzabel, who was long-haired and short-legged and horribly difficult to house-train, was quite the most adorable creature.

Arbel also liked Janet, who had helped her set the sleeves of her new gown. Aunt Margaret was always very busy, which was useful, as it meant that Arbel, with Christie for company, could do more or less what she wanted. Aunt Margaret had quickly discovered Arbel's incompetence in the kitchen and brewhouse, and had soon, to Arbel's relief, given up trying to do much about it. Eggs broke, yeast failed in Arbel's pretty hands: her skills in the kitchen were equal to her skill with a needle. Aunt Margaret had eventually remarked (rather tartly) that it was fortunate that no man would have the sense to inquire into Arbel's housekeeping abilities, and had then plunged her own capable hands into the bread dough, while Arbel ran, carefree at last, to the stables. And because it irritated Margaret beyond endurance to see Arbel sitting in a window-seat, aimlessly humming and plaiting and unplaiting her long fair hair, she had also released Christie, which pleased Arbel greatly, because Christie was her dear, dear sister. So they rode to Wooler market, and visited the Collingwoods, and skirted round the great glowering heights of the Cheviots. With Geordie's Will, of course, or Tom Dodd. Tom was only fifteen, and would have run to the moon and back for Arbel; Geordie's Will was of somewhat sterner stuff, but she was working on him.

In the middle of May, the Dixons and the Craws raided Adderstone. Richie had called the raid a rather ramshackle affair, and with the help of his brothers and his men had beaten off the raiders within the hour, losing nothing more than a couple of ageing mares. Ramshackle or not, Arbel had found it all very exciting, and had watched from a window as the Craws and the Dixons buzzed round Adderstone, lances in hand. The Forsters had enjoyed it too: Janet had waved her bony fist, and emptied something rather unpleasant out of a window on to the head of one unfortunate Craw. The only person who had not enjoyed it had been Christie, who had thought the whole thing foolish. But then, Christie wanted to go to France to find her family, and besides, one of the Craws had found his way into Christie's bedchamber, sword in hand. Arbel had almost wanted to giggle when she had seen Christie ready to defend herself with a three-legged stool, but then she had seen Christie's expression, and had screamed very loudly instead. The next day Christie had been tired and sad, so Arbel had made sure she played with the puppy. No one could be unhappy when there was a puppy or a baby around.

Arbel had found only one flaw in Adderstone's otherwise perfect vista. That flaw had amber-coloured hair, and light eyes, and a habit of calling at an unconventional hour. The thought of Luke Ridley had begun to trouble Arbel: the memory of his head bent over Christie's hand in Rothbury High Street, the expression in his blue, shadowed eyes as he backed away from Arbel down Adderstone's moonlit landing. Arbel wasn't used to men ignoring her or walking away from her – unless they were shy or uninterested in women, that was. And she did not think that Luke was either shy or uninterested in women.

She could have wed Rob tomorrow if she had wanted to, and be hanged to the fact that they were first cousins. But Arbel did not wish to wed Rob Forster, nor did she wish to wed John Grey or Mark Selby, or any of the other hopefuls that had knocked at Adderstone's door since her arrival. She did not even wish to wed Luke Ridley.

But she did want something else from him.

ESCORTED by Tom Dodd, the Forster girls rode to Wooler, and from Wooler to Kirknewton, to see the Magi carved out of the granite wall of the church. Arbel was quickly bored with the Magi. She looked once at the stone folds of the kilts, the devout, ancient figures, and yawned, and walked back to her horse. She was halfway up the hill beyond Kirknewton by the time Tom Dodd and Christie caught up with her. At the top of the hill they reined in, and Tom Dodd pointed out the landmarks. Wooler, and The Cheviot, and Adderstone itself, like a small black claw between Wooler and the coast. Black Law lay to the south, masked by the rise and fall of the hills. 'And Catcleugh?' asked Arbel, carelessly, and Tom Dodd thought for a while, and said, 'Oh, a couple of miles. Maybe more.'

He did not want to take them there at first. Luke Ridley was a bad man, and Catcleugh no place for ladies. Neither did Christie, eyeing Arbel knowingly, wish to call on the man she had seen only once, horribly sick in Rothbury High Street.

'He'll be busy,' she said patiently. 'Rob said he's very busy. And it's a long way and difficult country, Arbel. We should go back to Adderstone.'

'It's still light.' Arbel's voice was obstinate. The sky was a

55

clear sapphire blue with only a few puffy clouds. 'And it isn't that far – only a couple of miles. We could have something to drink – I'm thirsty, Christie. And' – leaning over, she murmured in Christie's ear – 'I'll give you my pendant. The pearl one. I hate it – you can sell it. *Please.*'

She spurred her horse in a vaguely westerly direction before Christie could reply. Christie, aware of a faint but unmovable feeling of guilt, rode after her. Better, she told herself, that Arbel should visit Lucas Ridley with herself and Tom Dodd in tow, than alone and unprotected. Christie did not like these hills, and nor did she like Lucas Ridley. The landscape grew rougher and stonier as they climbed; the broad slopes thick with heather. There were adders in the heather, waiting for a carelessly placed hoof or foot. Luke Ridley had blank eyes, like a snake's, and Christie had no doubt that his tongue could sting just as acidly. He had orchestrated that little scene in Rothbury High Street: he had probably even intended to be sick. Christie recognized deliberate offensiveness when she saw it. She hoped he would be out.

There were still small flurries of snow curled in the most shadowed hollows of the hills, and the great dark outcrops of rock broke haphazardly through the grass like teeth in an old man's mouth. Kestrels lunged like black darts through the sky: Dowzabel, on Arbel's saddlebow, whimpered. There was something to fear here, thought Christie, shivering despite the warmth of the afternoon. The sort of men that had called so unexpectedly on Adderstone only a fortnight ago lived in these hills. With swords and lances in hand they traced paths across the Border at midnight, respecting neither life nor property. Luke Ridley was one of those men, Christie understood that even if Arbel did not.

Catcleugh was backed by the great slopes of the Cheviot itself. Stephen Ridley had been right: it was nothing more than a tumbledown pele-house, with moss on its walls and two small shutterless windows. 'It looks empty,' said Christie, hopefully, and Arbel turned, and smiled, and continued riding towards the doorway.

The door was at the top of a flight of stone steps. Tom Dodd shuffled up the steps and beat on the door. The windows were black and empty, and Christie prayed that they would remain so. But the door swung disobligingly open, and there he was, Luke Ridley, bareheaded and in his shirtsleeves, leaning against the doorjamb.

'The Forsters' boy,' he said, his gaze travelling slowly over the three of them, 'and – Devil take it – the Miss Forsters themselves. Both dark and fair.'

Briefly, Christie wondered whether an exceptionally ugly pearl pendant would compensate for the obvious unpleasantness of this visit. But there was France, and a flicker of memories, all as tantalizing as a gallery of partially seen paintings, and Arbel's suitors, already lining up, and an embarrassing, if expected, lack of suitors for Christie herself. Husbands wanted money and birth as well as a pretty face. Christie did not intend to grow a nameless old maid at Adderstone.

Arbel, as always, was unaware of undercurrents. 'Good day, Mr Ridley,' she said, and produced her best smile.

He was supposed to fall at her feet, enslaved. They generally did, acknowledged Christie. But instead, Luke walked down the steps to take the bridle of Arbel's restless horse, Tom Dodd glowering all the while.

'It isn't convenient, is it?' said Christie, brightly, gathering her reins. 'We must beg your pardon, Mr Ridley, for having called so unexpectedly –'

'Unexpectedly?' He turned to Christie, and smiled at last. As an adder might smile, thought Christie, when it sights its prey, asleep. 'Not unexpected at all, Miss Forster. We've been watching your progress for the past half-hour. If you wished to make a surprise call, then you should have ridden in the shadow of the hill – and not made quite so much noise.'

We. Christie looked up. There was another man in the doorway, small and dark, insolent black eyes studying first Arbel, and then Christie.

'Perhaps you should introduce us,' said Arbel.

'Ah.' Luke stepped back, and with a flourish of his hand gestured in the dark man's direction. 'Randal Lovell – Miss Arbel Forster. Miss Christie Forster.'

'Your brother,' said Arbel, cheerfully. 'Isn't he?'

The breeze, the leaves on the one stunted tree, seemed to still. Christie held her breath, and counted very slowly to herself. One, two –

'Possibly, Miss Forster,' said Luke Ridley. 'Or my uncle, or my cousin. Still, at least Randal isn't my lover – that might cause even greater consternation.'

Christie bit her lip. On Arbel's saddlebow, Dowzabel began to whine. 'Not *Miss Forster*,' said Arbel, only a little pink. 'We are cousins, after all. You said so yourself.'

The gypsy sniggered.

Luke said mildly, 'I seem to recall that Stephen did not agree with me on that point. Neither, I think, did Richie or Rob.'

'Oh, Richie was cross because he had quarrelled with his wife. And Rob is fond of me, you see.'

Mr Ridley was supposed to look jealous. Studying him covertly, Christie could not detect the smallest spark of jealousy. He looked a bit tired, perhaps – his hair was untidy, his eyes shadowed. His shirt was half unlaced: he looked, in fact, as though he had just got out of bed.

'I don't know that Rob,' said Luke, thoughtfully, 'being fond of you, would approve of this visit.'

'Oh, he doesn't know!' Arbel's eyes were bright, her hair, unrestrained by any cap or caul, flowed gold in the sunlight, 'He's busy – with the sheep or the cows or something –'

Tom Dodd still glared at Luke; the gypsy had disappeared back into the darkness of the house.

'In that case,' said Luke, releasing Arbel's bridle at last, 'perhaps you should return to Adderstone before Rob ceases to be busy, Miss Forster.'

The sky had not even begun to darken. Christie saw Arbel struggle to keep her temper, her cheeks reddening at last, her eyes dark and angry. Arbel had her father's temper, a temper that seemed sometimes thoroughly at odds with such a precise, fragile, beauty.

'Perhaps you could let us have a cup of water before we ride on,' said Christie, hastily. 'If it is not too much trouble, of course, Mr Ridley.'

Mr Ridley, too, recognized sarcasm when he heard it. But he said nothing, merely bowed and handed first Arbel and then Christie down from their horses. Released from confinement, Dowzabel cavorted and chewed at the scrubby grass. Tom Dodd leaned against a wall, scowling.

Inside, the single room was long, with a fireplace at one end, and a set of wooden steps leading to an upstairs platform. There were stools and chests and a table, and weapons heaped in one corner. The gypsy was nowhere to be seen; Christie watched as Luke kicked open the trapdoor and disappeared into the ground-floor byre, returning shortly with a bottle of wine. Arbel perched on a stool near the table, her small hands knitted together, her loose hair catching on the embroidered bodice of her gown. Christie had embroidered that gown: blue, with silver swans sewn all over the bodice. Arbel's skin was flushed, her eyes moved restlessly around the room. Outside, Christie could hear Dowzabel snuffling, and Tom Dodd whistling some unrecognizable tune.

Luke set the bottle and three cups on the table. Arbel watched him uncork the wine, her eyes fixed on his face. 'Don't you keep any servants, cousin?' she said. Her voice was as brittle as glass.

'Like Stephen, you mean, Miss Forster?' The wine bottle was returned to the table: the three cups jumped in unison. 'Did you like Black Law? Well, yes, I'm forgetting my manners – of course I have a servant.' And called, 'Mariota!'

There was silence, then a muffled groan and a curse. Christie looked over to the wooden ladder. Eventually the trapdoor slid aside, and one bare, dirty foot was placed on the top step.

'Mariota,' said Luke, gently, 'Miss Forster would prefer her wine from my servant's hand.'

Another foot appeared, and then a shapely leg, naked to the knee, and a vast gathering of grubby blue cloth. Luke Ridley's servant climbed slowly down the ladder, yawning. At the foot of the ladder, Mariota hitched up her skirt with one hand, and clutched the shirt – a man's shirt – unlaced at her neck with the other. Her black hair tangled round her face, and her eyes, as dark at the gypsy's, inspected both Christie and Arbel from

59

head to toe. Swaying across the room, Mariota let one arm curl around Luke's shoulders as she poured, unhurried, three cups of wine.

Which was why he looked tired and as though he had just got out of bed.

Christie heard herself begin to talk, loudly and inanely, to fill the appalling silence. There were two scarlet marks on Arbel's cheeks, as though someone had hit her, and the air inside the pele-house had become very hot, as if the still summer afternoon had penetrated even those stony walls.

Christie, taking Arbel's hand, tugged her to her feet as soon as they had choked down the wine. Luke opened the door for them, Mariota still clinging behind him. Christie could see Tom Dodd, standing by the horses, but there was no sign of Dowzabel.

'Over there,' said Luke, at her shoulder. 'Being sick. I think something must have disagreed with her.'

'AND what', said Luke, watching the three riders as they disappeared over the hillside, 'did they want?'

'The dark one wanted to go home,' said Mariota, pulling down the collar of his shirt to caress the back of his neck. 'And the fair one wanted you.'

Luke said nothing.

'Didn't you want her?' said Mariota, and bit him, hard.

'Bitch,' said Luke, without animosity. He yawned. 'I want a good meal, and a bottle of wine, and a night's sleep for a change. You can provide me with all those, Mariota, and no strings attached. Arbel Forster has a whole cat's-cradle of strings wrapped around her lovely little person.'

Mariota bit him again. Disentangling himself, Luke turned to face her. 'Bitch,' he said again, and pulled her down with him to the grass.

Chapter Four

GEORGE Stevenson, who liked a drink, had almost reached the end of his unexpected windfall. The three rials, taken from the purse of Robert Snowdon's itinerant dentist had, with the help of the landlord of the Golden Bull and the ladies in Molly Turner's shack on the edge of town, shrunk to a handful of silver and coppers. George Stevenson drank the last four crowns in Otterburn's Golden Bull on the night before the horse races, interspersing the ale, appropriately, with an increasingly mournful rendition of 'The Battle of Otterburn'.

Otterburn was busy in anticipation of the races: glistening mares, stallions and geldings crowded the Golden Bull's stables while their owners, optimism increasing by the gill, drained the Bull's barrels dry. Horse-racing was like eating or drinking – or reiving – to the Borderer: a necessary pleasure, a sport that had its roots in the need for a nimble horse that would take its rider across the hills as rapidly as possible. The Lord Warden himself might attend a race-meeting, but so might the lowest outlaw, the most desperate broken man. Thieves, kidnappers, assassins, all could be hired at the races.

But the crowd in the Golden Bull was good-humoured tonight. Generous in his extremity, George Stevenson had collected a varied assortment of drinking companions, all clustered under the Bull's low plaster ceiling, ale in hand. And then there was Johnnie Forster, of course, who knew the inside of the Golden Bull better than he knew the halls and great chambers of his father's house. But Johnnie was curled in a darkened corner of the taproom, and George Stevenson, unwisely, had forgotten his existence.

He had reached the most affecting part of the ballad: large tears quivered at the corners of his eyes.

'*My wound is deep – I fain would sleep,*' mumbled George, and staggered to his feet as his ale ebbed and flowed over the brim of his tankard to the Bull's dirty floor. '*Take thou the vanguard of the three –*' Jockie Milburn, taking the tankard from his swaying hand, placed it, kindly, on the table.

Losing his balance rather suddenly, George sat down hard on the wooden bench. '*And hide me by the bracken bush – that grows on yonder lily lee* . . .' he murmured, and cradled his head in his hands.

The words of the next verse were not to be found. Something about a blooming briar, thought George, vaguely. Calling to the potboy, he felt in his purse for a coin.

His purse was empty, which was odd when you considered that there had been four crowns and an angel there at noon. Turning it inside out, George discovered nothing more than a worn pair of dice, and a rather grubby scarlet ribbon. Someone whistled at the sight of the ribbon, and a hand reached out and grabbed the dice and tossed them into the air.

'Lost my damned money,' explained George, half of his mind still pondering the blooming briar. Squinting, he held the purse up to the light of the Bull's small window. 'Rob Snowdon had the most of it,' muttered George. 'Damn his black eyes.'

Someone else found a coin for the potboy. The denouement of 'The Battle of Otterburn' continued to worry George: so did Robert Snowdon's greed. 'And Matty Wilkinson, I daresay,' added George, obscurely, and spat on the floor. He recalled the looking-glass and the dentist's instruments. He could have sold a glass like that and had money to put on the horses tomorrow; he had a good eye for a horse when he was sober. But Robbie Snowdon had taken the glass for his wife. She was half Robbie's age, and a wanton creature. 'A silver looking-glass, by God,' George said. 'Bastard.'

'And what would you be wanting with a looking-glass, George?' asked Jock Milburn as the potboy poured more ale into their cups. 'You're a sight for sore eyes, man – you'd crack any glass you looked into.'

It was unfair. George rose, jabbing his finger into Milburn's

62

chest. 'Rob had the mirror,' he said. '*And* a third of the money. That wasn't right, was it? We all found that damned dentist, didn't we?'

Jock Milburn grinned, and handed George his tankard. 'Then you'll just have to do another honest day's work for the Warden, won't you, George?'

George shuffled to his feet, somewhat comforted, because he had remembered about the blooming briar and the bracken bush, and besides, Milburn was right, there was always another day's work for the Warden.

Johnnie Forster, the Warden's illegitimate son, who drank in company when there was company, and alone when there was not, sipped his ale thoughtfully and fingered his own empty purse.

R o b Forster liked horses, and he liked a wager. He liked the thud of hooves on the springy turf, and the impatience in the horses' eyes as they shifted and shivered at the starting-line. Most of all, he liked the rush of blood to his head as his horse forged ahead of the rest and crossed the line. Rob had kept his black gelding safely through winter and spring, without ever having to ride across the border to retrieve it from some damned Kerr or Robson. Rob had great hopes of the black gelding. He had taken it to Bewcastle early in the year, and it had done well for him.

The day was clear and fine. The ale-booths were already up and doing good business when Rob arrived, the black gelding on a leading-rein at his side, a stable-boy behind him. He could smell hot pies and oatcakes, and see, on the outskirts of the field, a gypsy caravan. Anis or Mairenni or some such name, telling your fortune with a flick of a tarot. Rob did not need a mumbling old crone to tell him his future. The gelding's coat shone like sea-washed basalt as it pulled and shook at the leading-rein.

Even so, he walked slowly round the field, assessing the opposition, nodding to the faces he recognized. He saw some fine beasts, but none better than the one he led at his side. Jackie Laidlaw eyed the horse, and Rob smiled as he thought of poor Richie and his spitfire of a wife. Rob was glad it was Richie and not he who had been required to repair the feud between the Forsters and the Laidlaws. Jackie Laidlaw was gazing at the black gelding as though he wished his sister's marriage had never taken place.

He picked out other faces from the crowd. Collingwoods, Greys, Herons, some Grahams from the West March. And Stephen Ridley, his uncovered head golden in the sunshine, standing by the winning-post. As the first race began Rob rode across the field to Stephen and, touching him lightly on the shoulder, made his presence known.

By mid-afternoon, Rob's interest – the gelding having fulfilled all his expectations – had wandered from the race-course to the gaming-table.

The game was primero, and Rob's opponents were varied in both appearance and aptitude. The clerk sniffed and dabbed at his nose as the cards began to go against him, the gentleman in the blue-feathered hat was more interested in the bottle of aqua vitae at his side than in the cards in his hand. The red-haired fellow, whose name was Archie, played intelligently enough, but he had poor cards. Sometimes it went like that. Archie drank steadily, but not to excess, and played without a shake of the hand or a slur of the tongue when he called. Archie was six foot of elongated, muscle-packed limbs, and could probably drink three pints to another man's one.

The clerk and the inebriate gentleman were disposed of within the hour. Rob's horse was not due to race again until the late afternoon – the premier race of the meet, for a fine, cast-iron bell. The game had become sufficiently interesting for Rob to ignore the noise and bustle outside the tent, and to concentrate only on the changing suits and colours before him. The pile of coins on his side of the table was twice as high as Archie's: Rob could feel himself approaching the winning-post, could feel the satisfaction of taking everything from a man who was almost as good as himself. He decided to up the stakes a little, and he pushed a crown across the rough wood instead of a shilling. He saw Archie grin – ruefully, Rob thought – and delve in his purse for a coin.

He won the next hand as the crowd's wail of excitement announced that another horse had passed the winning-post. Rob disregarded the cheers, shifting impatiently as he was jostled by a sudden intake of men. Rob could see that Archie's purse was almost flat: he watched Archie rub his outsize palm across his chin. Then, 'Wait there, sir,' said Archie and, rising to his feet, he left the booth.

Rob half expected never to see him again. It did not matter, Rob had his winnings. There was only the lingering sense of frustration in a pleasure incomplete, an absence of consummation to an enjoyable afternoon. Rob raised his hand to call the potboy, and then stopped, statue-like, in mid-air, as he saw what Archie was attempting to lead through the tattered canvas flaps of the ale-booth.

It was a horse, a beautiful chestnut gelding, a hand bigger than Rob's black, its coat burnished to coppery glass, its dark mane and tail flowing like a maid's unbound locks. Rob rose to his feet as Archie said, 'I've brought a better stake, sir!' and then, as tables, benches, stools and cups tumbled to the grass below, he added, 'but I don't think he'll fit on the table –'

Rob was at the creature's side before fat Maggie, red with indignation and laughter, could push Archie and his wager out of the tent. Placating Maggie with a coin for the broken plates and cups, Rob examined the gelding's mouth and ran his hand along the velvety red coat.

'Can you match him?' Archie's voice whispered in his ear, and Rob felt his heart pause, and then restart again, and his mouth go dry.

But sentience returned soon enough. He heard himself answer, 'Aye. Wait here awhile,' and his legs took him in the direction of his stable-lad and his own black gelding. The lad was asleep when Rob reached him, but Rob kicked him awake, and the boy, wide-eyed, fumbled at the knotted reins and passed him the horse.

By the time Rob returned to the tent and to Archie, there

were more people cluttering up Mag's ale-booth than watching the races. A girl squeezed his arm as he passed, someone else called his name. Looping the black gelding's reins to the tent-post, Rob looked at them both one last time, the chestnut and the black. Then he pushed his way through the men and women and squalling infants, and the dogs that yelped round their heels, and sat down opposite Archie, and took up his cards.

He had a good hand, he had had good hands all afternoon. He was not a fool, to wager a horse like that on a losing hand. Rob recognized the desperation that had led Archie to act rashly – he, too, sometimes felt like that, but he generally had the sense to throw down his cards and walk away. He waited, calmly confident, for Archie to reveal his losing hand, for Rob Forster to become the possessor of two of the finest horses on the Border.

He could not believe it at first when he saw that Archie's hand was not a losing one, but damnably, inconceivably, a winning one. The array of aces and court cards shifted before Rob for an instant, as though the table had rocked, or the earth had moved. He put down his own cards with hands that felt made of wood, and he hardly heard Archie say, 'My game, sir, I believe.'

He knew that someone had sat down beside him, and that that same someone had pushed a cup into his empty hands. But Rob did not respond, the pressure did not register, until he heard Stephen Ridley say,

'Red Archie is Lucas's man.'

Rob looked up sharply at Stephen's handsome expressionless face, and he felt his mouth open, even though no words came out.

'That's right. Cousin Lucas of Catcleugh. Who now owns your rather nice black gelding as well as the chestnut he took last month from the Trotters.'

Rob found his voice at last, and a considerable number of adjectives to express his feelings about cousin Lucas of Catcleugh. Stephen listened to it all patiently, and at the end of it, hauled Rob to his feet and led him out of the tent into the open air.

The last race was about to begin, the race in which Rob should have rode the fine black gelding he had guarded so well for the last year. Or that great chestnut brute that had trampled Maggie Robinson's ale-tent. Rob would not have put it past Luke Ridley's pet to use marked cards.

'There's your horse,' said Stephen.

Rob stared across. He saw the chestnut first, and the small dark figure seated on the chestnut, his black curls blown about by the breeze. 'Randal Lovell,' said Rob, softly, through a throat that seemed oddly constricted.

'No doubt Lucas spent the day amongst his own kind.'

The gypsy caravan. Neither Anis, nor Mairenni, but Randal Lovell and a stolen chestnut gelding tethered beyond, out of sight. Rob looked for the black and found it next to the chestnut, and cursed again at the sight of the rider, who had, Rob knew, eyes of a lighter blue than any other Ridley.

The flag dropped, the race began. An eight-furlong tour of field and valley, weaving in and out of the long shadows the setting sun had begun to paste on the Cheviots and their foothills. Rob had run out of curses, but his eyes tracked the black and the chestnut as they traced their circle in the grass at the head of the mottled, thundering horde. Rob heard the bastard's name and the gypsy's name on every other tongue, but he was silent, his nails dug deep into his palm, the pewter wine cup distorting in his grasp.

Rob saw the black horse inch before the chestnut just as they reached the finishing-post, and he hurled the cup to the ground, where the wine stained the grass with red.

It was still half-light when they reached Black Law, Rob and Stephen ahead, their servants behind.

Rob had scarcely spoken since they had left Otterburn, for it had occurred to him that since the chestnut gelding had been stolen in the first place, then Luke might be required to return it at the next day of truce. Keeping, quite lawfully, Rob's own black. Rob chewed that thought from Otterburn to Black Law, and it tasted like gall.

The sight of Black Law, magnificent on the rise of a hill,

comforted him a little. Whatever else Luke had managed to secure for himself, this, at least, had been denied him. Black Law was twice the size of Adderstone, Black Law made Cat-cleugh look like the derelict hovel it was. But it was inside Black Law – after Rob had handed over his horse to Stephen's stable-boy and kicked the worst of the mud from his boots – that he was reminded of just how much Luke, in his wilfulness, had missed. Davey Ridley had been a traveller, to France, to Italy, to the Low Countries, even to Spain. Adjusting always to the demands of tide, custom and religion, for there had been times when to set foot in Spain, for instance, would have meant a somewhat hurried exit from this world, times when a journey through Italy would have found him nothing more than the inside of a Florentine or Genoese gaol. But Davey had had a genius for protecting his own skin, matched only by the genius he had possessed in seeking out the best – the most fascinating, the most rare, the most intriguing – that each country had to offer. Ironically, it had been his own country that had, in the end, killed him.

Stephen had sold nothing of Davey's, nor had he added anything. Stephen ran Black Law like one of Davey's more curious automata, a masterpiece of interlocking cause and effect. In Black Law's Great Hall, drinking from goblets of blue-green Venetian glass, Rob used the best Candian wine to disguise the taste of gall. Replying to Stephen's inquiries concerning his mother and brothers, he appreciated the fact that Stephen had not smiled, as others had, at the loss of a fine horse, but had offered sympathy and alcohol to dull the humiliation. It had not dulled it, though: Rob, draining his cup to the dregs, hardly heard Stephen's gentle inquiry concerning Adderstone's latest arrivals.

He had no difficulty, however, once Stephen repeated his question, in focusing his mind on cousin Arbel. Indeed, Arbel Forster, with her silvery hair and beckoning eyes, occupied most of Rob's thoughts, whether waking or sleeping.

'Christie is well,' said Rob, shortly. 'And so is Arbel.' Then, seeing nothing but darkness in the blackened depths of his glass, he added, 'She's a damnably lovely girl, y'know, Stephen. Damnably.'

Even then, Stephen did not smile. 'Then marry her,' he said.

Slowly, Rob shook his head. The candles had been lit, throwing pools of light over the tapestries on the walls, on the red-brown sheen of Stephen's doublet and hose. 'We're first cousins,' he said. 'Too close.'

'First cousins may wed.' Stephen's face, a succession of planes of black and gold, was underlit by the candles on the table to his side. Outside, a breeze had picked up, battering the heavily-leaved branches against the window-panes.

'I asked her,' said Rob. His words surprised him: he had not intended to tell anyone of his ill-fated proposal to Arbel Forster. 'She turned me down. She hardly even *listened*.'

He beckoned to the servant to refill his glass. He could feel the anger rising in him as though that scene in Adderstone's parlour – a month ago now – had happened only yesterday. He had not expected outright rejection – a little suitably feminine prevarication, yes, but not a cool 'Oh no, I don't think so, Rob' while she hardly bothered to stop in her search for some damned bauble she had lost the previous day. It had angered him even more that Arbel had then noticed the expression on his face, and had turned to give him a kindly, sisterly kiss. He had had better kisses than that from Arbel Forster: she might look as pure and as cold as a church angel, but there was fire there, and Rob had tasted the flames.

'I should persevere,' Stephen was saying. 'Unless Margaret favours a different suitor for her niece?'

'Half the county has called at Adderstone since Arbel arrived.' Rob drained his glass, and grinned. 'Had you thought of adding yourself to the list, Stephen?'

The question was not entirely serious. Stephen was thirty-two, ten years older than Rob, and to the best of Rob's knowledge had never properly considered marriage.

But Stephen shrugged, and said, 'Again, there would be a relationship. But of marriage only, not blood.'

It occurred to Rob, through wine and anger and bitterness, that Luke was the only one left to bear Stephen's name, and Stephen would never, ever leave Black Law to Luke. He watched Stephen closely, and when Stephen said, 'And Arbel

– has she a husband in mind?' he almost answered immediately, *No*. Arbel appeared to care more for her dog than she did for other people. With the exception of Christie, acknowledged Rob, in a moment of alcohol-induced insight. Suddenly, gloomily, it occurred to him that Arbel Forster had probably never loved anyone in her entire life except her dear, dear sister Christie. Who was, of course, no sister at all. Only –

'Luke,' said Rob, softly, and hardly knew that he had spoken.

For there had been that small, apparently insignificant incident that Rob had put out of his mind until today. Now, released by Stephen's wine and the afternoon's mortification, it resurfaced, like a grotesque, drowned body at the banks of a lake. If Rob had looked up, he would have seen Stephen signal his manservant to leave the room, and would have seen also the flicker of interest in his dark blue eyes, the twin of Rob's own. But Rob's eyes were fixed on the golden aureole of the candle, and in that haze he saw Arbel, her body outlined by moonlight, walking the length of Adderstone's landing to offer her hand to Luke. Rob felt sick with desire and misery. He heard Stephen say,

'Arbel can have no interest in Lucas, Rob. Lucas has nothing – is nothing.'

'Luke lives well enough when he pleases. And besides –' Rob stopped, unable to express his half-formed suspicion that Arbel might not have the sense to consider money, position, or power when it came to marriage, but might just choose her husband as she appeared to choose everything else, on the strength of a whim.

'Luke was at Adderstone,' he said, at last. 'He turned up after midnight to see Arbel.' And Rob found himself describing the whole ridiculous scene, a scene that had been enjoyable, entertaining, even, until Arbel had appeared on the landing, backed by moonlight.

It sounded lame, until he recalled that Stephen, too, had been at Rothbury, and that Stephen, after all, must know Luke better than anyone. By the time Rob had finished his story (slurring his words a little now, struggling to keep himself from invective or self-pity), Stephen had left his side to stand by the window, where the gold of his hair and the rich patina of his silks and satins were lost in the setting sun.

'Arbel is very young,' said Stephen, his back to Rob. 'She may need to be protected from someone like Lucas.'

Rob stared at him. 'He couldn't –' he said eventually. 'Luke couldn't –'

Stephen swung round to face him. 'Lucas could not have Black Law. Perhaps he intends to have a little of Adderstone instead.'

Rob's eyes, blue and dark, fixed on Stephen. Adderstone – Mark Forster, Arbel's father, had owned some Adderstone land. It was still there, farmed by Richie, waiting for Arbel to marry. Rob laughed uneasily.

'Mother – Richie – would never allow it.'

Stephen shrugged. 'Margaret is fond of Lucas, Rob. She still thinks of him as one of her family. And Richie has problems of his own at the moment. It might be left to you –'

The sentence, unfinished, hung in the air between them.

Rob's face burned. At last he said, 'Luke'll likely die young with a sword between his ribs or a rope round his neck. Or maybe he'll crack his skull falling from a horse –'

He laughed at that, briefly breaking the tension, and Stephen joined in the laughter, and called for food to be brought. Over bread and rabbits, woodcock and carp, Rob said carelessly,

'Perhaps Luke should consider marrying Christie. She's pretty enough, and they'd be well suited, don't you think?'

He had expected an answering smile. But Stephen did not smile at all, his face was as cold and fixed as the stone walls that surrounded them.

'Lucas wouldn't *marry* Christie,' said Stephen, wiping his fingers on a damask napkin. 'She has nothing – she is a bastard, like himself. You misread Lucas if you think he will marry to get a pretty girl into his bed.'

SIR John Forster, Warden of the English Middle March, knew all about ambition. More than seventy years old now, he had occupied his profitable post since 1560, spending much of that time fending off insinuations about his own integrity. A younger son, the lands he now owned throughout the Middle and East March included the mighty fortress of Bamburgh, commanding the coast between Warkworth and Berwick. It really didn't do to be over-scrupulous about honesty on the Borders – not if you wanted to reap the rewards of your office, not if you wanted to live out, like Sir John, your threescore years and ten.

It had infuriated him, though, to discover that some of his own officers had followed his example. It had infuriated him even more to have to learn of their greed through his illegitimate son Johnnie, and to have to reward the idle fool for his tattle. Robert Snowdon, Matthew Wilkinson and George Stevenson could spend the rest of the summer in Haddock's Hole, Berwick's distinctly unpleasant gaol, pondering the fruits of dishonesty.

Meanwhile, Sir John Forster had a breviary, a looking-glass, and a set of dentist's instruments to inspect. The breviary was battered and well used, some of the pages beginning to come away from the binding. Standing by the window of his house on the outskirts of Alnwick, Sir John Forster examined the dentist's instruments one by one.

He had no distaste, like Robert Snowdon, for such things. He had seen far worse in his seventy years – indeed, if the gossip were true, he had, in his own variegated past, not been averse to inflicting pain on his fellow-men. Physical pain, real or imagined, had long ceased to hold any terrors for Sir John Forster. He replaced the instruments in the leather roll, and turned to the looking-glass.

The glass was engraved silver, inlaid with tortoiseshell. Sir John could understand why Robert Snowdon had been so reluctant to part with it, for it was as fine a glass as any that Lady Forster owned. Too good for a travelling dentist. Forster turned the glass in his hands to inspect the front, aware of the sunlight filtering through the mullioned window, aware of the column of his own riders approaching from the street. Then, jarringly, he ceased to be aware of anything but the silver and tortoiseshell mirror, and the paper he could see, neatly folded, beneath the glass.

Pulling up a stool, Sir John sat down at the table and began to prise the looking-glass apart with his dagger. At last the glass came away from the metal backing, and he was able to take out the papers hidden inside.

The papers he had found were letters, but he could not understand a word of them, for they were in code.

Reaching for pen and paper, he began to write to Sir Francis Walsingham, in London.

PLEASANT and easy-going though the Forsters were, Christie had no intention of remaining forever at Adderstone. Even if the entire Border area had not been infected with a particularly incomprehensible sort of insanity, then she would have still quietly schemed and saved and planned. If she let herself begin to tolerate (and then, insidiously, to enjoy) the nights inter-rupted by sword and lance, or the vicarious excitement of a hot trod, then she knew what fate would eventually be allotted to her. Everybody's aunt, an old maid, good-natured because that was her only form of payment, passionless, because passion, like birth and independence, had been denied her.

Waiting inside the small jeweller's shop in Alnwick High Street, Christie pushed a stray lock of hair back into place and began, again, to plan. You could hire a post horse for three-pence a mile – how many miles were there between Adderstone and Dover? Too many threepences, suspected Christie. Far too many.

Arbel, a cloud of rose-coloured silk in the doorway, hissed, 'Aunt Margaret's coming down the street – she's talking to Rob. She looks so *cross* –' Arbel smiled, and the jeweller's boy, crouched in a corner of the room with a polishing rag, dropped his jar of beeswax. 'I'll say I'm buying a pair of ear-drops,' said Arbel, helpfully, coming into the shop as the jeweller's boy scrabbled under the table. 'Aunt Margaret knows I lost one the other day. *Hush*, Dowzabel,' she added, kissing the crown of her dog's beribboned head.

How long did it take to value a rather horrid pearl pendant?

'Your ear-drop's on top of your chest,' said Christie, glancing quickly out to the street again. 'Rob found it.'

She could see Rob now, standing next to the blacksmith's, gazing black-browed round the market-place. Rob had lost his best horse to Luke Ridley a week ago, in some ridiculous wager. Richie had unsympathetically told Rob that horse-theft was, after all, Luke's trade, and Arbel had laughed and played with her dog. But Christie had seen how Rob had looked at Arbel, sitting on the floor in a pool of sky-blue silk, singing nonsense rhymes to a puppy.

'She's gone to the draper's,' said Arbel, poking her blonde head out of the doorway. 'For more black mockado, I expect. Do you think that Aunt Margaret *courted* in black mockado, Christie?'

Christie, walking to the foot of the stairs, called, 'Mr Reade!' Her voice bounced and echoed on the winding wooden stairway. She had, of course, told no one but Arbel of her plans, because anyone other than Arbel would try and stop her. They would say, 'France? Don't be ridiculous, my dear,' or more gently point out that her mother must be long dead. Only with Arbel, as with Anne, did you never get the conventional answer. There was, though, a small part of Christie's own eminently practical soul that saw it, as Arbel did, as an adventure.

'Black ribbon,' said Arbel, gazing down the street again. 'Do you think she thinks we've been kidnapped?'

Christie, adding pennies, did not answer. Even if she gathered her ten sovereigns, there was still Arbel's future to settle. Arbel had received proposals a-plenty since she had arrived in Northumberland, and had turned down every one of them. Arbel had a ridiculous obsession with Luke Ridley. The unpleasant scene at Catcleugh had not, as Christie had hoped, discouraged Arbel. Arbel was not used to rejection: Arbel regarded Luke Ridley's uninterested blue eyes and slatternly mistress only as a challenge. Christie never wanted to see the man again.

She heard, with an exhalation of relief, the clack of the jeweller's pattens on the stairs. Even at midsummer Simon

Reade wore layer upon layer of shirts, doublets, jackets and robes. He held the pearl pendant in one hand, and a spy-glass in the other.

'I'll give you three sovereigns for it, mistress. It'll need resetting, so I can offer no more.'

'I'll take them.' Christie took the three gold coins and hid them in her sleeve. She glanced uncertainly towards Arbel.

Arbel threaded her arm through Christie's.

'What would I want with a pendant that looks like something Dowzabel has coughed up?' she said, comfortingly, and smiled.

Sir John Forster's letter was delivered to Sir Francis Walsingham at his home in Barnes near London, by his undersecretary, Thomas Phelippes.

Phelippes had ridden from Whitehall that afternoon, travelling alone through the stultifying heat of London in July, a satchel slung over his shoulder. He reached Barn Elms in the early evening, his pale, untidy hair stuck to his scalp with sweat, the plume of his velvet cap drooping like an unwatered flower. Trees cast their long shadows over the pathway and the front fascia of the house; Phelippes, young enough not to feel tired from the hours in the saddle, threw his reins to the stableboy, and knocked at the front door.

He was taken to a back parlour overlooking the garden, where Sir Francis sat beside an open window, writing. Phelippes grinned to himself: words were their trade and their lever, with words they conjured secrets, with words they could persuade a servant to sell his master, a sweetheart to betray her lover. Thomas Phelippes enjoyed words, numbers, and puzzles. His work for Queen Elizabeth's Secretary of State was the most glorious, exhilarating puzzle of them all.

He received no answering smile from Sir Francis, and expected none. But he had a nod and a greeting, and refreshments were brought into the room as Phelippes placed the satchel on the desk.

When the servant had gone and Phelippes was seated, his fingers cradling a goblet of wine, Walsingham opened the satchel. The candles were not yet lit, but the setting sun underlined the long, ascetic face, the dark brows and beard, the cold, shadowed eyes. Sir Francis Walsingham was in his fifties and in poor health, but his network of spies and informers threaded across Europe as far as Constantinople and Tripoli. Much of the satchel's contents were letters: the quiet of the house and gardens was broken by the scratch of pen on paper, the making and breaking of seals. Phelippes rose and lit a candle and placed it on the desk. Walsingham did not even look up.

He paused, though, halfway through the documents, a letter and its enclosures spread out before him. Several of the enclosures he took and held up to the candlelight.

'Sir John Forster has found a dentist who carries enciphered letters,' he said. 'My good Thomas – you are not too tired?'

A CIPHER was the most perfect puzzle to Phelippes, as intricate as a chess game, more rewarding than a round of dice. Seated alone in one of Barn Elms' many rooms, with only a flagon of wine and a candle for company, Thomas Phelippes applied himself to the dentist's cipher. He was not in the least tired, he was never tired, it was only boredom that crushed him, sending him yawning and groaning into a deep, unsatisfying sleep. If his mind was occupied he was alive, fed by the pleasure of adjusting letters and numbers until they formed a recognizable pattern, until, finally, there were words where there had been nonsense. It was a pleasure, he sometimes thought, comparable only to the pleasure of lying with a woman, a comparison he could never have suggested to Sir Francis.

He had the contents of Sir John Forster's letter by nightfall. The wine-bottle was empty, but Thomas Phelippes's head was perfectly clear as he laid the ciphers and their key on Sir Francis Walsingham's desk. 'The Sieur d'Aubigny has mislaid his correspondence,' he said, softly, and was rewarded by a gleam of light in the dark, opaque eyes.

Phelippes waited in silence, sitting, his long legs flung out before him, his doublet loosened because of the warm evening, while Walsingham studied his decoding. He thought of the Sieur d'Aubigny, now the Duke of Lennox, resident in Scotland for the past three years, and a letter, received only the previous month, from Sir Henry Woodryngton in Berwick. '*The King altogether is persuaded and led by the Duke, for he can hardly suffer him out of his presence, and is in such love with him, as in the open sight of the people oftentimes he will clasp him about the neck with his arms and kiss him.*' Esmé Stuart, Sieur d'Aubigny and Duke of Lennox, was a handsome, sophisticated man in his thirties; the young James VI of Scotland was barely seventeen years old. Thomas Phelippes did not give a damn about the King of Scots' sexual inclinations, but he knew, as Sir Francis Walsingham also knew, that Esmé Stuart was French and a client of the powerful Guises. And Mary Stuart, Queen Elizabeth's prisoner, was the daughter of a Guise . . .

At last, Walsingham put down the papers and sat back in his chair. His eyes were fixed neither on Phelippes nor on the letters, but on some darkness he saw before him. Sir Francis said,

'The hounds begin to gather, Thomas. Yelping and scraping at the Border. Philip of Spain, the Guises in France, Mary of Scotland . . .' He paused for a moment, his hands folded, his eyes hooded. 'The priests from Douai, as well. Who was our dentist, do you think, Thomas – Father Watts, Father Holt – Cardinal Allen?'

'Dr Allen is in France, sir, we believe.' Briefly, Phelippes considered the Jesuit priests and their whereabouts. 'The others – it could have been any one of them. Or none.'

'None?' Walsingham rose, and went to stand by the open window. 'Explain, if you please, Thomas.'

Phelippes' brows drew together, and there was an unquenchable glint of joy in his pale-fringed eyes. 'You recall the letter we received from Berwick a month or two past?' he asked, and Sir Francis nodded. Phelippes could see that letter in his mind's eye, from the greeting at the top of the page to the final flourish of the signature.

'Woodryngton's man followed a rider across the Border into Scotland, to a tower where letters and money were exchanged. The letters were from France, transported on a galleon whose activities are now, of course, carefully watched. The destination of the letters – well, the name of d'Aubigny sprang to mind, I recall.' Thomas leaned back, knitting his fingers in front of him. 'Now, we have known for some time that Sir John Forster has an informer whose face he has never seen. Letters are left in prearranged places, or passed in a crowded tavern or brothel. Money is likewise duly collected. It occurred to me, sir, that Forster's informant and the cloaked gentleman of Woodryngton's letter are both motivated by rapacity, not principle. What if Sir John Forster's dentist was not a priest, but a man short of a few shillings?'

Walsingham was silent for a moment, considering. Then he said,

'You are suggesting that all these – incidents – have concerned the same man?'

Phelippes nodded.

'Perhaps.' Walsingham laid his hands on the window-sill and gazed out to the garden. The heavy night-fragrance of honeysuckle drifted into the room, masking the more prosaic scents of beeswax and ink. 'Perhaps – but I don't think so. Cast your mind back, Thomas. Consider this helpful gentleman's career. Easing the task of the priest, the informer, the agent. Working for both sides, for any side, for money. Enabling letters to be carried from the Continent to Scotland through the most desolate of God's lands. The most desolate, Thomas.'

'By all accounts he led Sir Henry Woodryngton's man a merry dance.' Thomas looked across, thoughtfully. 'Then – not the sort of man, you think, sir, to lose his way in a Middle March bog?'

'Nor,' said Sir Francis Walsingham, 'the sort of man to part with his money and letters without an argument. No, it is a tempting thought, Thomas, but I believe that our travelling dentist was a priest. By God, I would give much to know which priest.'

'Although,' said Phelippes, obstinately, 'nor would a priest, motivated by belief, part easily with such documents.'

The papers on the table began to rustle in the slight breeze from the open window. Sir Francis closed the shutters, but the incongruous scent of honeysuckle still lingered in the night air.

'Whoever it was – whether there is one man, or two, or a hundred – we must *know*. The gentlemen in Berwick gaol did us a grave disservice in letting this "dentist" go. The *"Enterprise of England"* that these letters refer to – what is it, Thomas? And when – and where?' Sir Francis shook his head. 'We are embattled on every side – the serpent in Sheffield Castle has her supporters in France, in Spain, in Italy, and Scotland – and, of course, in England itself. Remember Pope Gregory's words of only two years past.*"Since,"'* quoted Walsingham, softly, *'"that guilty woman of England rules over two such noble kingdoms of Christendom and is the cause of so much injury to the Catholic faith and loss of so many million souls, there is no doubt that whosoever sends her out of this world, with the pious intention of doing God service, not only does not sin, but gains merit."* An incitement to assassination, Thomas – a blessing on the assassin of our Queen. An assassination to be preceded or followed – I know not which – by the invasion of our country.'

And Phelippes saw it no longer as a game or a puzzle, but as the gathering tides of war, gaining momentum by the hour.

'Invasion,' he said, putting his wine goblet aside. 'Landing troops in Scotland with d'Aubigny at the Scots king's connivance. Crossing the Border –'

'Possibly. But we do not know, Thomas, we do not know!' Walsingham's fist struck the table once: the papers jumped and the candle flickered. 'We do not know times, dates, places – names of financiers in Europe, of the paymasters at the embassies. We do not even know the names of our own traitors. We must know – and yet, I fear from these' – and he gestured towards Sir John Forster's letters on the table – 'that our time is running out. We must find a way of knowing, Thomas.'

For once, Phelippes was a half-step behind. Walsingham said, patiently, 'Woodryngton's letters. Forster's letters. What, Thomas, in such a dangerous, ticklish situation is the last thing that we want?'

The smile reappeared on Phelippes's face. 'Some damned freelance playing for both sides,' he said.

'Exactly.' Walsingham sat down at last, his hands balanced on the table. 'Let us assume for a moment that Sir John

Forster's courier and Sir Henry Woodryngton's cloaked gentleman are in fact the same man. What sort of man do you think he might be, Thomas?'

Phelippes enjoyed this almost as much as he enjoyed the ciphers. He leaned forward in the chair, itemizing his thoughts by ticking them off on his fingers.

'A man of no religion – like many a Borderer. Something of a gentleman – he travelled abroad with the Berwick galleon, so one would think he must speak some French. And he can write, of course. He must know the country well – both the English and the Scots Marches. Clever – some of those ciphers were damned clever,' added Phelippes, acknowledging kinship, perhaps, even, superiority. 'But his purse must often be empty, I think.'

'An unprincipled scoundrel,' said Sir Francis Walsingham, softly, and Phelippes nodded, unable to keep the glee from his eyes.

'A local man,' he said. 'A reiver.'

There was a taut silence. Then,

'I would like to meet this clever gentleman,' said Sir Francis, gently. 'And if I can, I will use him. And if not – well, then, he will hang, like any other traitor.'

He indicated the paper, the ink, and the quill pen. Phelippes rose and took the chair opposite him.

He wrote three letters, one to each of the three Marches. To Sir John Forster, the Middle March Warden, to Lord Scrope, Warden of the West March, and to Sir Henry Woodryngton, Deputy Governor of Berwick.

Chapter Five

THE fair at Berwick was an affirmation of the town's sovereignty, a well-thumbed nose at Scotland, less than five miles away. A jumble of squealing pigs, strutting cockerels, and fat, wool-padded sheep, you could hear the fair before you saw it, smell the gingerbread and new ale on the salt-scented air as you rode across the bridge into the High Street.

The fair was held on a grassy field on the outskirts of the town, within sight of the new, half-finished fortifications, Brightly coloured stalls and tents were patched with open areas for jugglers and tightrope-walkers; coins moved from pocket to purse, purse to gaming-table. In the courtyards and alleyways close by, less public transactions took place. A nice horse brought illegally over the Border from Scotland; weapons and saltpetre, carried in someone's carefully designed hold across the North Sea; half an hour in Nan Salter's upstairs room, with the noise of the street outside chinking through the shutters, and a stool wedged against the door to guarantee a little privacy.

The Forsters toured the fair at midday: Margaret, Rob, Arbel and Christie, with John Grey from Berwick, and an assortment of squealing, fractious Grey children, each with their pockets already overflowing with ribbons, comfits, and peg dolls. The child clutching Christie's hand began to wriggle energetically at the sight of a hobby horse cavorting through the crowd ahead of them.

Margaret, at Rob's side, said wearily, 'Were I six years old, the prospect of a horse covered in ribbons and bells would seem a wonderful thing. As it is, I can think only of a comfortable seat and a glass of sack in Susannah Grey's parlour.'

Rob, already burdened with comfits, a basket of feathers, and a box of face powder, gave his mother his arm.

'We'll show them the bear. That should do – unless you'd like your palm read, mother, or a few verses from the ballad-monger?'

'The ballad-monger's verses are a touch scurrilous for my ears, I'm afraid,' said Margaret, fanning herself. 'And any gypsy worth her silver would tell me that I will be perfectly content when I have my wine and my comfortable seat.'

The sun touched the North Sea with silver and lightened the grey stone walls of the town. Margaret, heavy with buckram and cramoisy, looked enviously at the village girls in their light skirts and lawn bodices, and the men in their shirt sleeves. Even the wind had dropped. In Northumberland you could usually rely on the wind . . .

They walked on through the crowd, past the horse-traders and ribbon-sellers, past the mutton-pie stall, and the dog with two heads. Christie, cluttered with small Greys, bought a whistle, the same eggshell blue as the sky, for the younger child, and a drum for Tom, the elder one.

The bear looked moth-eaten and irritable to Christie, but to Susannah Grey's seven-year-old son it was a thing of wonder, a towering, magnificent, fabulous beast. The bear began to dance, lumbering from one leg to the other, turning in a heavily swaying circle as the keeper, a wizened, swarthy man half the size of his charge, played a penny whistle and stamped his foot. One of the bear's hind legs was manacled and chained. The youngest Grey hid her face in Margaret's skirts; Dowzabel, in Arbel's arms, began to whine. John Grey, who carried a length of tawny silk, a spool of gold thread and an ivory comb, offered to hold the dog as well: Arbel smiled and shook her head, and treated Dowzabel (only Dowzabel) to a kiss. Dowzabel, scenting bear and hearing the clamour of drum, whistle and people, howled. Arbel patted her head and whispered in her ear. The dog's growl became full-throated, Tom Grey struck his drum with both sticks at once, and the bear danced closer, evoking some half-forgotten race memory of fear inside Dowzabel's curly head. With a squeal like a stuck pig, she sprang out of Arbel's arms and launched herself across the circle of grass: past Tom Grey, with his drum, past the bear, which dropped, startled, to all fours, and past the keeper, who cursed in Italian.

The little girl began to cry, the crown roared louder than the bear, and Margaret Forster found a pile of silks, feathers, comfits and thread dropped at her feet as John Grey and Rob hurled themselves after Dowzabel. 'Gingerbread,' said Christie, meeting Margaret's impatient eyes, and led her two noisy charges away through the crowd.

It was easy enough to find the gingerbread stall: Christie merely tracked the warm, sticky smell through the constantly changing maze of people and animals, two small hands gripped firmly in hers. The gingerbread, shiny with gold paint, was modelled into birds and moons, fish and kittens. Christie bought a fish and a bird, which temporarily silenced both the drumming and the sobbing. Standing on tiptoe beside the gingerbread stall, she peered back through the crowds, looking for Rob, or John Grey, or Arbel.

'Scattered like skittles,' said a soft voice at her side. 'No doubt still looking for this.'

'This' was Dowzabel, her small pink tongue dangling from her mouth as she gasped in the heat. And holding Dowzabel firmly by the scruff of her neck was Lucas Ridley.

'A little gold paint might do wonders, don't you think, Miss Forster?' Luke surveyed the dog without enthusiasm. 'She was about to get her throat cut for worrying the sheep.'

The thought of Dowzabel, not much larger than a rabbit herself, worrying sheep, made Christie, reluctantly, want to laugh. The little girl still held tightly to Christie's hand: gold paint dripped down the folds of her best gown.

'I'll take her back to Arbel,' said Christie, wiping the child's sticky face with a handkerchief.

Luke Ridley, leaning against a tent-post, hardly moved. Only his fingers stroked Dowzabel's quivering neck, so that the dog's eyelids began to droop, heavy with sleep.

'I expect she prefers the pavane to the volta,' he said. 'Or thought that dancing bears might prefer small dogs to gingerbread.'

There was still no sign of the Forsters. The little girl leaned heavily against Christie's skirts: Christie could not possibly carry both the child and the dog.

'And are you here,' asked Christie, briskly, 'for the dancing bear or the gingerbread, Mr Ridley?'

He smiled. It was almost a nice smile, it almost warmed his eyes. His hand continued to caress Dowzabel's neck: the shivering stopped, and the dog, like the little girl, closed her eyes.

'Neither,' Luke said. 'To earn an honest penny, Miss Forster, at the archery and the wrestling. Preferably both, for I need a great many pennies to satisfy my profligate tastes for dancing bears and gingerbread.'

He was, like many of the men at the fair, hatless and in his shirtsleeves. At his feet on the grass was a bow and arrow and a mug of ale. It was all so easy for a man, thought Christie, crossly: wrestling, archery, card-playing – any one of which might multiply three sovereigns into five, or ten or twenty.

'And have you won your honest pennies, Mr Ridley?'

Luke shrugged. 'The wrestling is in the afternoon. But the archery was quite adequately rewarding – a whole purseful of pennies. And I am now about to succumb to the unmitigated conceit of wagering on my own likelihood of winning the wrestling. Which may make me as rich as Croesus, or leave me without enough to buy a gingerbread cat.'

'Would you – ?' began Christie, and then stopped, her face burning red. She couldn't possibly – he'd only be offensive. And if the Forsters ever found out –

But on the other hand – as rich as Croesus . . .

'I've three sovereigns, Mr Ridley,' she said. 'Will you win?'

She saw his eyes, startlingly blue against his tanned skin, widen slightly.

'I don't see why not. But there is always a large measure of chance in these affairs. The Herons might field some giant who merely has to lift his fingers to send everyone else tumbling like ninepins. And Gib Elliot is, I believe, the favourite. But if you put your three sovereigns on me and I win, then your return will be greater than if you wagered on Gib. It depends whether you like a gamble, Miss Forster. Personally, I prefer a safe bet.

And I'd wager all I have that Rob, who is just over your shoulder, is not in the best of tempers.'

Christie glanced quickly behind her.

'Gallant as ever,' continued Luke, ecstatically, 'scouring Berwick in search of cousin Arbel's dog. Well, I have no doubt he'll be *delighted* to find her safe with me.'

Rob, very red in the face, said, 'Give me the dog, Luke, and be on your way.'

The tone of his voice, his hands clenched, fisted, at his sides, jarred Christie. 'Mr Ridley found Dowzabel in the sheep pen,' she said, soothingly.

'Then Mr Ridley can hand over Dowzabel,' said Rob, not looking at Christie, 'and go.'

Luke stepped forward. Christie bit her lip and put out a hand to steady the child at her knee. Tom Grey stopped drumming and stared up at the two men.

The moment passed. Dowzabel, fast asleep, tumbled in a heap of hair and ribbon into Rob's arms.

'There's Arbel,' said Christie impatiently, giving Rob a shove into the crowds. And, turning rapidly, reached inside her sleeve. 'Three sovereigns, Mr Ridley,' she whispered. 'Please win.'

In the cool, dark, interior of Martin Grey's house in Berwick, Margaret Forster drank wine and ate sweetmeats, and fended off Susannah Grey's more incisive questions.

Coming on top of the heat and an indigestible meal of boiled mutton, neat's tongue, Dutch pudding and brawn, Margaret felt less able than usual to deal with Susannah Grey's vast curiosity. Susannah was three years younger than Margaret, with nine children still living, and pale grey eyes that seemed too large for their sockets. Margaret had already heard the details of Martin Grey's digestive problems and Susannah Grey's troubles with the unfortunate tradesmen of Berwick. Now, Susannah, her eyelids stretched even wider than before, turned to romance.

'You've a very bonny niece, Margaret.' This in a tone half the room could hear. 'I daresay you'll be finding her a husband soon.'

'No doubt.' Margaret's eyes, like Susannah's, rested on Arbel. Not that much of Arbel was visible: Arbel was hedged with besotted men, as usual, so that only an occasional glimpse of blue satin and silver-fair hair could be seen. Arbel's future should have been settled by now. There had been admirers a-plenty – what was the girl waiting for?

Fashion seemed a safer subject. Margaret, for the first time in her forty-eight years, regretted that she had not taken a greater interest in clothes. 'Do you like Arbel's new gown, Susannah?' she said. 'Janet helped her with it.'

Susannah Grey's pale eyes scythed through the crowd to inspect Arbel Forster's unnecessarily low-fronted gown, and then moved quickly to Janet, seated by a window next to her husband.

'She's good with a needle, then, is she?' Susannah's eyes narrowed slightly. 'But it doesn't look as though she's breeding yet. How long have they been married? A year, now, isn't it?'

'Seven months,' said Margaret, firmly, helping herself to another quince tart. 'These are delicious, Susannah – you really must give me the recipe –'

'John was born before I was ten months married,' continued Susannah, undistracted. 'And Bess before the next year was out. I've always thought a family would be good for Richie – settle him down a bit.'

The quince tart was not sweet enough: there was a sour taste in Margaret's mouth. 'Does Bess prosper?' she asked. 'Is she well?'

'Oh *yes*.' Susannah slid another almond biscuit on to her plate: crumbs had begun to gather round the ruffs at the end of her sleeves. 'Her baby is due before Christmas. Though she's so big I wouldn't be surprised if there were two.'

Several little Greys, each heavily jowled, had gathered around Christie. Margaret reserved judgement. Susannah followed Margaret's gaze and tactfully lowered her voice.

'What of your niece's little friend? I hear from Maggie Selby that she's of your sister-in-law's blood. Though she lacks her name –'

Susannah's eyes gleamed. Margaret mentally disembowelled

the loquacious Mistress Selby. Christie had pulled one of the children's knitted stockings over her hand, and had, with the aid of a chalk, turned it into a puppy that yelped and wriggled all over the children. Three little Greys howled with pleasure and crunched biscuits into the polished floor. Outside, Arbel's wretched Dowzabel registered her protest at her exclusion.

Margaret turned back to Susannah Grey. 'There will be a home for Christie at Adderstone for as long as she needs it. And she is young yet.'

'Your Rob seems fond of his cousin,' said Susannah, helping herself to a piece of spice cake.

'So does your John,' said Margaret, pleasurably, and Susannah choked and sprayed cake crumbs as she picked out her eldest son's head from the gathering around Arbel.

'John is promised to Lettice Selby,' said Susannah, when she had recovered, and Margaret smiled and wished the afternoon were over. She could hear, through the hubbub of the Greys' upstairs parlour, the distant sounds of the fair.

Margaret had first met her husband at Berwick Fair: not an auspicious meeting, some would think, because there had been a scuffle between the Ridleys and the Forsters in one of the side-streets, ending when Davey, with all the many gifts that had been his, had turned a confrontation into a reconciliation, and a reconciliation into a celebration. Six months later Margaret Forster had married Richard Forster, and really, when she looked back on it, those twenty years had not been un-happy. She hoped that one day Janet Laidlaw would be able to say the same.

But Susannah was rising now, fiddling with an unnecessary silk shawl, brushing down the weighty folds of her embroidered gown.

With one last, annihilating salvo. 'My Dorcas's Jack says that he saw your cousin this morning,' said Susannah. 'In Berwick, coming out of that dreadful Salter woman's house.'

And when Margaret, standing, looked blank,

'Lucas, my dear. Catherine's bastard.'

CATHERINE's bastard was lying on the grass in a Berwick

field, with a rather large Elliot sitting on his head. The wrestling took place in a small area to the side of the main fairground, a field already well trodden by archers, swordsmen and cudgel-fighters. The earth had been baked to the consistency of unfired pottery, and the sparse remaining grass was yellowed and twisted by the sun and the pressure of many boots, all hoping for a fat purse, or a barrel of ale. The crowd had tightened to a circle: men's voices, and not a few women's, penetrated to Luke's consciousness even through his hefty covering of Elliot. It was his third match of the afternoon: it was, he thought, as he wriggled his toes to get some purchase in the dry earth, an uncomfortable way to earn his bread. But at least he was, for once, fighting on the right side of the Border. With an effort, Luke twisted his shoulders and dislodged Gib Elliot. A kick to the softest part of his unprotected stomach and Gib lay on the ground, groaning.

There was a roar from the crowd, someone slapped Luke on the back, and someone else upended a bucket of water over Gib. Luke beat the dust from his hands, and spat the blood from his mouth, and took the cup offered him.

'Tame sport today,' said Randal Lovell, at his side. 'A whole two hours' fighting, and not a single death to show for it.'

Luke took the shirt that Lovell held out, and threw it across his bare shoulders. The sky was a deep blistering blue: no sudden sea-mist had appeared to dull the day's clear light. Luke's arms and shoulders ached, his lip was split and his skin stiffened and cracked with sweat and dust. Yet he felt pleased with himself: using his fists and not his brains for a while always had something to recommend it.

Then a voice from behind him said clearly, 'Not going yet, are you, Luke? Why, man, you haven't finished yet –' and a hand gripped his shoulder, hard.

Luke swung round.

Rob Forster was removing a rather expensive doublet, and a shirt, undoubtedly silk.

MARK Forster saw them first: Rob and Luke, beating each other to a pulp on a field outside Berwick. With a good thirty –

no, forty – people watching. He squirmed forward to the front of the ring, and watched Luke's fist hit Rob's jaw, Rob's head butt Luke's stomach. It was *years* since Rob and Luke had fought each other. Then, Rob had always won. Mark clenched his fists as Rob tripped Luke and pinned his shoulders to the ground. Rob was going to win again – for a moment Mark wished that he was a few years older, and that he, too, was out there, with half Berwick watching.

He stayed just a little longer, and then ran off as fast as he could.

ARBEL and Christie sat under a tree at the side of the field, with John Grey for company. John had spread his saddlecloth on the ground for Arbel: her embroidered skirts flowered over it, white cornflowers on a blue background. Looking down at her own gown's passementerie of gingerbread crumbs, gold paint and chalk, Christie concluded that a few grass stains would make little difference.

She was tired now. She would have happily ridden back to Adderstone, weary of quince tart and dancing bears and brown-skinned men that swallowed fire. But Margaret was still with the Greys, and Richie and Janet and Rob were nowhere to be seen, and John Grey was in the middle of an interminable story about horse-racing. The sun beat down through the oak leaves: Christie lay on her back on the grass, and closed her eyes.

A small voice whispering, *Rob and Luke Ridley are fighting each other, Christie*, woke her. Christie opened her eyes, and saw Mark Forster.

'Luke and Rob are wrestling,' hissed Mark again. 'You must come and see – Rob's going to win!'

Christie sat up, blinking, while Mark crawled away to Arbel. Hours ago – aeons ago – she had given Luke three gold sovereigns to wager that he might win the wrestling. But not against *Rob*. Rob should have been here, dallying with Arbel; or at the horse-trader's, finding a beast to replace the one he had recently lost.

To Luke Ridley.

Christie sighed, and tucked her hair back behind her ears. She saw Mark stoop to whisper to Arbel, and Arbel's swansdown fan paused, and then resumed its rhythmic beating.

'I think this weather is too much for Dowzabel,' said Arbel. 'Would you be very sweet, John, and take her back to your house?'

A few muttered protests and then John who, after all, had no objection to being considered sweet by Arbel Forster, disentangled his reins from the tree and mounted his horse. Arbel, standing, deposited Dowzabel on the saddlebow, and waved prettily as rider, horse and dog were lost in the tired remains of Berwick Fair.

'Come on,' said Arbel, who did not look in the least bit weary. 'Let's watch.'

There were a thousand objections that Christie, running down the slope to catch up with Arbel, could have made. But, looking at Arbel's face, she knew that Arbel would not even trouble to listen. Arbel would watch Rob and Luke beat each other's brains out with or without Christie's company. Arbel did not mind the cattle-raids, had been thrilled by the men who had broken through the gates at midnight to encircle Adderstone, had been unafraid of the intruder who had appeared in Christie's bedchamber, sword in hand. Arbel enjoyed every second of it, Arbel thrived on excitement, could not tolerate boredom. It was only Christie who hated the foolishness and waste of it all.

At the sight of Arbel and her silks and ruff and jewels, the throng around the wrestling ring parted like a noisy Red Sea. Christie, pulled and pushed to the centre of the circle, found herself next to Arbel, and within six feet of Rob and Luke.

If she had been able to see an art in the spectacle of two men mauling each other like wild beasts, then Christie would have supposed this the quintessence of that art. The audience certainly seemed to think so: it whooped and shouted and groaned like a many-headed beast itself, surging forward so that sometimes Christie felt scarcely able to breathe, at other times ebbing back in a collective sigh of relief. Rob and Luke were stripped to the waist, barefoot, their skin dyed a uniform dun-brown by the earth, their faces streaked with rivulets of sweat and dust. Much the same height, Rob was a little thicker set than Luke, Luke lighter on his feet. A great purple bruise suffused Luke's ribs, and Rob's face was smeared with blood from a cut above his eye.

Christie dropped her head, sickened. Yet, even if she did not watch, she could still hear the voices calling around her. *In the guts – right in the guts, man! Break his bloody neck!* She, too, had invested something in this brutality. And there were the spare, spontaneous noises of the wrestlers themselves – a gasp, a flurry of over-fast, painful breathing, a dull thud as a head or an arm or a back hit the baked earth. Raising her head, Christie glanced at Arbel. Arbel's eyes had not left the glistening, contorted figures before her, and she did not move when Christie tugged at her sleeve.

A voice to her side said, 'He's going to kill him!' and Christie, looking up at the centre of the ring again, saw that what was taking place before her had gone past the stage of mere male foolishness, and had hardened into something irretrievably bitter. Luke had dropped to his knees, his hands spread on the earth for balance, and Rob, his back to Christie, was pummelling his face, over and over again.

Christie saw Rob pause long enough to lean forward and say something, his voice audible only to Luke. Luke swayed, and Rob upraised his fist for a final blow.

She heard her own voice cry out, and believed it lost in the tumult.

LUKE hardly ever lost his temper: he had learned the folly of that years ago, with Stephen. If you lost your temper, you lost your judgement; if you lost your judgement, then you had not a hope in hell. He had learned what happened to men who thought with their spleen or their balls: they ended up with the hangman's noose for a collar, or the life choked out of them in some secluded murder hole.

And he did not lose his temper now, even when Rob leaned forward and hissed, 'Take after your mother, don't you, Luke – *she* couldn't resist a pretty face –'

Even then, he did not, as others might have done, let fly anyhow, wasting what little thought and strength he had left in a futile gesture. Instead he waited for the precise moment when Rob's concentration would slip, when Rob, losing judgement, would overreach himself. For Luke did not intend to lose. There was a red haze before his eyes, and a persistent buzzing in his ears, and he knew exactly how to finish Rob, it was only the damnable weakness of his limbs that made him pause, waiting for just the right moment. Years ago, Rob had won every time; but those times had changed. For five years Luke had depended on the strength of his fists and the agility of his brain for simple survival: Rob had wined and dined and danced at Adderstone. In spite of the pain and exhaustion, he was going to enjoy this –

He heard a girl's voice cry out his name, and felt surprise, and then amusement. *She wanted her three sovereigns' worth.*

Rob heard her call, too: his arm pulled back, and his eyes shifted for a fraction of a second from Luke to the crowd that surrounded them.

A fraction of a second was long enough. Long enough to get to his feet, long enough to hear the *click* as his bare foot jabbed Rob's knee in just the right place. Rob collapsed like a hamstrung colt to the ground, and Luke grabbed a handful of dark Forster hair before he could turn. Then he struck the back of Rob's head against the hard earth so that the dark-blue eyes closed, and the open fingers twitched once and then relaxed.

Luke did not move, because he could not. He was aware of the silence that somehow seemed more shocking than the noise, and then the wail of triumph closely following the silence. Hands struck him on the back, someone threw a bucket of water over Rob, and Luke let his torn fingers trail in the slow brown rivulet as it trickled past him. He looked up, but could not see. Covering his face with his wet hands, fighting nausea, he stood up. Someone pressed a purse into his loose fist, and he stared at him, murder in his eyes. Then he heard Randal Lovell say, 'You haven't killed him.' And he let the gypsy pull him through the crowd, careless of whom he pushed or shoved, making for the sanity of the horse-trader's tent.

*

SHE was there, though, waiting for him in the cool, dark silence.

He had half expected it: he had glimpsed Arbel's face at the wrestling match, taut and intense. Then, the thought had crossed his mind that she had wanted to see someone die. Which one of them? He had seen that expression before, but rarely in a woman's eyes.

'You should not have come here,' he said, flatly.

His lips and tongue felt as if they belonged to someone else. There was aqua vitae in a saddlebag to the side of the tent: Luke uncorked the bottle and drank deeply. And added, wiping the blood from his mouth with the back of his hand, 'You should go.'

Arbel did not go. Her hair tumbled in a hypnotic swathe over her slender shoulders, the skirt of her blue gown was clouded with dust, and yet her fine pale face, framed by a fragile white ruff, was unmarred. Arbel reached up and touched Luke's damaged eye. Then she drew her hand away and studied her tapering scarlet fingertips, and put them to her own small mouth and kissed them, one by one.

He knew then what he had seen in Arbel Forster's eyes that night at Adderstone. He knew also why he had slighted her at Catcleugh. Arbel did not think in quite the same way as other people; the rules that she applied to life were not those of her fellow-creatures. She was an innocent in the oldest sense of the word, one who recognized neither good nor evil, who saw neither cause nor consequence. A child's morality and a siren's body: a dangerous union.

He took her arm and led her, gently, out of the tent.

From the doorway, he watched the most beautiful girl in the Borders cross the emptying field to greet John Grey.

'You'll need something on that eye if you want to see tomorrow,' said Randal Lovell, seated on the grass in the shadow of the tent flap.

There was still a purse in Luke's hand. Opening it, he counted out thirty gold sovereigns. 'For the other Miss Forster,' he said. 'Tell her the odds were high.'

*

93

NAN Salter's rooms were always busy after the fair. There was a room for drinking and card-playing and singing, and other rooms upstairs, for when you didn't want an audience. The piper from the fair played, sitting on the big table in the centre of the downstairs room: he wore a kilt, and a steel bonnet, and not a great deal else. A Grey and a Heron insulted each other over gills of aqua vitae, and a fair-haired man with a black eye sat in the corner of the room, Nan's prettiest girl at his side. And on a bench, his thin hands threaded round an untouched tankard of ale, his knees hunched up to his chin, Malachi Ratsey watched.

Malachi had no particular convictions about either politics or religion. He attended church on Sunday because he would have been fined if he had not, and besides, there had been times in his life when there had been no one to scream to but the Almighty. But he would have worshipped the Papists' God as happily as he worshipped the Protestants', had he been called upon to do so. As for the exiled Scots' queen, now incarcerated in Sheffield Castle with Lord Shrewsbury and his she-devil of a wife, if it ever came to it, Malachi would be Queen Mary's loyal subject, just as he was now Queen Elizabeth's. The game he played, he played not out of conviction, but because he enjoyed it.

Malachi wore an overlarge doublet and a misshapen felt hat, and his eyes were half closed, as though he was almost asleep. No beards or false moustaches for Malachi Ratsey; it was enough, he knew, to hold yourself differently, to let the muscles of your face relax, taking on someone else's expression. Tonight he was careful, tonight he sensed (a squeeze of excitement to the stomach, the merest flicker of a heavy eyelid) vengeance, sweet and satisfying.

Vengeance for the month's sickness he had endured after the five-mile walk back to Berwick; vengeance for the slight to his professional pride. He had never, to his knowledge, been discovered before, had never been bested so casually, so efficiently. That man had not even thought him worth a pistol shot.

Older faces, stupid faces, Malachi disregarded, having formed a picture of his enemy from the minute clues that had plagued him since April.

Another man might have found it hard to remember the changing, interweaving pattern of the busy room, but to Malachi it was like a story. Malachi had always liked stories. You listened, and recalled every word, knowing that it would all make sense in the end. On the table, the piper began to squeeze his bellows with a naked elbow. Malachi smiled to himself: he liked songs, too. The piper began to play 'The Hen's March', and Nan Salter waddled down the stone steps and pulled the fair-haired man to his feet.

He wore breeches, a torn shirt, and a leather jack. He had a short sword at his side, and he was, Malachi had no doubt, a reiver. The man Malachi looked for was a reiver, Sir Henry had said so.

But Malachi's quarry could also pass himself off as a gentleman. When he had spoken in the tower, his voice had been clear and accentless. '*Sweetheart*,' Nan had said when the fair-haired man had first come into her house, over an hour previously.

'An argument with a battering-ram,' he had answered, 'called Forster.'

A Northumbrian voice, a reiver's voice, but still it had made Malachi shiver with recollection. He was not sure, though. Memory played tricks on you, sometimes, seducing suspicions into certainties.

Now Malachi watched Nan and her partner dance to the piper's tune. Nan wore lime-green tonight and had feathers stuck in her hennaed hair; her arms encircled the fair-haired man like fat, white, dimpled pythons. The reiver must have been three parts drunk, or he would not have been able to dance for bruises. He had taken off his jack and wore only breeches and shirt, and there was hardly an inch of unimpaired skin to be seen. The sailors from the *Elizabeth*, newly docked in Berwick quay, had come into the room: they, too, joined in the dance. The *Elizabeth* made regular trips to the Continent. The Heron and the Grey had drawn their knives: one of the larger sailors seized them both and hurled them out into the courtyard, where the noise of the scuffle was lost in the piper's music and the sound of boots on a straw-strewn floor.

'Luke!' called the large sailor, returning into the room.

The fair-haired man looked up from Nan Salter's vast bosom. *Luke*, thought Malachi, and let his eyes open a fraction wider.

'They said ye'd won the wrestling, man,' said the sailor, clapping the reiver on his back.

Luke winced and turned round. The light from the torches in the walls underlit the spilt lip, the black eye, the cuts and grazes. 'My,' said the sailor, admiringly. 'I wouldnae like to see the other fellow.'

Luke might have been smiling. 'He's awful bad, Sandy,' he said, his hands buried deep in Nan's coppery hair. '*The blood ran down Duncalie's banks, and owre Duncalie's brae,*' he added, cheerfully, in the broadest Scots accent.

Malachi's hand, circled round the tankard, began to shake. He took a mouthful of ale to steady himself, and tried not to stare.

Malachi was sure, now. Malachi did not need to hear Luke speak French, he did not need to hear him talk in that galling, cultured, gentleman's voice. Malachi knew, because he had heard that lying tongue take on another guise.

And because Malachi Ratsey, one-time cutpurse, had seen in that brief exchange, a letter passed, and as quickly hidden.

Chapter Six

*Y*OU could set out across the Border on a half-hour's notice, inspired by nothing more than an empty ale-barrel, or the rumour of a fine chestnut gelding. Or you could plan for days in advance, using all the intelligence and skill at your disposal.

Riccarton lay thirty miles to the south-west of Catcleugh, in the Scottish Middle March. Snug in the hills surrounding Liddesdale, Riccarton Tower looked down on the dark moss and streams of the most troublesome valley on either side of the Border. Tynedale, Redesdale, Teviotdale: all were bowers of peace and tranquillity compared to Liddesdale. The spoils and the risks were equally magnificent, which was why Luke planned when he rode to Liddesdale.

He had gathered his men, dispersed over the summer months: Red Archie, Dand's Jock, Willie Graham, and all the rest of their violent, quarrelsome, useful breed. They had grown fat in the summer, like the sheep, but the hunger born of boredom and empty pockets was already in their eyes, and they welcomed the notion of Riccarton on a fine September night. Crozier horses and cattle and sheep would justify the difficult trek through the hills. Crozier men were a more worthy opponent than a few drunken Trotters. In the room over the byre at Catcleugh, they sprawled on the straw and on the benches, and listened, reasonably quietly, to Luke's talk of Border crossings, fords, and the sort of valley likely to hide the Crozier cattle in the event of a trod. Mariota was away, which was a pity, as she was easier on the ear than Luke, who was in his most unsympathetic frame of mind, stone-cold sober, impatient with inattention or stupidity. Luke had the remains of an impressive black eye, and a string of bruises from shoulder to waist.

Dand's Jock glanced across the room to Randal Lovell, crouched by the open door, sharpening his knife on a stone. Lovell would be visiting the Croziers for the horses, for Scots nags were infinitely superior to English ones. At Dand's Jock's side Willie Graham belched intermittently and picked at his teeth with a straw. Dand's Jock had been half surprised to see Willie Graham again after last spring's episode in Rothbury. Willie Graham must have a forgiving soul. Willie had spent much of the summer in the ale-house, and the rest of it in Berwick gaol, because drinking gave him a temper and loosened his tongue. Willie was not drinking tonight. No one was drinking tonight.

Outside it was raining, and a wind had picked up, throwing fine droplets of water into the pele-house. A little rain was no bad thing – Dand's Jock wanted enough moonlight to see his way across the Cheviots, but not so much that anyone else would see him. Luke would be there, besides, and Luke did not need moonlight.

At Dand's Jock's side, Willie Graham had abandoned the straw and had settled down against the pele-house's stone wall, his eyes closed. Lovell had gone, and there was only the sound of the horses in the byre below, and Luke's voice listing escape routes and contingency plans. Long Martin was cooking: unpleasant smells rose from the centre of the room. Dand's Jock sighed and wished once more that Mariota were here.

It was only later, when they were all fed and ready to ride, that Luke drew Dand's Jock aside and gave him his message.

OR part of his message. That he had a call to make, and that he would rejoin the rest of them before they reached Riccarton. Luke watched Dand's Jock's brows rise until they almost met his intermittent hairline, and was thankful that Dand's Jock asked for nothing more than the time and place of their meeting. Willie Graham would have cursed and said that he could do it better himself. Red Archie would have logically pointed out that Luke knew the hills better than anyone. Luke thanked God or the Devil for prosaic Scots like Dand's Jock.

Outside, Luke saddled his horse, aware of the fine needles of rain, blown by the squally weather. A voice from the pele-house called out, 'Give her a kiss from me, Luke!' and he lifted one hand in salute and spurred his horse towards Downham. The grass was already slippery; the peaty shallows in the valleys would soon be a quagmire.

He had not told Dand's Jock that he had not the least idea who he was going to meet, or what he was going to find. Neither had he admitted that, for the first time, the two halves of his varied career seemed to have collided, jarringly, opening up all sorts of possibilities, most of them unpleasant. He had already considered and quickly rejected the option of ignoring the note that Long Martin had handed him. The mere fact of receiving the letter denied him that option, forcing him to discover the limits of his vulnerability. A boy, Long Martin had said as he wiped the grease from his hands on to his dirty shirt, had given him the paper a day ago. Or maybe two days – he was not sure. Briefly, Luke had wondered why he kept Long Martin. He could not even cook.

Riding down the rounded, shadowed hills, Luke considered, coldly and methodically, the possibilities conjured by one unsealed, unsigned letter. There were many who could have sent it. The Warden's agent, the Warden himself. Unlikely. The single sheet of paper had been a misspelt, blotched scrawl: Mariota, with a little help, could have done better. More probably its source was one of the reptilian creatures on either side that he had dealt with. There were more than a few who would like to see Luke Ridley dance his last dance on the gallows.

He had chosen to ride alone: if that letter had been written by one of the Warden's men, or by some other disappointed customer, then he would need more than his own small band of malefactors to save his neck.

The Blink Bonny Inn stood on the outskirts of Downham, not far from Flodden Field. It was a gabled, rambling building of grey stone, inset with courtyards, straggling with outhouses, gardens and hedges. You could have hidden a man with a sword or a pistol there, there and there. Three – no, two – men could take the simpleton who walked the exposed hundred yards between the copse and the stables.

Luke tethered his horse in the copse, looping the reins around the damp, gnarled branch of an oak tree. The stables were about thirty yards from the inn, backed by disused kitchen gardens rank with the remains of last year's cabbages, fronted by a cobbled courtyard. The sky was velvet black, a watery half-moon flickering fitfully between the ragged gaps in the clouds. Light showed through the slatted shutters of many of the Blink Bonny's windows; distantly, Luke could hear voices and laughter. And singing. *Where have you been my long lost love, these seven long years and more?* Luke did not feel like singing. Silently, well hidden by the thick dark-green early autumn leaves, he slid his back against a beech tree's smooth silver trunk and sitting on the ground, his knees bunched up to his chin, settled down to watch.

For almost an hour he saw no one but stable-boys, contented patrons, and giggling servant girls. He studied the face of every one of them under the lamplight, consigning them to memory just as he always did. He did not mind the wait, he was used to waiting, in quiet alleyways or in the corners of crowded taverns. His ability to wait had been one of the guarantees of his success. You failed if you broke too early and startled the coverts. He had learned to wait since Davey had died, but not, as Rob Forster believed, for Black Law. He had not set foot in Black Law since he had ridden out after Grace's funeral – *ridden*, mark you – and Stephen had not, as Rob Forster chose also to believe, sent him on his way with the point of a sword. Stephen had never lifted a finger to Luke. He had never had to.

No, what Luke had waited for, and over the past few years had won, was his independence. He was indebted to no man, he need call no one his master. Grace's death had severed him from anything he might owe the Ridleys, and Catcleugh, that laughable, fitting inheritance, had permitted him a trade, if not a name. Twenty men rode for him, twenty men thieved for him, not caring a damn about his birth or his lack of affinity to any surname. Twenty men followed him for one reason only: they believed that he could bring them back across the Border in safety.

And his other little diversion? Well, that had been partially for money, and partially for entertainment. Or intellectual satisfaction, or the pleasure of involving himself with a greater foe than a band of marauding Armstrongs. His involvement had been purely fortuitous at first, but then he had nurtured it, manipulating it, refusing to let himself be answerable to either side. He had been careful, but though he knew that the rope he had made for himself was a long one, sometimes he could feel it tightening about his neck. Tonight, it choked him.

The inn had been quiet for some time when he heard the footsteps. Running steps, loping and uneven. Thin shoes on hard cobbles, thought Luke, and stood up.

Someone shapeless in a long, dark cloak left one of the Blink Bonny's side doors, and ran towards the stables. He saw a shaft of moonlight on fair hair, but no face: the face was muffled in the folds of the cloak. He heard the stable door creak as it was pushed open, and saw the figure, cloak trailing in the straw, disappear into the darkness. He looked for a last time towards the tavern, the fields, the road, and then moved out of the copse.

The walk to the stables seemed to take an aeon. If this was to be someone's trap, then now was the time when he would hear the drumming of horses' hooves, the clink and scrape of bit and bridle, sword and leather jack. Now was the time when he might look up and see that the long game was over, and that Stephen's predictions of a bastard's birthright were justified.

He kept his sword lightly balanced in his hand as he reached, at last, the cobbles. Slowly, with his left hand, Luke pushed open the stable door. His dark-cloaked correspondent had lit a candle: the thin white light glimmered on the horses unmoving in their stalls, the tack hung on the walls. The candle flickered. Someone had lifted it.

Looking up, Luke saw the pale face and spun-silver hair of Arbel Forster.

HE let the tip of his sword fall slowly to the floor, and heard the stable door swing shut behind him.

'Arbel,' Luke said. 'How unexpected.'

The relief made him light-headed, as though he had drunk, too deeply, of some potent wine. He found that he wanted to laugh at the incongruity of it: Luke Ridley, armed to the teeth for a midnight assignation with a silly girl. Then, looking more closely at Arbel, he no longer wanted to laugh.

She wore something long and red, clutched round her neck with one hand. Her feet were bare, which accounted, thought Luke, for her odd gait across the cobblestones. Her dress and the halo of light cast by the candle gave her the look of one of Davey's portraits: a saint or an angel, perhaps, with trumpeting amoretti hanging from the corners. Arbel's eyes were not angelic, though, they were dark, lightless, and did not even cast back the candle's aura.

'You received my letter, then, Mr Ridley?' she said.

A hot wave of anger closely followed the relief.

'I did. Why didn't you sign it, Miss Forster?' Luke let his sword slide back into the scabbard: his heart was beating, he discovered, rather fast. 'Did you think I might decline your invitation? Ah, no – how foolish of me. You wished to protect your reputation, of course. A cloak –' his eyes travelled the length of Arbel's body from her loose hair to her bare feet, and came to rest on the generous folds of material gathered at her throat '– no, a *curtain* of secrecy. Just in case my poor lamb could read. Well, he couldn't, I'm afraid. And neither had he the wit to recognize your servant – your Hermes, I should say.'

Sarcasm, and classical allusion, were wasted on Arbel. 'The Forsters' stable-boy,' said Arbel, 'who hasn't a great deal of wit either, Mr Ridley.'

'Whereas you, my dear, are positively overflowing with it.'

Arbel smiled. 'Well, you are a remarkably difficult man to see, Mr Ridley. You do not call at Adderstone, or dine with the Greys, or visit the market at Wooler. What else was I to do?'

She sat down on the bale of straw, and placed the candle on the flagstones. Folds of red damask settled around her: Arbel still smiled.

'Well, you could pass the time with embroidery – or even improve your writing –' said Luke, carefully. 'Couldn't you?'

Her great grey eyes rested on him, perfectly calm, perfectly in control. 'I don't think so.'

He took a deep breath.

'I do not call at Adderstone – or at Black Law, or at any other decent address – because I would not be welcome there. You have not lived long in the Borders, Miss Forster, or you would know that there is a difference between a man who rides to defend his name, and a man who will ride against anyone – Scots, English, friend, or foe. I am one of the latter.'

Arbel adjusted the folds of material about her shoulders. 'Do you think I care, Mr Ridley?'

He had not taken his eyes from her. He could not take his eyes from her, any more than he could turn and walk from the stables.

'No,' he said, flatly. 'I don't. But you *should* care, Miss Forster. There are rules, you see.'

She looked at him, considering. 'You do not keep to rules,' she said. 'Why should I?'

He thought: because you are a woman, and the penalties exacted on a woman are infinitely greater than those suffered by a man. As his own mother had discovered.

But he said only, 'Where's Rob?'

He saw her thin arched eyebrows lift. 'Rob is asleep in the inn. So are Stephen and Christie. We went to Wark today, and I was taken ill on the journey back. Rob was most concerned, and agreed that we should stay here for the night. How did you know he was here, Mr Ridley?'

Because it would make it even better, wouldn't it, to know that Rob is sleeping only a few yards away. To know that Rob, damn him, is probably *dreaming* of you. And Stephen –

Luke shook his head. 'I guessed.'

His heartbeat had not lessened despite the apparent absence of danger. There was, he knew, just as much danger, just as many appalling consequences contingent on this rendezvous. But he had ceased to care, had ceased to see anything but Arbel Forster, swathed in crimson like a damascened succubus. A bed curtain, he thought, absently, its dark-red fabric streaked and faded by the sun. He could see the curve of her white neck under that incredible fall of hair, almost feel the heaviness of her breasts. He had no doubt whatsoever what Arbel wanted of him, this time.

'But there *are* rules,' he said, gently. 'And it really wouldn't be a terribly good idea, would it? *You* might find yourself hastily wedded to some ageing squire, and I'd probably end my days with a sword in my belly. There're too many damned Forsters, you see.'

She stood up, and he saw her lips curl into a smile. Then Arbel said softly, 'Are you afraid, Luke?' and relaxed the hand that held the material around her neck.

She was naked, as he had guessed, beneath the crimson curtain. The moiréed damask slithered to the ground, encircling her bare feet with red. 'I thought the straw might be a little rough,' said Arbel, but he did not hear her. He wanted to drink of a different sort of wine: his eyes were dragged from Arbel's shadowed throat to her breasts, to her belly, and to the haze of hair, a darker gold than the hair on her head, between her legs. She held out her arms to him, and he found that he had crossed the flagstones to stand before her. His hands shook slightly: he bent his head and kissed her, letting his fingers thread through that impossibly fine, bright net of hair before they tracked the hollow that ran the length of her spine. He felt Arbel's hands slide beneath his leather jack, pulling apart the laces of his shirt, so that her fingernails seared against his skin. He could hear the sobbing of her breath as his tongue found the hollow at the base of her throat, then her taut pink nipple, then the flat softness of her belly.

It was she who pulled him down to the ground. The clatter of his sword on the flagstones, the sharp cut of straw on his arm and face. Her eyes, wide and darkened at first, and then closed, so that the candlelight smudged the shadow of her lashes black against her cheekbones. Her hair, fanned across the stone like riverweed. Her hands, tearing at his clothes: skin against skin, bone against bone, the oldest dance.

She did not want to wait. Her fingernails pierced his flesh, pulling him into her until, at last, in exquisite agony, he ceased to know where she ended and he began.

When he opened his eyes, he saw that Arbel's own eyes were closed, her lips slightly parted. Wisps of straw had tangled themselves into her hair, and the bed-curtain had rucked up into a tattered scarlet rag.

In the hills overlooking Liddesdale, they waited. Dand's Jock, Red Archie, Willie Graham and the rest of Luke's men, and a handful of broken men and outlaws picked up en route to thicken their numbers. The sky was velvet black, and they had neither lanterns nor firelight. Not far away in the hills was Riccarton, and its nest of thieving Croziers.

Randal Lovell could see in the dark, though. Dand's Jock heard the gypsy before he saw him: horse's hooves on wet grass, a whisper of coal-black mane and tail. 'All's quiet,' said the gypsy, softly. 'The gate's locked, and they've dogs in the courtyard. And the bonniest little mare in the stables.'

Dand's Jock, who had been resisting the temptation to doze, struggled to his feet. He took hold of the gypsy's bridle.

'Ye can have the mare, Randal, if ye'll quiet the dogs. One of Crozier's dogs damn near bit my leg off last time we paid Riccarton a visit.'

Randal nodded. The only visible parts of him were his teeth and the whites of his eyes and the thin silver chain round his neck. 'The hounds won't so much as whisper,' he said.

Aye, thought Dand's Jock, who was not a superstitious man, but who recognized witchcraft when he saw it. 'We'll hide the horses in the brake, then. And –' he glanced round quickly at Willie Graham, who lay full length on the ground, his hands cushioning his head '– Luke said to take a dozen over the wall. The rest to wait in the moss.'

He saw the gypsy's black eyebrows rise inquiringly. 'Aye,' added Jock, crossly. 'The damn fool's nae here yet.'

Randal grinned. 'Trouble?' he said.

Behind them, Willie Graham stirred and muttered in his sleep. Jock scratched his bristly chin and lowered his voice.

'Luke had business of his own,' he said, and shrugged.

Randal's smile spread like a brushfire.

'Willie was all set to ride to Riccarton an hour past,' added

Dand's Jock. 'He said he'd be damned if he'd ride behind a man who cannae keep his breeches on for a single night.'

'Willie Graham', said a new voice from out of the darkness, 'would ride behind the Whore of Babylon herself if he thought she'd keep him in food and ale.'

Luke reined in his horse next to the gypsy's.

Far from being unbreeched, he wore, like the rest of them, a leather jack and steel morion, and carried a sword and lance at his side. His eyes rested benevolently on Dand's Jock.

'If Willie finds my company distasteful,' said Luke, gently, 'then he can always seek solace with the sheep. The sheep, Willie,' he continued, raising his voice, 'that are to be your charge tonight. The sheep. Not the horses, nor the cows, nor the wenches. Remember?'

Willie Graham's reply, as he struggled through rain and overweight to rise to his feet, was vulgar in the extreme. But Dand's Jock only gave him a slap on his back and pointed him in the direction of his horse, because just over there was Riccarton Tower, and it was only a couple of hours until dawn.

HAVING ridden as if the three fates were behind him – Clotho, Lachesis and Atropos, each one with Stephen's voice, Arbel's eyes and a Forster's sense of vengeance – Luke Ridley still reached Liddesdale more than an hour later than he had intended to.

He had crossed the Border just south of Pawston, riding parallel to the Border line, avoiding Cessford and Ferniehurst, and all other haunts of Kerr and Scott. The shortest route, but not the safest, for most of the journey he rode on the wrong side of the Border. But he had seen not a soul, and heard only the sound of his own horse's hooves and the occasional nighthawk out, like him, hunting. The hills had surrounded him and protected him. He would think about Arbel later.

They left the horses and half the men in the thicket of trees at the valley mouth. Long Martin, who was good with horses, gentled them, keeping them quiet. Quiet was essential: to make no more than the ordinary sounds of the night. A Crozier might close his eyes and sleep, but his ears never ceased their vigilance.

Crossing the moss in the darkness, they felt their way through the morass of stone and marsh that moated Riccarton Tower. Removing their spurs, they steadied their swords against their sides so that the betraying chink of metal should not rouse the wary Croziers. Dand's Jock slipped to his knees in the yellow-green mire, but he kept his curses silent and his sword-edge clean. The moon, emerging briefly from behind a cloud, lit the squat shape of Riccarton Tower, square and blunt against the curve of the hills. The man who had built Riccarton had considered neither grace nor beauty in his architecture, but only occasions such as this, when twenty thieves in the night might pick their way delicately through the moss, swords in hand.

Luke was first over the barmkin wall, closely followed by Lovell. There were no tumbling stones or clumsy falls this time. Inside, Randal Lovell bent over the sleeping hounds, whispering. Magic muttered into pointed ears, so that the dogs might dream of the chase, misty mornings and a plump hare coursing through the hills. Dand's Jock shivered and crossed himself.

In the sleeping quarters they found two pretty armfuls, one of whom spat, one of whom cursed. Dand's Jock would have liked the task of guarding the wenches, but that was left to a more fortunate soul. Instead, he helped Randal Lovell and Luke Ridley tie sacking round the horses' hooves. So that Dickie Crozier should not wake when the gypsy led a dozen good Scots nags through the gate in the barmkin wall and across the Border to England.

WHEN the dawn was no more than a whitening of the sky and a glimmer of sun through the clouds, Dickie Crozier yawned and climbed to the tower-head, and looked out over the valleys and hills. Clad in shirt and breeches, he checked that the gate was still secure, the stable door shut, and the surrounding scrub and stone populated by nothing more sinister than a bird or a rabbit. Shuffling back downstairs, Dickie woke up Isa, who pulled a shawl over her woollen nightgown and set off down the steps to the outside kitchens, grumbling. The Tower was cold: Isa wished, as she made her way down the stone steps, that she had worn her pattens.

There were two doors at the base of the Tower. The inner door was of iron, and the outer of wood, scorched a little where the Fenwicks had tried to burn Riccarton out last spring. Isa unbolted the inner door, and then turned to the outer one. Rubbing her eyes with the back of her plump, freckled arm, she drew back the bolt and began to pull the heavy wooden door open, sniffing a little at the chill early morning air. There was no sound from the kitchens: the kitchen-maids must still be asleep. Isa opened the door a little further, her heavy gaze wandering over the distant hills, the variegated emerald of the moss, and the over-eager eyes of Johnnie Irvine, looking straight at her.

She almost managed to close the door, for she was a strong girl. But the door was heavy, and soon more than one arm was pushing at it, so that eventually Isa had to give way and devote her energies to raining curses on the intruders loud enough for Dickie Crozier to hear. Isa stopped cursing when faced with a pair of light-blue eyes and a voice that gently told her to hold her tongue. A realist at heart, she allowed herself to be led outside to join the kitchen-maids. Meanwhile, there was the clash of sword on sword on the curving steps of the Tower, the creaking of iron hinges as the barmkin gates were opened to allow the sheep and cattle to begin their journey across the Border, and Dickie Crozier's voice rising above it all, telling Liddesdale what he thought of the English, the Ridleys, and the whoreson renegade Scots that rode with them.

It was all over soon, however, because there were, in the end, little more than a dozen Croziers, all under the disadvantage of being taken by surprise. Dickie Crozier, just as much of a realist as his daughter, did not insist on fighting to the death. There were easier ways of taking vengeance: let Catcleugh beware the long moonless nights of winter. Meanwhile, Mark Crozier had a knife-wound to his shoulder, and Red Archie a bump the size of an egg on his forehead where Mary Crozier had hit him with a warming-pan. And Johnnie Irvine bore a scarlet weal across his face, but no Crozier had been responsible for that.

The Croziers, with the profits of their own excursions, had

bought fine clothes for their women, and filled their larders as though it was Yule already. The unloading of Riccarton Tower was an orderly affair, completed in the shortest possible time. Dand's Jock hugged to himself all the way back across the moss and into the valley the recollection of Red Archie, staggering under the impact of the warming-pan. The sheep and cattle swarmed before them, a carpet of black and white and red, hedged on either side by riders with lances. Soon they were halfway down the valley to the Border.

It was only when they were almost within sight of the Border line that they saw the Elliots, fifty of them, each with a lance in his hand.

HE almost wanted to laugh: Luke Ridley with a flock of Scots sheep, Anthon Elliot driving some poor Englishman's beasts, two improbable shepherds facing each other across a sea of bleating white wool. Well, it had been a fine night for it.

But, again, he did not laugh. Instead, raising his voice to cut through the wind and the noises of the animals, Luke called to Willie Graham. Willie *should* have been halfway up the hillside, driving those accursed slow sheep to safety. But, damn his black eyes, he had done nothing of the kind. Instead, he slid his sword from its scabbard, and grinned mutinously at Luke over a dividing river of ewes and cattle.

'Willie likes tae fight, and he doesnae like the Elliots,' said Dand's Jock, helpfully, at Luke's side. And Luke, consigning both Willie Graham and his charges to the Devil, groaned, and drew his own sword.

Picking out Anthon Elliot's greying head from the throng, Luke yelled, 'Hey, Anthon – found a few more cattle for us, have you?'

And Anthon Elliot, delight in each experienced eye, shouted back, 'Naw, Ridley – but we'll take a few of yon beasties, and make the journey home a mite easier for you –'

Then there was the soft, unmistakable sound of a lance finding its way through the morning mist, and Johnnie Irvine, paying for his importunity a second time, slid from his saddle to the stone-pocked grass.

Liddesdale stirred itself into a witches' brew of sheep and cows, swords and lances. The cattle began to bellow in protest, the sheep to look for leadership and find none. Sword in hand, Luke sought Anthon Elliot, and found him, barricaded by ewes, efficiently dispatching one of Luke's less talented riders.

'Ye shouldna left your puir woman at hame last night, Ridley!' bawled Anthon, and, incongruously, Luke's mind jerked back to Arbel, candle in hand, with a bed-curtain gathered round her throat. There had been joy of a sort then, and there was joy of a different kind now.

Then, all unnecessary thought left him, just as it always did, and there was only balance and strength, and a need to search for a way through his opponent's guard. Anthon Elliot was nearing fifty, and had survived longer than most in his precarious trade. His seamed face under his steel bonnet was a mask of grinning, sweating pleasure, his right arm strong and skilful. It was not for their pretty faces that the Elliots, along with the Armstrongs, were the chief clan of Liddesdale. Elliot pele-towers pitted the Borders like a smallpox, every one a fitting monument to the success of force and guile.

But Luke had first blood, a scratch the length of Anthon Elliot's upper arm. Anthon's grin widened at the sight of the scarlet, washed to pink by the rain. 'Ma gude shirt,' said Anthon ruefully. 'The wife'll kill me for that.'

It was the sheep that complicated things. A few funnelled to freedom through the bottle-neck of the valley, but most surged round the battlefield, hemmed in by the grey-green heights of the hills, straggling sometimes up the scree to slip and slide, bleating piteously, back to the grass. Willie Graham had long lost control of them; Willie was enjoying himself, sword in hand, an Elliot to either side. The sheep churned the wet ground to a quagmire, a soup of mud and grass and moss. Luke's horse stumbled and, though he ducked, losing his steel morion, Anthon Elliot's sword found its home at last, jabbing him sharply in the side. The sheep bleated and the cattle bellowed, and soon there was a dampness that wasn't rain spreading over the faded remnants of Rob Forster's fistmarks.

Luke's sword had locked with Anthon's when Anthon's arm

froze in mid-air, when Anthon's narrowed grey eyes focused no longer on Luke, but on some not-too-distant point behind them both. Luke followed the direction of Elliot's gaze, and did not even bother to curse.

The English intended to reclaim their property.

A hot trod, complete with horn and hounds, hue and cry, and a lighted turf speared on the point of a lance. The Elliots' victims had been quick to seek their lawful revenge, enlisting, realized Luke, as he made out colours and faces from the crowd, the help of Sir John Forster's men on the way.

'The bastards have got the Keeper, too!' hissed Anthon Elliot. He swung round his horse. 'I'm for the hills, Ridley. We'll settle our account another time –'

The hills, indeed, seemed much the best option. There came a point, Luke had always been prepared to acknowledge, when events favoured retreat. That point had arrived when the English and the Keeper of Liddesdale had doubled the number of men on the battlefield. On another day he might have stayed and enjoyed the ironic insanity of it all, enjoying the glorious spectacle as they tumbled headlong into the great cauldron of the valley, English and Scots, soldier and reiver alike. But, today, he knew that the wound in his ribs had already begun to extract its dues from his strength and judgement. Today, he knew that there were many other knives waiting to finish off what Anthon Elliot had begun. Or, much worse, the hangman's noose that Stephen had always lovingly predicted for him. The hills, England, Catcleugh, were there, waiting, to offer him the only sort of sanctuary he knew.

Dand's Jock and Red Archie were nowhere to be seen. Willie Graham could, for all Luke cared, meet his Maker tonight; the others must look after themselves.

Retreat was not simple. There were too many sheep, cattle, horses, and distinctly unfriendly faces between him and safety. Gathering his reins, he used his sword to fend off only his more determined aggressors. Slowly, steadily, aware of the beginnings of a treacherous lassitude, he threaded his way towards the outskirts of the mêlée. Somewhere not far away he could hear Anthon Elliot, still cursing.

It was a sheep that felled him. He held his reins in his left hand, for blood had begun to seep through the slatted covering of his jack, and he still needed his sword-arm. A voice called his name, a sword met his and then retreated, and he struggled to keep his balance.

And when half a dozen ewes tangled themselves with his horse's hooves, Luke had not a hope in hell. Even then, if the wretched creatures had provided him with something soft and woolly to land on, it might not have been quite so final. But Fate proved disobliging, and the ewes, bleating hysterically, did not stay long enough to witness their revenge on their abductor, and the back of Luke's head, already deprived of its morion, struck nothing more forgiving than a lump of granite.

Chapter Seven

THE effort of opening just one eye was equal to all the travail – pleasurable or otherwise – of the previous night. But eventually Luke managed it, and then discovered that it had not been worth the trouble, because there was still nothing but blackness.

He was about to abandon the unequal struggle and let himself sleep again, when a voice said, 'I see ye're nae deid, then.'

A second blue eye opened, drifted a little, and then finally focused with the first.

'No, Jock, I am nae deid. Neither,' said Luke, 'am I in heaven. Or I would doubtless be denied the pleasure of your company.'

'Oh, aye. I'm bound for the other place.' Dand's Jock chuckled. 'I thought ye might be deid, ye've been lying there sae lang.'

If Luke concentrated, and refused to let his eyes close again, he could remember. There had been Catcleugh, and no Mariota. There had been the Blink Bonny Inn, and Arbel, wearing nothing but a bed-curtain. Then there had been Riccarton, and the Elliots, and the hot trod ... '*Where?*' said Luke, eventually. 'Where have I been lying so long, Jock?'

'Hermitage,' said Dand's Jock, and Luke swore, and tried to sit up, and decided rapidly against it.

'Aye.' Dand's Jock's voice reverberated lightly against the thick stone walls, the wooden ceiling. 'The Devil's own place if ye're nae wanting to stay.'

Luke had begun to see at last, to pick out the edges of stones and straw, and the outline of Dand's Jock's blunt profile from the darkness.

'I'd hoped Alnwick – or even Bewcastle. The Hermitage –

God's teeth, man, Satan himself couldn't find his way out of here.'

'Ye're right there. It was just our bad luck that the Keeper should bother himsel' with the Elliots and their quarrels. Forster must have picked him up at the Border.'

Dand's Jock fell silent, pondering life's mischances. Luke thought, when the pain in his head and his side allowed him to think, of Hermitage. The grimmest fortress in all the Border, Hermitage Castle stood at the head of Liddesdale, its dark, almost windowless walls reminding you of its black history. When you saw Hermitage, you were not surprised to learn that one of its lords had sold his soul to the Devil, and had been rewarded, eventually, by being boiled alive in a cauldron. No one left Hermitage unless the Captain of Hermitage intended them to.

Luke tried to sit up again, using the other arm this time, digging the heels of his boots into the earth. What little light there was issued from a latticed trapdoor a good ten feet above them. There was no other exit: only a cell of about six feet square, scattered with dirty, rank-smelling straw.

'The others,' he said, at last. 'Archie – Long Martin –'

'Red Archie was making for the hills last time I saw him. And Willie Graham was halfway down the valley with a dozen sheep. He always had the Devil's own luck. Dickie Grey – Long Martin –' Dand's Jock shook his head and watched Luke wriggle himself upright until he was leaning against the wall. 'I wonder if they'll give ye a physician before they hang ye?' he added, conversationally, nodding to the dark stain on Luke's side.

'You think it's the rope for us this time, then, Jock?' One-handedly, Luke began to disentangle the muddy fastenings of his jack.

'Oh, aye. I was always for the noose if they found me in Scotland, and I dinna think they'll let ye go with only a smack on your hand.'

'In that case –' gingerly, Luke unthreaded the laces of his shirt '–I think I'll forego the physician. I've always thought a quick death would be preferable to a lingering one.'

Dand's Jock laughed, a sound like a rusty saw cutting through unseasoned wood.

'But they were good years, weren't they, man? Do ye mind the time Red Archie found that lassie in bed with Dickie Hall? Or when Randal Lovell –'

He stopped, and looked across at Luke. 'Mebbe Lovell'll find us a way out of here.'

Anthon Elliot's blade had made a gash about four inches long across Luke's ribs. 'Randal will be well away by now,' said Luke. 'Selling the Croziers' horses to the English.'

'Aye, but –'

The sides of the gash had knitted quite well; if he didn't have to move too much when they hanged him, it should stay together nicely. Luke looked up.

'Since you so delicately refrain from putting your thoughts into words, I will answer your questions anyway, Jock. Yes, Randal Lovell may well be my brother, my uncle, or my long-lost cousin for all I know – my mother didn't live long enough to discuss my parentage with me. And no, I don't think even Randal could arrange for our release. And, though the thought of Randal Lovell and all the rest of the Lovells and Faas and Herons appearing to cut us down at our execution is a fetching one, it really doesn't seem all that probable. Sorry, Jock.'

'Nae matter.' Dand's Jock shrugged his shoulders philosophically. 'Though ye've some other fancy relations –'

Luke retied his shirt. 'I can't see Stephen pleading with the Keeper of Liddesdale for my reprieve. He'd more probably offer him the shilling for the rope. And Margaret – well, if Margaret's been talking to her darling son, then she, too, might have tired a little of my bonny blue eyes. I see my mistake now. I should have cultivated my relatives. Though, to be honest, I'd sell the lot of them to the Sultan of Turkey himself now for just a mouthful of water.'

'Aye,' said Dand's Jock again. 'It's a damned thirsty place, Hermitage.'

LUKE slept frequently and woke as often, startling out of terrifying, multicoloured dreams, believing that he had

115

screamed and learning from Dand's Jock's untroubled face that he had not. It was the fever, of course, the fever that frequently followed knife wounds or a rather hard knock on the head. A fever that could quite simply have been eased by a bucketful of water, but which burned unabated because he could not assuage his thirst. Often he dreamed of water: brackish water lacing the valleys, falls of ice-clear water tumbling from the hillsides. Sometimes Arbel Forster, as naked as a baby, stood by the waterfalls; sometimes Rob or Richie jabbed a sword between his ribs. Once it was Stephen's face he saw reflected in a still pool, staring back at him where his own should have been.

And then there was the black, destructive weight of Hermitage itself. He could almost feel the stones bearing down on him, choking the breath from him. *Peine forte et dure*: the slow squeezing of life from a tortured body. He had always known that if they reserved for him that particular treat he would, like Hermitage's former master, barter them his soul.

In the end, therefore, it was easier to keep awake. Dand's Jock had a pack of cards, a little dog-eared and very dirty, but complete. There was just enough light from the trapdoor, so Luke pulled himself into a sitting position, took the hand that Dand's Jock dealt him, and waited.

THE wait ended when the metal grid in the roof slid aside, and a wooden ladder was let down into the cell. There was a small heap of straw to one side of Luke, and another next to Dand's Jock. The movement of air as the ladder thumped to the floor dislodged the straws, scattering them like chaff to the wind.

'Damn,' said Dand's Jock, clutching at the straws. 'I was winning. Just you remember that, Ridley – you owe me three shillings.'

A voice called Luke's name. Rising unsteadily to his feet, Luke heard Dand's Jock add apologetically, 'They were offering tae use thumbscrews if I didna give them your name. I thought ye were deid.'

'Not yet, Jock, not yet.' For a moment, Luke's fingers

touched the crown of Dand's Jock's balding head. 'Three shillings, by God –'

He began to climb the ladder, willing his feet to remain steady on the rungs, his hands not to slip on the rail. Reaching the top, he followed the soldiers through dark passages and into the sunlight. It was easy enough to walk, Luke found, if you concentrated on putting one foot in front of the other and kept an even distance from the wall. Anyway, if he swayed too far they simply shoved him back into place. It was the shivering he could not control: the intermittent, violent shaking that bounced his brain against his skull and threatened to rip Anthon Elliot's sword-cut apart again. He had no control whatsoever over the shivering, which was annoying, because it was not this short journey and its inevitable end – though, God knew, he had little enough taste for that – which caused him to shake, but simply the fever that alternately burned and froze his skin.

He found himself singing the song that had rattled through his head since Downham and the Blink Bonny. *Where have you been, my long lost love, these seven long years and more?* and received a cuff across the face. Well, he didn't much like that song, either. The remainder of the verse pounded through his head in rhythm with his footsteps as they led him upstairs and through one of Hermitage's bleak ante-rooms. *I've come to seek the former vows you granted me before.* He told himself that he had made no vows to Arbel Forster, but somehow he didn't quite believe it. At the end of the ante-room, which contained a tapestry that Davey would have coveted, were a pair of wooden doors. They meant to do it correctly, then, with some sort of trial, and perhaps the Captain of Hermitage himself reading out the sentence. In deference to Luke's fancy relations. Who really were no relation at all.

When they opened the door he saw that he had guessed right. He recognized the Captain, who was, ironically, an Elliot of Redheuch. The Warden and the Keeper were Maxwells, but the Warden and the Keeper had better things to do than hang a handful of unimportant English reivers. The Captain was elegantly dressed in black and white puffed doublet and hose, and seated at a table across the room. He had a glass of wine in his hand, the sight of which made Luke's tongue stick to the roof of his mouth. There was another man – Robin Elliot's secretary, he guessed – sitting at a desk, scribbling. And in a soldier's garb of buckskin breeches and leather jack, Sir John Forster, Warden of the English Middle March.

Luke had not expected to see Sir John. Perhaps Forster had stayed to sample Hermitage's cooking, or to reap a few hours entertainment at the gibbet. Sir John Forster eyed Luke as a hawk might eye a carelessly placed rabbit. 'Lucas Ridley. Lucas Ridley of Catcleugh,' said Sir John Forster, and Luke bowed, and regretted it.

'Sir John Forster. What a pleasure. You are – let me see – my great-uncle once removed. My third cousin's brother-in-law's father. My –'

'I doubt it, laddie,' said Sir John, as one of the guards, suspecting insolence, cuffed Luke on the other side of the head. 'And the pleasure, I think, is mine, Ridley.'

'Probably.' Luke let his eyes wander around the room. *Two* tapestries this time, one with a squint-eyed unicorn that would have given Davey the utmost delight, another a hunting scene that dragged Luke back, suddenly and painfully, to the Great Hall at Black Law. Himself, six or seven years old, and Davey at his side, saying, 'An elephant, Lucas, and a giraffe. And the spotted one is a cameleopard.'

The Ridleys had a habit of coming to a bad end. Davey, with an arrow through his neck, falling from Black Law's tower-head; Davey's cousin Johnnie, Catherine's husband, his throat cut on one cross-Border venture too many. And soon Luke Ridley, swinging from a hastily erected gallows in Hermitage's courtyard.

Despite the tapestries, the fire, the Turkey rug, the room was cold. Or perhaps it was only he who was cold, thought Luke, struggling to collect his thoughts. He stared across the flagged floor to Sir John.

'I've waited a long while for this meeting, Ridley,' said Forster, pleasurably. 'And Mr Elliot here, and the Keeper have, I believe, waited even longer. So yesterday's affair was quite a piece of luck.'

Luck. Somewhere, yesterday, between Catcleugh and Riccarton, Luke's luck, good for five years now, seemed to have run out. Like sand through a glass, water through cupped fingers. *Water* – my God, what would he not have given for a cup of water, for a mouthful of the Captain of Hermitage's wine.

Sir John Forster, no fool, tracked his prisoner's gaze.

'You look thirsty, laddie,' he said, and going to the table, poured out a fresh goblet of wine. 'Drink.'

'Venice's finest,' said Luke, raising the glass to the square of fading light through the window. 'Via England, no doubt.'

He ducked, that time, before the soldier could hit him. And Sir John Forster put up one warning hand to the guard, and said softly, 'Keep your wit to yourself, Ridley. You were clever enough the night before last, don't you think?'

Luke drank, and the shivering stopped at once, and the edge of his headache was dulled. 'Not clever at all, I'm afraid, Sir John,' he said, 'or I would not be sampling your hospitality.'

'You've had a good run, though, haven't you?' Sir John Forster's eyes were level with Luke's, sharp grey soldier's eyes, neither rheumy nor overcast with age. 'You've lived fine these last years.'

'Aye – on Scots cattle and ewes,' said the Captain from behind him.

'And horses,' said Luke helpfully, having drained his glass. 'Scots horses are so much better than English –'

They hit him that time just where it hurt, so that he tottered forward and the glass slid from his hands, fragmenting into shards on the stone floor. 'Venice's finest,' said Luke, mournfully, and blinked to clear his vision.

He looked up. There was, improbably, something that might have been understanding in Sir John Forster's old grey eyes.

'Keep your head clear, lad,' said the Warden, softly. 'You're going to need it.'

At Whitehall, Thomas Phelippes studied letters, depositions, confessions. He held the disparate pieces of a puzzle, but not the key. He could still hear Sir Francis Walsingham's voice saying, *The hounds begin to gather, Thomas,* and know – dammit, almost *smell* – that Sir Francis was right. Yet he lacked, frustratingly, the evidence that must one day take him to Walsingham at any hour of the day or night, the evidence that would allow him to say, *See, this is how they intend to do it.* Throughout the summer he had sensed the intricate cat's-cradle of intrigue, but had been unable to lift it, triumphantly, with all its separate skeins and strands visible.

Yet there had been developments. Events tumbled like a poorly dealt pack of cards: queens, kings, and knaves, and all their shifting play of allegiance and alliance. The seventeen-year-old King of Scots had had a most eventful summer. In August, the schemes of Alexander Douglas, the Earl of Angus, delicately nurtured by Queen Elizabeth herself, had finally come to fruition. The young James VI, hunting near Perth, had found himself the hare, not the courser: captured and imprisoned by three of his earls, Mar, Gowrie and Glencairn, in Gowrie's stronghold of Ruthven Castle. Instability in Scotland was the easiest thing to provoke: you merely whispered in some dissatisfied lordling's ear, or placed a purseful of gold in his pocket. And there were dissatisfied lordlings a-plenty across the Border.

Phelippes' pale eyes had gleamed when he had read of James's abduction, his separation from the seductive, influential Esmé Stuart. Then the light had gone, and his eyes had hooded, and his hands caressed his ragged, pointed beard. He had read Stuart's confession, obtained under duress, and he had known that the game was not yet over, that they had merely been permitted a short respite. In his brief but glorious ascendancy in Scotland, Esmé Stuart had dealt with not only the Duke of Guise in France, but also with Mary Stuart in Sheffield Castle. He had communicated with the imprisoned Queen through the obliging medium of Michel de Castelnau, Seigneur de la Mauvissière, the French Ambassador in London. The Seigneur's correspondence would be watched even more carefully now.

The French, the Spanish, the priests. The priests stirred up the lingering adherents of the old faith in the north, where Catholicism refused to die. There was another letter, a hastily scrawled note from Sir John Forster, Warden of the Middle March. It had arrived only that morning, delivered by special courier, landing on Phelippes' untidy desk because Sir Francis Walsingham was sick in his bed in Barnes. Well, thought Thomas, gleefully, Sir John's letter should do more for Sir Francis than all the physicians' remedies of calves' turds and sulphur.

Sir John Forster's prisoner arrived in London only three days after the letter. Thomas Phelippes rode to Hendon, as requested, to meet him. Dozing on and off for a day and a half in a huge, sprawling riverside tavern, Phelippes had allowed his mind to dwell on Forster's captive. Had Forster's travelling dentist been a traitor by conviction, or a man who juggled with treason for his own ends?

The small cavalcade arrived in the late afternoon, when Phelippes, itchy and restless with boredom, had almost decided to seek distraction with one of the prettier serving-maids. Her name was Emmot, and she had a small, pinched face, a laugh like an ass's bray, and a habit of wiping her nose with the back of her hand. Yet she was obliging enough. But there was Sarah, of course, and Thomas had no wish to give Sarah a present of the pox. Still, Hendon was so damned dull, and the river, catching the first autumn leaves, was positively hypnotic in its monotony. So Emmot was on Thomas Phelippes' lap, and her small reddened fingers beginning to stray to the laces of his doublet, when diversion arrived in the form of three of Sir John Forster's men, and their prisoner.

Emmot bounced off Phelippes' knee, and he gave her a coin: for services offered rather than rendered. Grabbing his hat, retying his laces, Phelippes was down the stairs and into the courtyard before Emmot, biting the coin with small, sharp teeth, could follow the gentleman out of his room and return to her dusting.

One of Forster's men dismounted and went to greet

Phelippes. Thomas took the proffered letter and read it, but his eyes strayed to the other three men in the courtyard, from the two in Forster's livery to the third, clad in anonymous brown and black, seated on a restless chestnut. Phelippes could contain his curiosity no longer: stuffing Sir John Forster's note inside his doublet, he crossed the cobbles.

The prisoner wore no hat, and his fair hair was blown about by the brisk October wind. He was young, between twenty and twenty-five, estimated Phelippes, studying with interest the pale, high-cheekboned face, mottled with bruises across the jaw, and the eyes, an intense light blue, which met Phelippes' own.

'Mr Ridley.' Phelippes' hand stroked the chestnut's arching neck. 'My name is Thomas Phelippes.'

The blue gaze rested on him for a moment, and then Lucas Ridley said,

'I would bow or offer my hand, Mr Phelippes, but it's a little impractical.'

Phelippes looked downwards. Ridley's hands were bound together and looped to his saddlebow. His face was impassive, devoid of rancour.

Thomas heard one of the guards call out, 'He didn't like our company, sir. We almost lost him in Cambridge.'

Which accounted for the bruises, no doubt. The prisoner's eyes met Phelippes' again.

'They wouldn't tell me my destination, Mr Phelippes. It was all a touch enigmatic for my taste.'

'Really?' Phelippes grinned broadly. He signalled to the stable-lad to ready his own horse. 'I would have thought the enigmatic appealed to you, Mr Ridley. I would have thought enigmas – puzzles – ciphers – were just to your taste.'

Ridley said nothing, at first. Then, 'And to yours also, Mr Phelippes?'

THEY had drunk ale and eaten bread in the courtyard of the inn at Hendon: Sir John Forster's men finishing every crumb of white manchet bread, draining pints of Hendon's rather splendid ale, and then exorcizing the aches and pains of a week in the saddle by a walk to the Thames's sandy bank.

But although Lucas Ridley had drunk, he had scarcely eaten. 'Nothing else?' Phelippes had asked, and the prisoner had replied, 'Hobble this damned horse,' and had dismounted from the bad-tempered brute and followed the guards to the riverside. One of the guards, returning to the wooden bench in the courtyard, called out, 'Watch he doesn't try to swim for it, sir!' and Phelippes, dismissing the man's concern with a wave of his hand, walked to the river's edge.

Lucas Ridley stooped and splashed his face with the Thames's icy water. So, he wanted his wits about him, thought Phelippes – no bad thing when you were going to meet Sir Francis Walsingham. There were questions Phelippes would have liked to ask: the dentist's ciphers were not as good as some of the others – which were yours? Which did you devise? How do you work? Methodically, or by the bright unreliable candle-flame of intuition? But he asked nothing, because those questions were for Sir Francis, and Thomas Phelippes had infinite respect for Sir Francis.

The ride to Barnes was pleasant: autumn's fading of the countryside had scarcely begun. A few dusty flowers still lingered in the ditches, and the fields were heavy with spindle and whitebeam. If Lucas Ridley found the lush southern countryside different from his native Northumbria, then he did not say so. He hardly appeared to be looking about him, but Phelippes knew that he was. Phelippes rode to one side of him, Sir John Forster's man to the other. It would not do to lose him now. So he pointed out spires and towers, towns and villages, and Ridley answered politely, and all the time, Thomas knew, his mind was estimating cause and effect, probabilities and possibilities, chance and error. Just as Thomas Phelippes himself would have done in the same situation.

It was late evening when they reached Barn Elms. The sun had shrunk to a salmon-pink disc behind a threadwork of leaves and branches; the wind had picked up a little, rattling the drying grasses and teasles. The soldiers were yawning and talking of food and wenches: they'd feed them at Barn Elms, thought Thomas, and then pack them off to an inn in Barnes. And if Sir Francis Walsingham was already abed, then he would rise for Lucas Ridley; Thomas Phelippes knew that he would.

But Walsingham was not in bed when Thomas, leading soldiers and prisoner into Barn Elms' Great Hall, reached the end of his journey. Sir Francis was in the parlour again, in anticipation of their arrival, letters, documents and writing materials spread out on his desk, just as before. He greeted Phelippes with a nod, and a, 'Bring him in, Thomas,' only adding, 'You have done well, Thomas,' as Phelippes was about to close the door behind him. But Thomas Phelippes had time to notice the new shadows on Walsingham's dark, saturnine face, the loss of weight on an already spare frame. Then may Lucas Ridley speed his recovery, he thought.

Lucas Ridley was sitting on a bench to the side of the Great Hall, his eyes resting calmly on one of Barn Elms' tapestries. He was tired, then, that was good, people talked better when they were tired. And he did not know where he was, or who he was going to meet: Sir Francis's name would, Phelippes guessed, shake him from any assumed self-composure. Let's see then, thought Thomas Phelippes with a grin, let's see what a half-educated Northumbrian reiver makes of the Queen's Secretary of State.

Ridley had regained his feet before Phelippes reached his side. He followed Phelippes through the double doors, into the Great Chamber, and through the withdrawing-room, until they were at the door of the parlour. Phelippes knocked, and pushed open the door.

'Sir Francis Walsingham – Lucas Ridley,' he said.

THEY did not let him sit. Sir Francis took the chair behind the desk, Phelippes the cross-strutted stool in the corner, his legs folded before him, the back of his head resting on his threaded hands. You did not let them sit when they had ridden for a week, half expecting the gallows at the end of it, with no certainty of their destination. Sooner or later they might ask for a chair, or for water, or even just for an open window, and when they asked for anything you were almost there. The evening was drawing in, a windy, clouded autumn evening, when there wasn't even the reminder of blue skies and summer sun to tell you that out there, somewhere, was freedom.

Lucas Ridley stood easily enough, his hands loose at his sides, the candlelight glinting gold on his uncovered hair. No one lived long in his profession without possessing both intelligence and physical strength. Phelippes, scenting a fascinating interview, settled back against the wall and waited for Sir Francis Walsingham to speak.

Walsingham sifted through the papers on the desk, studying them in silence for a moment. Then, looking up:

'Lucas Ridley of Catcleugh? Thieving – burning – the unlawful taking of prisoners . . . Do you know the penalty for crimes such as yours, sir?'

The blue eyes flickered once, but Ridley answered easily, 'For March treason, my lord? The gallows, of course.'

Walsingham's hands left the papers, his eyes rested on his prisoner's face. 'We'd need not discuss only *March* treason, Mr Ridley. There are other kinds of treason – perhaps we should consider them. Yes, I think so. We will discuss treason against your anointed sovereign, the Queen Elizabeth. We will discuss what recompense may possibly be due to a man who passes information to an enemy state.'

Phelippes saw Ridley's hands tighten, but when he spoke his voice was level. 'The gallows again, my lord, but with a little refinement.'

'Tell me the refinement, Mr Ridley.'

Phelippes knew the penalties for treason well enough. If you were sufficiently fortunate to have been born into the peerage, then you merely lost your head on Tower Green. Phelippes had witnessed a beheading: he had also seen a commoner hanged for treason at Tyburn. In the event of his being offered to choose between two such abrupt endings, he knew which he would prefer. Not a squeamish man, the sight of a living person cut down and disembowelled had put Thomas Phelippes off his food for an afternoon at least.

Now he hardly listened to what the reiver was saying, he merely watched his face. Ridley's skin had drained of all colour, intensifying the shadows under his eyes.

Walsingham pointed to the letters.

'Your hand, I would hazard, Mr Ridley. Here, and here and here. And these, I believe, you intended to carry across the Border in May.'

Phelippes did not move. He watched Ridley step the pace to Walsingham's desk, and saw him pick up and study the dentist's encoded letters. 'No, my lord,' said Lucas Ridley, and put them down again.

'No?' Walsingham did not so much as glance at Phelippes. 'Can you be sure, sir?'

'I am sure. I have never seen those papers before.'

The long shadows that daubed the lawn outside had found their way into the room, stippling floor, walls and ceiling with darkness. Sir Francis nodded, and pointed to the letters.

'Then let me tell you about these papers, Mr Ridley. They were discovered hidden in the back of a looking-glass. Three of Sir John Forster's men took them from an itinerant dentist they had found lost in a marsh near the Border. Unfortunately, they let this – dentist – escape. Sir John subsequently sent the letters to me, and Mr Phelippes kindly decoded them.' Walsingham glanced up. 'I daresay you, Mr Ridley, could, if asked, perform the same service as my good Thomas.'

A silence. Sir Francis continued, 'These letters were intended for Esmé Stuart, Duke of Lennox in Scotland. Do you know anything of that gentleman, Mr Ridley?'

Ridley had stepped back from the desk. 'Esmé Stuart was the Sieur d'Aubigny, a client of the Guises in France. Stuart laid a successful claim to the Lennox estates in Scotland three years ago. And has been a guest of King James since then.'

Walsingham's dark head inclined a little. 'That is correct, Mr Ridley. No doubt you also know that the Guises, if not an enemy state in themselves, constitute an unfriendly force within a very unstable state.'

The silence was almost tangible that time. Lucas Ridley's forehead and upper lip were jewelled with sweat. He said, 'The Guises favour the claims of Mary Stuart to the English throne. But Esmé Stuart is now, I believe, in hiding. In Dumbarton, it is rumoured.'

Phelippes struggled to suppress a smile. Well done, Mr Ridley, he thought, and shifted his legs.

'You are well informed, sir. Esmé Stuart was, of course, only a means to an end – a cat's-paw. If his star is indeed diminished, then our enemies will look for other means of assailing us. The Guises, the Spanish, the priests, will not abandon their efforts to put the Scots Queen on the English throne. Rather, we fear they will redouble them.'

Lucas Ridley's face was shadowed by the fall of his hair. 'The letters were from Spain?' he said, and Thomas Phelippes held his breath.

'The dentist's letters were from Bernadino de Mendoza, the Spanish Ambassador in London,' said Sir Francis Walsingham. 'Do you still say you have not seen them before, sir?'

'I have not.' Ridley looked up, a single candle-flame reflected in each pupil. 'If I had, I would hardly have been so foolish as to lose myself with them in a Middle March bog.'

There was something almost like a smile on Sir Francis Walsingham's face. Almost. 'I don't believe you would, Mr Ridley,' he said.

'I do believe, however, that even if you had nothing to do with these letters, you have had a great deal to do with others. Let us, for instance, consider my agent in Berwick, Sir Henry Woodryngton. Sir Henry, in turn, has various agents of his own. One of them – his name need not concern you – met a ship from France at Berwick docks last April. He followed a man from that ship to a rendezvous in the Merse where letters and money were exchanged. I think that you were the man our agent followed, Mr Ridley, and because of that, no, I don't think you would lose yourself in a Middle March bog. But let me continue. Both Sir Henry Woodryngton and Sir John Forster have also received information concerning the movements of the Jesuit priests and the activities of Esmé Stuart himself in Scotland. One of Woodryngton's or Forster's servants – in a tavern, at a fair, even in a brothel – might find themselves leaving with an unexpected letter in his pocket, or the next piece of a cipher they had been following for months. Did it amuse you to play for both sides, Mr Ridley? Did it amuse you to let Woodryngton's man follow you across the Border one month, and to sell him information the next?'

There was wine on the table, and a bench to one side of the room. *Now* he would ask for one or the other –

But Lucas Ridley only said, 'These are mere children's tales, Sir Francis – maid's prattle of bullbeggars and bogles. There is no substance in them.'

'There is substance a-plenty in the dentist's tale,' said Sir Francis, glancing at the papers on his desk, and Ridley looked up sharply.

Traps are yawning for you, Mr Ridley, thought Thomas Phelippes, and watched Sir Francis lean back in the chair, his hands folded in front of him.

'Let me explain why we were so anxious to meet you, Mr Ridley. No – let Thomas explain.'

Phelippes rose and poured himself some wine from the flask on the table. 'These letters – assignations – secret journeys across the Border. We wanted to meet the man responsible for them. We wanted to meet him very much, for we wished to talk to him about his future.' Phelippes sat down on the stool again, glass in hand. 'So we began to consider what sort of a man he might be. And we thought – well, he is the sort of man who knows the Borders well. Who knows where to hide a herd of cattle when the Elliots or the Armstrongs are in hot pursuit. The sort of man who could take a dozen horses across the Border one day, and have no trace of them in his byre the next. You have a little experience of that sort of trade, haven't you, Mr Ridley? And although you found yourself in Hermitage Castle a week ago, I think you were perhaps unlucky. There were the Elliots, and the Keeper of Liddesdale himself, I believe.'

'And the English.' The strain, Phelippes noted with satisfaction, had begun to tell. Every so often the prisoner's hand would creep for support towards the window-sill, and then jerk away, as though ashamed of betraying vulnerability. 'And the sheep –'

The man's wits had begun to wander. 'We are agreed, then,' said Thomas Phelippes, 'that you know the Borders as well as any man, and would be unlikely to lose yourself in the moss. But, you see, we were also looking for a man of some education – someone who could read and write and encipher a letter or two. I believe you have had some education, Mr Ridley?'

'You were brought up,' said Sir Francis Walsingham, 'as a gentleman. You are illegitimate, of course, but you were brought up by David Ridley of Black Law, in the Middle Marches.'

The betraying hand ceased to wander. With a visible effort, Ridley straightened himself.

'Latin, sir?' said Walsingham, softly. 'Chess? Mathematics? Such disparate arts, don't you think, Mr Ridley, yet each with that element of the obscure, the enigmatic. Are you a good chess player, Mr Ridley?'

'Passable.' The man's face was the colour of the paper on Walsingham's desk. 'And I'll write you ciphers in Latin, French or Italian if you wish, my lord. But that proves nothing.'

Another silence. The servants had gone to bed: there was only the sound of the wind in the dead leaves.

'Latin, French and Italian, Mr Ridley?' said Walsingham, shuffling papers. 'How erudite.'

'Davey travelled,' said Ridley, softly. 'Davey believed that with a gentleman's education a bastard could redeem himself.'

Which told Thomas Phelippes more about Lucas Ridley than all the guarded, careful conversation of the rest of the night. He almost rose and offered the man his seat. But instead, cradling the wine goblet in his short, spatulate fingers, he said, 'Then you must see how useful you could be to us. You know your country well, and you are educated, aware of the dangers England faces. You are also –' and he glanced at the prisoner's frayed, anonymous clothing '– in need of money. And you do not appear to have a great many loyalties. You thieve for yourself, and not for the chief of your name.'

There was a ghost of a smile on Lucas Ridley's face as he turned towards Thomas Phelippes.

'The chief of my name, Mr Phelippes, does not consider me entitled to that name.'

The house was silent. Even the wind had ceased to pull and

drag quite so savagely at the elm trees that bordered the garden. 'Bogles and bulbeggars,' said Lucas Ridley. 'Nothing more.'

'But enough to hang you,' said Sir Francis Walsingham. 'Please do not forget that at Hermitage they had enough to hang you. If I choose to send you back to Scotland tomorrow, then at the end of your journey there would still be the gibbet.'

The threat hung heavily in the night air. You are a dead man, Lucas Ridley. It is only a question of whether they let you die before or after they cut you down.

'Tyburn or Hermitage,' said Phelippes, very gently. 'We'll fabricate the evidence if necessary.'

The blue eyes closed, and then opened again, looking at neither Phelippes nor Walsingham, but at the dim, dying garden beyond. 'What', said Ridley, carefully, 'do you want?'

So they told him. To discover the channels between the Scots Queen and her supporters in Scotland, England, and the Continent. To find out details of the enemy's plans. Where and when, times and dates, ports and Border crossings, Mr Ridley.

'If there is an invasion, it may well come through the Scots Border,' said Sir Francis. 'There are a hundred secret byways across the Border, and a hundred rogues – Scots and English alike – who would escort a messenger through them. You would do it yourself, Mr Ridley, would you not? The Warden's men cannot watch the entire Border, and those who know the land well cannot be trusted. You see my dilemma, sir? But I can trust you. With a sufficiently large price on your head, even your erstwhile friends would betray you.'

Walsingham paused, watching the prisoner, and then added, 'You will continue to live in the Borders. Continue, if you wish, to ply your trade of horse-thief. And you will keep me well informed – you will be sure to hear a great deal, Mr Ridley. Oh – and no more unauthorized trips to France, of course. You will remain in this country.'

Ridley said nothing.

'It's quite simple,' said Phelippes, putting aside his glass. 'If you do not work for us – and only us – then you will find yourself with a rope about your neck. We are interested only in the safety of the realm. Your loyalties – your commitments – do not concern us. Our assurance of your loyalty lies at Tyburn.'

And Lucas Ridley accepted, just as Phelippes had always known that he would. Some day Thomas would discuss ciphers and addresses, priest's holes and safe houses with him, but now was not the time. The reiver merely nodded. His head had dropped again, his hair fallen over his face. Then he looked up, his eyes focusing, with an effort, on Phelippes.

'There was a friend with me at Hermitage. John Graham of Bonshaw. Known as Dand's Jock –'

Walsingham flicked through the papers in front of him. He studied a list: Phelippes recognized Sir John Forster's crabbed angular handwriting.

'John Graham, known as Dand's Jock . . .' Walsingham looked up from the letter. 'Hanged two days ago, Mr Ridley. I have the list – you may see it if you wish.'

Ridley said nothing. He walked to the window and laid first his palms and then his forehead against the cool, mullioned panes.

It was the slow sliding of the palms down the glass that alerted Phelippes. Younger than Walsingham, he was on his feet and across the room before Sir Francis had risen. Ridley's eyes had begun to close and his skin to turn a peculiar bleached white as Phelippes reached him. Lowering him into a chair, they gave him wine and his eyes opened briefly again, and then closed, as though he did not choose to see. But by then Thomas had opened his shirt and seen the soaking, poorly applied bandage covering the old sword wound. Phelippes looked at Sir Francis.

'A dead spy is of no use to me, Thomas,' said Sir Francis Walsingham. 'And he cannot stay here. It would be too dangerous.'

Phelippes thought quickly. 'I know where to take him, sir,' he said. 'I know the very place.'

Chapter Eight

SARAH Kemp, having been married three times and widowed as many, and having been careful with her widow's thirds, now lived happily in Shoreditch. Almost forty, she had no wish and no need to marry again: she had seen three ailing, difficult husbands to the grave, had worn black for each of them, and had then settled down in silver-greys and crimsons to a supremely happy widowhood. Her house was a four-storeyed, cantilevered building, hanging over the cobbled courtyard like a new mother over her baby's cradle. At night, the light glowed through the slatted shutters; indeed, the shutters, the beams and the window-panes seemed to dance in rhythm with the music and laughter inside.

For Sarah Kemp was a collector. She did not collect miniatures (though she had already sat for Nicholas Hilliard), and neither did she collect glass, not even Venice's finest. She had belongings enough, amassed over the grey, husbanded years: heavy oak linen chests and faded, unfashionable wall-hangings cluttered every crooked, low-ceilinged chamber and parlour.

Sarah Kemp collected people. Poets, playwrights, musicians and printers, people who could make a party out of a dull October evening, an adventure out of the last spiteful dregs of a London winter. Sarah provided the setting: the warm welcome, the equally warm fire, the spinet and lute, the plentiful food and wine.

She collected oddities, too. Those – both men and women – whose looks had caught her discerning eye, or whose minds worked at a different speed or in a different fashion from others'. Thomas Phelippes was one of those: Sarah had a shrewd idea of how her sweet Thomas earned his living, but she had never inquired too deeply. She would have lost many of her more interesting visitors had she been over-curious. But she liked to watch Thomas play chess or backgammon or primero, to hear him calculate the odds on a game of hazard, turning the dice with his square, workman's hands while his voice listed numbers, proportions, possibilities.

It was to Thomas Phelippes that Sarah, who had not had a lover since her third and final husband, had opened the door of her bedchamber. Thomas Phelippes was no figure of romance: he was short, lean, his yellow hair generally untidy, his eyesight poor from too many figures, too many puzzles. But then, Sarah Kemp was no longer a young girl, and she had learned to appreciate, and even love, an original mind, just as much as she had always appreciated a beautiful face. And Thomas had not made love like a mathematician. In Sarah Kemp's richly curtained bed (a legacy of her second husband, a successful, if achingly dull lawyer) Thomas had forgotten his numbers and his devices, and said only her name over and over again while his body gave her more delight in one night than she had found in twenty-five years of marriage.

There was no contract, written or otherwise, between them. If Thomas was free, then he would visit, and be assured of food, entertainment, and the opportunity to sleep in Sarah's second husband's comfortable bed. If Thomas, as often happened, worked through the nights, then there was still the beauty of a Dowland air, or the steps of the latest dance at court to keep Sarah content. Sarah Kemp was finished forever with contracts.

She had not seen Thomas for several weeks when he arrived, late one night, a clatter of horses' hooves on the cobbled courtyard outside, a light tapping on the front door. Sarah was still fully dressed, in a long-bodiced gown with a lot of silver lace that made the most of her unsilvered chestnut hair. A poet was asleep on the floor in front of the parlour fire, the last couplet of his sonnet still on his lips. Sarah removed an empty glass from the inside of the spinet, and had Joseph unbolt the front door.

She thought that Thomas's friend was drunk, at first. Then, when Joseph had closed the door, and Thomas's friend was leaning against one of the drearier hall tapestries, his eyes shut,

Thomas said, 'He's got a sword wound under the ribs. Is anyone else here?'

'Only Nicholas, and he's fast asleep in the parlour,' said Sarah. Thomas's friend had opened his eyes: they were a clear light blue.

'Help him upstairs,' she said. 'The little room with the daisies – I'll fetch water and linen.'

She did not see Lucas Ridley again until the following afternoon, for one of the pleasures of Sarah Kemp's widowhood was to rise late. She had woken, briefly, in the morning to bid Thomas farewell. 'I'm sorry, my dear,' he had said between kisses, 'but I couldn't very well find him a room at Whitehall.'

She invited Mr Ridley to dine with her. Joseph brought him to the withdrawing-room, and she saw that he had washed and shaved and slept, and looked a little better than when she had last seen him. The brightness of fever had gone from those remarkable eyes, the cold anger had not. He still wore the same doublet, but the silk shirt beneath was the property of Sarah's third husband. She had left an embroidered doublet and a starched ruff with the shirt (her third husband had had expensive tastes in clothes) but they must have been discarded amongst the daisies on the coverlet. A pity. She would have enjoyed seeing Lucas Ridley in black silk with a diamond in one ear.

'You slept well, Mr Ridley?' said Sarah, brightly. 'You are recovered?'

'Perfectly, thank you, madam.'

It would be like dining, Sarah thought, with an unreliably primed pistol: a clumsy movement, the wrong word, and even Joseph would feel the heat of the explosion. Mr Ridley would doubtless have preferred to have been left to his pique and the daisies in Sarah's spare bedchamber. But Mr Ridley was Sarah's guest, however unwilling, so Mr Ridley would, at least, talk for his supper.

'The shirt fitted adequately well, then.' Sarah sat down at the table, Joseph poured the wine. 'I thought the doublet might be a trifle large – my third husband was overfond of his food. Pigeon pie, Mr Ridley?'

She watched him (covertly, she thought) while they ate in silence. She was intrigued: she could not place him. The gentlemen of Sarah Kemp's acquaintance had close-cropped hair and small pointed beards and ruffs like lace cartwheels round their necks. Mr Ridley's hair – the colour of old amber, Sarah decided – touched the collar of his borrowed shirt. His only jewels were the string of bruises around his jaw.

He looked up and smiled, but the smile did not touch his eyes.

'Let me guess, Mistress Kemp,' he said. 'You are waiting for me to drink my soup from the bowl, or wipe my nose with my napkin?'

Sarah smiled as well, unruffled. 'Not at all, Mr Ridley. Some might believe the north of England to be still populated by blue-painted savages, but not I. I am not considering your manners at all. Only your temperament. Have some rabbit.'

He refused the rabbit. 'My temperament? And what conclusions have you come to, madam?'

Putting down her knife, Sarah considered him briefly.

'My second husband excused his rages,' she said, 'by saying that he had a passionate nature. What is your excuse, Mr Ridley?'

For a moment she thought that he might rise and leave the room. But the serpent's smile returned, and he shook his head.

'Intemperance, Mistress Kemp, is the chief of my faults. Wine, women and bad timing. Particularly the latter.' His fingers curled round the stem of his glass. 'And what of you, Madam? Do you usually dissect your fellow-diners like a Michaelmas capon? Or –' picking up the glass, Lucas Ridley rested it between his threaded fingers '– perhaps you are merely continuing Mr Phelippes' trade.'

Meaning, she thought, seeing for the first time something other than anger, that you have had enough of questions.

'Mr Phelippes' trade is no concern of mine,' she said. 'Mr Phelippes juggles with numbers. Nicholas Browne, who also slept here last night, writes sonnets. Mark Faunt, who you will meet this evening, plays the virginals. I like music, poetry, and juggling, you see, Mr Ridley.'

She saw him push aside his plate, half finished. His eyes met hers.

'Mr Phelippes juggles with quantities other than numbers,' he said. 'And I am neither a poet nor a musician. I am a thief. Didn't Mr Phelippes tell you?'

Sarah was beginning to enjoy herself. 'Then I should guard my silver, Mr Ridley, and lock up my gold plate?'

'If you wish.' He had abandoned all pretence of eating, his wary eyes rested on Sarah's face. 'Or you could imprison me with all those damned daisies upstairs.'

'Mr Ridley. I stitched every one of those daisies myself!'

She saw the corners of his mouth curl very slightly.

'A labour of love,' he said, 'for the passionate husband?'

'A labour of loathing,' she replied, gently, abandoning the game. 'So sleep in his bed, Mr Ridley, wear his shirt, drink his wine. And remember that I choose the guests that I entertain in my house. No man chooses them for me – not even Thomas. If I wish to entertain a thief, then I will do so!'

She reached across to refill the glass. His hand trapped hers, and she looked up.

'Why?' he said, softly.

'For your eyes, Mr Ridley, your eyes,' she said, and reclaimed her hand.

SHE watched him again that night as one of her famed evenings (controlled chaos, exquisitely orchestrated by Mistress Kemp herself) gambolled gloriously along. The Shoreditch withdrawing-room – all low timbers, slanting walls and decorated plasterwork – seethed with the most interesting and beautiful of London's literary and artistic world. Sarah's cool eyes ranged from Nick Browne, scribbling a scurrilous verse on the misted window pane, to Mark Faunt, annihilatingly drunk, bawling out the verses of the latest ballad over the ale-spattered virginals, to the players from the Lord Admiral's company, who had turned Sarah's chambers into a playhouse, pulling tables and chairs aside, taking tapestries from the walls to serve as cloaks, the sails of ships, a shroud for a corpse.

Lucas Ridley played backgammon when he was invited to

and spoke when he was spoken to, perched on a window-seat to the side of the room. An obedient man, Lucas Ridley. Sarah did not ask him to dance, because she knew what lay beneath her third husband's carefully pressed shirt, and she did not ask him to sing, because to sing requires joy or sorrow, and she saw no emotion at all in those beautiful, empty eyes. But she watched him, because she thought that at some time the ice would shatter, and she still wished to see whether there was anything, or nothing, behind the façade.

In the centre of the room the players acted out the latest tragedy, with Letty Hawkins in the heroine's part instead of a shrill-voiced boy. Letty had stabbed herself: red wine flowed over her bosom and trickled to Sarah Kemp's polished wooden floor. Mark Faunt played William Byrd perfectly, despite the alcohol: William Byrd always made Sarah, who had not cried since her first marriage at the age of fifteen, feel tearful. For waste, she thought. For the way fate twisted and turned you, and eventually gave you, for a while, what you had always wanted. Mark Faunt had brought his hawk: it perched on a curtain-rail, surveying the company with cold, clever disdain. One of the players hauled Letty Hawkins to her feet. Speechless with laughter, she tumbled against him, clutching the worn velvet of his doublet for support. The player bent his head and kissed Letty's wine-stained skin: Sarah saw her push him away and run to the virginals, where she rested her hand on Mark Faunt's silk-shirted shoulder.

'*Then may chance thee to repent, the time that thou has lost and spent,*' sang Letty Hawkins in her husky boy's voice.

Sarah saw Lucas Ridley rise and walk to the far end of the room, so that he stood silhouetted against the night sky. Sarah continued to watch as he fisted his hand and struck it once against the mullioned glass so that the small lozenge-shaped pane cracked and shattered into a myriad jagged pieces.

She stopped Nicholas going to him, and went herself. At his side, Sarah said, 'A foolish song, I have always thought. Music should be a comfort, not a torment, don't you agree?'

He turned to face her, but she did not think he had heard what she had said. He opened his palm, and a thin trail of blood trickled over his fingers.

'What do you repent, Mr Ridley?' she said.

He shook his head. His eyes had focused again, and the anger had returned, masking what had briefly taken its place.

'Nothing, Mistress Kemp,' he said. 'I've just been meditating on my unpaid debts, that's all. A gentleman should always pay his debts.'

'Debts, Mr Ridley?' said Sarah Kemp. 'To what value?'

Above the window, the hawk blinked its topaz eyes and, lifting its wings, glided smoothly down from the rail to land on the fingerboard of the virginals.

'Three shillings,' said Lucas Ridley, softly. 'Three lousy, stinking shillings.'

THE absence of one Lucas Ridley, reiver, was noted with varying degrees of concern or relief throughout the Border.

Rumour, spicing the gossip like cinnamon, drifted, as it always had, around Catherine Ridley's only son. Luke Ridley had left the country, Luke Ridley was riding for the Scots, Luke Ridley had been hanged at Hermitage. Serve the bastard right, not a few voices had said to this last, and most interesting, supposition; he'd had a good run, said his more sympathetic compatriots. Margaret Forster, on hearing of her distant cousin's suspected demise, had sent her eldest son to make discreet inquiries: of the Warden, of the Governor of Berwick, of the Captain of Hermitage himself. Richie, meeting with a cloth-yard volley of indifference or uncooperation, had returned to Adderstone, patted his mother on the back, and told her that Luke would be all right, he was born to his chosen career, and he always fell on his feet. And Margaret had smiled, and wished that the Ridleys had been lawyers, of farmers or clergymen.

Neither Arbel nor Christie, walking one afternoon through Berwick to escape the confines of Susannah Grey's overheated parlour, paid much attention to rumour: Christie, because she knew rumour's limitations and extravagances; Arbel, because she had, after all, unfinished business with Luke Ridley. He could not be dead, because sooner or later he would call on her, write to her, beg to see her. They always did.

Arbel carried her dog in her arms; Tom Dodd trailed behind, picking up pebbles from the gutter. Christie's feet took her, inevitably, to the magnet of the sea, a thick, grey November sea that stormed the bastion of the harbour-wall, pushing and shoving at the ships jostled around the quayside. The carracks, galleons, barges and pinnaces were a source of great joy to Christie. She knew now that she did not need to travel to Dover, or Greenwich or Southampton, for ships sailed to France from Berwick.

At the harbour-wall, Dowzabel ran up and down chasing dead leaves, and Tom Dodd skimmed stones on the jagged surface of the sea. Christie and Arbel watched the sailors unload barrels and bales from Berwick's latest arrival, a small galleon called the *Elizabeth*. The *Elizabeth*'s name was painted on her bows, gold chevrons to either side of the lettering. Christie followed Arbel along the harbour-side. Arbel's hair was threaded with red ribbons; the wind caught and tossed the ribbons into the air, the heavy blue embroidered folds of Arbel's skirts brushed the cobbles. The sailors had stopped working long before they passed the *Elizabeth*: barrels rolled untended on the stones, untied lengths of cloth flapped in the breeze. Someone whistled, and Arbel smiled and tossed back her glorious hair.

A man working on board the ship called good-day; Arbel paused and directed her smile more carefully. He was black-bearded, almost bald, dressed a little better than the rest of the crew.

Arbel said, still smiling at the black-bearded man, 'How much money did you say you had, Christie?'

Christie's dark eyes had not left the bobbing galleon. 'Thirty sovereigns,' she said.

'Shall I ask him?' Arbel's small face was vivid with excitement. 'Shall I ask him if he sails to France?'

She did not wait for Christie to reply. Scooping up a muddy Dowzabel, Arbel Forster walked up to the *Elizabeth*'s gangway. Men dissolved from her path like wraiths, eyes tracked the sway of her skirts, the swirl of lace at wrist and throat. On the foredeck, the black-bearded man spat on his hand and smoothed back non-existent hair.

Tom Dodd, alert only where Arbel was concerned, dropped his pebbles. 'It's all right,' Christie said, taking his arm, stopping him running after Arbel while her heart pounded like the cannon that hedged the town walls. Arbel might trust her secrets to a muddle-headed stable-boy, but not Christie.

It all seemed to take an unreasonably long time. The *Elizabeth*'s pennants alternately flicked and trailed in the wind, the sea juggled the little boat like a fairground sideshow. The man with the beard met Arbel at the top of the gangway. He must be smitten, thought Christie: he had even gingerly patted Dowzabel's head.

When Arbel and the master disappeared down some unseen hatchway in the ship, Christie had to grip Tom Dodd even harder to stop him running after her.

But soon Dowzabel was skittering up the quayside towards Christie, and Arbel was following after her, a small box in her hand. 'Suckets,' said Arbel, on reaching Christie and Tom Dodd. 'French suckets,' she added, looking at Christie, opening the box, unwrapping layers of waxed paper from marzipan, jellies, raisins in sugar and cinnamon.

THE *Elizabeth* sailed to France and the Low Countries regularly. The master, said Arbel, licking sugar from her fingers, was not a superstitious man. His name was Sandy Lawson, and he'd take headless men from Africa if they paid their passage. He'd take a woman if she didn't get sick, didn't complain, and kept to her cabin. His crew had to keep their minds on their work. Mr Lawson, added Arbel, was a nice man. He had given her a box of sweets.

Tom Dodd was happy with a handful of marzipan and Arbel within sight again. The sky was clouding over, a wet rain, picked up from the sea, had begun to dew the ends of Arbel's bright braids. They began the uphill walk back to the Greys' house.

'Twelve sovereigns,' said Arbel, threading her arm through Christie's. 'He said fifteen at first, but then he changed his mind. So you'd have plenty left for France. And when you find your mother, she'll be rich, I dare say. All the French are rich, and they have beautiful castles, and the loveliest clothes. And they colour their hair. Pink, I believe.'

Arbel, breaking marzipan into little pieces for Dowzabel, began to sing. '*Handy spandy, Jack-a-dandy, loved plum cake and sugar candy.*'

'I won't go,' said Christie, gently. 'Not yet. We'll find you a husband with a castle, first, Arbel. And pink hair, if you wish.'

Arbel laughed. 'Pack your bags, Christie. I've found someone already – though he hasn't a castle –'

Rob, Mark Selby, John Grey – ?

Arbel began to dance in the street, whirling round and round, Dowzabel in her arms, the sweets spilling from the box into the gutter.

'A Ridley,' said Arbel. 'Margaret should be pleased, don't you think?'

And started to sing again, while Christie's heart beat in time to the dance, and her stomach turned to ice.

A FOG assaulted London, throwing a damp, grey-feathered coverlet over streets and houses, extinguishing fires, aggravating chilblains and lumbago, blurring window-panes with a stream of dirty droplets. Paul Carnaby, mixing pigments in Nicholas Hilliard's Gutter Lane house, did not generally care a jot about the weather. But fog and gloom were difficult, they stole the light, sucking it dry, leaving only shadows and an absence of colour. A miniaturist needed light.

But still, despite the fog, Paul Carnaby was content. A cheerful disposition and a knowledge that he was, at last, where he wanted to be, meant that even the grimy sea-coaled mist could not put him out of humour. He ground his pigments and mixed them with gum arabic and stored them in mussel shells: lapis and malachite and ochre and umber and masticot and the carbon blacks. And silver and gold, ground to a powder, and all the bright, difficult lakes and blues, expensively obtained from flowers and insects. A multitude of colour, a world away from the muted shades of the Borders, the subdued tones of northern hills and valleys.

The name of the day's first caller brought Paul abruptly

back to his origins, though. 'Ridley,' said the boy, and Paul Carnaby looked up from his paints and his brushes, interest in each sharp hazel eye.

Ridley, thought Paul again, his heart beating rather fast, as the visitor entered the room. He wore unassuming dark clothes, and had a face that Paul Carnaby, artist, would not have forgotten. *Had* not forgotten. Nicholas Hilliard, thought Paul, rising and returning his caller's bow, would have welcomed that face, would have all but dragged its owner through the doorway and sat him in the best light, and seized a squirrel-hair brush and began to sketch. Paul's disquiet was of a different nature.

'Mr Ridley.' Paul stood and bowed awkwardly. 'How unexpected.'

Luke Ridley smiled. Paul remembered that smile. There were Ridleys throughout the English Middle March. Woodryngton, Haltwhistle and Black Law. And Catcleugh, of course. Eighteen months ago, Paul had been glad to see the last of both Catcleugh and its owner.

'Mr Hilliard is away at present,' he said. 'I expect his return tomorrow.'

'I am not here to see Mr Hilliard.' Mr Ridley's eyes glanced briefly over the studio (eighteen feet long, so that you could paint a sitter full-length), the apparently haphazard jumble of colours, cards, parchments and brushes, and the miniatures in various stages of progress. 'I was hoping to speak to you, Mr Carnaby.'

Paul smiled, and shrugged his crooked shoulders. 'Then speak, Mr Ridley.'

Mr Ridley did speak. Mr Ridley, perching on the window-seat from which, on a fine day, you could have seen all the great houses of Goldsmith's Row, spoke at length. All Paul's chequered history, all the folly and misadventure that he had abandoned, with a little hope and even less money, over a year past. 'You could not fulfil your ambitions in the north,' said Mr Ridley, his sky-blue gaze moving from the misted window-pane and back to Paul. Blue bice, thought Paul, for a background, but not too strong. And said,

'The prospects for a crippled portrait painter in the north of England were none too promising. And my expertise in other areas was, as you remember, poor. Thus the journey south.'

'You couldn't shoot straight and you lost a dozen good sheep in the moss.' Lucas Ridley neither smiled nor wasted time with unnecessary expressions of sympathy. 'So you went to London. But not, at first, to Mr Hilliard. I have spent the last fortnight searching for you, Paul Carnaby.'

The dismal weather made Paul's shoulder and the crooked part of his spine ache. He disregarded it, just as he always did, because he had learned long ago that there was nothing to be gained in giving attention to the unalterable. His hands were good, and his eyes, and they were what mattered to a painter.

'Mr Hilliard took me as his pupil three months ago,' he said. 'Before that, I did what I could. I have begged, Mr Ridley, I have served, but I have not thieved. I gave that up when I left the north.'

He had ridden with Luke Ridley briefly eighteen months ago, an experience he would have preferred to be able to forget. He had sketched them all before he had left, though, a piece of Luke's paper in one hand, a feathered quill in the other. Perhaps those sketches still existed, long-forgotten at the bottom of a chest.

Paul sat down and began to cut parchment, mix paste.

'It's the serving I'm interested in,' said Luke Ridley. 'I heard that you served for the French ambassador for a while.'

Paul said casually, 'The Seigneur de la Mauvissière. I was as poor a serving-man as I was a horse-thief, Mr Ridley. I was with the unfortunate Seigneur for only eight weeks. I resigned – hastily – from my post after christening the man with a pigeon pie.' He looked up, parchment in one hand, cutting-knife in the other. 'Are you in need of a clumsy serving-man, Mr Ridley?'

Luke shook his head. Mentally, Paul mixed the pigments to paint his hair.

'I am in need of information, Mr Carnaby. Gossip, names, faces – that sort of thing.'

'Gossip,' said Paul, spreading a pack of cards on the table in front of him, 'from the French Embassy?'

Mr Ridley did not reply. Mr Ridley, when Paul glanced up, only inclined his fair head. Paul began to select cards from the table.

'We paint the miniature, Mr Ridley, on the plain side of the playing-card. First we cover it with parchment, and then we colour the parchment with a wash of carnation, and sketch in the features. But because the ciphers of the playing-cards can still be seen, we have to colour over the spades. They're bad luck,' said Paul, softly, 'and it's my job to cover them up.'

In Paul Carnaby's well-shaped hands the entire suit of spades fanned like a peacock's tail. 'I had you down for a horse-thief, Mr Ridley,' said Paul. 'Not a spy.'

Luke Ridley was much the same height as Paul, but his body was straight. His arrows did not miss their targets; he would never lose a horse in the murky, difficult byways of the Cheviots.

'Like yourself,' said Luke, 'I do not find thieving entirely fulfilling.'

There was a small silence. At last Paul Carnaby, taking a brush and beginning to paint out the ace of spades, said, 'Then we have something in common, Mr Ridley.'

And smiled. Paul's face was neither twisted like his back, nor graceful like his hands. Just plain, and pleasant.

'We are countrymen,' he said. 'Perhaps we should drink to that.'

In the Bear and Ragged Staff in Cheapside, a mere cock's stride from Nicholas Hilliard's Gutter Lane house, they talked. Hedged by card-players, dice-throwers and a gaggle of apprentice-boys in search of mid-morning refreshment for their masters, their words – treasonable, compromising or just plain scurrilous – were lost in the laughter and talk of a London tavern.

'Gossip,' said Luke, catching Paul Carnaby's bright hazel gaze. 'Extravagance, greed, seductions, courtship. You're an artist, Mr Carnaby. You know the sort of thing.'

'I,' said Paul, taking two tankards of ale from the potboy's tray, 'am a painter. I paint what I see, Mr Ridley, that's all.'

'Then what did you see?' Outside, the fog had dewed every brick, every falling leaf with a string of bright diamonds. 'In detail, mind – but then, as a miniaturist, you should specialize in detail.'

Nicholas Hilliard's pupil grinned and attempted to pull his crooked body into a more upright position. Some talked because they wanted money or favours. Some talked because they liked to talk, because it gave them, even for the shortest time, the attention they craved. Some talked because he forced them to talk by holding a knife to their quaking throats. Paul Carnaby would talk because he did not see politics as reality, but as a fleeting pageant of colour and faces, less real than the minute representations on the table in Nicholas Hilliard's studio.

'I wonder', Paul said, meeting Luke's eyes, 'if I should inquire what side you are on – but it doesn't really much matter, does it? Well, then –' his brow creased, he rubbed at it with long, clean fingers '– I assume you are not interested in the Seigneur de la Mauvissière's diet. He drinks an uncommon amount of claret, Mr Ridley, but do not assume that clouds his judgement. Nor, I think, do you wish to know which of the grooms beds which of the serving-maids. People pair on the basis of appearance,' he added, looking up. 'The handsomest man to the prettiest wench. Have you noticed that? My paramour had recently recovered from the smallpox, poor creature.'

He took a mouthful of ale.

Luke said softly, 'Neither the highest nor the lowest, Mr Carnaby. I cannot approach the ambassador himself, and an illiterate serving-girl knows nothing. Tell me, if you can, about those between.'

Paul Carnaby was staring at him. There was that small kernel of excitement. Paul Carnaby would give him what he wanted, because Paul Carnaby was an observer of life, not a participator.

'Monsieur Cherelles,' said Paul, and his smile flowered. 'You, Mr Ridley, would wish to speak to Monsieur Cherelles, who is a secretary of the French Ambassador. Monsieur Cherelles writes and receives the Seigneur's letters – letters from Scotland, Spain, France –'

The apprentices had left the tavern, jostling each other, spilling ale into the gutter.

'You wouldn't get near him, of course. Keeps himself buried in the Embassy. Regards anyone but his countrymen with the utmost suspicion.'

'And I cannot stay in London,' said Luke, drily. 'You disappoint me, Mr Carnaby.'

Paul grinned. 'Patience, my friend. Listen. The serving-maid with the smallpox told me about Monsieur Cherelles.' He drained his tankard of ale. 'Before she'd had the pox, she'd had a love-affair with Cherelles's own body-servant. When I say *body-servant*, I mean it, perhaps, a little more literally than the term is usually applied. Cherelles's servant was jealous of a certain Henri Fagot, friend to Monsieur Cherelles. Note the somewhat appropriate name, Mr Ridley. *Fagot*. A London term for a woman only one step up from a whore. Although you mustn't think of our Henri Fagot as a common harlot – oh, no, far too selective, far too clever. Anyway, Fagot was at the Ambassador's house throughout the summer, and Cherelles was besotted with him. Most of the Embassy were, in fact – male and female alike.'

The small kernel of interest blossomed into an entire tree of possibility.

'Go on,' said Luke, evenly.

'They quarrelled, I think. Or, rather, Fagot quarrelled, Cherelles wept. And begged. And has pined ever since – thus his manservant's resentment.'

The potboy paused at the table to refill their tankards. Carnaby began to draw patterns in the spilt ale on the table. 'Yes. If I were you, Mr Ridley, I would look for Monsieur Fagot. Monsieur Fagot has no loyalties and would sell anything. For the right price, of course.'

'And where is Monsieur Fagot now?' said Luke.

Paul threaded his long fingers together. 'Henri Fagot went back to France shortly before I left. In September. To Paris, Cherelles's servant thought.'

'Do you know why they quarrelled?'

Carnaby shrugged his crooked shoulders. 'Fagot engineered

it – he enjoyed it. I should imagine that he had discovered better things to do in France. He was ambitious – he wouldn't waste time on someone like Cherelles if he had no further use for him. He is a manipulator of human souls, Mr Ridley.'

The smile had utterly disappeared. Carnaby added, thoughtfully, 'I saw him at a banquet – I tried to draw him, then. But I was never completely happy with the result.'

The tavern had begun to empty. One of the dice-players slept in the corner of the room, his mouth slightly open, the dice still nestling in the palm of his hand.

'I'll show you the sketches, though,' said the portrait painter. 'But if you look for him, remember that it won't be like looking for Elliots and Armstrongs in Liddesdale. For myself, I wouldn't ride in pursuit of Monsieur Fagot, not if you offered me a shipful of gold. But then,' and his eyes met Luke's, 'you always were better at that sort of thing.'

The grin had returned. On the table in front of them, sketched in ale on the scuffed oak surface of the table, was a cat's face, bright-eyed.

'Henri Fagot had a nice little pet. A wildcat. When I tried to draw Monsieur Fagot, I kept giving him the wildcat's eyes. They were,' said Carnaby, 'like jewels.'

Chapter Nine

CHRISTIE Forster rode past Wooler, through Lanton, and into Kirknewton. Past the crumbling, turf-roofed cabins, and the black-windowed houses, and the church with the stone Magi. Christie never got lost: pick her up and place her anywhere from Kholmogory to Media, and she would know north from south, an honest face from a deceitful one. Like a homing-pigeon, Anne Forster had once said, wings extended, fluttering reliably back to the dovecote.

But today Christie felt uncomfortable. The streets were empty, yet she felt eyes watching her from every window, saw half-glimpsed figures in every open doorway. It was the weather, she told herself, the black clouds that gathered over the Border, the sting of winter in the bitter wind. That, and the fear of what Arbel's thoughtlessness, Luke Ridley's licentiousness, might provoke. Disgrace for Arbel, and the crushing of all Christie's fragile dreams.

Because, whatever Arbel might think, Luke had no intention of marrying her. Luke was certainly not the marrying kind, Christie recognized that, even if Arbel did not. She had talked to Arbel, had even, gently, scolded Arbel, and Arbel had paid no attention whatsoever. 'He'll come and see me soon,' Arbel had said confidently. 'When he comes back.'

Christie hoped Luke would never come back. She did not quite hope him hanged in Hermitage Castle, merely well out of the way. In Italy, perhaps. Or Africa.

But he had, of course, come back. Yesterday, one of the Forster servants had seen Luke in Wooler market, and had gleefully imparted the news to the Forsters over dinner. Margaret had then looked happy for the first time in weeks. Rob had been out, and Christie had not dared look at Arbel. She had spoken to her later, in private, calmly, patiently, and

Arbel, combing Dowzabel's tangled hair, had not listened at all. 'Handy, spandy, Jack-a-dandy, loved plum cake and sugar candy . . .'

Christie had thought, then, briefly and hopelessly, of telling Margaret. But Margaret did not know Arbel as Christie knew her, and Margaret was, after all, Rob's mother. Margaret had not seen Rob and Luke at Berwick fair. She had only seen the results of that encounter.

Which was why Christie rode the hills beyond Kirknewton. Today Margaret, Janet and Arbel had ridden to Berwick to see Bess Grey's new baby. Christie, falsely pleading the beginnings of a cold, had stayed behind, swallowing nerves and pride and an instinctive dread of the lonely Cheviots in winter.

She still felt eyes watching her as she rode steadily up the hillside, head bent against the gathering wind. But when, frequently, she turned, there were only the thickening rainclouds, and the heather, and the sheep, dotting the distant slopes like puffballs. Streams edged with the paper remains of summer's reeds and flags laced the valleys with thin, dark cobwebs. Some of the hillsides were scattered with steeply falling cascades of scree, others threaded with narrow paths, like webbed skeins of wool. Sometimes the black outcrops of rock seemed to Christie to take on the blurred shape of a rider on horseback – a Craw or a Dixon, perhaps, with a lance in one hand and a sword in the other.

The rain began to fall more heavily as Christie skirted the steep side of Yeavering Bell. She should have taken a thicker cloak, she should have worn more sensible gloves. She had ridden this path in the summer before, with the warmth and light of the wide blue sky and Tom Dodd for protection. Now, the sky seemed already to be darkening, and she was alone. The best sense of direction in the world could not make the Cheviots a safe place for an unescorted woman.

She rode doggedly on. The hillside was a tracery of tiny rivulets: Christie's pony slipped in the mud, sending her ricocheting against its neck, her feet flying from the stirrups. Sliding out of the saddle, she scrambled up the slope, reins in one hand, bunched skirts in the other. Her blue velvet trailed heavily in the mire. Christie Forster hated Northumberland.

At the peak of the hill she paused to regain her breath. There was still the awful sensation that there was something – someone – behind her. She did not feel that she was alone. But when she looked, there was only the dim grey outline of the hills, their moiréed silhouettes seeming to shift and shimmer in the rain, as though someone had gently moved a length of silvered fabric. For a fraction of a second, Christie thought she saw something else move: her heart paused, waiting, and then restarted. A bird or a rabbit, or just the wind in the endless dying heather. She was not usually prone to ridiculous fancies. It was only this place – these hills, with their memories of violence. Rain trickled down Christie's face, rain squelched between her toes. Climbing back into the saddle, telling herself not to be foolish, Christie continued to ride in the direction of Catcleugh.

IT had been raining in the small village of Wark as well, a steady ice-cold rain with a hint of sleet. Rain trickled from the hills to the streets, filling the gutters, so that the rotten apples, vegetable peel and straw bobbed in the muddy water like a half-drowned flotilla of tiny boats.

Luke Ridley, having met an anonymous gentleman in the back of a Wark tavern, was returning to Catcleugh. He had ridden out with Randal Lovell the previous day, crossing the Border overnight. Neither for sheep nor encoded letters this time, but in search of the surviving relatives of John Graham of Bonshaw, known as Dand's Jock. They had found Jock's widow in the outskirts of Bonshaw, living in a hovel that made Catcleugh look like a palace, a gaggle of small children about her skirts, their ragged clothes hemmed with mud. She had accepted the news of her husband's death with no obvious emotion, pausing only to wipe one child's face with the edge of a grubby apron, and to smack another's head when it whined. The light had come to her reddened eyes when she had seen the money – a purseful of gold, realized by Randal Lovell for the Croziers' fine horses. She had taken the purse and thrust it into the folds of her sagging bosom as though she feared that Luke might change his mind. Then, one of her children, looking from Lovell to Luke and to his mother, had begun to cry again, and she had hustled them back into the shack and shut the door tight.

They reached Wark the following midday. Randal Lovell left Luke to his ale and his black mood and his uncertain assignation in the tavern and rode into the hills, whistling. He had found a good horse in Yetholm, a little beaten about the flanks, but a fine animal none the less. To Randal Lovell, horses were more important and better company than most human beings.

The uncertain assignation – an old acquaintance – arrived, and was duly, if pointlessly, voluble after a quart of ale. Luke said the right things, his hand felt in his pocket and drew out the correct number of coins, but his mind's eye saw a turf-roofed cottage with no glass in the windows, and a huddle of whey-faced, shoeless children. He drank ale with the thirsty gentleman, and aqua vitae when the gentleman left, because aqua vitae generally worked better than ale. He left the tavern soon after his informer, his head uncovered in the pouring rain, the half-empty bottle in his hand. The roads were busy, the streets congested with squirming grey sheep, children playing in the gutters, dogs rooting for scraps outside the kitchens. The oily smell of sheep's wool in the pouring rain reminded Luke of September and the Croziers and Hermitage.

He took the road south-west from Wark, riding towards the hills and Catcleugh. A bottle of aqua vitae rested on Luke's saddlebow, his reins, spongy and oozing water, slipped a little through the gloved fingers of his right hand. At first there was no one: even the ravens had taken shelter in the rocks, and then, as Luke skirted the curve of the hill, there was Rob.

Rob Forster, riding a large bay horse, his servants spread out in his wake behind him. No, not Rob's servants. Luke's hand tightened on the reins: there was an almost irresistible temptation to turn tail and make for the hills. Most of the servants wore jade and white. Stephen's colours. And Stephen himself rode behind Rob, his golden head covered by a feathered black hat, his short cloak falling elegantly to one side of his equally elegant horse.

There was nowhere to go but forwards. Luke corked the bottle and slid it into his saddlebag, but Stephen would have seen it anyway. There had never been any part of himself he could hide from Stephen. Six of Stephen's men dispersed themselves across the track, barring Luke's way. The rain had darkened Luke's hair and the grey cloak that he wore, but on Stephen's brimmed hat two feathers nodded, miraculously untouched by the weather. Stephen rode forward. He was smiling.

'Glory to God, it's Lucas, my own sweet cousin. Riding home, are you, Lucas? I should get those wet things off, and warm your feet by the fire, and have your servants bring you claret and capons.' Stephen's eyes moved slowly from Luke's face to his saddlebags. 'Or perhaps a scrawny fowl and a half-bottle of spirits – that's more your style, isn't it? With some pox-ridden slut from the nearest village on your knee –'

Rob chuckled. 'We thought you were dead, Luke. Someone told us you'd been hanged at Hermitage.'

'Risen from the dead like Lazarus, perhaps,' said Stephen, coolly. 'Miraculous, don't you think, gentlemen?' His voice, his gesture, embraced the liveried servants and Rob Forster's stable-boy. 'Although miracles come thick and fast where Lucas is concerned.'

There was a small silence. Then Stephen said, 'My cousin is, after all, the product of the world's only twelve-month gestation. A miracle indeed, don't you think? Who knows what such a wonder might have spawned – our Lucas might have entered the world with two heads, or scales, or breathing poison like a cockatrice –'

'Or fish-tailed, like a mermaid,' said Rob.

'Fish-tailed. Yes,' said Stephen, thoughtfully. The crimson feathers still bobbed in the rain; water polished the jewels on Stephen's gloves. 'You must be thankful you have not a fish-tail, cousin, or you would find some of your indulgences more problematic. Or course –' Stephen's brow creased, his eyes moved briefly to Rob and then back to Luke again. 'There is a simpler explanation.'

'For a twelve-month pregnancy?' Rob's voice was innocent. 'Go on, Stephen.'

'His mother might have been the sort of whore who couldn't endure three months widowhood without a man inside her.'

For once, Rob said nothing.

Then Stephen, leaning over until Luke could feel the heat of his breath, added, 'Go on, Lucas, you've a sword and a knife. Use them. Why don't you use them?'

One of Luke's hands stayed flat against the horse's neck, the other still gripped the reins. Stephen's sword hung in a jewelled scabbard at his side: Luke could see the hilt of his knife under the dark folds of his doublet.

'You look sick,' said Stephen, gently. 'Are you going to be sick again, Lucas?'

The hot breath ebbed away, leaving only the rain. The taunting voice was replaced by the sound of horses' hooves, dimming to silence. Luke shut his eyes very tightly, and drew in one long, painful breath. A rhyme from childhood drummed through his aching head.

> *Bow, wow, wow*
> *Whose dog art thou?*
> *Little Tom Tinker's dog*
> *Bow, wow, wow.*

AT last Christie saw Catcleugh, lost in shadows, almost touched by the low rainclouds. Rain dripped from the brim of her hat, rain found its way into the fingers of her gloves, the toes of her boots. The sky had darkened to tortoiseshell tones of grey and mauve and purple.

There was a light behind Catcleugh's one small window, and a plume of smoke rising from the chimney. If the thought of the ride back to Adderstone had already begun to trouble her, then Christie did not admit that even to herself. The rain and the wind were unpleasant enough without fancying hobgoblins round every corner. Looping her reins round Catcleugh's single bare tree, Christie climbed the steps to the door.

At the top of the steps, fist poised to knock, her heart sank even further. The noise that found its way through the window, through the tiny chinks between the stones, and round the stout wood of the door, was the sort of noise you expected to hear in the rowdiest tavern. Men's voices, shouting, singing, whooping: men at their least lovable, *en masse*, and with a quart of ale in their bellies. Taking a deep breath, screwing up the last soaking dregs of her courage, Christie knocked at the door.

She had to knock twice before anyone heard her, and then she heard a movement above, and a voice called out, 'It's a lassie, Archie! Let her in – quick!'

Christie looked up and saw a man leaning out of the window. He wore a woman's bonnet over frizzy brown hair, and clutched a pewter cup in his hand. He was not Luke Ridley, and the cup was not held straight: ale waterfalled from the window to the grass below.

The doorbolt was pulled back, and the door opened. A hand reached out and seized Christie's fingers and kissed them noisily. Someone called, 'Bring her in, Archie – don't be so damned greedy, man!'

Archie had red hair, a pale, freckled skin, and lashes and brows of white sand. Archie's shirt was unlaced, and he was slipping slowly sideways down the doorjamb. Christie, sickened of rain and wind, and having no patience with lack of balance, stepped over Archie as he slithered to the floor to lie across the doorway.

If Catcleugh when she had first seen it had had no pretensions to elegance, at least it had been reasonably clean and tidy. Now the pele-house looked as though a cyclone had scythed through it, scattering swords and lances and ale barrels haphazardly over the stone floor. Men lounged on the ale-soaked straw, hundreds of them, it seemed to Christie on an initial, dazed glance. Someone lobbed a peat turf into the flagging fire: ash scattered, thick black smoke belched from the feeble flames, and Christie coughed.

All the sentient heads in the pele-house turned and stared at her, all male, and not one of them Luke Ridley.

'I'm looking for Mr Ridley,' she said, weakly. 'Is he here?'

A large man with half a chicken in his hand hauled himself unsteadily to his feet. 'Luke's away,' he said. 'Will I do, sweetheart?'

Christie shook her head and edged a little closer to the wall. There was no sign of the black-haired girl – Mariota – or the gypsy.

'Luke should have been back a while past,' said a slurred voice from the doorway. Archie, his hair wet with rain and ale, struggled into a sitting position, and added, 'You can wait for him if you want, darling.'

'There's a nice dry bed upstairs –'

'I should get out of those wet clothes –'

'Come over here and keep me company, sweetheart. What's Luke got that I havena?'

'A bonnier face,' said someone, and, with a roar, the man with the half chicken hurled himself across the room.

Christie, sitting in the only free corner, gathered her skirts respectably round her ankles. Should she leave a letter? But what she had come to say was too delicate to put in a letter. Should she leave at once? The rain and the dark frightened her.

Archie, another bottle of wine in his hand, stumbled across the floor and sat down beside her.

'Archie Grey,' he said, extending a free hand, 'or Red Archie, if you wish.'

Red Archie had been instrumental in depriving Rob of his best horse ... 'Christie Forster,' said Christie, briefly taking Archie's hand.

'Forster ...' said Archie, with a frown. 'There's Sir John, the old devil ... and the Forsters of Blanchland ... and Alnwick ... and Adderstone, of course.'

'Adderstone,' said Christie, removing Archie's more adventurous hand from her knee. 'I'm an adopted Adderstone Forster. A temporary, adopted Adderstone Forster.'

'You don't look like an Adderstone Forster.' Archie screwed up his pale eyes. 'Oh aye. I remember. Like Luke – I mean –'

'Yes, that's right, a bastard like Luke.' It had never served Christie well to be anything less than honest in the matter of her birth. Archie had wedged himself up against her. 'Where has Luke gone, Mr Grey? And if you don't take your hand off my knee this instant, I shall bite it. I've very strong teeth.'

Archie hastily withdrew his hand. 'Luke's over the Border,' he said. 'Or at Wark – I'm not sure. He was only back last night, you see, sweetheart. That's what all this' – with a sweeping gesture, Archie indicated the ale, the wine, the scattered remains of food strewn over the pele-house floor – 'is for. To celebrate his return. We thought he was dead, you see. Mind you,' said Archie, thoughtfully, righting the wine bottle which had toppled over into the straw, 'it might have been easier if he had been dead. He's not in the best of tempers.'

Which comforted Christie not one bit.

'Have a wee drink,' added Archie, wiping the neck of the bottle with his sleeve. 'You're awful wet, Miss Forster.'

Christie took the bottle and drank, not just because she was wet and cold and tired, but also because she must soon decide between Luke Ridley (in a temper), and the rapidly darkening Cheviots, with some nameless *thing* following behind her. On the whole, Christie thought, she might prefer the hobgoblins.

'Of course,' said Archie, accepting the bottle back from Christie, 'as Rob Dunne says, why wait for Luke? If you're wanting a wee bit of help with anything, darling, then I'm your man. After all,' continued Archie, reasonably, 'he got himself into an awful mess at Riccarton, didn't he? Not that I'm saying that it was all Luke's fault, but still –'

The door opened. Cold air, cold rain, and an even colder voice.

'Well, well, my pretties. We must be thankful that the Elliots and the Armstrongs do not choose to ride tonight. A watch on the hillside – or even the door?'

Luke Ridley shut the door gently behind him. The question hung in the air, steel-edged, the sudden silence broken only by the hiss of the fire and someone's intermittent retching.

A voice said tentatively, 'We'd a little to drink, Luke.'

'So I see.' He removed two soaking gloves and flung them on to the table. He looked slowly round the room, taking in men, and ale, and wine bottles, until, at last, his cold blue gaze came to rest on Christie.

'God's teeth, the second Miss Forster. Two ladies of such different complexion, yet of remarkably similar habits.'

She must look a sight, Christie realized – her dress dishevelled, Archie leaning amorously against her, a half-empty bottle between them.

Scrambling to her feet, she said, 'I wanted to speak to you, Mr Ridley. That's all.'

Which sounded, even to Christie's ears, horribly equivocal. Luke's cloak followed the gloves, and the sprawling bodies cleared quickly out of his way as he crossed the room. He was as wet as Christie, his hair and his leather jack dulled to dark brown by the rain, his boots heavy with mud. Halfway there, he paused and looked around him.

'Do continue your play, gentlemen. There's more ale in the byre.'

The hubbub restarted as though it had never stopped. Luke, dripping rain from every fibre of his clothing, reached Christie's side. He had smiled at her in Berwick, but he did not smile now. Leaning against the wall beside her, his eyes surveyed her once, comprehensively, and he said, 'There's sheets on the bed upstairs, Miss Forster. Or straw in the byre, if that's what you prefer.'

Biting her lip, Christie resisted the temptation to slap his beautiful, insolent face. Foolishly, it had not occurred to her that he might be insulting. But of course he might, of course he would assume that Arbel's standards, Arbel's tastes, were also hers.

'Neither, thank you,' she said, tightly.

His eyes focused deliberately between her chin and her waist. 'Really?' said Luke.

If only he would look at her face rather than her bosom, it would be easier to talk to him. 'I wanted to speak to you about Arbel,' said Christie. What she really wanted was to shake him. 'I wanted,' she said, crossly, 'to tell you never to go near her again.'

All wrong, all wrong. If there was a tactful way of saying what she had come to say, then Christie knew that she had not found it.

'Ah,' said Mr Ridley, softly, scuffing one muddy boot in the straw. 'Did you now?' He looked up, his eyes finding, at last,

Christie's face. 'Then I'd better be obliging, hadn't I, Miss Forster?'

It was then that Christie realized that he was drunk. He did not slur his words as Rob did after a bottle of wine, nor totter like some drunkard in a mummer's play. But there was a light in his eyes that reminded Christie of her first encounter with him in Rothbury, a scarcely restrained violence, a dangerous nonconformity.

Luke smiled. 'Tell Arbel,' he said, 'that I have no intention of seeing her. Tell her I'm dead. Tell her I've the pox. Tell her I've a wife.' His hand touched Christie's cheek, quite gently. 'Yes. Let me demonstrate the strength of my attachment to your sister. Let me show you how much I covet her lands and her money.'

The tips of his fingers trailed slowly down Christie's cheek, along her jaw and neck and on to her breast. 'Archie,' called Luke. 'Marry us.'

Christie's head jerked up, her eyes wide.

Red Archie was sitting against the wall on the opposite side of the room, the wine bottle still in one hand, playing-cards in the other. Crossing the floor, Luke pulled Archie, unresisting, upright: cards tumbled from his loose hands, ace, king, knave. 'Come on, Archie,' said Luke, releasing Archie's bunched shirt. 'You've a sober tongue in your head sometimes. Miss Forster and I are to be wed.'

Most of the occupants of the pele-house turned and stared at Christie. Christie felt sick. Her knees were the consistency of a quaking pudding, her heart hammered distressingly fast. It was all a joke, of course. All a crass, stupid, male joke.

But Luke, flanked by Archie, was back at her side. He had taken off his leather jack: his shirt, half-dried by the heat of the fire, clung to his back. His face was like a mask, Christie thought, an exquisite, callous mask.

With an effort, she found her voice.

'Mr Ridley – this is foolishness. I'm sorry – I should not have come here. I'll go.'

'But we are to be wed, Miss Forster!' Luke's hand grasped Christie's wrist, she tried to pull away, but could not. 'You wouldn't leave me standing at the altar, would you?'

'There is no altar,' said Christie, firmly, trying to shake off his hand. 'No altar, no priest, no wedding. Let me go.'

'Your church,' said Luke Ridley, gesturing expansively to the squalid pele-house. 'Your wedding-guests, your wedding-breakfast. We have a convenient custom in these parts, Miss Forster, called handfasting. We make an agreement to live as man and wife for a year, and at the end of that year we are legally wed. A delightfully simple arrangement, don't you think? No need for churches, marriage-portions, or even' – frowning, he lifted a fold of her gown and rubbed it between forefinger and thumb – 'dry clothes.'

His hand was hurting her wrist. 'You're drunk, Mr Ridley,' said Christie, coldly.

'Lucas. Or, since we are to marry, Luke. And you are quite right, my dear, I am drunk.' Turning aside to Archie, who had slithered down the wall again, Luke added, 'Archie, you bastard, find your feet and your wits and witness my marriage to Miss Forster.'

She could not believe that he intended to lead the charade to its conclusion. But Luke's grip was sliding from Christie's wrist to her fingers.

'Your hand in mine, my dear. I've even a ring – see? I, Lucas Ridley of Catcleugh, take thee – what's your name, Miss Forster? – oh, yes, Christie – Christian, is that it? – take thee, Christian Forster of Adderstone, to wife. I assume the surname will do – no doubt it's as accurate as mine.'

Christie hated him. Christie hated Luke Ridley, Catcleugh and Northumberland.

'Girouard,' she hissed, glaring at him. 'Christiane Girouard.'

'Girouard,' repeated Luke, thoughtfully, and pushed a ring on to her third finger. '*Félicitations*, mademoiselle. Go on, then. I, Christiane Girouard –'

'No!' Desperately, Christie tried to pull away.

'*Yes,*' said Luke, softly.

He held a knife in his free hand. The blade of the knife was six inches long and winked wickedly in the firelight. The tip balanced delicately on Christie's soaking velvet bodice. 'Luke –'

said Red Archie, nervously, and the blade moved and skimmed Archie's throat, and Archie stepped back, the palms of his hands upraised in submission.

'Go on,' said Luke.

And Christie heard her own voice, a little cracked and halting, repeat the ridiculous words.

Her skin was on fire and there was a hollow where her stomach and lungs should have been. She heard Luke say, 'Tell *that* to Arbel, Miss Forster,' and she felt him raise her hand so that her finger with his ring was almost level with her eyes. Then, suddenly, he let her hand drop. 'It's a damnably wet night to be married,' he said.

Christie found that she was shaking with anger. Running across the room, she was through the door of the pele-house before Luke, climbing the ladder, had banged the trapdoor shut, and before the ring had stopped rolling and spinning on the ground, its gold muddied by the dirty straw.

Luke let the trapdoor drop behind him, shutting out some of the noise and laughter below. He found a dry shirt and a reasonable doublet – black, with one of Mariota's inaccurate patches on the elbow. There was a petticoat and bonnet of Mariota's on the floor, and someone had spilt ink on the table. It had dried to a thin black line, a circle of black on the floor. The sky was almost dark: kicking the petticoat out of the way, Luke tried to light the candle. His hands shook, the spark flared and flickered around the wick, and then died. He sat down suddenly on the edge of the bed, his fists balled against his forehead, his eyes closed.

But he still saw a woman hedged with white-faced, hungry brats, a turf-roofed shack behind her. And he still heard Sir Francis Walsingham's voice saying, *John Graham of Bonshaw, known as Dand's Jock. Hanged two days ago, Mr Ridley.*

Not that he, or anyone else, had responsibility for Dand's Jock. He had merely been late at Riccarton, so Willie Graham had been insubordinate, and Dand's Jock had hanged for it. Which was nothing more nor less than Dand's Jock, outlawed reiver, would have expected. Luke had no responsibility for

Dand's Jock. Luke had no responsibility for anyone or anything.

And then there had been Stephen, of course, providing the perfect *coup de grâce* to an appalling day. He had allowed – virtually begged – Stephen to insult him, and had been unable to make any reply. He had not said a word, he had not moved his hand from the reins to the hilt of his sword. He was (admit it, Luke) afraid of Stephen. He had always been afraid of Stephen, would always be afraid of Stephen. If, out there, Stephen had lifted his knife to cut his throat, Luke could not have stopped him. Steal all the horses you want, Lucas Ridley, work for the Queen's Secretary of State if you must, but there will still always, *always*, be Stephen. Measure your worth by your cousin's yardstick, see yourself in the dark-blue eyes of Davey's heir. Little Tom Tinker's dog, rooting in the gutter for leavings from a rich man's table.

Tying the laces of his doublet, Luke opened the trapdoor and slid down the ladder. He heard Red Archie say, slurring his words a little, 'The wife's gone, Luke. Mebbe she wasn't looking forward to the wedding-night,' and he hauled Archie to his feet for the second time that night, and dragged him to the pele-house door. The rush of cold air and rain hit Luke in the face as he let Archie find his own uncomfortable way down the steps. 'It's blowing a gale, man,' said Archie, self-pityingly, from the grass, and Luke went back inside the pele-house.

He didn't need to manhandle every one of them. He had his sword in his hand, and that, and the expression in his eyes was enough to convince most of them that they had outstayed their welcome. When they had gone, Catcleugh was silent, and only the scattered floor and the circle of ashes round the fire gave any evidence of celebration.

LUKE found Christie near the byre, huddled in her cloak, perched in the doorway. He was glad that she had had the sense to remain at Catcleugh: he did not wish to spend the night scouring the hills in search of a foolish girl. She did not look up at him when he rounded the corner, but pulled her cloak further round her face, and stared resolutely ahead into the darkness.

The wind and the rain had begun to clear his head.

Luke said, 'You may as well come into the house, Miss Forster. They've all gone.'

She did not turn round. 'So that you can insult me again, Mr Ridley? Or to consummate the marriage?'

He shook his head. 'Consummate the marriage, Miss Forster? No. You are unwilling, and I am probably incapable. As for insulting you – well, you did invite it, don't you think?'

She scrambled to her feet, the hood of her cloak slipping from her head. 'I didn't know that you intended to spend the evening celebrating, Mr Ridley. I didn't know that you would be drunk – although from past experience I might have guessed –'

It was Luke's turn to walk away them, to let the endless rain fall on his uncovered head, to dig his nails into his palms so that he should not lose his temper again. Twice, in so short a space of time. My God, Christie Forster. Wine, women and bad timing are my failings, he had said to Sarah Kemp, a long time ago, in a London withdrawing-room. Well, Christie Forster (no, *Girouard*) shared the last of those failings. Christie's timing was damnably bad.

'All I do know is that you have seduced Arbel,' said the small, nagging voice from behind him.

Arbel, naked except for a bed-curtain; he, true to form, making love to her. Straw in her hair, cold stone beneath his elbows.

He swung round. 'My dear Miss Forster,' he said, coldly. 'How well do you know your sister?'

Luke saw her frown, her great brown eyes staring at him like some damned puppy-dog. She was shivering: he'd take her back to Margaret with the quinsy, and that, no doubt, would be his fault as well. Seizing her by the elbow, Luke dragged Christie towards the steps.

'If we're going to quarrel, we may as well quarrel in comfort, don't you think?'

Inside the house, Christie sat herself on a stool near the fire,

162

and Luke slammed the door behind them. The fire was crumbling to ash; carefully, he stooped and fed the small flames with peat.

Without turning, he said, 'I wasn't the first. She knew exactly what she was doing.'

Christie should never have come here; his exasperation increased ten-fold at the thought of the inevitable fuss her fumbling interference might provoke from the Forsters. 'For God's sake,' he said, angrily. 'What would you expect me to say? "No thank you, Arbel, not tonight"?'

He saw her eyes close tightly. She was silent, motionless, for a long time, and then she said, 'Arbel's always had a lot of admirers.' Her voice was not quite steady, she was, he thought wearily, going to howl. 'Here – and in Salisbury. Well, she's beautiful, isn't she? All men fall in love with Arbel. But I didn't realize . . .'

Christie's words trailed tremulously back into silence.

'You should have thought of yourself, Miss Forster. To ride through the hills alone is not very sensible – anything could have happened to you.'

She stared at him again, eyes wide. Her chestnut hair had untied itself from whatever style it was supposed to have: it trailed wet and tangled to her waist.

Luke said, twisting the knife, 'It's dark, Miss Forster. Hadn't you noticed? It's going to look damned bad, you know, arriving back at Adderstone at midnight with me for an escort.'

He saw Christie begin to shiver more violently, as though all the inevitable, tedious consequences of her meddling and his ill-humour had suddenly occurred to her. 'Margaret –' she whispered. 'And Arbel –'

And Arbel. Arbel of the pale silk hair, and the enchanting grey eyes. Arbel of the straw and stone, and a dozen clever, tantalizing tricks of the trade. Luke took a reasonably clean cup and poured some wine into it. 'My God, Arbel,' he said, more thoughtfully, and handed the cup to Christie.

She held the cup between her threaded fingers, but did not yet drink. 'Margaret may still be in Bamburgh,' said Christie, with no great optimism. 'Oh dear,' she added, and began to blink rather rapidly.

'Drink the wine, Miss Forster,' he said, suppressing his impatience, 'and then I'll take you back to Adderstone. Perhaps Margaret is still in Bamburgh, and Rob drinking himself to insensibility in Wark. Perhaps. As for Arbel – well, she's just a spoilt brat who's a little too used to having her own way. And you will be delighted to know that I have no intention of ever seeing her again.'

Christie did not look delighted. Her eyes, Luke decided, were her only foreign feature, dark brown, almost black.

'Arbel is not used to rejection,' she said, uncertainly. The tips of her hair had begun to dry, to dance about in the heat of the fire. 'I am afraid –'

He was weary of Arbel. Arbel had made trouble enough already. 'Oh, no doubt Arbel will soon be making some rich man's life a misery.'

Turning away, Luke picked up his cloak. He felt tired, suddenly. The effects of too much alcohol had begun to wear off, leaving only the flat aftermath of a day and a night in the saddle, an unsatisfactory interview in a tavern in Wark, and a considerably less satisfactory interview with Stephen. 'Finish your drink, Miss Forster,' said Luke, 'and I'll take you back to Adderstone. I'll make peace with Margaret – she has a very forgiving soul. We'll tell her you got lost. Or something.'

Somewhere in the straw that littered Catcleugh's floor lay his own gold ring. He had not apologized for the early evening's extravagances, he had not found the words. He heard Christie squeak about not needing an escort, being perfectly able to find her own way home, and he ignored her. He opened the front door to go and see to their horses.

It was then that he saw the riders, ten -- no, twenty – of them, the light from the pele-house fire and the rainswept half-moon catching on bridle, bit and sword.

'Devil take us,' said Luke Ridley, neatly, closing the door. 'The Trotters have come to call.'

The Trotters have come to call, Luke said, as he bolted the front door.

When he reappeared through the trapdoor in the floor,

ramming the latch shut, Christie, her velvet still damp, her thoughts in a hopeless jumble, said feebly, '*Why?*'

'I visited them in May.' Luke dragged the table to the far end of the room. 'I borrowed a horse. I expect they've come to get it back.'

Christie watched Luke select bow and arrows from the pile next to the wall, testing the tips and feathers with his fingers, feeling the tautness of the bow. 'A *horse –*' she said, as he gathered up the arrows. 'How many Trotters are there, Mr Ridley?'

'About twenty, I think.' Luke paused for a moment, and then frowned. 'They're not all Trotters, though – they must have found someone fool enough to ride with them.'

Christie found that she had lost the use of her voice. *Twenty.* From some distant night Richie Forster's voice filtered back to her, saying, *Luke's had a good run.* And Stephen had answered, *Even Lucas must run out of breath soon, don't you think? Twenty,* thought Christie, rising, remembering the Craws and the Dixons last May; twenty out there and two of them in Catcleugh ... Taking a deep breath to steady herself, she said, 'What can I do, Mr Ridley?'

He didn't waste time.

'Put out the fire. Smother it – keep the water in case they try and fire the place. If you can find any more arrows, put them on the table. And keep well away from the window. Oh –' he paused halfway through the trapdoor. 'If a fire does take hold, then get out. The Trotters won't hurt you, they'll only ransom you back to Adderstone. It's me they're interested in.'

Luke disappeared upstairs. Smothering the ashes with someone's discarded cloak, Christie could hear the sound of horses' hooves echoing through the walls of the house. And then the unmistakable whine of an arrow slicing through the rain, and a grunt of protest followed by a dull thump as someone slithered from the saddle to the ground. She set to work: dragging water-buckets into the centre of the room, tipping any remaining ale and wine into an empty bucket, hauling it up on to the table, and emptying it from the window over the byre door. Keeping well aside, as Mr Ridley had ordered, of course, but there was a satisfying yell and curse a fraction of a second after she upended the bucket. Jumping down from the table, Christie surveyed the room. She began to kick the dirty straw into a heap in the corner of the room, away from the wooden platform and ladder. Anything to give a fire a smaller chance of spreading. If only Mr Ridley had possessed a broom ... Mariota had been very pretty, but an abominable housekeeper ... *twenty* ... work, Christie Forster, don't think ... leave the warfare to the foolish, foolish men .. *twenty* ...

'Seventeen,' said Luke, jumping through the platform to the floor below. He glanced round approvingly. 'Well done, Christie, we'll make a Borderer of you yet.'

Christie watched him climb on to the table, lean against the wall and nock an arrow to the bow. Someone was hammering at the door with what sounded like a battering ram, and a loud Scots voice was yelling, 'Where are ye, Ridley, you bastard? Come out of there, and I'll murder ye!' The door shuddered, but stayed shut. Luke called, 'In here, Jamie! And the horse was a winner –'

There was a sound like a small clap of thunder. 'Christ,' said Luke, swinging quickly away from the window, shaking his hair back from his eyes. 'Jamie Trotter's got himself a pistol. I didn't think he knew how to load one. What will we have next, do you think? Cannon? A mangonel?'

He fitted another arrow to the bow, and aimed it downwards. 'Come and get your nice horse, Jamie,' said Luke, softly, and let the arrow fly. There was a howl of protest, a shout, and then the hammering at the front door abruptly ceased. 'Idiots,' said Luke, happily.

'You'll lose your horse.'

Christie heard another arrow hiss through the air.

Luke turned. His hair clung to his face with rain and sweat, but his eyes were joyous, his hands steady.

'So will you. They've taken your pony, I'm afraid. Dear me, I *am* going to have to do a lot of explaining to Margaret ...'

'You mean, "Sorry, Margaret, but I've handfasted with your adopted niece, and the Scots have stolen her horse?" said Christie, unkindly, handing him up another arrow.

'Something like that.'

Luke accepted the arrow and flattened himself further against the wall as a Trotter arrow rebounded off the sill. There was a more regular thundering noise now, gathering in intensity so that the pele-house itself seemed to shake. 'Damn,' said Luke, glancing quickly back out of the window. 'The door's going. The byre door. We're down to thirteen now, I think. I wonder if they'll just take the horses and leave?'

He did not sound very optimistic. *The Trotters won't hurt you, they'll only ransom you back to Adderstone.* How much would they charge for an illegitimate, adopted niece?

Luke was staring out of the window again. Then, '*Randal,*' he said, suddenly, and jumped down from the table. He took Christie's arm for an instant. 'I'm going out. Remember – look after yourself first. I don't give a damn about the house.'

Christie, open-mouthed, watched him disappear up the ladder and through the trapdoor. She felt deserted, cold. A few seconds later she heard a thump as he dropped from the upper window to the grass below. Then, running feet, horses' hooves, and the continual, ominous, crashing and splintering of the byre door.

OUTSIDE, in the darkness behind Catcleugh, Luke put two fingers to his mouth and whistled. He was, he realized, as he waited for Randal Lovell and his brothers, enjoying himself. There were only the hills and the sword in his hand, and his property to protect. In spite of what he had said to Christie, he did care about Catcleugh. It was his, he had fought for it, over and over again, and he intended to keep it.

He picked Randal Lovell from the darkness, a glint of moonlight on a hooked nose and curling hair, the wind and rain feathering tattered layers of gaudy clothing.

'Selling horses?' said Luke, and Randal grinned, and nodded to Johnnie Lovell and the Faa brothers at his side.

'Five of the bonniest you ever saw. For the Warden himself, mind.' His dark eyes surveyed the pele-house, the tangle of Trotters at the byre door. 'The Warden likes to conduct his business at night,' continued Lovell, drawing his sword, 'so we mustn't be late.'

They divided, Janus-faced, into two, skirting each side of the pele-house. As Luke reached the far corner of the house, he heard the byre door fall through. 'There's your nag, Jamie!' yelled someone. Smoke was belching from a small pile of brushwood to the side of the house: the Trotters intended to fire Catcleugh, and would waste no time in striking the tinder. Luke waited until half the Scots were in the byre, and then tapped the nearest remaining Trotter on the shoulder.

The first of the horses were dragged through the shattered doorway just as Luke's sword found a suitable home between Dandy Trotter's ribs. By then the Lovells and the Faas had joined in, and the flames of the bonfire were rising higher, catching fire on sword and lance, dyeing everyone's features orange. Luke did not even attempt to stop them taking the horses. They took the chestnut, and Rob Forster's black, which was a pity, but there were other horses to be had. And Christie Forster's pony: *Sorry, Margaret, but I've handfasted with your adopted niece and the Scots have stolen her horse* ... God's teeth, Luke Ridley, talk your way out of that one. Luke found that he was smiling, even though he had a sword in one hand and a knife in the other, and Mark Trotter was coming towards him in a distinctly unfriendly fashion.

'Warm enough for ye, is it, Ridley?' said Mark, nodding towards the bonfire. 'Don't fret yourself, man, we'll make it warmer yet –'

The swords met in the night air. Sparks and fragments of burning straw, gold thread on black velvet. The rain, damn it, had almost stopped. The light from the bonfire underlit Mark Trotter's sweating, straining face: feint and parry, balance and speed, but no time for fancy swordsmanship because someone would soon throw a burning branch on to the dry straw in the stables. Mark Trotter slipped on the muddy ground, Luke's sword drove into him just below the shoulder. He wasn't dead, but he was Jamie Trotter's eldest son, and Jamie Trotter was there, somewhere, for Luke heard the roar of fury as Mark collapsed to the grass, his hands clutching his shoulder. The horses were gone, which took care of some more of the Scots, who were herding them away to the hills. 'Bonny nags,' said a voice behind him, and Luke spun round to see Jamie Trotter, his fingers curling round his lance. 'And a bonny wee hoose –'

Jamie speared a tangle of flaming brushwood and hurled it through the broken doorway of the byre. Luke lunged at him, and something large and heavy struck him on the back of the head. He felt his knees buckle, and he clutched desperately at his retreating consciousness, groping through the black, the red, the suffocating grey mist. Jamie Trotter, dropping his lance, seized a handful of Luke's shirt in each square palm. 'D'ye think the Warden'll mind another bale-fire, Ridley?' said Jamie, softly, and Luke thought: *Christie*. My God, *Christie*.

He felt Jamie shake him as a terrier shakes a game bird, and heard his own voice call Christie's name. But then Jamie's handhold slipped, and Jamie began to do what Luke himself had only just resisted: to slide to the grass, his empty hands pawing at the folds of Luke's clothes. Something dark smeared Jamie Trotter's scalp, and Randal Lovell stood over him, a thick unburned branch in his hand. Jackie Faa was dealing very capably with the Trotter who had hit Luke on the head. Luke hurled himself through the gaping aperture of the byre door.

The fire had already begun to take hold, thick white plumes of smoke skirled to the ceiling. Luke took a deep, choking breath and fought his way through to the buckets of water in the corner. It wasn't the heat that was unendurable, it was the smoke that clogged his lungs and his brain, making his reactions sluggish and his thoughts jumbled and inconsequential. If the fire took hold and the flames burned through the trapdoor, then the house would be lost, for the dry wood upstairs would ignite like gunpowder. But still – Luke upended the trough so that the brackish water streamed all over the floor – as Stephen had so often said, Catcleugh was nothing but a tumbledown shack . . . not like Black Law . . . not an inheritance worth mourning . . .

The foul air was making him lightheaded. He pulled off his jack and his shirt and, dipping his shirt in one of the buckets of water, threw it round his face. The dirty straw in the centre of the byre no longer burned, but tongues of flame had begun to lick at the bales around the perimeter. Luke's eyes streamed: the flames blurred and shifted, *there was not enough water* . . . He emptied the buckets over the bales, but patches of stubble still singed and sparked, fire still crackled. Someone was beside him in the byre: Randal, he thought, as he smothered the flames with his jack, his boots, his bare hands. And Randal had water: God, brother or no, he owed Randal Lovell several lives . . .

Christie. Abandoning the byre to Randal, Luke ran out through the doorway and towards the front steps. The Trotters were retreating, loading their dead and wounded over saddle-bows, driving Luke's horses towards the Border. Luke saw the front door open, smoke clouding round its rim, and Christie, framed in the doorway. Then there was the soft sigh of an arrow, piercing the cold air, and he called out. Luke saw Christie turn, halfway down the steps, and then she tumbled to the ground, to lie, a tangle of blue velvet, on the soaking grass.

SHE did not move. Luke, running, saw the arrow skirl impotently into the wet earth a few inches from Christie's shoulder. It had not hurt her – why, then, did she not stand?

He understood why when he crouched down beside her and said her name. Her hands were covering her face, and she shook like the reeds in the marshes. She was saying something to herself, very softly: he heard only a few words and realized that the language she spoke was not English.

He caught her up in his arms and carried her into the house. Placing her on the straw, wrapping an abandoned cloak around her, he found a half-empty wine bottle in the corner of the room. He had almost to force the liquid down her throat, but eventually Christie coughed and spluttered and opened her eyes.

'The fire –'

'The fire is out,' Luke said, firmly. 'The Trotters are gone. It's all over, Christie.'

Her eyes were bleak. Slowly, she shook her head. 'So foolish,' she said. 'All this –'

Her wide dark gaze took in the scorched, dirty straw, the

bow and remaining arrows on the table. Luke rose, and shut the door.

He made no attempt to defend himself. 'It's a way of life,' he said, flatly. 'My way of life.'

He saw that she was crying, that tears made tracks through the mud and soot that grimed her face. He found that his own hands hurt, that he, too, shook, as the events of the night started to take their toll.

'I'll take you back to Adderstone tomorrow,' Luke said, and went to find Christie a blanket.

Chapter Ten

*M*ARGARET Forster had never allowed herself to watch and wait, and she did not do so now. But the strain was beginning to tell: it was almost mid-morning, and there was still no sign of Christie. She had already snapped at Arbel and sent her away to Janet, and had, against her better judgement, released Mark from his studies to ride the fells, like his elder brothers, in search of Christie. Every able-bodied Forster servant also rode. She could do no more.

They had returned to Adderstone the previous night, Bess Grey's plump baby having provided sufficient entertainment. And Christie, sensible, reliable Christie, had been absent. Since the afternoon, the servants thought. Or possibly midday. It would have made more sense, thought Margaret, as she threaded her needle, if Arbel had disappeared. Christie was such a sensible girl. It was Arbel, impulsive, thoughtless Arbel, who knew no fear. But Arbel, questioned, had no idea of Christie's whereabouts.

There remained the unpleasant possibility that Christie had been kidnapped, a common enough occurrence on the Borders. A part of Margaret, the part she could not control, waited for a letter, or a messenger. Only, again, why not Arbel? Arbel had land and money, Christie neither birth nor fortune. Margaret picked up her sewing, and tried not to think of Christie, alone and frightened in someone's desolate pele-tower.

But her sharp ears caught the sound of the barmkin gate opening, horse's hooves on Adderstone's cobbles. She stood up, needlework in hand, and went to the window.

She recognized Lucas at first, from the hair that was neither Stephen's gold nor Forster brown. Then she saw Christie, her gown muddy and torn, sitting side-saddle in front of him.

Feeling faintly sick, Margaret ran down the stairs to meet them.

SHE attended to Christie first. Christie was shocked and tired and incoherent: Margaret sent her to bed. Then, hardly having spoken a word to him, she took Lucas to her room, thanking her own good angel that both Rob and Richie were still out on the hills, and that Janet had taken the distracting Arbel out for a walk.

In her parlour, Margaret sat, straight-backed, in her box-chair, and studied Lucas. He had never looked less a Ridley, she thought. Davey's feelings – joy, or (rarely) anger – had showed in his eyes. Rob was the same. But she could tell nothing from Lucas's eyes, nothing at all.

'Sit down, Lucas,' said Margaret. And then, watching him, added impatiently, 'Christie is well. Very tired, that's all.'

Still he did not sit. 'Christie spent the night with me at Catcleugh,' said Luke, and Margaret's hand paused in the middle of pouring the wine.

She did not let herself spill a drop, though. She filled the glass and held it out to him, and poured, unusually, another for herself. There were times when she felt very alone.

'I think you had better start at the beginning, my dear,' she said, and saw him walk to the window, and lean against the sill, glass in hand.

'Christie went for a ride yesterday, and got lost – I think she went further than she intended. Anyway, she found herself at Catcleugh.' Luke looked up, his eyes focused, briefly, on Margaret. 'I was going to take her home, but the Trotters appeared. They took all the horses, including Christie's.' His mouth twisted in the smallest of smiles. 'They owed me a visit. They were a long time coming – I'd almost given them up. I will, of course, recompense you for the horse.'

'I don't think we need worry about the horse.' Margaret, no fool, had seized upon the omissions in his story. 'You lost all your horses – you were alone, then, Lucas?'

He put his glass down on the sill. For the first time Margaret noticed the shadows under his eyes, the tension in the muscles around his mouth.

'The Lovells and the Faas arrived in time to prevent the Trotters razing Catcleugh to the ground,' he said, evenly. 'But yes, Margaret, I was alone.'

'With Christie.' Margaret put aside her glass and folded her hands carefully in her lap. 'I think there is something you have not told me, Lucas.'

'Yes.' He did not avoid her gaze. 'When Christie turned up at Catcleugh, I was very drunk. My men were there – I sent them away later. There was some – nonsense.'

Margaret thought: Richard should have lived. And Davey also. To sort out these unreasonable, squabbling children, who were children no longer. 'What sort of nonsense, Lucas?' she asked.

'Christie and I handfasted. I forced her. It was inexcusable, I know.'

Margaret turned her face away. Her hands were knotted, rigid, like wicker fencing. She took a deep breath, and said,

'And –?'

'Nothing. We said the words, that was all. Nothing else happened, I swear it, Margaret.'

She breathed out, slowly, painfully. He had turned away from her, she saw the line of his shoulders, the fair hair feathering the edge of his collar. '*Nothing,*' she said. 'It is enough, though, Lucas, don't you think? There are many who would now view Christie as your wedded wife.'

'If we lived together for a year,' he said, evenly, still facing the window. 'Which prospect Christie, for one, would view with extreme distaste. Otherwise – it was foolishness, as I said. That's all.'

He had, sometimes, an arrogance unmatched by any other Ridley or Forster. Margaret wanted to shake him. 'It was very wrong of you, Lucas,' she said. 'Christie has no one. We are her only family.'

'Yes.' He swung round. 'Listen, Margaret – is there anyone who might want to hurt Christie? Rejected lovers, that sort of thing –'

'Rejected lovers are more in Arbel's line,' said Margaret, crisply. She frowned, and shook her head. 'No. Why do you ask?'

He did not answer at first. Margaret noticed the difficulty he had in keeping still, the effort that went into standing easily by the window.

At length, he said, 'The Trotters had pistols – and extra men. One of them tried to shoot Christie. She was running from the house – because of the fire. If I hadn't called out –' He stopped. 'It was all over by then, you see, Margaret. There was no need – they had my horses, they had fired the house, and most of their riders had already gone. So why shoot at a defenceless girl?'

'Revenge?' said Margaret. 'You do have a talent for annoying people, Lucas.'

'They thought that Christie was mine? Perhaps.' There was an edge to his voice. 'Anyway, that was why I didn't take her back to Adderstone last night. She'd had a bad fall, and was very upset. And some of the Trotters might have lingered.'

He looked, and sounded, very tired. How much had the Trotters' raid cost him? All his most valuable property, and his house burned into the bargain. But, still – *handfasting*.

'How could you, Lucas?' she said, 'How could you? You, surely, should understand Christie's position better than anyone.'

She saw him visibly straighten himself, his eyes harden a little. 'Christie knows it was nothing but drunken foolishness,' he said. 'And that I regret it.'

'*Cruel* foolishness.' Margaret was surprised at the passion in her voice. 'If Stephen should hear of it –'

'I was hoping you would not find it necessary to tell Stephen.'

She looked up at him then, her eyes meeting his.

'Really, Lucas?'

It was his turn to frown. 'What do you mean, Margaret?'

She rose from the chair and stood face to face with him, almost his height. She had always felt big, graceless, near Lucas.

'I mean, are you sure that you don't want Stephen to hear of it? Are you sure that isn't exactly what you want? Are you sure that wasn't why you did it in the first place?'

He drew his hand across his forehead. She could see the fine white lines underneath his tan. Her own hands were bunched by her sides.

'I know what you are trying to do, Lucas,' she said, very softly. 'You want to offend Stephen. You want to offend Stephen so much that he loses control with you. What then, Lucas? Will you fight him then? Will you show Stephen that when it comes to it you are no lesser a man than he?'

She saw his eyes flicker once.

Margaret whispered, 'And Rob? What of Rob? Stephen will take Rob with him. I know Rob's faults, but he is my son. Don't use him to try and hurt Stephen. Don't do it, Lucas. Please. I could not bear it.'

'I have no quarrel with Rob.' Luke had moved away from her, taking his cloak from the back of a chair. 'I have no quarrel with any of the Forsters.'

He threw his cloak over his shoulders. Again, Margaret wanted to shake him. Or to hold him against her: anything to change the expression in his eyes, anything to make him look at her, just once, with something like his old affection. But she, who spent a lifetime erasing the impulsive from her nature, merely said, 'Stephen will not hear of this through me. And neither will anyone else,' and she watched him bow, and kiss her hand, his eyes veiled.

At Adderstone's front door, Luke looked up, too late, and saw Rob and Richie Forster, newly arrived in the courtyard. And Arbel. My God, the whole bloody lot of them.

His horse was in the stables on the far side of the courtyard. Rob and Richie had dismounted, Arbel was at Rob's side: she stared from him to Luke. *I've come to seek the former vows you granted me before.* Richie was untying his saddlebags, the stable-boy leading Rob's horse away. Arbel whispered something to Rob, and Rob began to walk towards Luke.

He could tell from Rob's face something of what Arbel had

176

said. Luke's chief emotion was exhaustion, a simple reluctance to go through explanation, abasement, again.

Rob's hand was already folding round the hilt of his sword.

'Enjoyed your ride, Rob?' said Luke, strolling a few feet out of the doorway. 'It's a fine day for it –'

Rob's eyes had darkened; he had, impossibly drawn his sword. 'You bastard,' he said gently. 'Couldn't have the pretty one, so you took the plain, eh, Luke? Was it a fine night for it?'

'Christie isn't plain,' said Luke, consideringly. 'A little less gaudy, perhaps, but not *plain*. Quite the opposite, in fact.'

'You little –'

'Bastard, as you've said already, Rob.' Luke felt suddenly very tired, and the desire to tease, to taunt, evaporated. 'Listen, Rob – for once in your life just *listen*. Christie stayed the night at Catcleugh, yes. But I slept downstairs by the fire, and she slept upstairs in the bed. And there were a couple of dozen Trotters visiting for most of the night. Chaperone enough, don't you think?'

'I think,' said Rob, slowly, resting the tip of his sword against Luke's doublet front of quilted black, 'that you should draw your sword. *Now*, Luke.'

Richie was still there, looking irritable, and Arbel, no doubt enjoying every minute of it, and half the Forster servants, back home for their dinner and wanting nothing more than to witness a good fight. Luke spread out his hands in front of him, palms upraised.

'I've burned my hands, Rob. Can't hold a sword.'

He saw Rob glance down at his reddened, blistered palms, and felt the sword slip a couple of inches, nicking the laces on his doublet front.

Then Margaret's voice from behind him said sharply, 'Put up your sword, Rob.' And to the waiting servants, 'Well, what are you all about? You have work to do, haven't you?'

The sword slid a little further, and then was returned, resoundingly, to the scabbard. Rob said softly, 'Don't come back, Luke. You're not welcome here,' and then he pushed past Luke and his mother, and disappeared into the house. Luke gazed after him for a few seconds, and then went to fetch his horse.

*

It was evening before Arbel was able to talk to Christie in private. It was not a moment Christie had looked forward to as she had slept, her dreams exhaustingly vivid, her body bruised and aching. It was not physical pain that concerned her, though, it was her soul that was sore, scraped to rawness by the previous night's events. The awful ride to Catcleugh, the hand-fasting, the raid. The arrow that she had heard, serpent-toothed in the darkness, the wet grass rushing up to meet her.

But now Arbel was in the doorway, Dowzabel dangling over her silk-sleeved arm.

'Why did you go to Catcleugh?' said Arbel. 'What did he say? He's gone – why has he gone? Is he afraid of Rob?'

'Luke?' Wearily, Christie shook her head. 'No, he's not afraid of Rob. I don't expect he's afraid of anything.'

She remembered Luke Ridley standing by Catcleugh's small stone window, firing his arrows, his eyes joyous and steady. And she remembered the sour echoes of fear she had found to accompany the smoke, the flames, the shouting.

Arbel sat down on the edge of the bed, her loose hair falling around her face. She said, brightly, 'But he'll come back, won't he?'

Arbel had everything: money, beauty, her own name, but she wanted Luke Ridley as well.

'No,' said Christie, flatly. 'He won't come back.'

'Rob wanted to fight him in the courtyard – did you see, Christie?' There was an edge to Arbel's voice that, another time, Christie would have recognized and tried to do something about. 'Luke wouldn't. He said he'd burned his hands –'

The room was too hot. Christie slid off the bed and walked to the window. She tried to force open the stiff catch, but it would not budge. She closed her eyes for a moment, but she could still smell the awful, suffocating stench of burning straw.

'He won't come, Arbel,' she said with an effort. 'He won't ever come. He *married* me there at Catcleugh. Oh, not a proper ceremony, nothing that counts. Just some stupid thing called handfasting. Luke doesn't care for you, Arbel, and he doesn't care for me. You should forget him.'

The window opened at last, letting in the cold air.

Christie did not cry, but closed her eyes tightly, and breathed in the bitter pure air of Northumbria.

LUKE reached the gypsy encampment late that night, stopping only briefly at Catcleugh. The small circle of fires was bright against the black of the hills and the sky. He nodded to old Ashena, and to Johnnie Lovell, seated on the front step of their wagon. Randal Lovell met him, and he pressed something into Randal's palm.

'For the horse,' he said, nodding to the mare he had tethered to the tree.

Randal dropped the gold coin into his pocket. 'The Warden wasn't too pleased to be one short,' he said. 'When do we call on the Trotters again?'

'When they're half asleep and in their cups,' said Luke. 'Anytime. But not for a while. I'm going away.' Taking Randal by the sleeve, Luke led him beyond the circle of tents and caravans.

'The gentleman with the bow and arrow,' said Luke, when they were out of earshot of all Randal's second cousins and half-sisters. 'What do you think?'

Lovell's eyes were dark, glittering. 'I think', he said, 'that a woman running in the darkness is not an easy target. And I think that he wasn't a Trotter.'

'So do I.' Luke frowned. 'Christie thought she was followed from Adderstone to Catcleugh. Do you think you could discover our over-eager friend's name, Randal? Quietly, mind.'

They had reached Luke's horse.

'How's the bride?' said Randal, grinning.

STEPHEN Ridley arrived at Adderstone the following morning. He spent a half-hour with Richie and Janet and Margaret, received a finely sketched version of the events of the last two days, and then, at Margaret's request, went to see Arbel.

She's a little out of sorts, Margaret had said. Arbel was in her room, alone except for her dog. Her door was open very slightly, so Stephen pushed it a few inches further and allowed himself the luxury of watching Arbel Forster unnoticed. She sat by the window, the backdrop of hills and lapis-lazuli sky etching her profile in bas-relief. She had not put up her hair, it looped, pale and rippling, over her narrow shoulders, fine tendrils curling round her cheeks and brow. Her eyes, dark and expressionless, looked at nothing, her severely sculptured lips were still, silent. Only her fingers moved, very slowly, scratching the dog's neck. A shawl was draped around her arms and chest, disguising the contours of her body, negating the fact that she was female. She could have been anything: boy, woman, sexless angel, a pure beauty that transcended all the futile, degrading drudgery of adult love and sex.

He opened the door a little further, and allowed his footsteps to be heard. Arbel turned, and he saw then what he had not seen before: that she had been crying. A single tear glistened, diamond bright, on the exquisite curve of her cheek. She smiled, though, looking up at him, and said his name.

He did not offer her physical comfort because it was not in his nature to do so.

He stood before her, and said, 'Why did you not come to me, Arbel, if you were unhappy? Surely you know me to be your friend?'

A second tear overflowed her eye, and coursed, unchecked, down her satin skin.

Stephen knelt: he almost took the silk hem of her gown and pressed it to his lips. 'Let me help you, Arbel,' he said. 'I am at your disposal. I am always at your disposal. What can I do to make you happy?'

She stared at him. 'Take me *out*,' she said, fiercely. 'Take me away from here.'

He stood, and looked out of the window. The temperature had dropped; there had been a frost that morning, and the sky was a pure, wintry blue. 'I am yours for the day,' he said. 'Where would you go?'

'The sea.' Her eyes had focused, there were no more tears. 'Oh, Stephen, take me to the sea. Please.'

THEY rode to the long, flat swathe of sand between Embleton and Craster. Dunstanburgh castle perched on its rocky, sea-bound promontory to the south, Bamburgh, black and forbidding, was lost in the curve of the coast to the north. The sea was as flat and shining as a tortoiseshell looking-glass, scarcely a breeze moved the dying sea-pinks and marram-grass.

They followed the fishermen's path through the sand-hills and across the streams, riding down to where the sand was firm and smooth. Emerging from the final barricade of the dunes, gaining their first uninterrupted view of the water, Stephen heard Arbel's small sigh of delight, saw her lips part and her hands tighten on the reins.

Arbel had changed her silk gown for a warmer riding-habit: black velvet, with a stiff, white half-ruff that curved round her slender neck and shoulders. She had put up her pale, corn-silk hair under a velvet coif, neatly, so that not a single silver strand was out of place. Stephen had told her to leave her dog at Adderstone and, obediently, she had. She had not carped and squawked as Janet Forster would have done, had not, despite her impatience to leave Adderstone, bundled herself anyhow into an old cloak and hat like one of Lucas's promiscuous harlots. Lucas had not known how to behave, faced with someone as pure and unspoilt as Arbel. Lucas had puked and wallowed in the gutter, showing the stuff he was made of.

Down at the sea-strand, the white foam laced about the horses' legs. Arbel was silent, and Stephen let her remain so. There was only the cry of the gulls, soaring above the dark basalt foundations of Dunstanburgh castle, and the gentle lap of the sea, slipping on the silver sand. Arbel looked out to the horizon like a dreamer, her grey eyes fixed on the almost invisible line between sea and sand. She began to walk her horse forward, into the waves, so that the sea churned and seethed almost to the level of her stirrups. 'Arbel, you will wet your gown,' said Stephen, and seized her bridle. Arbel, turning, looked down at the incoming tide, and he saw that she was crying again.

He led her horse back to the shelter of the dunes. Arbel's hands no longer even touched the reins; she wept silently, not snuffling and gulping as so many women did: her nose was unreddened, her eyes still clear and unswollen. When the dunes had taken away the sound of waves and gulls, Stephen said, 'Arbel. What is it?'

He thought at first that she would not answer him, that, like a painted angel, she would keep her own counsel. But she said, with sudden passion, 'Adderstone! I hate it!' and he felt his heart begin to quicken, and his tongue moisten the inside of his dry lips.

He did not yet answer. Stephen waited, unable to speak, while she looked up at him, her grey eyes meeting his dark blue ones.

'I hate Adderstone,' said Arbel. 'I never want to go back there.'

He found that now he could answer quite easily; the loss of control had been temporary, scarcely noticeable.

'You don't have to stay at Adderstone,' Stephen said. 'Come to Black Law with me.'

Her eyes did not leave his face. Only the dreamer's expression began, slowly, to return, as though Arbel Forster, having made brief contact with reality, had abandoned it, finding it not to her taste.

'Come to Black Law as my wife,' said Stephen.

He knew she would not refuse.

He knew that she would do whatever he told her, that she had no will of her own, that she was as malleable and unresisting as the dunes that edged Embleton Bay. He did not yet regret his impulse. Arbel's transparent chastity might distance him from what he would have to do. Besides, he needed an heir. He needed a son to take his name and to inherit his lands, and to erase what Davey, Catherine and Lucas alike had done to the name of Ridley.

QUEEN Elizabeth's court had returned to London, having emptied the cellars and larders of many honoured gentlemen, having traced a slow, noisy path through flagged and flowered streets, having watched masques and country weddings and sat, unyawning, listening to madrigal and motet, lute and cittern.

Now that the splendour of Elizabeth's majesty had been

demonstrated yet again to the people, they could put pomp, if not aside, at least on a slightly lower rung, and return to the business of government. Which had, of course, continued unabated throughout the summer.

Meanwhile, Sir Francis Walsingham's men rooted through England and Europe like so many inconspicuous truffle-hounds, picking among the whispering leaves of Catholicism for the priceless fungus of information.

Disguised as fellow-prisoners, they won the confidence of Papists in the English gaols. They wormed their way into the services of Catholic agents and sympathizers. The serving-man, perhaps a little clumsy with the plates and ewers, was not clumsy at all when it came to copying a carelessly placed letter, recalling a treasonable conversation. Working their way higher up the ladder, Walsingham's men might even find themselves accepted as one of their host's own kind. What treasures, then, for their master back in Whitehall: exchange a little fools' gold in the form of unimportant snippets from Queen Elizabeth's court, and a wealth of fact and figure might tumble into the open hands of Sir Francis Walsingham.

It was never enough, though, never enough. Station a man at every port, outside every recusant's house, and there was still, always, the possibility that he might play you at your own game. If you bought an unprincipled man for money, then there was always the risk that someone else might be prepared to pay him just a little more. Always the risk that, whatever he knew about you, he might betray to your enemy.

Some people Sir Francis Walsingham could almost trust. The ambassadors, the lords-lieutenants, the bishops. Some of them were men of principle, others had earned too much to throw it away on a political gamble. Some might recall, as Lucas Ridley had done, treason's reward. But the others, the freelances, the men he used for a year or so and then dropped, those he could not trust. And he needed them, those little local men.

So he must watch the watchers. He must watch for any hint of a double game, any suggestion that greed, or ambition might overreach itself. He must know all the minute causes and effects of provincial life, the temptations, the betrayals, the payments offered, services rendered.

And he must watch the ports and the ships. Including the *Elizabeth*.

THE Forsters, a family accustomed to drama, had, one evening in early December, two pieces of news to assimilate. The first, that Janet (refusing her dinner yet again) was pregnant, they had guessed, the second, that Arbel was to marry Stephen Ridley, they had not.

Relief and unease mingled unequally in Margaret's bosom. The relief was simple: she had never understood Arbel, had not, if she was honest with herself, become attached to Arbel, as she had once been attached to Anne. Margaret blamed only herself for that: the years, the times, had hardened her. No, she had hardened herself, carefully and deliberately. For survival. Stephen was landed, wealthy, and respected throughout the Borders. A good catch for any girl.

The unease she could not quite identify. It centred, un-focused, around the past, round Davey, Grace, and of course, Lucas. She should be pleased, she told herself: a troublesome niece and an unwed brother had solved each other's problems neatly. She *was* pleased, she had told them so, Arbel and Stephen, when they had come to ask her permission for their marriage. Which Margaret had given, because she saw the sense in it, and because, after the unfortunate affair of Lucas and Christie, she wanted one niece at least happily settled. But when she tried to imagine Stephen and Arbel happy together, she failed. She had become accustomed to the thought that Stephen would never marry, that Black Law would be left, eventually, to some distant relative. Not to Lucas, that much was certain. But of course Stephen would marry, for he needed an heir. And of course, seeing Arbel, he would secure himself what every other man had wanted. It was in his nature to do so. And surely Arbel would be happy when she had a baby to replace that dreadful dog.

Christie's emotions were a little more defined.

After dinner, in the seclusion of her bedchamber, Arbel said,

'You can come and live with us at Black Law, Christie. Stephen won't mind. I asked him.'

Christie remembered Stephen's eyes when she had first met him at Hexham, that instant, unalterable hatred. She shook her head.

'It wouldn't do, Arbel,' she said, gently. 'I'd be in the way. You do see that, don't you?'

Neither would she stay at Adderstone, though. She had arrived at Adderstone as Arbel's sister and, with Arbel gone, there would be no place for her.

Instead, there was France, the past, and a bundle of fleeting, fragile memories. Staring out of the bedchamber window, she could not see the hills, the valleys, but she could hear the wind, recollect all too clearly the drumroll of horses' hooves, the whistle of an arrow in the darkness.

'I'll go away,' Christie said, firmly. 'It's time, Arbel. We won't tell anyone – it'll be our secret. You must help me.'

And she felt Arbel's arm thread through hers, Arbel's silken head rest on her shoulder.

THREE days later, Christie stood on the quay at Berwick, bag in hand. What had once seemed so impossible had, when it came to it, been ridiculously easy. Arbel had requested a visit to Berwick to buy her wedding-clothes, Margaret, administering to a horribly sick Janet, had suggested that she and Christie stay with Susannah Grey. In Berwick, Tom Dodd had been sent to the docks to search out the obliging *Elizabeth*, times of sailings had been ascertained, money handed over. The *Elizabeth* sailed with the tide at mid-afternoon on Monday; any passengers must be on board by three o'clock.

In some ways it would, thought Christie, shivering on Berwick quayside, have been easier if the ship had sailed at night-time. Then the sense of adventure that had buoyed them both up since the announcement of Arbel's betrothal to Stephen and Christie's decision to sail to France might have been maintained. But there was little adventure in standing on a wind-swept, dirty quayside, a bag in one hand and Arbel firmly clutching the other, watching the ships bob up and down on the restless sea like children's playthings, while her stomach slithered, cold and uncertain, down to her boots.

'That one's pretty,' said Arbel, hopping from one foot to the other, tossing back her windswept hair from her face. 'It's got the dearest little flags. Don't you think so, Christie?'

Christie nodded and tried to smile. 'They're lovely little flags. It's from the Low Countries, I think –'

'Pirates, perhaps,' said Arbel, enthusiastically. 'You might be abducted by a pirate, Christie. He'd have long moustaches and scarlet breeches and one of those curved swords. It would be terribly romantic, don't you think?'

'Terribly,' agreed Christie, and tried not to shiver. 'Well, perhaps not *scarlet* breeches . . .'

They stood in silence for a moment. The sailors were loading the *Elizabeth* with unfinished cloth.

Arbel said, uncertainly, 'Do you think Dowzabel will like Black Law?'

Christie looked down to where Dowzabel slept, cradled in one black velvet arm. Christie's eyes ached.

'I'm sure she'll like Black Law,' she said, gently. 'She'll eat her food out of a golden bowl, and lose herself in the knot garden. And she'll *adore* the ship clock –'

Arbel giggled. 'She'll hide from it. She hid from it last time we were there. I told her it wasn't real, but she wouldn't listen.'

The master of the *Elizabeth* was walking up the quayside towards them.

Christie turned and faced Arbel.

'I won't go. I'll stay here – I'll come to Black Law.'

At first, Arbel did not speak.

Then she smiled, and said, 'You're to bring me back some cloth of gold and golden lace and a pair of golden slippers. Then I'll match Dowzabel's drinking-bowl. And you're to let me come and stay with you in your castle. *Please*, Christie.'

FROM her cabin on board the *Elizabeth*, Christie could see neither Arbel nor Berwick itself through the single small porthole, for the waves rushed against the bows of the ship, green-grey with a lacing of white.

The cabin was tiny, its outer wall the curving hull of the ship, the only furniture a small wooden bed, stool and table. Christie's bag stood on one end of the bed, Christie herself, her knees hunched up to her chin, sat on the other. Arbel's parting gift, a penknife in a leather sheath, was clutched in Christie's hand. In case of pirates, Arbel had said, hopefully.

Christie hoped that Arbel would walk straight back to the Greys, that Arbel would remember to deliver the letter that she, Christie, had written with such difficulty. The letter to Margaret, thanking her for her kindness over the months at Adderstone, apologizing for the anxiety she knew she must inevitably cause. Trying, and failing, to explain what she herself had never fully understood, her compulsive need to understand the past and its manipulation of the present. She had a lingering memory of a another voyage, a child then, bundled into a heavy cloak, a hand waving to her on a different quayside as she sat on wooden steps looking out to a calmer sea. Sometimes Christie thought those memories nothing more than inventions, dreams, incorrect answers to unanswerable puzzles. Now she curled up on the narrow wooden bed, her cloak pulled over her head, trying to forget Arbel's face when she had said, *Do you think Dowzabel will like Black Law* . . .? Who would look after Arbel now? Would Stephen?

Of course, Christie said to herself sternly, Stephen would look after Arbel. He liked Arbel, he must do, because he had offered to marry her. She sat up and blew her nose. This, after all, was the easy part of the journey, there was no excuse for snivelling now.

It was only that she seemed to have forgotten quite how violently a ship moved. That awful lurch, bounce, lurch, bounce, until she thought the tiny galleon would be tossed and whirled into the air to fall broken like matchwood. Or like an eggshell. Christie thought of eggs rolling from Adderstone's huge kitchen table to the stone floor, smashing one by one on to the flags. Her stomach lurched in rhythm with the ship: she was beginning to feel rather odd. She was sure she would feel better if she could go on deck, but the master had expressly forbidden her to go on deck. A woman would distract the crew . . . She would have to wait until after dark, would have to stay in this tiny, cramped, stuffy cabin for another *hour* at least. The sky was dimming already, but not quickly enough . . . Oh God . . .

Christie closed her eyes, sank down to the bed again and concentrated very hard.

To her suprise she slept, and did not wake until dark. By then the black beast that mauled her usually obedient stomach had crouched in the corner, snarling, waiting for any careless movement. The *Elizabeth*'s lurching seemed to have lessened somewhat: peering out of the porthole, Christie could see nothing but darkness, but knew, instinctively, that they had paused in their journey, weighing anchor. To change sails, she thought, vaguely, thankful for the comparative calm. Or perhaps the master had decided to put in at a port further down the coast – Scarborough, perhaps, or Whitby. There were no lights, though, no indication that they were in a harbour. She could hear, through the susurrant, sucking sounds of the sea, the clatter of feet on wooden planks, men's voices calling. She could not catch the words, the waves and the ship's creaking timbers smothered them, extracting their meaning and throwing the ragged syllables to the wind.

Eventually the ship began to move again. Lurch, bounce, lurch, bounce, and the black beast crawled across the floor to lurk threateningly by the bed. Footsteps outside, coming nearer. A knock on the door.

'Dinner, miss,' said the sailor, and dumped a bowl on the small table.

Lumps of beef in a barley gravy, and two biscuits. The biscuits had little holes in them. Weevils, thought Christie, horribly, and ran as fast as she could out of the cabin.

There did not, she thought at first, as she climbed the ladder and began to breathe in great gulps of cold, salty air, seem to be anyone else on the quarter-deck. Then, as the single lantern swinging from the yard-arm began to draw for her the deck, the rim of the gunwale, and the taut, swollen sails, she heard a sound.

A footstep. Boots on scuffed wood.

Christie turned, and saw Luke Ridley.

Chapter Eleven

*H*ER only consolation was that he looked as horrified as she felt.

There was a short, ridiculous silence in which they stared at each other, frozen. Luke was the first to speak.

'Arbel's disguised herself as a cabin boy? The master's morals are as deficient as mine? You've taken up gun-running?'

The nausea had not retreated. Christie's heart hammered like the tiny cannon on Stephen's ship clock.

Luke had drawn level with her, standing by the gunwale. He wore jerkin and breeches, boots and cloak. His breeches were wet past the knees. 'Rowed on, a half-hour past,' he said. 'And you, Miss Forster?'

'Berwick,' she whispered, and then was silent again. Somewhere, there were questions to be asked, but she did not feel like asking them now. She did not feel like speaking, or moving, or even thinking.

'Sandy Lawson,' said Luke, bitterly. 'The avaricious bastard.' He stared at Christie.

He did not, she thought weakly, look as he had on that awful night at Catcleugh. Shocked, perhaps, but not yet angry. There was even a faint edge of amusement overlaying the light eyes, the long mouth.

'Miss Forster,' said Luke, 'did you know that there's a storm picking up?'

She shook her head, and then regretted it. As if to emphasize his words, the ship pitched violently, jarring her against the gunwale.

He took hold of her elbow to steady her. 'You do look rather pale,' he said, considerately. 'Are you a good sailor, Miss Forster?'

And by then she had no answer, no answer at all. Christie leaned her head over the gunwale and was horribly sick into the uncaring North Sea.

When she did, eventually, return to her cabin, it was not because she had stopped being sick, but only because her stomach was empty – turned inside out, in fact – and it seemed preferable to lie on a bed than to sit on the *Elizabeth*'s heaving decks. Her body heaved and her head pounded.

The storm reached its peak the following midday. The *Elizabeth* was a solid little ship, not top-heavy like so many others of her kind, and kept in good repair. But the finest ship on the seas could founder in a gale on the North Sea in December, caught on sandbanks, or simply whisked to kindling by the wind and the waves. Seamanship might lengthen the odds against the *Elizabeth*; luck, or prayer, depending on your point of view, would be the make-weight that dipped the balance in the ship's favour.

Luke had no time for prayer, and had recently lost faith in luck. He was, however, enjoying himself. He had grown used, over the past five years, to a certain element of danger, so that he almost missed its absence.

The only inconvenience the storm caused him was connected with Christie. Had the weather been calm, he would have coerced Sandy into parting temporarily with the ship's boat and a reliable man, and Christie would have been rowed back to the next convenient headland and returned to Adderstone as quickly as possible.

Outraged Forster voices echoed dimly in his ears, intermingled with wind and waves, during his uncomfortable attempt to untangle a jammed topsail. And his own voice, *I, Lucas Ridley of Catcleugh, take thee, Christian Forster* teased him as he cut ropes and slid back down the mizzen mast, the knife jammed between his teeth.

At some point during the day he found time to go down to her cabin. She did not answer his knock, and when he pushed open the door he saw that she was asleep face down on the bed, her hair spread stickily over the pillow, the blanket slipped to the floor. Her skin had no colour, her hand, when he tucked the blanket round her, was ice-cold. He stood for a moment, steadying himself against the doorjamb. Over the battering of the sails and the booming of the waves against the galleon's wooden walls, he could hear only the sound of an arrow whistling through the darkness, and his own voice calling a girl's name.

SHE dreamt that she was on horseback, riding from Adderstone to Catcleugh, and someone was shouting to her. She did not recognize the voice, but knew, without being told, that it was her father's voice. *Christie*, he said, *Christie*, but she could not see him. So he took her by the shoulder and shook her, forcing her to open her eyes.

She was lying on her front on the small truckle bed, one cold hand fisted against her mouth, the other loose at her side. The ship still lurched and bounced; her stomach, scoured raw, lurched and bounced too. Something was pulled across her back; she turned slightly and saw that she was covered with a blanket and her own cloak. They felt heavy, not warm. And there was someone else in the cabin; Christie turned again, and, recognizing Luke, groaned.

He was sitting on the edge of the bed, and he wouldn't let her go back to sleep. She hated him then just as much as she had hated him in Northumberland, for all she wanted was to close her eyes and drift away again, back even to Catcleugh if that was where her dreams took her.

But he would not let her. He took hold of her shoulder and shook her again, saying her name. That had been Luke Ridley's voice, a Northumbrian voice, not her father's. She hated him for that, too.

She felt herself hauled upright, and a cup put to her lips.

'Drink some water,' he said. 'You haven't had anything to drink for two days, Christie – you'll make yourself ill.'

She wanted to tell him that she was dying already, but she did not have the strength. Besides, his arm was round her shoulders, and something was trickling down her chin. She took a mouthful, and coughed and choked because it wasn't just water, there was aqua vitae as well.

'Finish it,' said Luke.

She did, because, miraculously, her stomach had stopped its terrible gyrations and her heart had stopped pounding quite so violently. Even the *Elizabeth* seemed to have stilled a little.

When she had finished, he took the empty cup and placed it on the table. She felt cold when his arm left her, and she began to shiver. 'You're a lousy sailor, Miss Forster,' said Luke, standing up. 'I'll find you another blanket.'

He left the cabin, returning shortly with two more blankets and his own cloak. 'If you're not sick again, you can have something to eat in an hour,' he said, arranging blankets and cloak over her as she shuffled into a sitting position. 'Meanwhile, to pass the time, you can tell me what on earth you are doing here.'

Christie stared at him furiously. He had perched on the stool, his back against the *Elizabeth*'s hull, his legs flung out before him. As though he *owned* the bloody ship.

'I might ask you the same question, Mr Ridley,' said Christie, tightly.

'I'm going to France,' said Luke, unconcerned. 'Surreptitiously, because I'm not supposed to leave the country.'

She didn't know what to make of that, so she ignored it. 'Well, so am I going to France, Mr Ridley. I paid Mr Lawson twelve sovereigns for my passage – Arbel arranged it.'

'I bet she did . . . Twelve sovereigns, by God. I told you he was an avaricious bastard.'

There was nothing to say to that, so Christie just scowled.

Luke added, thoughtfully, 'How long have you been planning this, Miss Forster? Since Berwick Fair, perhaps?'

She felt her face go red. 'Before that,' she said, eventually. 'I never intended to stay in Northumberland.'

He said nothing for a while. Then, 'You have family in France, I take it, Miss Forster?'

If she had not been feeling so tired, so ill, so utterly beaten, then she might have given a better answer.

'I think so,' said Christie.

'You *think* so?' He was staring at her, frowning. 'You don't know?'

She shook her head. Her hair trailed lank and limp around her face. Her clothes smelled sour.

He continued, mercilessly, 'You are travelling to a foreign country – alone – on the off-chance that you might still have some surviving relatives? Is that right, Miss Forster?'

She nodded. '*Christ,*' said Luke Ridley, adding, 'I should have had you put off at Scarborough.'

There was a short silence.

Then Christie, finding her handkerchief at last, and blowing her nose, said defensively, 'Well, I could hardly stay at Adderstone, could I? Not now Arbel's going to Black Law.'

It had not occurred to her that he would not have known. Nor that he would care. But of course he would not know; for Rob had banned him from Adderstone, and of course he would care, for Luke and Arbel had shared something once.

She saw the shock on his face, in his eyes.

'Arbel is to marry Stephen?' said Luke, and rose, and went to the door.

He said one more thing as he left, but she thought, closing her eyes again, that she must have misheard him.

'Poor bitch,' said Lucas Ridley, softly. 'Poor, silly bitch.'

CHRISTIE did not see Luke again until, weak-legged, she walked that evening up to the *Elizabeth*'s swaying mizzen-deck. She had eaten some bread and drunk a little wine, and the prospect of imminent death seemed to have retreated a little.

He was leaning against the bows, looking out to sea. The greying horizon was featureless, sky and sea smudging endlessly together. He was looking at nothing.

She crossed the deck and went to him.

'Your cloak, Mr Ridley.' And, gathering her courage, added, 'Arbel will be happy, I'm sure. It's a lovely house – she'll be very comfortable.'

He stared at her. '*Comfortable*, Miss Forster? Do you really think that Arbel gives a damn about comfort?'

She could not meet his eyes, she stared down at the deck-planks.

'Do you think she loves Stephen?' said Luke. 'Do you think she even *likes* him?'

She looked back up at him. His cloak was slung over his arm, his hair blown back from his face by the wind.

She said, at last, 'Arbel likes Stephen as much as she likes anyone.'

She had not intended to hurt him, but the words – the truth – were out before she could stop them. But he did not look hurt, he only said, 'Except yourself, Miss Forster. Except yourself.'

'You don't understand.' Christie pulled her own cloak around her; the wind, bitter cold, hurled droplets of sea-water on to the deck. 'You didn't know Anne – Arbel's mother. You don't know how it was –'

Her voice drifted away to silence, as cold and as sad as the winter wind.

She heard Luke say, 'And you, Christie? Do you like Stephen?'

She could not have lied, even if she had wanted to.

She shook her head.

'I disgust him,' she said, simply.

'And you think that Arbel will be happy with *that*?'

His hair was darkened by the sea-spray, his face bleached of colour by the evening sky.

She said, sharply, 'Stephen dislikes me for the same reason that he dislikes you, Mr Ridley. Because I am a bastard.'

'Yes. There is that, too, of course.'

She did not understand him; she was not even sure that she wanted to understand him. But she recalled their first meeting in Rothbury. Stephen had been there, too, and she had been forced to witness that awful hatred. She had seen the blanched whiteness of Stephen's face, his hands as they clenched the reins. And she thought of Arbel, thoughtless, beautiful Arbel. Arbel had seduced the object of Stephen Ridley's hatred, had slept with the man her future husband loathed. *Handy, spandy Jack-a-dandy, loved plum cake and sugar candy* . . .

Christie turned away, biting her lip.

She heard Luke say, dismissively, 'Arbel must take care of herself. As for you, Miss Forster, you had better return to England.'

She swung round. She could hardly see his face now, but his tone had been practical, almost bored.

'Return to England, Mr Ridley? Certainly not! I apologize if I have been a nuisance during this voyage, but that was hardly my intention. As soon as the ship docks, we need never see each other again.'

'My dear girl –'

'*No.*' She had gathered up her skirts, flung back her cloak. 'I've waited ten years for this – I'm not going back now. I am perfectly able to look after myself.'

THE *Elizabeth* docked in Dieppe three days later.

From the galleon's small fore-deck, Luke Ridley and Sandy Lawson watched Christie walk down the gangway, bag in hand, on to Dieppe's bustling quayside. It was afternoon; the sky was a clear, cold sapphire, unmarred by clouds. Dieppe, with its docks and its shipyards and its castle spread out before them, a gateway to the muddled, beautiful country of France.

'Someone should keep an eye on that lassie,' said Sandy, watching the determined chestnut head bob through the crowds. He scratched his beard, and leaned his huge fore-arms against the pin-rail.

'Someone', said Luke, repressively, 'should never have let her on his bloody ship.'

Sandy grinned. 'I was in need of a few shillings – trade's always bad at this time of year. Besides, the wee one asked me – her sister. A man couldnae refuse her anything.'

He glanced sideways at Luke, but Luke's eyes were also on Christie. 'I heard', went on Sandy, 'that she's some sort of relation. Cousin, was it?'

High on the chalk cliffs, the great mass of Dieppe Castle glowered down at them, licked with gold from the dying sun. Luke did not answer. Christie had reached the far side of the harbour.

'A man should look after his relations,' said Sandy.

*

196

SHE had forgotten her French, she did not know where she was going, and Dieppe's cobbled streets still heaved and swayed like the *Elizabeth*'s wooden decks. As she left the quayside and started up the road a man took her arm and gabbled incomprehensibly: she did not understand a word he said, but she understood very well his intention. So she shook him off and continued smartly up the street, praying that he did not follow.

It was cold, and the weak winter sun was already fading from the narrow alleyways. She felt ravenously hungry for the first time in a week, yet she did not know what to eat, where to eat. A tavern, said Christie to herself, sternly, she must find a tavern. Then she could have an evening meal, and a good night's sleep, and continue her journey the following morning. She must not give in to the impulse to stand here and weep, and wish herself back at Adderstone with Arbel.

Yet Dieppe, unlike Berwick, did not seem particularly rich in taverns. There were the docks, and the vast shipbuilding yards, and the Place du Puits-Sale with its well and its large open square. And the handsome church in the Rue St-Jacques. Standing on the cobbles, bag in hand, Christie stared at St-Jacques' exquisite rose window, and sniffed.

'Qu' est-ce que vous voulez, mademoiselle?'

A woman's voice, this time. Christie turned.

She was Aunt Margaret's age, but more smartly dressed than Aunt Margaret, with a French-cut black satin gown under a fur-trimmed cloak. She had Aunt Margaret's shrewd, sensible grey eyes, a long, narrow Valois nose, and brown hair in tight curls around her temples. The hand that rested on Christie's arm was kindly, comforting.

In rusty French Christie explained her situation.

'A tavern?' said the lady. 'Ma petite, I own a small hotel. You may have a bed for the night, and some good French food, and a warm fire. Yes?'

THE lady's name was Madame de Bordenard, but Christie could call her Marie. Madame's house was a tall, thin affair, not far from the fish-market, whitewashed and green-shuttered.

The room Christie was shown to was small and neat, with a very comfortable curtained bed and, as promised, a warm fire in the grate. There was a crucifix and a figurine of the Virgin Mary on one wall, and a rather strange woodcut on one of the others. A man and a woman, unclothed, in a forest. Adam and Eve, thought Christie, vaguely, and knelt by the fire to warm her hands.

Through the shutters came the smell of fish and salt and the cold dry scent of winter. It was not like Berwick, it was different, foreign. Some of Christie's sense of adventure, battered out of her by the rough sea voyage, began to return. She was in France at last; she felt a rush of triumph and expectation at the realization that years of planning and scheming had paid off. Tomorrow – or the next day (for Marie had intimated that she could stay for as long as she liked) she could ride to Rouen. And then from Rouen to Paris.

She had almost finished the tray of soup, bread and wine, kindly provided by Marie. Mopping up the last of the soup with a piece of bread, Christie unlaced her boots, put her cloak and hat over the chair, flung herself on the bed, and slept.

SHE was woken by a knock at the door. It was pitch-dark. She had to stoop and light a candle to see her way. Opening the door, candle in hand, the thin light flooded on to a familiar face.

'Well, at least you know me,' said Luke Ridley, and was inside the room, the door closed, before she could stop him.

The house had woken up during the time she slept. There had been a glimpse of bright lights down the stairs, and music filtered through the floorboards. *Well, at least you know me* . . . anger and unease mingled equally in Christie's bosom.

'Oh, do leave me be, Mr Ridley!' she said.

He grinned, and sat down on the edge of the bed.

'I've paid for this pleasure, Miss Forster. An economical girl like you would surely expect me to have my écu's worth. Marie was going to let you have a night's sleep, but I insisted – I was most particular. Untouched English virgins for me, nothing else.'

She did not speak because she was not able to.

But the candle-flame was flickering unsteadily, so he took the stick from her and placed it on the table, and said blandly, 'My dear, you are in a whorehouse. A very high-class whorehouse, but a whorehouse nevertheless.'

She sat down then because her legs would no longer hold her. 'But Madame –'

'– is a business-woman, Christie. You were a lost, penniless English girl – in need of employment, as she saw it.'

She stared at him. There was, infuriatingly, a glint of amusement in his eyes.

'How did you –? You didn't –?'

'I followed you from the ship.'

'You followed me from the ship?' Pieces began to fall into place. 'You *knew* who Madame de Bordenard was, didn't you? You've been here before!'

He did not look the slightest bit ashamed. His mouth twitched almost imperceptibly at the corners. 'Well – yes. Once or twice. When I'd money to spare –'

'And you let her take me here –'

She could hear the fast accelerating rise of her voice. Clenching her fists, Christie walked to the window and forced open the shutters. Light streamed out of the downstairs windows, bands of light on the cobbled streets.

'I thought you'd be all right for a while,' he said, his tone one of reason, patience. 'Besides, I had some business of my own.'

She did not answer. The light blurred a little; she folded her arms around herself.

'Christie.'

She did not turn. She said, 'I'll leave tonight.'

'And go – where?'

A headache had gathered tightly round her forehead, and she had never felt so foolish. 'Paris,' she said, tightly.

'And I don't suppose it would make the slightest difference if I pointed out that France has been at civil war, on and off, for twenty years now, and that your home is Adderstone, and your family the Forsters?'

She shook her head.

'Sensible, practical, Christie Forster,' he said, wearily. 'You're as obsessed as the rest of us, aren't you?'

Christie said nothing.

Eventually, Luke shrugged his shoulders. 'My business takes me to Paris. We may as well travel together.'

She turned round, slowly. 'I'm sure –' and Christie recalled an earlier conversation, on board the *Elizabeth* '– that whatever you are *surreptitiously* doing in France, you will do it a great deal easier without me. If you would be so kind as to recommend me a respectable hotel, Mr Ridley, then I would be most grateful. I don't think either of us would find each other's company tolerable for any length of time.'

Her eyes met Luke's.

'As you wish, Miss Forster,' he said, and rose, and waited while she packed her bag.

THREE days later, Christie left the respectable hotel, and rode with two equally respectable wine merchants for the city of Rouen.

The sky was clouded; a cold rain began to fall on the rolling fields and orchards as they left the town for the open country. Christie had only to think of her first night in Dieppe, though, for a wave of hot colour to take the sting of winter from her face. *Untouched English virgins for me*, Luke Ridley had said, following that remark shortly with an equally awful *we may as well travel together*. She would as soon travel with a nest of vipers. Two portly, plain wine merchants and their entourage would be much less exhausting.

The countryside was softer than Northumberland; in the gently wooded valleys there was green grass instead of dying heather. The trees made a tracery of black against a steel-grey sky, dead leaves gathered in the mud at the roadside, wide puddles drowning the ruts and pot-holes. The wine merchants talked of grapes and vintages, bouquets and noses. Christie (widowed, she had decided, donning black) rode close behind, silent to befit her mournful status.

The trees thickened into a forest that clung to the slopes of a shallow gorge. Wet branches dripped on to dying bracken and dead leaves; the quiet was broken by the sounds of running water, bird calls and the damp clatter of horses' hooves. The merchants discussed the cost of shipping, and Christie wiped the rain from her nose, and guided her horse carefully over the twisting roots that broke through the soft, dark earth. One of the servants by her side, a gangling youth with a cloth cap, sang a rather rude song under his breath.

Then there was a whistle, a sound which Christie found she remembered all too well, and the song ceased, and the youth slid forward in his saddle. In the frozen seconds it took for the remainder of the servants to draw their swords, another had tumbled from the saddle to roll, covered with leaf-mould, down to the stream. And by then Christie had seen the grey shapes crowding out of the dark thickets, the swords that caught the poor light from the filtering branches.

The merchants had not even time to draw their swords. Christie saw one protesting throat slit, and then she closed her eyes tightly, her mind too numb for prayer, her brain knowing the futility of crying for help, or mercy.

When she felt her horse jar, she knew that someone had taken her reins, and, unwillingly, she opened her eyes.

The man had lost most of his teeth, and some of the fingers of his right hand. He held a knife in that half-fingered hand: the blade rested on the swathes of black velvet covering Christie's thigh. He said something in guttural French that Christie did not understand until he waved the knife and spoke again. Then she began to pull the ring from her finger, the handkerchief from her pocket, her purse from her saddlebags.

'J'ai rien d'autre,' she said, as firmly as she could, and the half-handed man, who wore, like the reivers of Northumberland, a soldier's leather jack, looked at her, and then glanced back to his companions, and laughed.

The merchants' servants sprawled on the forest floor as uselessly as the merchants themselves: a hand trailing in the shallow stream, bloodied hair mingling with dead leaves and fern spores. The merchants' baggage was strewn about the ground; ridiculous, colourful silks had been dragged out and stuffed inside leather doublets, saddles and saddlecloths ripped open for gold and silver. One sort of violation. There were others. She could still try to ride away down the slope. That would earn her an arrow in the back: that deadly, familiar whistle, a sting worse than any viper's, the reins slipping through her hands and the earth rushing up to her face. The arrow that should have been hers in Northumberland would be hers now, in the land of her birth, on an unknown wooded hillside. Rain beaded her horse's mane, rolled in small balls down her own chestnut hair and her eyes looked at anything other than the ten – twelve? – pairs of eyes that stared at her.

'Demontez,' said the half-handed man.

She had raised her spurs when she heard the horses' hooves, and the voice. 'Christiane!' it called, and, 'Mignonne!'

The sound of that voice made her heart squeeze and jump, her feet pause. Her reins were still held, the knife still rested on her thigh, but the half-handed man had turned and was staring upwards, through the thickening trees, to where a horse picked delicately down the slope.

'Sweetheart,' cried Luke Ridley, affectionately, as he drew level with Christie. Ignoring the raised swords and murmurings from the brigands, he slid from the saddle, and held out his arms to her, so that she, too, dismounted. 'Sweetheart, forgive me,' he said, and threw his arms around her. And when he had for a second time begged forgiveness, and she, weakly, had accepted it, he lifted her face, and kissed her passionately.

'You're my wife and we've quarrelled,' he whispered. 'For God's sake look pleased to see me.'

That wasn't too difficult, for she found that she was, for once, extremely happy to see Luke Ridley. She flung her head on his chest and snivelled a little, while the half-handed man muttered beside them.

The half-handed man was called Nonette, and the black-bearded man who had slit the first merchant's throat was Le Corbeau. There were other names and other faces, but Christie, Luke's arm about her shoulders, Luke's hand fondling her hair, forgot them as soon as she heard them. Nonette spat on the ground and still stared at Christie, but Le Corbeau said one word in angry and incomprehensible French, and the half-handed man stepped back, his dagger sheathed.

Beside the muddied, bloodstained heap that were the wine merchants and their baggage, were three new, shining hand-guns and a sack of white powder.

SALTPETRE, said Luke, as they rode, not looking back, away from the hillside. The white powder had been saltpetre, principal constituent of gunpowder, mined in Germany, received in France, intended for England. England was short of saltpetre. Luke had not originally intended to exchange the sack and pistols for one rather damp, very frightened, distant adopted cousin. The saltpetre had been for Sandy Lawson and the *Elizabeth*, when she next put into Dieppe harbour. Men like Le Corbeau and Nonette and the rest of them infested France like a disease, feeding off terrorized villagers, legacies of civil war. France was weary of war, yet unable to halt it; England daily expected war. There were profits to be made.

She glanced up at him then, at his profile, clear against the murky sky, at his eyes, looking not at her, but at the track ahead. 'The *Elizabeth* —' she said, uncertainly. 'I thought she was a wool-merchant's ship —'

They had ridden out of the forest and on to the open ground.

'On her outward journey, perhaps,' said Luke. 'Coming home, the finished cloth will only be a few inches deep. The calivers and dags and saltpetre will be a little more substantial.'

She had begun to shiver: cold and reaction, and the answer she knew she would receive to the question she must ask.

'*Why?*'

He turned and looked at her at last.

'For myself — well, for money, of course. And entertainment. And because England will be at war soon — today, tomorrow, next year, maybe. It's inevitable.'

Christie bowed her head. The countryside had blurred, the greys and greens and browns misting together. The pony followed the track: she did not guide it.

'You can't travel by yourself, Miss Forster,' he added. His tone was utterly matter-of-fact. 'You must see that.'

She nodded. She did see it now: Nonette and his knife and the expression in his eyes and her own blank, useless fear, had stripped her of any illusions of independence.

She said, squeezing the words out as though they hurt, 'If Aunt Margaret will have me, I'll go back to Adderstone.'

'You won't reconsider my other suggestion?'

She did not understand at first. 'What do you mean?' she said.

'That we travel together. A mutually beneficial arrangement. You need an escort, and my venture might have a considerably better chance of success if I were a respectable Scots gentleman. The chances of an unaccompanied Englishman remaining unnoticed in France are not too good. The chance of a Scottish gentleman married to a French wife are considerably more promising.'

Married. The tears stopped. I, Christiane Girouard of Adderstone, take thee, Lucas Ridley of Catcleugh . . .

'You are suggesting we travel as man and wife?'

He looked across at her. 'Why not? If I take you back to Dieppe we might have to wait a month or more for Sandy to re-appear.'

He seemed to be waiting for some sort of an answer. He added, impatiently, 'If it is the proprieties that trouble you, I could find a priest in Rouen, I suppose.'

Christie nearly fell off her horse. The rain had begun again, the cold wind whipping it into needles against her skin. She realized, for the first time, that they were still heading for Rouen, that they had not turned back to Dieppe. She almost wanted to laugh.

'Don't be ridiculous, Mr Ridley.' Her voice did not seem to be working right. 'We can't possibly marry.'

'Why not?' Luke had slowed his horse to a walk, but Christie still felt bone-weary, scarcely able to breathe.

'In the eyes of half Northumberland we're married already. In the eyes of the Forsters – well, a priest might help a little, perhaps. And I'm running out of reasonable alternatives.'

He looked at her again. His face was unchanged, but his eyes, shadowed by the clouds above and the wind-blown strands of his hair, held just the smallest hint of mockery.

'A marriage in name only, Miss Forster,' he said, softly. 'When my business is done, and you have found your family, then we shall part and the arrangement shall be dissolved. On grounds of non-consummation, of course.'

She felt her face redden, and her eyes avoided his.

'Well, then,' he said. 'Will you marry me, Miss Forster?'

And, weakly, she said, 'Yes.'

THEY were married two days later, in an over-furnished Rouen parlour. Christie had rediscovered sufficient sanity to specify that the priest be Protestant, not Roman Catholic.

She had brought two gowns with her, and she was married in the blue velvet she had worn for her ride to Catcleugh. The same gown, the same gold ring, Luke's ring, a little large for Christie's finger. Different words, in a language that was fast becoming familiar to her again, bringing with it a trawl of ragged memories, and an ache that had never quite left her in ten years of exile.

The room was stuffy and overheated, their only witnesses the minister's wife and an array of stuffed birds. Popinjays, glassy-eyed and open-beaked, attended Christie Forster's marriage to Lucas Ridley, gentleman, of Catcleugh in Northumberland, England. Briefly she wondered, as the minister muttered the words of the blessing, how Luke had persuaded a Huguenot priest to marry two strangers at a day's notice. Had he held a knife to that quivering throat? Had he bribed him with Armstrong silver, Crozier gold?

The air was cold, the hour late as they walked back out into the street. It was already dark: flares cast a shadowed light over the shops and houses that still bore the scars and scorch-marks of civil war. Luke took Christie's arm to steer her up the road.

'So now you're Mistress Ridley, of French extraction, lately of Edinburgh. I'm a Scots gentleman trading in – let me see – yes, books. Good French books for the decent, *douce* citizens of

Edinburgh. *La Chanson de Roland, La Roman de la Rose.* We have been married a year, and we still cannot bear to be parted.'

They had reached the turning to their hotel in the Place du Vieux-Marché. The sky was already darkening, casting a bleak December pall over the city. The bell began to chime the nine o'clock curfew as they entered. Inside, they ate fish in a sauce, and a long loaf of French bread, and drank tart red wine while the wind rattled the shutters and funnelled down the chimney just as it had at Adderstone.

Luke refilled their glasses, and said, 'Our errands have something in common, Christie. We are both looking for something – someone. Your quarry may well be long-dead, mine may have vanished, or simply be unrecognizable. So perhaps we should combine our efforts, share our information.'

He had a sketch to show her. Drawing the candle closer, Christie smoothed out the paper and studied the face before her. A remarkable face, a compelling face, even. Yet frightening, as well. Christie blinked to clear her eyes. It was only a face, after all. She was tired, she had ridden all day, she had married a stranger that morning . . .

'Who is he?'

Luke rose from the table. 'In London he was called Henri Fagot. But if he is the sort of man I think he is, he may well have a different name here. I am not sure. But the face is memorable enough, don't you think?'

The pencilled, oblique eyes watched Christie from the table. Carefully, she folded the paper and returned it to Luke.

'Why are you looking for him?'

'To free myself.'

She glanced up at him. He was seated on the windowsill, his back resting against the shutters. She realized that, until he had spoken those last words, she had heard none of the bitterness, none of the anger, that she had once encountered at Catcleugh. When she had spoken of Arbel's betrothal on board the *Elizabeth* he had been shocked, but not angry. And as for their own hasty travesty of a marriage: well, it was he who had suggested it, he who had engineered it; but she who had consented. A marriage of mutal convenience.

'Free yourself of what, Mr Ridley?'.

'Luke – *please*. We are married, after all. I don't think our present masquerade will be too convincing if you persist in calling me 'Mr Ridley''.'

His voice was level again, light and uncaring. 'I don't think you need to know who I wish to free myself from. I like to be my own master, that's all. Not to be beholden to anyone, not to be bound to anyone.'

Again, that annoying pricking of the eyelids, that troublesome lump in the throat. Because he had expressed what she had thought, unvoiced, for years? Not to be beholden, not to be bound.

'And if you find this man?'

He smiled. The serpent's smile, reminding her of heather-swept valleys, stony hillsides.

'Then he must be persuaded to help me.'

She felt cold, suddenly.

Seeing her shiver, Luke stooped and put more logs on the fire. Business-like, he began to ask her about her own prospects. She had a ring and a name, she told him. The ring she wore on a chain about her neck: slipping it over her head she passed it to him. It was made of jet and gold, no initials, no mark. An uninteresting, unhelpful ring.

'The name, then,' he said, returning it to her. 'Girouard. Do you know your mother's baptismal name?'

'Louise,' she said. 'It's my second name, also. Christiane Louise Girouard.'

'Anything else? Memories – and Anne Forster must have known *something* –'

She tried to be as objective, as practical, as he was.

'I came to live with Anne early in '73. I can remember the voyage a little.'

''73?' He frowned. 'And your mother was a Huguenot?'

She nodded. She heard him say:

'The Blood-Red Wedding – the Massacre of St Bartholemew's Day – was in '72. *Poor* Christie.'

She had to look down at the table again. He had that awful knack of getting under her skin, right to where it hurt.

'No wonder you were frightened when they fired Catcleugh,' he added, and she had to take a very large gulp of wine.

'Two thousand Huguenots were put to the sword in one night in Paris alone,' she said, when she could speak. 'Ten thousand more were killed throughout France in the following months.'

He said, very carefully, 'The odds are against you, then, Christie. The odds are that you were shipped out of France for safety, and that your mother did not survive the slaughter.'

She stared at him, eyelids blinking rapidly, wanting to explain that it did not fit, that there were too many disparate parts of an impossible puzzle, too many loose ends which, try as she might to seize them, would not join. But she only said, 'But I need to *know*.'

She saw that he was about to speak, and she said, savagely, 'Don't you need to know, too, Luke?'

His eyes were expressionless. 'I *do* know,' he said. 'I am the son of a gypsy and a whore. Stephen's told me often enough. Oh – Davey put it differently. *Le rossignol est mon père, qui chante sur la ramée. La Sirène elle est ma mère, qui chante en la mer salée.* Only they weren't a nightingale and a mermaid, were they? They were a stranger who saw a pretty girl, and a woman who was very lonely, and perhaps a little bored. Bastards can be born from loneliness and boredom, you see, Christie, just as much as they can spring from uncontainable passion.'

She whispered, 'You should not be so hard on her.'

'My mother? I'm not hard – I know I'm no different. Society does not forgive that sort of error in a woman, that's all.'

There was silence; no sound except the crackling of the fire, the wind threading through Rouen's roofs and chimneys.

Christie heard Luke say, 'Why Anne Forster? Why were you sent to live with her?'

She shook her head. 'I don't know. But Anne was happy to have a companion for Arbel. Perhaps my father was one of Anne's relatives – a Sibley.'

'Didn't she tell you?'

'Anne told me nothing.' It felt odd to explain that small,

domestic tragedy to this man, in this room, this country. 'I shouldn't think she could remember. By the time I was old enough to ask questions, she was no longer capable of answering them. She was ill, you see. She had been ill since Arbel was born, I think, and of course she became a lot worse after her husband was killed. Margaret told me that. And Arbel and I looked for letters – anything – after Anne died, but there was nothing.'

Christie was silent for a moment, and then she added, quietly, 'Arbel is like Anne. Only Anne was afraid of everything. Her horrors did not confine themselves to her dreams.'

'And yours do?' He had moved away from the window and sat again in the chair opposite her. 'Unless, that is, people set fire to your house and shoot arrows at you.'

Christie folded her hands in front of her, and tried to focus her mind on the past. 'I was brought up in Paris – I know that, I remember it. I know my mother's name, and her religion. I need to know whether she is alive or dead, I need to know if I have a family – brothers, sisters – a father, even. I need to know who I am.'

SHE slept in the curtained bed, he on the floor. A strange wedding-night. She slept, and did not dream, as so often, of fire and sword, shouting voices and the sour smell of burning. When she woke, the sun was streaming through the slats of the shutters, filtered by the pale faded yellow bed-curtains. She knew that there was no one else in the room; she knew also that last night, for the first time in days, months, years, she had felt safe.

THEY arrived in Paris three days later. Monsieur and Madame Ridley installed themselves in lodgings not far from the market at Les Halles, in a small but respectable set of rooms a mere stone's throw from the banks of the Seine.

The weather had deteriorated on the road from Rouen, the bright skies turning first to rain, then sleet. The chill, dirty sleet matched the mood of Paris. Paris had two kings; one, the Valois Henri III, who alternated between bouts of dissipation and religious mania; the other, another Henri, the powerful Duc de Guise. Penury and sickness racked Paris, just as they racked Catherine de Medici's tortured second son.

Walking through Les Halles' muddy streets, Luke Ridley reflected on the impossiblity of the task he had set himself.

He would take an afternoon to find his bearings in a city he already knew well, and tomorrow he would begin to search more methodically. If he could find his way through the Cheviots in a snowstorm, then he could surely find a libertine with a wildcat and a sense of humour in Paris. Meanwhile, there were the flower-sellers, and the fishmongers, and an old witch selling improbable prophylactics against the plague. Luke was looking neither for rabbits' tails nor for a bunch of holly for his sweetheart.

He heard the sounds of a scuffle in the street ahead, followed by a cry of outrage. Running feet, voices shouting and a dog barking. A small body cannoned head-first into him, and he felt hopeful fingers briefly brushing the pocket of his doublet.

Luke, recovering his breath, seized one thin, bony wrist.

'Mignon,' he said, and smiled.

Mignon did not smile back. Mignon was about thirteen years old, with black curls and a length of sarsenet under one arm. Mignon was trying, very single-mindedly, to free himself from the grasp that imprisoned him.

Luke Ridley's understanding was equal to the stream of gutter French that assailed him.

'My mother may be an incestuous whore, and my father a farmyard animal, but I am fond of my handkerchief. My handkerchief is useful, mignon. I might have a cold – or something in my eye – or merely wish to keep the stink of the city from my nostrils –'

Dark eyes, angry and intelligent, stared up at him. Sharp teeth prepared to sink into his wrist.

'There's the pillory –' said Luke, seizing a handful of dirty black curls with his free hand, '– and there, I believe, is the man from whom you stole the cloth. I could give you to either, or, more probably, both. Alternately, if you could promise to be a little less obvious in future, I could offer you a job.'

The mouth closed, the expression was a fusion of suspicion and hope.

'You name, mignon?' said Luke.

'Baptiste,' said the boy, and grinned.

Chapter Twelve

ARBEL Forster and Stephen Ridley were married in January, at the church of St John the Baptist, in Edlingham. The church, all arrow-slits and pale stone, and a tower of almost Mediterranean starkness, seemed doubly cold inside. The mist of ages seeped through the stones along with the fog, so that the wedding-guests pulled their cloaks about their ears, and shivered in their finery. The bride did not shiver, though: her responses were as clear as the church bell's, as clear as her new husband's. Arbel wore crimson and silver, her wide velvet sleeves slashed and the gauze undersleeve pulled through, her unbound hair falling either side of a ruff of Valenciennes lace. The groom wore a deep dark blue satin and was a head and shoulders taller than his fragile bride.

Outside a dog whined incessantly.

Margaret shivered, too, but not with cold. She, who had spent her adult years immured in Adderstone's draughty walls, could withstand any amount of cold. It was perfection that momentarily distressed Margaret, the perfection of the golden couple before her, her niece and her brother. Kneeling awkwardly in her farthingale and brocade, Margaret began to pray.

But her prayers, she found, were for neither Arbel nor Stephen, but for Christie. Christie had left Adderstone six weeks ago, and sometimes, at night, Margaret could have cried for her. By the time Margaret had discovered from Arbel Christie's destination and the name of the ship she travelled on, it had been too late to stop her. There had been nothing she could do, except hope and pray that some kind and understanding deity might intervene and offer protection. Margaret had found that she had grown used to Christie's presence, and that she missed her. Arbel had missed her, too; Arbel had not sat still for as long as five minutes since Christie's departure.

Margaret prayed, at last, for Stephen and Arbel.

Richie voiced, softly, Margaret's other, blackest thoughts, as she rose from her knees and the bride and groom went into the vestry to sign the register. 'At least Luke didn't come. My God – can you imagine it, Mother? Spewing his way down the aisle with his latest light o'love on his arm. Still –' Richie ignored his mother's expression '– it might have livened things up.'

'Perhaps Lucas is beginning to learn sense.' Margaret's tone was clipped. She was voicing the half-truths she had become accustomed to dispensing in her attempt to keep the peace. Lucas had never lacked sense, Lucas capitalized on other peoples' idiocies, caused them, manipulated them. If Lucas had not turned up, like a spectre at Stephen's wedding, it was because it had not served him to do so.

Somewhere at the back of the church an ensemble of crum-horns and viols scraped and hooted dismally. She should not want to protect Lucas, thought Margaret, but she did, because she alone, who had known Davey and Grace and Stephen, recognized that Lucas had never truly belonged at Black Law. He was like his mother: beautiful, impossible Catherine, and he belonged to the hills and the moss and the heather. He was not, when it came to it, a Ridley: he might possess, when he chose, some of Davey's charm, but he had what Davey had always lacked – an unceasing calculation, a superb awareness of cause and effect. Davey, who had married Grace in this same church, had let consequences take care of themselves. Stephen, on the other hand, tried to force the future, to bend it to his design. Margaret thought of Arbel, who would sing, if she felt like it, at a death-watch, and she shivered again.

Outside the church, following in the steps of the newly-weds, it was a relief to be able to breathe in the cold, fog-laden air. Richie helped his mother into the saddle. Mark had gone to throw stones at the ice-covered duck-pond; Janet waited for her husband to lead forward her horse.

Rob stood apart, his eyes fixed hungrily on Arbel as she stood beside Stephen at the lych-gate.

*

BAPTISTE became Christie's escort.

There was a limit, Luke had told Christie, as he hauled the boy through the door of the lodgings in the Rue St-Martin, to how many brothels he had time to extricate her from. And his beloved wife could not, after all, wander the streets of Paris alone. And she wouldn't sit at home and wait for him, would she?

Baptiste did not remain Baptiste for very long because it was a ridiculous name for an undersized Parisian street-urchin. Emilie, the witless kitchen-maid who went, like the furniture, with the apartment, re-christened Baptiste in an unusual access of creativity, Mouche, because he was small and dark and angry and aimlessly energetic like a bluebottle. The name stuck, and Mouche, too, stuck, because he no longer had to steal his food, and besides, he loved Christie with an undivided adolescent passion.

Towards Luke, Mouche's emotions were a little less certain. If he drew his knife and spat on the floor, then Luke laughed at him and called him mignon until the rage subsided and he went to watch Christie make bread, or to accompany her on one of her endless walks round Paris. If, sometimes, the rage boiled over into physical violence, then Mouche would soon find that the knife was in Luke's hand, not his, and that his own matted curly head was breaking the ice in the horse-trough in the courtyard. Mouche respected and feared Luke in equal quantity.

He did not believe all this nonsense about booksellers, though. Mouche could not read, but you did not have to read to know that a bookseller would not regularly break the curfew, a bookseller would not best Mouche in a fight. As for Monsieur and Madame's sleeping arrangements, Mouche did not question the habits of gentlefolk. A man who caught fish on the banks of the Seine had told him that the King and Queen of Navarre had not shared the same bedchamber for three years. Mouche thought, privately, that Monsieur probably visited certain houses in the warren of streets behind Les Halles on his late nights. Mouche was glad. He loved Christie.

Every day, Mouche and Christie tramped the streets of Paris. Mouche did not mind: Christie had bought him a coat (only a little too large, and she had repaired the rip in the elbow), so he was no longer cold, and besides, he liked to be out of doors. She told him that she was looking for someone: *two* someones, and she told him their names. Neither of the names had meant anything to him, but he had looked interested and thoughtful because he knew that would please her. He knew faces, not names, but he did not recognize the face in the sketch that Luke showed him.

In January, the weather became worse. It snowed heavily, and the King levied a new tax: to pay for the Duc d'Epernon's new clothes, people said. Mouche did not envy the Duc d'Epernon his satins and silks; he was happy enough with his broadcloth, and his knife in his folded hand as he trailed the streets of Paris after Christie.

He understood that she had lived in Paris before, a long time ago. His breeches wet with mud and snow, he listened as she talked of memories. She remembered two houses. The first had been a tall house with a lot of rooms, and woodland near by. There had been a spinet, a big chair with carvings, a silver looking-glass in a frame, and a nurse called Lucrezia. Of the second, smaller house, Christie remembered little. A hilly, narrow cobbled street, herself sitting at the top of some stone steps, a bunch of dandelions in her lap. A large leather bag on the step beside her, a pony clattering up the winding hill. A woman's voice, sharp but kind. She had other memories, she had told Mouche once, when they stood in Les Halles in front of the mercers from whom Mouche had stolen the cloth. She remembered darkness, shouting voices and the scent of smoke, and the feel of slippery fabric against her face. Satin: cold and lubricious, like snakeskin. Christie would never wear a gown made of satin.

As for Mouche, he had no memories. Memories were made of other things than the struggle for food and a warm place to curl up for the night. Mouche did not pity loneliness because it was all he had ever known or expected. So he walked the streets of Paris with Christie, looking for hills and trees, not knowing that at last he was making memories.

*

In mid-January they went to the Bois de Vincennes. The Bois was quite a long way from the Rue St-Martin apartment, so Christie, who had a cold, hired a horse. Mouche perched uneasily on the saddle behind her, his hands gripping the quilted doublet she wore over her gown, his teeth clenched. Mouche was terrified of horses.

It was Luke who had suggested the Bois de Vincennes. The previous night they had, unusually, dined together, sharing, over Emilie's chicken in wine, their equal lack of success. Christie had sniffed and blown her nose, and described the house with the spinet and the wood, and Luke had unsympathetically recommended an onion stuffed with cloves under her pillow and the Bois de Vincennes. He had also told her that Henri Fagot was reputed to possess a wildcat. He was beginning to hate the wildcat.

So the following day, despite the snuffles and the cough, Christie hired a horse, coaxed Mouche on to the saddle, and set off for the Bois de Vincennes. Mouche, perched stiffly behind her, fingered his dagger as they rode through the frozen marshlands of La Marais. Every blade of grass, every reed, was furred with a fringe of frost, as brittle as glass. Land and sky were white, the only light the heavy, nacreous glow of the sun.

Reaching the Bois, Christie's heart sank. The wood was immense: to her pessimistic eye, it seemed as vast as the Cheviots. A forest of oak and beech, elm and sycamore, the endless leafless branches reaching up to a blank, white sky. The King's hunting-grounds sprawled around the eastern boundaries of the city, guarded by archers and swordsmen, thick with game. On fine cold mornings, surrounded by courtiers glittering with silks and satins, frosted with ribbons and lace, Henri de Valois hunted deer, boar, and the wanton hare.

Mist seared the leafless branches of the trees, drifting like a will-o'-the-wisp around dead bracken and leafmould. *Ignis fatuus*, false fire. She was searching for a false fire, thought Christie, as she slid from the saddle. She was searching for something that had long ago ceased to exist.

Still, she led her pony towards the railings, away from the city, conscious that she was wasting her time, that she should not be here, she should be searching the streets that bordered the wood, looking for a tall house with a spinet. Yet she found, somewhat to her surprise, that she was glad to be away from houses and streets, that she had grown used to Adderstone and all the wide desolation of the Borders. Frost crunched under her feet; the mist made her cough, yet the sudden silence was welcome, comforting. Mouche, at her side, had taken the knife from his belt. Mouche trusted trees and silence no more than he trusted horses.

She began to be aware of a new feeling as they climbed up the small incline towards the gate in the railings. She did not recognize it at first, but then she began to know it for what it was: the nagging, unreliable tingle of recognition. At the top of the incline she tried the gate, and found that it was locked. Standing with her fists clenched around the ornate metal bars, her nails dug into her palms, Christie tried to seize the moment of memory before it left her, as fleeting as the mist. Tree roots broke through the ground to one side of her, like bones through silvered skin. A child had stood here once, outside, looking into the valley that flowed smooth and pale beyond the railings.

Mouche touched her arm. 'I'll open it,' he whispered, and pointed with his small, narrow-bladed knife to the gate. Christie shook her head and looked down across the sweep of frosted grass.

A circle of large trees – beeches. Her imagination – memory? – painted summer's acid green leaves on them, clearing mist and frost from the silver-grey trunks. A slope (grass and flowers, *yes*), where a man now played with a dog in the basin-shaped valley below.

No, not a dog. Christie stood, frozen at first with cold and remembrance and possibility. Then she moved, hidden beneath a broad oak tree, and looked again, just to make sure.

The man was about Stephen Ridley's age, black-haired, elegantly dressed. Beside him, the creature clenched a writhing rabbit between its jaws.

Not a dog. A wildcat.

LUKE arrived back at the Rue St-Martin rooms at the same

time as Christie drew up, on horseback, but minus Mouche.

He made a great show of peering to both sides of the saddle, and then, as he handed her down, he said, 'You've sold him. He fell down a rabbit hole –'

'Mouche is busy,' said Christie, defensively, blowing her nose.

'Mouche is here for one purpose only. To act as your escort. He will have his hide tanned if I ever see him again.'

Christie's eyes were watering in the cold wind. 'You've had a bad day,' she said, and sneezed.

'I've not had a bad day.' He had the reins of her horse in one hand, he did not even bother to turn and look at her. 'I've had a dull day, a futile day. Where did you get the horse?'

At first she did not answer, but stood silently for a moment, struggling with her own temper. She had the beginnings of a headache, but the beginnings of hope as well.

She watched him attend to the horse, and then said, 'I've found your Henri Fagot. Mouche is watching him.'

Luke swung round. Christie saw that his eyes gleamed, that interest and calculation had instantly replaced the irritation and tedium.

'*Where*, Christie? Where did you see Henri Fagot?'

'In the Bois.' She sniffed. 'He had the wildcat with him. He didn't have a beard, and his hair was different, but I'm sure it was him. I came to tell you.'

Extracting a sodden handkerchief from her sleeve, Christie blew her nose very hard. 'We followed him from the Bois. He was playing with the wildcat in the wood. Then he went to a house in one of the streets near by. Mouche should still be there – I can tell you where to find him.'

Luke placed a clean handkerchief in Christie's hand. 'Have mine. Onions with cloves never work.'

He swung into the saddle as she told him how to find the house. Looking down at her, his cloak already dewed with mist, he asked, 'Did he see you?'

Christie shook her head. 'I don't think so. We were very surreptitious.'

She saw him grin briefly, and raise his hand in salute. Then he was lost in the crowds of Les Halles.

*

218

LUKE arrived back at the Rue St-Martin apartment in the early evening.

'He's changed his name and he appears to be rich,' he said, dismissing Mouche, flinging his damp cloak to the floor and placing a flagon of hot wine on the parlour table.

He looked, thought Christie, very pleased with himself. She had changed her gown and built up the fire, and sat, breathing noisily, on the floor by the grate. The parlour was pleasantly warm, the shutters closed to the frost and the mist.

'Twenty servants and a dozen horses in the stables. Randal Lovell,' said Luke, thoughtfully, 'would sell his soul for any one of those horses . . .'

He poured Christie out a cup of mulled wine, and another for himself. She could smell cinnamon, nutmeg and allspice.

'A much better cure for a cold than onions stuffed with cloves,' he said, handing her the cup. 'More sociable, too.'

He dropped down beside her in front of the fire, and pulled a handful of chestnuts from his pocket. The mist had curled his hair, darkening it slightly. Christie drank and watched him drop chestnuts into the embers.

'He has a very obliging kitchen-maid. Called Lisette.' Luke pulled off his damp doublet. His back was to Christie: she sniffed. 'Monsieur Fagot – or Blaise Lamarque, as he is now known – is a friend to the rich and famous. His social occasions have a reputation throughout Paris, offering such delights as a masque of John the Baptist and Salome, complete with naked dancers *and* a dismembered head. Personally,' said Luke, raking amongst the ashes, 'I can't help thinking that both would put me off my dinner.'

The wine went pleasantly to Christie's head: she giggled. She watched Luke pull a hot chestnut out of the fire, and crack the scorched skin with the hilt of his dagger.

'Madame.' The chestnut tumbled into her cupped palms. Luke, pushing back his shirt sleeves, poured more mulled wine into her cup.

'There – you're looking better already. I knew it. Anyway. Monsieur Lamarque.'

He sat down by the fire again, cross-legged, the knife still poised in one hand.

'Monsieur Lamarque is, I believe, quite promising. The kitchen-maid is enamoured of Monsieur Lamarque, and Monsieur Lamarque himself is enamoured of someone rather more important. A Duke, Lisette said, but she was rather vague as to which Duke. Guise, d'Epernon, or de Joyeuse, do you think, Christie?'

His eyes, though half-lidded, were bright; his fingers absently pulled more chestnuts from the fire and cracked the shells. Christie struggled to recall what she knew of French politics. There was the powerful Henri, Duc de Guise, leader of the extreme Catholic faction. And the Valois King's two favourite mignons, Anne, Duc de Joyeuse, and La Valette, Duc d'Epernon.

'The Duc de Guise seeks to rival the king. It depends how high your Monsieur Lamarque wishes to rise.'

'Or who he thinks will live longest. The Valois are a feeble dynasty, Christie. Not one of Catherine de Medici's sons is healthy in mind and body. Power in France is wielded now not by Henri de Valois, but by de Joyeuse and d'Epernon.'

A second chestnut was tossed into the air: Christie caught it, the creamy flesh was warm against her palm.

'Let's hope Monsieur Lamarque seeks the favour of d'Epernon or de Joyeuse. It would not suit me at all if he still pursues Monsieur de Guise.'

She remembered the man she had seen in the Bois de Vincennes.

'I thought he looked – dangerous.'

'I don't doubt that he's dangerous. His is not an old name, so he has achieved what eminence he has through his own efforts. Men like that are always dangerous.'

'Especially when they meet one of their own kind.'

The mulled wine had freed Christie's tongue; she watched the smile slowly spread across his face, his eyes find hers.

'Do you fear for my safety or my morals, Mistress Ridley? The second I abandoned long ago; the first is dependent on my success with Monsieur Lamarque.'

The hour was growing late, but Christie did not want to move from her seat near the fire. 'I don't mean to imply that you are not capable of looking after yourself,' she said, as carefully as she could. 'But it's different here, isn't it?'

'Paris?' The fire feathered the drying ends of his hair, and lit his light eyes with gold. 'The appearance is a little more refined, I agree. But the differences may be more superficial than you think. Too many people chasing too little wealth, and power, and security. It's just a little closer to the bone in the Borders.'

'The stakes are higher here.' She had drained her cup, her head was pleasantly fuzzy. She could have fallen asleep on the hearth.

Luke was still watching her. 'The Bastille – Hermitage Castle. I doubt if there's a lot of difference once someone locks the door on you. And as for the rivalry between the factions – well, in the Borders, as you know, you have to have the right name, too. You wouldn't be a Kerr in Branxholm, for instance. Paris glitters a little more, that's all.'

She blinked, trying to focus clearly on his face. 'Hermitage Castle. Was it horrible?'

'Averagely horrible.' Luke rose, neatly unfolding himself from the floor. He held out his hand to her. 'No more wine, my dear Christie. Your Aunt Margaret frightens me far more than any Blaise Lamarque.'

She took his hand, and found her feet. The room was not quite steady, she had to hold on to his shirt for support. She said, enunciating the words with difficulty, 'What do you intend to do now?'

'Me?' Luke felt pleasantly warm; Christie dropped her head against his shoulder. 'I intend to call Emilie to put you and your cold to bed. And after that, I intend to be invited to one of Monsieur Lamarque's parties. I'm sure I'd appreciate Salome, if not the dismembered head.'

THEODORE Brune owned a printing press on the Left Bank, not far from the Sorbonne. During the day, the press rattled and heaved and spewed out religious tracts, propaganda leaflets, and calls to arms. At night-time, though, when the ink-stained apprentices and cross-eyed typesetters had left, the press still sometimes heaved and rattled, but then the noise was safely masked by other, less treacherous sounds.

Tonight Theodore's press was printing a rather dubious pamphlet of Italian origin, complete with woodcuts. Michel was inking the type whilst sucking claret through a straw from the leather bottle that the Dutchman held for him; Angus, who was Scots, and huge, and who spoke only the Gaelic when he'd had a lot to drink, laid the paper on the tympan. Theodore himself set the type, because making the letters took a long time, and he wouldn't trust those bastards not to lose them down the gaps between the floorboards.

Blaise had arrived with the darkness, bringing with him all the usual crowd and a consort of musicians scraped from the streets. Three lutenists, a counter-tenor and a serpent. The serpent played when the boy, Armand, perched at the top of the stairs, shouted warning of passers-by. Then the press stopped its clacking and its banging, and Angus made ready to hurl himself on top of the pile of printed papers, and snore. Angus in a drunken stupor was a forbidding sight.

It was pitch dark and twenty identical sheets of paper were pinned up to dry, when they heard the knock at the door. Armand came scampering downstairs as Angus reached out one brawny arm for the line, and serpent, lutenists, and counter-tenor roared into an écossaise.

'He's by himself and he's got yellow hair,' gasped Armand.

'Tell him we're closed –' shouted Theo, above the serpent. 'Tell him to come back tomorrow.'

Armand ran back upstairs. Angus turned away from the press, and removed the knife from his belt. The press, silenced, gleamed with ink and polished brass. Over the tumult of serpent, lute and singer there was the sound of the door closing in the next room, and footsteps on bare boards. 'Monsieur Ridley, Monsieur Brune,' said Armand, smugly, and scowled at Theo. Armand had a gold coin in his hand.

Theo clipped the boy neatly round the ear, and studied his unexpected caller. Monsieur Ridley had fair hair and light blue eyes, and was rather well dressed in a tasteful and restrained black silk, quilted and lined because of the cold weather.

Monsieur Ridley bowed, and said, 'It's good of you to receive me, Monsieur Brune. I'm a bookseller, from Scotland. Looking for –' and he surveyed calmly the printed papers slung over the line '– interesting texts.'

'Daytime's the usual hour for trade.' Theo, equally calm, was aware of Angus at his side, knife in hand. 'You could come back tomorrow morning, monsieur.'

'I've Montaigne and Machiavelli by the dozen,' said the visitor, heedless, apparently, of both Angus and his knife. 'I prefer to specialize in the esoteric.'

Theo grinned, then, and pushed his black, bushy hair out of his eyes with an ink-stained hand. There was an element of the esoteric about Mr Ridley: he would introduce him to Blaise Lamarque.

He kicked Armand back upstairs first, because Armand was sulking, and there was always the possibility that Mr Ridley had been followed by, or had led, the King's men. Though they weren't printing Huguenot literature tonight.

Armand slouched his way upstairs: Blaise had favoured Armand once, before adolescence had begun to inflict its toll of pimples and short temper on Armand's small, dark, southern frame.

Theo waved a hand, and the press began to heave and clatter again. Someone brought the visitor a glass of wine, and Theo unpinned a particularly interesting page from the line and showed it to the bookseller.

'The Scots have a reputation for being dour,' said Theo. 'Do you think you'd find a market for such texts?'

Ridley glanced down.

'We've a poor climate, Monsieur Brune. A good book can brighten up a foul winter evening, don't you think?'

Theo grinned, and touched Angus on the shoulder. The part of Theo that was the artist, not the artisan, enjoyed the contrast of the two men. It was hard to believe that they were of the same species, let alone countrymen.

He left the two Scotsmen talking, and went to Blaise's side.

'He's Scots and he likes obscure Italian books,' said Theo. 'And he appears to be friendly.'

The wildcat's eyes were closed; Blaise Lamarque's hand lazily scratched its jewelled neck.

'If he isn't, there's always the Seine,' said Blaise, slowly. 'Though that would be a waste.'

Someone was filling the serpent with claret; Michel, Theodore's brother, had abandoned the straw and returned to the bottle. The Dutchman, at his side, smiled, and tried to read the first page of the book upside-down as it fluttered from the line. Blaise Lamarque's hooded golden eyes rested on Lucas Ridley, black-clothed and fair-haired in the centre of the room.

'He speaks good French and reads Italian,' added Theo. 'Are you thinking of adding him to your collection, Blaise?'

The wildcat stirred and yawned, showing its teeth. Blaise said, 'That depends on whether he would be an asset, does it not, my dear Theo?'

The serpent was beginning to bubble. Theo, who was not afraid of Blaise, said, 'I'm sure you will form an estimate. You have such a head for figures, Blaise,' and, refilling Blaise Lamarque's glass, he returned to the printing press.

By midnight, they were too drunk to load the press, and Angus and the Dutchman hand-wrestled on one of the thick oak tables.

A crowd had gathered round to watch, yelling and cheering until the Dutchman's elbow slipped and his fist hammered into the table-top. There was a pile of coins to Angus's side of the table; half a dozen other wrestlers had gone the way of the Dutchman.

Luke also watched. He watched the hand-wrestlers, the printer and his brother, and, of course, Blaise Lamarque. He had watched Blaise Lamarque, formerly Henri Fagot, for more than forty-eight hours now, dozing curled up in a doorway near the house by the Bois de Vincennes, tracking the black-haired man's footsteps through the streets of Paris. Tonight, Lamarque had led him to the printer's shop on the Left Bank of the Seine. Tonight, Luke knew he had his best, perhaps his only chance.

The wildcat, a clump of black and yellow, slept folded on the seat of a chair. *Guise, d'Epernon, or de Joyeuse?* thought Luke. He must know.

He became aware that Blaise Lamarque had risen and was standing behind him, that a hand touched the black silk sleeve of his doublet. 'The Scots are a quarrelsome race,' said Blaise, clearly. 'We have two of them in this room. I should like to see them fight.'

The Frenchman's fingers were like claws, pressing into Luke's skin. 'Properly, of course,' added Blaise. 'To the death. I shall wager a hundred écus on Mr Ridley.'

Luke found himself stripping to his breeches, kicking off his boots. On the other side of the room, the Gael did likewise. The Dutchman had drawn a circle of black ink on the floor, and Michel, the printer's brother, took the bets. In one corner were three lutes and a rather wet serpent; the owners gathered, like the rest of them, round the circle.

It was silent outside, the shutters closing out the ink-black sky, but the cold still seeped through the cracks around the window-frames. The candlelight delineated the folds of fat and muscle on the Scotsman, the bulk of his forearms, the ham-like hands. He, like Luke, was treading the edge of the circle, his bare feet scuffing the boards, his thick fingers loosely fisted. It reminded Luke of Berwick. Only Rob Forster had been half the size of the Scotsman, and the stakes had not been quite so high . . .

Angus swung forward, his hands locking round Luke's shoulders. Luke twisted from his grasp, and the fight had begun.

For a while there was only the sounds of the wrestlers' breathing, the slap of bare feet on floorboards, the dull thud as a head, or a fist, made contact with flesh. A blow with the flat of the foot to the Gael's thigh, and Angus staggered, momentarily losing his balance and sinking to his knees in the centre of the ink-drawn circle. Then he regained his feet, and picked up Luke with his two huge hands, dropping him like a puppeteer's doll to the floor.

Luke rolled aside before the Scot could jump on him, crushing his ribs, spine, lungs, to papier mâché. The crowd had begun to howl: if he opened his eyes he could see a circle of faces above him, mouths wide, faces reddened, fists clenched. Except for Blaise, of course. Every now and then he caught sight of Blaise Lamarque, standing a little apart from the rest, a ripple of black and gold, a fleeting smile on his curved crimson lips.

No, he thought, as he lunged for the Scotsman, it was not like Berwick at all. Here, the reward for failure was death, the reward for success was – what? A chance to delay death, perhaps, a chance to begin to set in motion the complex game that might keep him from Tyburn, or from Hermitage.

He wished, as his fingers clawed a handful of the long greying hair that fringed Angus's bald head, that he had had the benefit of a decent night's sleep. As at Berwick, Luke knew that he must finish the fight quickly, that the two days he had spent trailing Blaise Lamarque round the city of Paris must soon take its toll in juddering muscles, in slowing reactions. Angus had forced him to the ground again, was leaning over him, his knees pressing on his thorax, so that Luke almost expected to hear the cracking of his ribs, one by one, like damply primed pistols. It was becoming difficult to breath: when he closed his eyes he saw a vast curtain of crimson, and a pair of watching golden eyes.

His head jerked upwards, butting Angus sharply on the chin. As the Gael's grasp relaxed, Luke twisted the heavier man sideways.

He was kneeling on the Scotsman's back, his thumbs poised at the base of Angus's neck. Great arms flailed like a windmill's sails, finding no purchase. He could hear his own breath squeezing out of his bruised lungs, he could feel the unmistakable excitement of a hunt almost over.

The room was no longer noisy, the silence was charged, expectant. If he flexed his thumbs, then there would be that small deadly *click*, and Blaise Lamarque would have won his bet. *To the death*, Blaise had decreed. *To the death.*

Luke smiled. He rose, leaving the Scotsman sprawled on the

floor, and, walking fairly steadily to the edge of the circle, began to pull his shirt over his head. From the circle of spectators, there was a hiss of expelled breath, a shuffle of movement, a ripple of laughter. Angus, ink-stained and bloody-nosed, his hair matted with sweat and dust, staggered into a sitting position, grinning for the sheer joy of being alive.

Luke heard a voice ask, as he began to thread a lace through its eyelet, 'Don't you kill, Mr Ridley?'

He turned slowly, and looked up. His muscles had already begun to stiffen, and it still hurt to breathe.

Blaise Lamarque was sitting on the chair to the side of the room, the wildcat curled on his lap.

Luke's voice was cold; he no longer smiled. 'Not for entertainment, monsieur,' he said, and finished lacing his doublet.

He went back with Blaise Lamarque to the tall, thin house Mouche had found two days previously. Somewhere in the basement of the tall, thin house was an obliging kitchen-maid called Lisette. The withdrawing-room was impressive: the walls rich with tapestries and hangings, several ornate mirrors multiplying the reflections, over and over again.

It was almost dawn; a heavy red touched the church spires and the tiled roofs of the houses. The snow that had begun to fall as they crossed from the Left Bank to the Right was thickening; great wet flakes dabbed their dark mark on the pavements.

In the withdrawing-room the scent of the candles almost removed the stink of printers' ink and sweat from Luke's nostrils. Blaise Lamarque sat in a chair opposite; the wildcat was not to be seen. Out hunting, thought Luke. Catching rabbits in the Bois de Vincennes.

'You are a bookseller, then, Monsieur Ridley?' said Blaise Lamarque, offered Luke a glass of claret.

He had topaz tiercel's eyes, hooded, slightly oblique. The small, neat beard of the miniaturist's drawing had gone, and the black hair was straight instead of curling, but Paul Carnaby's sketch had been a good one.

'You don't look like a bookseller, though. Booksellers should be fat and slow with good living. Theodore Brune tells me that a man who follows your trade can become rich within a year. How delightful – success can be such a gamble, n'est-ce pas? And how many other vocations can be as lucrative?'

'Piracy?' said Luke, gently. 'Prostitution?'

A bronze light had begun to crawl through the gaps around the shutters.

'Dangerous trades.' The Frenchman's voice was soft. 'So easy to end one's days in the gutter, or with a knife between the shoulder-blades. Bookselling is safer, don't you think, chéri?'

'On the whole.' Luke's mouth curled a little at the corners. 'Though it has its moments.'

The golden eyes gazed at him. Those eyes would have black, oval pupils like a hawk's. They would catch sight of you and Fate would fall out of the sky like a thunderbolt, allowing you no place to hide.

Blaise had walked to the window: he twisted the catch on the shutters so that they opened, and the dull, burnished light, pitted with snowflakes, flooded into the room.

'A wife, petit? Children? Little Ridleys to inherit the profits of their father's ambition?'

'I have a wife.' Blaise turned, the light from the glazed window dappling his dark skin. 'But in name only. We have – an arrangement.'

'Ah.' The golden eyes closed, the full mouth twisted a little at the corners. 'What self-control, Mr Ridley. Can we corrupt you a little, do you think? Can France corrupt you?'

He had moved to Luke's side. His jewelled hand rested on Luke's black silk sleeve. Luke did not move a muscle, only his pupils widened, black against the palest blue.

'Hunt with me tomorrow, chéri,' said Blaise, at last. 'Let us hunt the hare together in the Bois de Vincennes.'

Chapter Thirteen

ARBEL, most of the time, was happy at Black Law. She liked the square, high tower (taller than Adderstone's), she liked the initials (Davey's and Grace's) carved floridly over the doorway. She also liked having a maidservant to brush her hair and to lay out her clothes, a cook to take care of all the tedious offices of the kitchen, and a groom to fetch her horse. It was nice to be married and have all the overbearing matrons who had ignored her only a few weeks past call her 'Mistress Ridley' as they wheedled for invitations to Black Law's sumptuous dinner table.

Best of all, Arbel liked the ship clock, a wonderful, hideous creation of gilt and fantasy, with bells to strike the hour and a tiny cannon to fire the midday salute. Dowzabel did not like the ship clock: Dowzabel hid under Arbel's skirts and whined when the fearsome thing began to roll and lurch in rhythm with an imaginary sea. Dowzabel was suffering from a skin disease: she wept hairs all over the rugs and bedclothes and worried at the sore patches until they became raw. Arbel powdered the lesions with calendula and cradled her like a baby.

And there lay Arbel's only, but growing, discontent. Much as she loved her darling Dowzabel, she wanted a baby as well. She wanted Stephen Ridley's golden-haired, blue-eyed baby. It was very quiet in Black Law, sometimes, when Stephen was away. Arbel missed Christie dreadfully. She knew that Christie might be away for months, even a year, and she wanted to have a child of her own by the time Christie returned. But she wouldn't, because Arbel Ridley, the most beautiful girl in the Borders, had encountered an unexpected difficulty.

She was not yet truly Stephen's wife. She might have all the trappings – the house, the status, the clothes and ponies – but still she was not, in the eyes of the law or the church, Stephen's wife. He had come to her bed, and she had kissed and cuddled him and done some daring things, and each time he had parted from her with some excuse, leaving her hungry and unsatisfied. How the old gossips would laugh if they ever found out! And they would find out, inevitably, if the months began to go by and there was no baby. Arbel grew angry when she thought of that blue-eyed, golden-haired child. Sometimes she wanted to scream as she walked through Black Law's silent rooms, thinking of her husband who had not yet fulfilled his duty.

On the night Stephen returned from a week's absence, she decided to make a special effort. Her cambric nightgown was transparently fine, the lace collar shadowing her throat like sun-meshed leaves. The maid had brushed her hair until it shone and rippled like water running over stone, a clear fall almost to her waist. Her skin was perfumed with musk and rose-water, her cheeks pinched so that her pale complexion had some colour. Taking a candle, Arbel went to Stephen's room.

Pushing the door slightly ajar, she saw him, in shirt sleeves and hose, facing the window. Noiselessly, Arbel put the candle on the table and crossed the floor. When she laid her head against his broad back and let her fingers slide round his waist she felt his muscles grow rigid, heard the short indrawn breath. She did not speak, but pulled down his collar and kissed the smooth contours of his back. His skin was white, dotted with a few golden hairs. Gently, Arbel turned Stephen around to face her, and then she began to loosen the laces of his shirt.

He was shaking and his breathing was hurried. Inexperienced men were often unable to hide their arousal. And Stephen was inexperienced: the realization had surprised Arbel, but then she had begun to see it as a homage to her. Stephen had asked no other women to be his wife, had waited more than thirty years for her, Arbel Forster.

She would teach him, then. She had begun to want Stephen very badly: it had been months since she had lain with Luke Ridley in the Blink Bonny Inn. The recollection of that night excited her; Stephen's arms had folded round her, and he had begun to stroke, awkwardly, her silver-blonde hair. Arbel pulled him towards the bed.

He made no move to undo the laces of her nightgown, so she did it for him. The pale cambric rustled to the floor, and she saw Stephen's eyes move from her face to her breasts and her belly. As Luke's eyes had done. No: not quite like Luke – Arbel still had to take Stephen's hands and place them on her breasts, still had to loosen his clothing for him and pull him down towards her. His eyes were open, staring, but she could not do it all for him, so she whispered in his ear, telling him what to do.

Arbel heard Stephen cry out and thought at first that it had been with pleasure, and that he had not been able to wait. She felt frustration then, but when she opened her eyes and saw his face, the frustration receded and something more terrible began to replace it. Stephen's eyes were dark with loathing, not passion: he had sat up and was bundling his clothes together, trembling. Arbel knelt up, but did not cover herself.

'You have a duty, *husband*.'

Stephen stared at her. He had already masked over some of the disgust, but Arbel had seen it, naked and unforgivable.

'I'm sick,' said Stephen. 'The wine –'

'The wine?' Arbel laughed, but her eyes were filled with contempt. 'Perhaps you should have taken more wine, Stephen – it might have given you courage.'

Stephen's head jerked at the word 'courage'. His hair clung to his forehead with sweat, his strong, regular features were touched with gold by the candlelight. Arbel began to laugh again.

'A whole barrelful of wine, Stephen – would that give you courage enough?'

'Bitch,' said Stephen, under his breath. 'Bitch.'

Arbel did not cringe. She knelt on the bed, her hair tumbling like raw silk over her naked body, her eyes narrowed and hard. 'If I'm a bitch,' she said, deliberately, 'then what are you, Stephen? You cannot do what a dog can do.'

He hit her then, full across the mouth, so that his hand left a scarlet imprint on her white skin.

She did not cry, but said, clearly, 'Do you remember, Stephen, that night in Rothbury? Lucas said that the Ridleys were not a prolific breed. Well, we know why now, don't we?'

Seizing her thin shoulders, Stephen shook her to and fro so that her fragile body jerked like a marionette's. The rhythmic violence recalled to Arbel something else, something she had missed since that September night in the Blink Bonny. '*Lucas* is a man,' she hissed, 'not a rabbit!'

She heard him cry out again then, and felt his fingers bite deep into her flesh. The sheets and coverlet started to slither to the floor, and Arbel fell with them, enjoying the sensation of the stone through the cold silk, hearing the satin and brocade grate against the flagstones. Stephen's eyes were closed and his features contorted, his hands still gripped round her body. They were a tangle of limbs and sheets, and she could feel the cold stone through the thin material, just as at the Blink Bonny. Stephen's hands had reached for Arbel's throat, but Arbel's own small hands caressed his groin, coaxing that part of him to life. Her breath came in short gasps; she thought, as she straddled him, that he would choke her. She did not care: she felt him inside her at last, heard his deep groan, almost of pain, and knew that she was properly a wife.

He did not leave her immediately he was done, although he wanted to.

The stink of sweat and love-making choked the room: Stephen went to the window and pushed it open, leaning his head out to breathe in great lungfuls of cold, February air. He had pulled on his robe: the anger had receded, leaving only the familiar sense of revulsion. Turning, he saw that Arbel had not moved, that she still lay on the floor, her hair darkened with sweat and dust, her sprawling limbs uncovered.

He had believed Arbel to be as pure and gentle as Grace Ridley had been, like an angel. But even he, with his ignorance of such things, now knew that to be false. When he thought of what she had whispered to him, up there on that heated, tainted bed, he felt the sweat gather on his brow, and the hair on his scalp prickle and stand on end. Her unclean body was still pressed against his sheets, the candlelight shadowed the folds and hollows and crevices of her white flesh.

But he could not yet go. There was something he had to ask her. A possibility so appalling, so enormous, he could hardly make himself consider it.

'Arbel,' he said, and waited until her eyes had opened, her head had moved a little. 'You said that Lucas was a man. What did you mean?'

She did not answer at first.

It had hurt him even to say his cousin's name in this room, he almost regretted having asked the question. But the possibility her words had conjured had taken hold of him, and would, he knew, offer him no peace. Just as Davey's few, careless, angry words had taunted him so many years before. He had thought these past few weeks that the persistent ghost of the past had been laid: he could not bear loose ends, unclear futures, all the mess and chaos that people such as Davey, Catherine and Lucas created. But now a different spectre haunted him: Arbel and Lucas. No, it was not possible. He would kill her.

She said, 'I was angry, Stephen. Don't hurt me. I didn't mean anything.'

He said nothing, just waited, looking at her. Rob's earlier suspicions throbbed through his head in rhythm with the pounding of his blood.

Eventually, sitting up and wrapping one of the sheets round her, Arbel added, 'Lucas and Christie handfasted a few months back. He forced her.'

Her voice was brittle, slightly nervous. He did not even hear her second phrase. His immediate relief swamped him, but then a new horror, equally terrible, began to take its place. His face must have betrayed what he felt, for she said hastily, 'It was only a joke, Christie said. Lucas was drunk. Nothing happened.'

He had to pour himself a glass of wine, and drink it very fast. His face was turned away as he drank; he did not want Arbel to see him.

He heard her add, 'Anyway, Christie's gone away now.'

And he knew that he, too, had been careless, unprepared.

'*Where* has she gone, Arbel?' Stephen said.

In Paris, Christie watched the snow, made the bread and tried not to despair.

In two months she had found nothing. If there had been memories once, she knew that she had erased them now; that she had looked too long and had lost the unreliable, necessary flicker of instinct. She had stared at houses, hills and woodland until she thought she recognized everything, or nothing; she had listened for voices, searched for faces in crowds, knowing that dreams and inventions had made a mockery of the childhood she had once had.

She did not often feel despair, but she felt despair now, standing in front of the kitchen window, pounding dough into shape. She knew, if she was honest, that much of her misery had to do with loneliness, that she missed Arbel and Margaret and Janet. Rob, Richie and Mark, too: it had taken absence to show her that she had begun to think of those strangers as family. Here, there was Emilie, who alternately giggled and looked blank, and Mouche, who was no conversationalist. There was most definitely not Luke. The apartment seemed quieter, less alive, without him. She had seen Luke only twice since he had found Henri Fagot. The first occasion had been in the street, when she had seen him riding beside the dark-haired man she had glimpsed in the Bois. He had been dressed with untypical elegance then, and she had not thought he had seen her until he had winked at her. On the second occasion, he had appeared at the Rue St-Martin house late one evening, with money for the rent. He had been thinner, paler, darkly shadowed under the eyes, unnaturally bright with a sort of restless brittleness she had not seen before. He had left a whole purseful of gold; and he had been in a considerable hurry and extremely drunk. She had asked him how he was, and he had stared at her, slightly unfocused, before mounting his horse and saying, *I'm in heaven or hell, my dear, I'm not sure which.* She had wished, as she had watched him ride off into the Parisian night, that she had never seen Henri Fagot, nor that damned wildcat.

She had wondered, too, whether for her there would come a moment when she would simply accept defeat and go home. If she still had a home. She had rewarded Margaret poorly for her past kindness.

Mouche came into the kitchen as she left the bread dough to rise by the oven. She had not left the house for two days now: Mouche, reminding Christie momentarily of Luke, was looking restless. He was not used to houses, beds and tables. 'We'll go out,' said Christie, cheerfully. 'Fetch your coat, Mouche.'

He had put on his coat and was waiting for her at the door by the time Christie had tied her cloak and found her hat. She knew, as she left the house, that she had no real idea of where she was going. Her feet took her in the direction of the Bois de Vincennes, just as they had for the past month. There was a small market on the outskirts of La Marais. She would start there.

The market sold haberdashery and shoes and gloves. Christie bought a pair of gloves for Mouche, whose fingers were always chapped with chilblains; mumbling thanks, he thrust them into his pocket. Then she bought some thread from a large woman with a headscarf and a dog, and inquired after a lady by the name of Girouard. The dog reminded Christie of Arbel's awful Dowzabel, and she thought, painfully, of Arbel, perhaps already living in Black Law, with her dog, and Stephen.

The woman with the headscarf knew of no one called Girouard. Nor did the shoemaker, who grinned and peered at Christie's ankles until Mouche swore at him. Which left the lace-maker.

The lacemaker wore stiff, faded black, cracked and a little mouldy at the seams. Her face was seamed too and threaded with lines that were as delicate and complex as the minute pattern of lace on the cushion in front of her. She did not look up from her work as Christie asked her questions: her hands, blue with cold and deformed with gout, twisted thread round pins, so that the ribbon of lace grew infinitesimally longer. 'Girouard?' she said, her fingers not pausing for a second. 'By St-Gervas.'

Her voice unsteady, Christie bought a yard of lace.

*

235

THE snow began to fall again as she reached the Eglise St-Gervas. She searched, as the lacemaker had instructed her, for a house with lozenge-patterned shutters, and a flight of steps going up to the front door. Christie could hardly see the shutters for snow, and all the houses had steps. It was midday now, yet it scarcely seemed any lighter than dawn. The clouds were shaded with orange, heavy with snow, crowding Paris's jagged skyline. There could be a hundred Girouards living in Paris, ten of them in houses not far from the Bois de Vincennes.

From one of the houses candlelight glowed. Christie peered more closely at the open shutters, saw the diamond cut-outs, and her heart began to pound as she started up the steps.

The noise of the streets faded into the background. She realized, as she lifted the doorknocker, that she had no idea what she was going to say. If this was, at last, her mother, would ten years of another country, another family, have erased all familiarity? Might she look at her mother's face and see only a stranger?

A maidservant answered the door. The maidservant was smiling, and a little boy, three years old perhaps, was clinging to her skirts. The little boy had something sweet and sticky in his hand, and was distributing it equally over his face and the maid's gown. Another child, a girl, sat at the foot of the stairs, cradling a wooden poppet in her lap. In a different room, someone played the spinet, rather badly.

'Mademoiselle?' said the maid, disentangling the little boy from her apron.

Christie made her voice keep calm as she explained her errand. The maidservant looked blank, and said that she would ask Madame. Leaving Christie dripping snow on the doorstep, she disappeared into a further room. On the stairs, the little girl smiled and held up her poppet. Christie could feel the warmth of the house against her cold face, and see a half-cleared table in the next room, hear the distant sound of servants' voices in the kitchen. Children's clothes were scattered down the stairs, and someone had spilled a jar of pot-pourri in the centre of the bright Turkey rug. But the furniture and floors shone with beeswax, the little girl and her poppet were

236

doubled in the dark wood tread of the stairs. Christie looked, hungrily. Had she played with her own wooden doll at the foot of those stairs? Had she eaten marzipan and sugared almonds at that table?

A woman appeared, the maidservant and the little boy following behind her. The woman was about ten years older than Christie, well dressed, in a blue gown that matched her eyes. The Sibleys, Anne Forster's family, had been blue-eyed. Christie had always imagined her mother to have had brown eyes, like her own.

The woman introduced herself as Madame Charroux. Madame Ridley, said Christie, finding the name, as always, odd, and repeated her request.

'A lady called Girouard lived here before we took the house.' The woman's brow creased, she studied Christie coldly. 'She was a Huguenot, I believe.'

There was a curling of distaste around the word 'Huguenot'. Christie's heart began to pound very fast.

'Can you tell me where she lives now, Madame?'

Madame Charroux shook her head. Her eyes were hard, estimating the worth of Christie's gown, expertly judging her place in society.

'I believe she died in the wars like so many of her religion – eight or nine years ago, I think. Was she a relative of yours, Madame?'

The maidservant and the children had disappeared. For the first time since she had arrived in Paris, Christie felt threatened, endangered by the simple, limited facts of her own dubious birth. Paris was a Catholic city; they had slaughtered women, children, babies, on St Bartholomew's Day. Some of that horror was with her always, not as words, but as a selection of flickering, terrible pictures.

She was aware of Mouche beside her on the step. 'Just an acquaintance,' Christie said, and turned, stiffly to leave. 'It is of no importance.'

The door closed, shutting out the warmth and the light. The dull glare of the sun gleamed on the blade of Mouche's knife.

'I could talk to the old witch,' he said, helpfully.

Somehow Christie managed to smile and shake her head. If family was nothing more than a delinquent thirteen-year-old, a witless kitchen-maid, and an absentee husband, then so be it.

She wanted to be alone for a very long time.

BUT, returning to the Rue St-Martin apartment, Christie found that Luke had returned.

He was asleep on the floor in front of the parlour fire. He wore crumpled dark-blue silk, and one arm was half over his face, the other flung out to the side. Having managed not to howl the entire, awful journey home, Christie wanted to cry again when she saw him. They had sat in this room together, he shelling chestnuts, she watching him, drinking spiced wine. Talking almost, she had thought later, as though they were truly married. What nonsense: she hardly knew Luke Ridley at all.

She did not know why the sight of Luke asleep should upset her. It was not Luke, of course, it was the knowledge that her mother was dead; that, and that woman's cold, hard blue eyes. Christie stood in silence, watching Luke's long eyelashes flicker as he slept, his fingers clenching and scratching at the floor. He should not be here, she did not know why he was here. He belonged to Catcleugh; the one extraordinary night they had spent together there had shown her that. His hair was damp and tangled, dried a little by the fire, clinging to his forehead and cheekbones. He muttered something in his sleep, and then woke, sitting up so suddenly that Christie stepped back.

He looked at her and the room as though they were the nightmares he had only just left. Then, 'Christ,' he said and, rubbing his eyes, emerged, hair tousled, with some sort of sanity.

'My apologies. A long night and a longer day.'

She found a false smile for him. 'I'll tell Emilie to get you something to eat.'

'No. Thank you.' He stood up. His doublet was undone, showing the silk shirt beneath, half-laced. 'Nothing to eat. But I'll find myself a drink.'

He left the room, returning shortly with a bottle of claret.

He drank two glasses to Christie's one, and then said, 'Well, come on, Christie – what is it?'

And when she said nothing, but just stared into the uncaring crimson depths of the claret, he added, impatiently, 'You've a face like a February afternoon in Berwick, and Mouche tried to kill me in the kitchen. It can't just be my untimely reappearance.'

She could not speak at first. She could hear the distant sounds of Les Halles, the closer rattle of Emilie clattering pots and pans. She said, eventually, 'I found out this afternoon that there was a Huguenot woman called Girouard living in a house in St-Gervas. She died a long time ago.'

Her voice was steady, just small and factual. But it was hard to accustom herself to the death of a dream, to know that she had built her life upon an edifice of crumbling sand. She waited for the meaningless words of comfort. They did not come.

'Well, it was always a possibility. You'll need to know more, though, if you wish to be sure. Did you find out the woman's baptismal name?'

Christie shook her head. 'They were Catholics. I was afraid.'

'Ah.' Luke frowned. 'You must be careful. Paris is quiet now, but it may not remain so. Tell me the address, and I'll make inquiries for you. You shouldn't go back.'

Surprised, she told him, and then, at his request, described yet again the house, and the silver mirror, and the spinet, and the maid called Lucrezia.

When she had finished, he said, 'Now go and put on your other gown. The blue one.'

She stared at him as he threw the dregs of his wine into the fire.

'Why?'

'Because it suits you better. Old women with rosaries and knitting wear black. Because then we'll match. Because we're going to a banquet. Because I want to introduce my beautiful, elegant wife to Henri Fagot. Or Blaise Lamarque. Or both. Because,' he finished, softly, 'at the moment, the devil is winning.'

*

SHE not only wore her dark blue gown, she also let Emilie, who had once been a ladies' maid, dress her hair. Emilie, blessed with the endless patience of the utterly stupid, enjoyed combing out the dense chestnut mass and coaxing it into something reasonably elegant and curling, heaped on top of Christie's head. The blue gown, shaken and brushed into shape, *was* more becoming than black; nervously, Christie presented herself to Luke, waiting in the parlour.

'I've no jewellery. Will it be very grand?'

'You don't need jewellery. And it will be very grand and very decadent. It will make Catcleugh seem like one of Susannah Grey's dinner-parties.'

She giggled. 'I didn't think you went to Susannah Grey's dinner-parties.'

'Once.' He fastened her cloak around her shoulders, and picked up his own hat. 'Stephen was there. I took a horse of the Grey's back from the Armstrongs. The horse didn't like the dinner-party either. Stephen didn't like the horse.'

They had to ride past the Rue St-Gervas to reach Blaise Lamarque's house near the Bois de Vincennes. Christie pointed out Madame Charroux's house, and Luke nodded, but she knew that his mind was already elsewhere. The snow had stopped falling and the shutters were closed: diamonds in the stained wood, sealing in the light, keeping out the darkness.

They reached a wide street with tall houses either side. Not far away, Christie could see the trees of the Bois de Vincennes, tipped with moonlight. She could hear music and laughter. Christie thought of the man she had seen in the Bois de Vincennes, and the wildcat, and she shivered.

BLAISE Lamarque, though, was perfectly courteous. His eyes widened only slightly when Luke, having dragged an increasingly unwilling Christie through the throng, said, 'And this is my wife, Christiane,' and gently pushed her towards the man she had seen only from a distance through metal railings. Monsieur Lamarque took her hand and kissed it and said, 'How delightful, petit,' and Christie curtseyed, partially because it seemed appropriate, and partially because her knees had gone wobbly.

The delight seemed genuine: a sparkle in each slanting yellow eye. Blaise Lamarque had an Italian's dark, olive skin, hair that was straight and black and heavy, and features that immediately recalled to Christie the hotel in Rouen, and the spare symmetry of the miniaturist's pencil sketch. He was dressed in cloth of silver, the front of his doublet intricately meshed with embroidery. Green stones pitted the embroidery: emeralds, thought Christie, impressed.

'Greet my Lucifer,' said Blaise Lamarque when he had relinquished Christie's hand, and he bent, and lifted the creature chained to the chair-leg.

The wildcat had a collar of emeralds about its neck. Its eyes opened briefly as Christie touched the dense, harsh hair on the crown of its head. The golden eyes watched her coldly, but the creature did not bare its teeth. Lucifer, thought Christie. A familiar spirit if ever she'd seen one.

A dangerous analogy. If the wildcat was Blaise Lamarque's own private demon, what then was Luke? Ten years younger than Blaise, perhaps, and as fair as the older man was dark. A fanciful woman would have thought of fallen angels, bright wings beating into dark pits. But Christie was not fanciful, and Luke Ridley was no angel.

The room was magnificent, far outdoing Charles Webster's house in Salisbury, Stephen Ridley's castle at Black Law. The tables and benches were inlaid with silver, their cushions and covers embroidered and tasselled, coloured stones and tiny mirrors set into the embroidery. Coverings of crimson sarsenet trimmed with gold fringes were thrown over the tables, tapestries of embroidered silk flowers fluttered on the walls. Light from the banks of candles caught and shimmered on silk, on fringes, on mirrors, on jewels. And on the breast of every woman, in the ear of every man, more jewels, their facets seizing the light and playing with it before throwing it back in waves and waterfalls of shade and colour. She looked plain, decided Christie, glancing down at the dark blue gown, with its restrained cuffs and collar and modest farthingale. Everyone

241

else was brightly dressed, many of the women wearing stiffened lace collars the height of their heads, like rays emanating from the suns of their faces. Some of the men had *pink hair*.

A servant offered Christie a glass of wine.

Blaise Lamarque smiled, and said, 'Madame is French – a Parisian – I believe? Madame must find all this utterly dull –'

Madame did not find it dull at all. Madame could have watched the Great Chamber and its guests for hours. It was fascinating, awful, compelling, like Monsieur Lamarque himself.

'I am French, monsieur,' said Christie, after taking a reassuring mouthful of wine, 'but I have not lived in France for many years.'

'Ah.' Blaise Lamarque's eyes glittered. 'You have sailed from the heathen north, then, like my little Luke?'

Luke was seated; Blaise's hand rested on his shoulder. Christie assented.

'So will you return, Madame, to your hills and your castles – or do you intend to remain in the country of your birth?'

The slanting golden eyes, heavily lashed with black, watched her attentively.

'I am looking for my family, Monsieur Lamarque,' Christie said. 'When I find someone – or when I know that I will find nothing – then I shall think about the future.'

Lamarque smiled, briefly. 'To prosper – to survive – in Paris, you must know particular people and cultivate particular friends. You must also have an appropriate history.' He paused, then added, 'I am trying to persuade your husband that he could have a promising career in France. There are great rewards for gifts such as his to be found in Paris. Don't you agree, Madame Ridley?'

A servant murmured in Blaise Lamarque's jewelled ear. His hand still rested, possessively, on Luke's shoulder. Looking up at Christie, Blaise said,

'We should eat now, Madame. But perhaps we may talk again later.'

THE white ceiling of the banqueting-chamber was interlaced

with violet-blue bands of lapis lazuli, studded with silver. On the walls, painted people paraded in superbly executed perspective, their parti-coloured Italian hose and high Renaissance foreheads clear and unfaded, silhouetted against skies of Mediterranean blue. Gondolas bobbed on foreign waters in the shadows of squat, bulbous churches; a black-skinned man held a bare-breasted woman's hand as she stepped on to a barge from a narrow pier.

The clink of glasses, a woman's brittle laughter, fragments of conversation filtering through scented air. *The King is to go on a pilgrimage, but the Duc de Joyeuse will not accompany him because it would ruin his shoes . . . Adultery? I leave that to grooms and serving-maids, chérie. I have the prettiest page . . . Madame d'Aubespine wears a veil, they say, because her face is so scarred by the smallpox . . . One never went to bed with d'Aubespine for her face, mon cher. She has other attributes . . .*

And at the top of the table Blaise Lamarque sat between Luke and a man with a monkey on his shoulder. Luke did not, as Christie once might have supposed, look out of place in this company. Covertly, she watched him. He no longer looked tired: his eyes were bright, his movements quick. He had adopted their manner, their dress, as far as was necessary. Different enough to be noticeable, not so different as to be unacceptable. Clever Luke.

She lost count of the different dishes. Cows' feet, soused ham, cinnamon pies, oysters, eels and boar, and a hundred others, glazed and beflowered and sprigged with rosemary. There was a cake modelled into the shape of Notre Dame, surrounded by a Seine of ice with boats of floating marzipan. There was a huge golden pie, and when Blaise Lamarque cut the pie a child unfolded, a boy, of nine or ten perhaps, gilded, wearing only a golden loincloth.

Christie sat beside a man with a lovelock and a nose like a kestrel's beak: someone had told her his name, and she had forgotten it instantly.

'Frumenty?' he said, wearily, to her. His hair was frosted, glittering. 'Syllabub? Pomegranate seeds for a returned Persephone –?'

Christie shook her head.

The woman next to him said, looking pointedly at Christie's gown, 'Whom do you mourn, Madame?'

Before she could answer, the man with the lovelock answered, 'The spring, of course, chérie. What else should Persephone mourn?'

'I'm not in mourning,' said Christie, firmly. 'I've two gowns, dark blue and black. My husband prefers this one.'

'Hades should favour black.' The man with the lovelock let his bored gaze trail the length of the table. 'Where is Hades, Madame?'

She showed him Luke, and his eyebrows raised a little. 'He has the wrong colouring for the Prince of Darkness. But the right tastes.'

The woman giggled. Her hair, netted with pearls, was the same colour as Arbel's. 'He makes love like an angel, not a devil, mon cher. Did you not know?' Her eyes, still laughing, moved slowly to Christie. 'Oh, pardon, Madame. Just gossip, je vous assure.'

The man with the lovelock had taken a pomegranate and was splitting it with a knife. 'Now, I should dress you in jade green, Madame Ridley. Jade, not emerald. There are so few ladies who can wear jade, don't you think? Claude, here, for instance, could not. She would look like a vegetable. I am not sure what type of vegetable, but then, I have never been well acquainted with vegetables.'

He had prised out the seeds, and was placing them, like pearls in pink glass, around the edge of his plate. His face was painted; in the flickering candlelight Christie could see where the paint met the frosted hairline. At the far end of the table, close to where Blaise and Luke sat, a group of musicians played, dwarves every one of them, tiny hands clutching miniature viols, shawms, and tabors. Luke always drank and his glass was always full.

Claude said, 'There is no need to be unpleasant, Fernand. Madame's marriage to Blaise's new darling is one of convenience, n'est ce pas? Blaise told me.'

There was an entire circle of pomegranate seeds round the rim of Fernand's plate.

'The marriage is to be dissolved.' Claude leaned towards Christie, a fan of ivory and swansdown half-covering her face. 'Has it not occurred to you, Madame, that you have the poor end of such a bargain? That in order to achieve your annulment, you must keep that pearl of dubious worth – your virginity? While your husband – well, see your husband.'

Christie followed, unwillingly, Claude's careless flick of the fan. The Seine of ice had begun to melt, staining the white damask tablecloth. One of the dwarves sat in the ruins of the golden pie, the child's loincloth in his hand. Someone was pouring claret over his head; it glistened as it trailed along his thickened arms and shoulders, scaling over the crumbling gilt pastry. And at the end of the table, a woman with peacock feathers in her hair drank wine, and placed her lips on Luke's, so that the dark red liquid trickled down their chins and breasts.

She saw Luke bend his head to kiss the woman's wine-stained throat, and she turned quickly away.

'Your husband is a little unpredictable, is he not, chérie?' said Claude, untangling the spun sugar on a basket of marzipan roses. 'He will sleep with whomsoever Blaise tells him to, but he has not slept with Blaise himself, it seems. Nor with his own wife. I wonder why? He is not fastidious. He slept with the Comtesse de Braque – no man can claim to be fastidious who sleeps with the Comtesse de Braque. And I wonder why Blaise does not kill him? He does not like to be rejected.'

They had begun to throw bread at the dwarf in the pie: crusts soared through the air to splash, floating and bobbing, in the claret.

'Blaise keeps him because he is decorative, my dear,' said Fernand, calmly. 'He does not need to paint his face, nor to bleach his hair. Blaise intends to find favour with the Duc d'Epernon. To do this he requires a little decoration. Your husband' – turning to Christie – 'is part of that decoration. You and I' – and he turned slowly back to Claude – 'are no longer as decorative as we once were.'

Claude's hair was not like Arbel's at all: in the bright candlelight it was yellowed, harsh, darkened at the roots. If Christie touched it, it would feel like the wildcat's coat.

Claude said, sharply, 'Even youth can drown itself in wine and self-indulgence. That would solve your problems, would it not, Madame? So much *simpler* to be widowed than to have a marriage annulled.'

Someone had thrown a goblet at the dwarf: it had struck him on the back of the head and he had slipped, half drowned in wine and pastry crumbs, to lie open-mouthed, eyes closed, curled in the bottom of the dish. Couples were dancing, some of them a little unsteady, their swaying shadows imprinted on those other, older shadows painted on the wall.

Christie looked down at the table, and blinked rapidly. Six pomegranate seeds were neatly circled in the centre of her plate.

CHRISTIE watched dark-skinned women dance, their jewelled arms fluttering like heavily leaved trees in a breeze, letting fall lengths of silk one by one to the embroidered rugs beneath their feet until they were as naked as the Venetian courtesans on Blaise Lamarque's wall-frieze. She watched the pie with the dwarf in it whirl through the air from hand to careless hand until someone let it fall and it landed on a golden tryptych, so that the blank, peaceful faces ripped and tore, and dull, ancient stones mingled with the pastry crumbs and wine. She saw swordsmen fight on the long wooden dining-table, kicking puddings and cakes aside like footballs, slipping on nuts and oranges, embedding their rapiers in half-eaten hams, quivering jellies. She could, however, see neither Luke nor the woman with the peacock feathers.

In the withdrawing-room, empty except for a man asleep in the corner, and a couple giggling behind the curtains, she examined Blaise Lamarque's spinet. The spinet was scented, and all of glass except for the gold and silver strings. Lowering her face, Christie breathed in the scent: rose petals, sandalwood, patchouli, all the heavy, exotic fragrance of the east. A voice behind her said, 'Play, Madame, if you wish.'

Blaise Lamarque. She was about to refuse gracefully, when she thought that she would not be intimidated by a man with yellow eyes and an undomesticated cat. So she sat on the stool, and let her fingers touch the keys: lightly at first, for it was many months since she had played. But the music began to return: Dowland, Byrd, a country air that she and Arbel had sung together, far away, long, long ago. Blaise Lamarque stood behind her, and every now and then she felt his cloth of silver brush against her velvet back. The tone of the glass instrument was poor, barely audible against the clamour from the banqueting-chamber. Beauty sacrificed for appearance, thought Christie, grimly, and finished with a flourish.

'Delightful, Madame,' said Blaise Lamarque. 'You must play later for my guests. Have you been married long?'

'Not long,' Christie said, replacing the lid of the spinet. 'We were married first in November and then again in December.'

'Twice?' She had moved round on the stool so that she could see his face. 'It seems a great deal of trouble to go to for so poor a reward.'

She willed herself not to blush. The topaz eyes glinted a little brighter, but the red, curving lips did not smile.

'The petit Luc told me that you have an arrangement,' added Blaise, gently.

Christie mentally cursed the petit Luc. 'An arrangement of mutual convenience,' she said, brightly. 'I lack fathers and brothers you see, Monsieur Lamarque. The marriage will be dissolved when we return to England.'

'Really?' Blaise held a fan in his right hand: with a flick of the wrist the segments spread, painted ivory, Zeus pursuing a rather fat Daphne. 'But you are in love with your husband, Madame. How will you bear to dissolve this marriage – these marriages, I should say?'

Leaves sprouted from Daphne's plump fingertips. The room had become too hot, Emilie had laced her gown too tight. It was difficult to breathe.

'You are mistaken, Monsieur Lamarque.'

He looked at her for a moment, and she did not drop her eyes.

'Really?' said Blaise Lamarque, and let his own golden gaze wander the length of the room.

'I wonder where your busy husband is, my dear. He has been gone a long time.'

*

CHRISTIE's husband was, at that moment, making love to Blaise Lamarque's guest in Blaise Lamarque's own scented bedroom.

The ceiling of the bedchamber was divided by bands of gold into lozenge shapes. In each alternate lozenge a well-proportioned classical nude reclined, fig-leaf conspicuously absent. The four-poster bed was draped, morbidly, in black silk. Blaise Lamarque's guest, whose name Luke had forgotten, slipped in the black silk like a seal in stormy waters, only her plump white buttocks visible over the dark waves.

'Otarie,' said Luke, vaguely, kissing each dimpled white thigh. 'Hippocampe.'

The seal giggled. Leaning one arm over the side of the bed, Luke picked up one of the three peacock feathers that lay on the floor. 'Paonne,' he said, softly, and heard the sudden intake of breath as he trailed the tip of the feather from the soles of her feet to the tops of her smooth white legs.

She did not even bother to roll on to her back. She was as drunk as a lord, and so was he: it had taken him fully five minutes to slip the lock on the bedchamber door. Her thighs parted at another touch of the feather, and he was on top of her, his hands reaching beneath her body to squeeze her flat brown nipples, his teeth sinking carefully into the fold of fat at the side of her neck. He heard her cry out as he entered her, felt her body arch in pleasure. Not a seal, he thought, a whale. A large, comfortable, blubbery whale who, thank God, was tonight as easily satisfied as he.

He waited until he was sure she slept, and then, planting one poorly aimed kiss between her shoulderblades, slid off the bed. Her face paint was smeared across Blaise Lamarque's pillow, and the sheet was half pulled off the bed where her fingers had gripped it. Pulling on shirt and breeches, ignoring the painted figures that stared pruriently down on him, Luke began to inspect the contents of Blaise Lamarque's bedchamber.

There were three chests and a rather fine court cupboard. He hiccuped as he opened each chest in turn, and found, as he had expected, clothes, fans, shoes. The court cupboard was locked, though: carefully, using one of the peacock-lady's hairpins, Luke began to pick the lock.

He had to concentrate hard, because his fingers were not as steady as usual. All the time he listened: to his own breathing, to the snoring from the bed, for footsteps in the ante-room outside. His face was beaded with sweat when finally the lock slipped and the cupboard door swung open.

He had not expected, and he did not find, anything as convenient as a letter from the Duc de Guise to Blaise Lamarque. There were letters, carefully tied with a ribbon, addressed to Monsieur Lamarque . . . mon cher Blaise . . . mignon . . . All useless.

He found something as he heard the far door of the ante-room open. A shopping-list. He relocked the cupboard, placed the folded paper inside his shirt, and returned to the peacock-lady.

The door swung open.

The wildcat jumped on to the bed first.

'Méchant Luc,' said Blaise Lamarque, smoothly, glancing at the sleeping woman. 'To share my bed with another.'

SOMETIME in the middle of the night, they left Blaise Lamarque's glittering house and walked to the nearby Bois de Vincennes.

Luke had a key for the heavy metal gate. Christie did not need to ask him who had given him the key. The gate swung open: Luke closed it behind them.

The sky had cleared, and the moon was a full round silver disc in the sky. Taking Christie's arm, Luke led her through the trees until they came to a valley.

It was the valley where she had first seen the man with the wildcat. The moonlight glazed the untarnished sweep of snow from the hillside, the trees and hedges shut off the noise of the city. Luke leaned his back against a tree and closed his eyes. It occurred to Christie that Blaise Lamarque would destroy him; he would take what was worthwhile in Luke Ridley, and would leave behind only the husk.

'Go home,' she said, at last. 'To your real home, I mean. To Catcleugh.'

He did not answer.

Christie stared at him, and felt despair. His white shirt was soiled with wine, his blue silk crumpled and dirty. His skin was pale, shadowed and slack around the eyes.

'You don't belong here.'

Her voice sounded hopeless, lost in the immense and exclusive loneliness of Vincennes.

Luke shook his head. 'Unfinished business,' he said, the words hardly slurred at all. 'Monsieur Lamarque and I have an arrangement. He calls and I answer. See?'

She saw the long lashes droop again. She watched him slide down the length of the tree-trunk, snow powdering from the bark, to sit, head in hands, on the bulbous curling roots.

'What do you want from him?'

Luke was silent; for a moment Christie thought that he slept. Then he said, 'I told you before – my freedom.'

She saw him run his fingers through his tangled hair.

'You have Catcleugh – you have your independence – what more do you want?'

'But I do not have my independence, you see, Christie. I lost that in September.' He was silent for a moment. 'I have worked for Sir Francis Walsingham since that month. If I do not work for Sir Francis Walsingham, then my life is forfeit.'

She had not felt cold until then. But suddenly she felt chilled, now the surface of her skin had iced as though the snow was still falling. 'Sir Francis Walsingham –' Christie said the name slowly, not wishing to accept its implications.

'Yes. I didn't intend to tell you. But – yes, Sir Francis Walsingham, the Queen's Secretary of State. You thought I sold horses, didn't you? Well, I do, but I have dealt in other commodities as well. Guns, saltpetre. And information. Information pays much better than horses.'

His voice was flippant, only slightly blurred. 'I found myself on the wrong side of the Border in September, you see. In Hermitage Castle. Until then, I had worked for whoever paid best, but after Hermitage I had to bind myself to Sir Francis. I do not like to be bound, Christie. Blaise Lamarque can free me from that, damn him. I just need to find the right way to persuade him. With his help I can achieve what Sir Francis wants of me – in rather spectacular style, I think.'

She knew that he spoke the truth.

'Espionage,' she said, flatly, pulling her cloak tighter about her shoulders. 'You are a spy, then. *Why?*'

'Because I enjoy it – because I am good at it.' Luke shrugged. 'Why do you play the spinet, Christie? I don't suppose Arbel plays – Arbel can barely write. Neither can Blaise, for that matter . . . Something else they have in common . . .'

She heard the laughter in his voice and saw the short, barely noticeable struggle to control himself. He drew his hand across his face. 'You play the spinet because it answers something in your nature. I play with other men's secrets because it answers something in mine. Also, it has paid well.'

She had played the spinet before she had lived in Anne Forster's house. In one of those dark streets, somewhere in this beautiful, cruel city, she had sat at a keyboard and picked out nursery rhymes and dances.

Christie looked up at Luke, and saw that his eyes were focused, inaccurately, on her.

He said, 'I began by travelling to France with Sandy Lawson. Davey had travelled – Black Law's littered with his things – and I suppose I wanted to see what he had seen for myself. Besides, I needed pistols, and I thought the odd bit of gunpowder might come in handy. That's Sandy's trade, as I told you. And the other things just happened – I fell into it. I was good at it. Ciphers and codes and different voices, different faces. It was entertaining. Yes, that was it. Espionage was to me as I am to Blaise Lamarque. An entertainment.'

He grinned, his eyes bright. Christie thought of the six pomegranate seeds circling the centre of her plate.

She said, 'Did you find this evening – entertaining?'

'Bits of it.' Luke shivered. 'I'm sorry – it was worse than I had expected. The man with the monkey – was the Duc d'Epernon. The French King's favourite. The whole delightful evening was for the benefit of the Duc d'Epernon. Henri III uses his mignons to keep the Guises out of power . . . which suits the English. Especially Walsingham . . .'

251

His voice had drifted away. Collecting himself, Luke added, 'But I shouldn't have taken you.'

'I didn't mind.' Christie found, a little to her surprise, that she spoke the truth. 'But I still think that you should go home.'

He stared at her. She saw that calculation was still there behind those bleached blue eyes. Luke calculated with Blaise Lamarque just as he had once calculated with her. A marriage to get the French authorities off his back, a little debauchery to free him from the English. Yet he was nearer the edge than he had been two months ago: she knew that. She had seen him lose control only once before, at the handfasting. Something had thrown him off his guard, then, shattering his defences.

He stood up, brushing the snow from his back, offering her his arm.

'I can't. Not yet. Shall we walk? Or are you cold?'

She shook her head and took his outstretched arm. The snow was blue-white, each crystal turned to diamond by the moonlight.

'He could hurt you,' Christie said, bluntly.

Luke looked down at her, and grinned. 'Yes, he might. But I don't intend him to. Look.'

The broad sweep of the moonlit valley below made her catch her breath. The trees were a filigree of silver and blue, the branches fringed with a lacework of frost. A circular pond, frozen to metallic dullness, reflected the moon. Christie could see a face in the moon in the sky, and another shimmering face in the moon in the pond. The only sound was the crunching of their footsteps in the snow: the snow took and stifled any other small movement. It was cold: their breath made opaque clouds in the icy air. Christie felt the silk of Luke's doublet brush against her face, the warmth of his body through the layers of material that divided them. She heard him speak.

'I remember standing like this at Catcleugh the first night it was mine. It was the day after Grace's funeral. I remember looking beyond the Border to Scotland, east to the sea, west to Liddesdale and Teviotdale, and thinking that now I had something that was mine. No one else's. I could feed myself, clothe myself, keep myself. And I did – and a few others as well. I belonged there.'

She found, to her surprise, that she was crying. She almost expected the tears to stiffen and freeze in the cold air. She felt Luke's fingers gently wipe them away, one by one.

'I'm sorry,' he said. 'Tactless of me. I'm not quite sober, my dear, or I'd choose my words more carefully.'

'I don't belong anywhere.' Her breath came in great clouded gasps. 'I'm like Mouche.'

'You're prettier than Mouche.'

His arm was about her shoulders. The tears dried at their source. When he held her the awful overwhelming loneliness dissolved, like the ice of Blaise Lamarque's miniature Seine.

'You could go home, if you wish, Christie. I could find someone reliable to take you to Dieppe.'

'*No.*' The single word came out more forcefully than she had intended. His face was close to hers, his bare fingers had curled round her gloved hand. She knew that if she had been a hundred miles away she could have sketched that face, have pencilled in the long, thin nose, the shadowed eyes, the curling mouth, drawing them just as carefully as the miniaturist's pupil had once drawn Blaise Lamarque. She knew also, with a terrible, overwhelming realization, that now she had a different reason for staying in Paris.

'Then – look for the nurse,' she heard Luke say. 'Lucrezia. It's an unusual name. You may be lucky.'

Chapter Fourteen

IT took Stephen over a week to find Willie Graham: a week of searching the taverns of Alnwick, Berwick, and Wooler.

He had used Graham before, because Graham, he had discovered, was loyal to nothing except a purse of coins or a few drinks. He despised Willie Graham for that, but still he made use of it.

He found him in Rothbury, eventually, in the Angel. Stephen wished it had been anywhere but Rothbury, for now Arbel's silvery voice chimed with Lucas's: *The Forsters are a prolific breed. Unlike the Ridleys. We know why, now, don't we, Stephen?*

Yet he had done his duty by her. He avoided Arbel by daytime and slept apart from her by night, but at least he knew that now there was the possibility of a son. A son for Black Law. He would call his son David, after his father, not his brother. He could picture them, sometimes, himself and his wife and child, riding through Black Law's gates, ordered and tidy. In his imagination Arbel's hair darkened a little and faded, until she looked like Grace. Grace's childlessness had been a great sorrow to her, but Stephen, once he had known of Davey's sin, had been glad. A child would have been an abomination. It was right that Black Law had passed, on Davey's death, to Stephen, and would then go to *his* children.

Which was why he sought Willie Graham in the Angel tavern. The Angel was not, generally, the sort of place which Stephen would have visited. When he was younger he had been to such places, and worse. The smell of woodsmoke and sweat and ale recalled those times: the squalor, the self-disgust. No matter how carefully he had washed himself, no matter how clean his silks and linen, he had thought that some of the stink of the night must cling to him, polluting him. Things were better now. And they must remain so.

He saw Willie in the corner of the room, his bulk slack on a three-legged stool, a tankard in his hand. Stephen put his handkerchief to his nostrils to cross to Willie's side.

He did not, as another man might have done, touch Willie's shoulder to get his attention. Willie's shirt clung to his back, his leather jack was stained and shiny. He bent to murmur in Willie's ear, and then, his gorge rising uncomfortably in him, he returned to the Green Man.

In Paris, the days passed, apparently just the same, but changed irrevocably.

If Christie went out now, it was not to search, as she still pretended, for yesterday; it was to look for a fair head, lost in the crowds of Les Halles, a familiar loved figure, riding through the streets. She went to places where she had been with him, because there was happiness in seeing the same commonplace streets and houses, and remembering. She went to the Bois de Vincennes, and stood, outside again, looking through the railings down to the valley, and she regretted the melting of the snow, even the tight budding leaves, because they altered what she and he had seen.

She dressed better, making, with Emilie's help, a new gown. It was a light blue, the sort of colour that someone pretty, like Arbel, would wear. She took more care with her hair, brushing it, and pinning it loosely back instead of attempting to tie it up. It had never tied up properly, anyway, no matter how many pins she and Arbel had used. Sometimes in the street strangers smiled at her, and she could not help smiling back. *You're prettier than Mouche* he had said, a dubious compliment if ever she'd heard one, and yet, for the first time in her life, Christie had begun to feel pretty.

She could not sleep and she could not eat. She sang, and she read, especially the poetry books that Luke had brought home with him in his first, unfruitful, days of searching.

Je plante en ta faveur cest arbre de Cybelle
Ce pin, ou tes honneurs se liront tous les jours:

255

If she could have reached the tree against which he had lain in the Bois de Vincennes, she, too, would have scratched his initials on the trunk. C. F. and L. R., etched on the smooth bark for all the world to see. But she could not reach it, she knew that it was too far away.

A week later, riding back to Black Law, Stephen had to use all his self-control not to vomit, like Lucas, into the gutter.

Lucas had left the Borders for France in mid-December. Willie Graham had heard that from Red Archie, who had heard it from the gypsy. Lucas knew the master of the *Elizabeth*, had sailed with him before. The *Elizabeth* had put to sea from Berwick in mid-December. And Christie Forster had travelled to France on the *Elizabeth*, to look for her family.

Margaret had showed him Christie's note; Arbel had told him the name of the ship.

Stephen had begun to plan, even as Willie Graham had confirmed his worst fears. He decided to call on Sir John Forster.

THE snow was thick on the Cheviots when Sir John Forster, Lord Warden of the English Middle Marches, came to dine with the Ridleys of Black Law.

Lady Forster accompanied her husband, and she, and Margaret, Rob, Richie and Janet Forster sat between Stephen and Arbel Ridley in Black Law's splendid Great Hall. Candles glittered in all four corners of the room, the heavy brocade curtains kept out the wind and the cold.

Janet Forster, no longer sick, ate happily for two. Pregnancy had given a little fullness to her face, softening her dark robin's eyes. She could still throw a chamber-pot with deadly accuracy, however, but it was less often Richie who felt the strength of her arm. Janet and Richie no longer worried Margaret: she could read their future as clearly as any gypsy might. Half a dozen children, most of them sons, and Richie would adore every one of them. Adderstone would prosper as well as any

Border inheritance prospered, and Richie would die, one night, an arrow in his back, because he had grown contented and careless. But that was a long time away, and she, Margaret, would be long dead.

She had not, as she had hoped, stopped worrying about Arbel.

Margaret, having eaten her cinnamon pudding, watched her niece. Arbel, though still beautiful, seemed to have grown thinner, her pallor almost transparent. Her eyes were darker, haunted, shadowed a little in the sockets. Arbel picked at her food like the pigeons in Adderstone's courtyard, her small, neat head bending to take a few mouthfuls, her tiny graceful hands pushing the plate away unfinished. The dog had been coiled on her lap throughout the entire meal, shedding hair on to Stephen's exquisite Turkey rug, whining if anyone but Arbel went near her. Arbel had begun to look like her mother, a beautiful, caged creature who had eventually nibbled away at her own sanity because of the unsuitability of the bars that surrounded her. Margaret had regretted the loss of Christie more than ever when she had seen Arbel. Christie, loving Arbel, had kept her in contact with reality. Stephen did not love his wife. Stephen, she thought with a shiver, had begun to loathe her.

The conversation had turned, as conversation sometimes did, to Lucas. Margaret had not seen Lucas since that memorable November morning when he had told her about the handfasting. His absence was nothing unusual, but she missed him, just as she still missed Davey. Black Law always recalled Davey to her: a flick of an eyelid, and there was Davey sitting at the head of the table, not Stephen; Grace, not Arbel, opposite him. When Davey had been there, there had been laughter, and Lucas had still been an enchanting, troublesome child.

'There's no one at Catcleugh,' Richie was saying. 'The house is half-burned and Luke's mistress has taken up with Dickie Grey. God knows what Luke's doing with himself.'

Rob did not, as Margaret might have expected him to do, venture a few suggestions for the silent Deity. Instead, Stephen, leaning back in his chair, said,

'Lucas is out of the country, I hear. He put to sea in mid-December.'

Rob, next to Margaret, looked up from his wine. Sir John Forster frowned, and said, 'Are you sure of this, Ridley?'

'Oh, yes.' Stephen nodded to the servants to begin to clear the table. 'Apparently he's sailed with the *Elizabeth* before. Though I've heard the ship's a gun-runner.'

Margaret's heart had begun to hammer uncomfortably loudly. She saw that Rob was looking hard at Stephen; that he had put aside his glass. Rob turned in his seat, and she lowered her eyes, unable to meet his gaze.

'Christie sailed with the *Elizabeth* in December,' said Rob, softly.

Margaret heard Stephen say, 'Christie is my wife's adopted sister, Sir John. She is of French origin.' And added, 'Is it possible that there was something between Lucas and Christie, Margaret?'

Looking up, she could not judge Stephen's innocence, could not tell whether he was taunting her or not. She could not speak at all at first, as the implications of Stephen's words began to crowd in on her. She heard Rob say her name, softly, at first, and then more urgently. She should have told the truth in November. She should have watched Christie more closely; she should have thought what effect someone like Lucas might have on a reserved girl like Christie. It was not only the Arbels and Catherines of this world who could lose their heads for a seductive face, a well-made body.

Rob said, '*Mother*,' for a third time, and Margaret, sick with a certain knowledge of disaster, said, 'Christie and Luke handfasted in November. I kept it quiet – for Christie's sake.'

'For *Christie*'s sake?' Rob was staring at her, and she could see the anger already burning in his dark blue eyes. 'Are you sure?'

'I thought it for the best,' she added.

'Best for whom?' Rob's hands were clenched on the table, his eyes hard and dark. 'I should have killed him at Adderstone. Christie was in our care, and Luke violated her.'

'Lucas did not violate Christie. He handfasted with her

because he was drunk – and in a temper, I would guess. He told me so, and Christie told me the same. I had no reason to disbelieve them. Besides –' Margaret paused, and then said steadily '– Lucas has never, to my knowledge, been in the business of violating innocent young girls. Every other sort of wickedness, no doubt – but has it ever occurred to you, Rob, that most of Lucas' misdeeds are simply an attempt to keep body and soul together? In a rather over-flamboyant fashion, I grant you, but still, we all must eat.'

She heard Rob, standing, say softly, 'God forgive you, Mother,' and she knew that she could not meet Richie's eyes, Janet's eyes. They would only, she knew, say the same as Rob's.

'So our Lucas has married a Frenchwoman,' said Stephen, clearly. 'Well, well.'

Rob rose from the table. The door slammed shut behind him.

There was an uncomfortable pause in which the lady of the house pulled a ribbon from her own blonde hair and tied it carefully around her dog's neck, and Janet, finding the silence increasingly awkward, thrust a bowl of syllabub in the direction of a startled Lady Forster. Sir John Forster still drank, but his sharp grey eyes were fixed on Stephen.

'I met your cousin a few months ago. I didn't think the lad was the marrying kind. Too wild.'

Stephen smiled, and beckoned to the servant to refill Forster's glass. 'People change, Sir John,' he said. 'Loyalties change.'

The goblet paused, halfway to the Warden's lips. 'Yes. Loyalty,' he said, thoughtfully. 'Young Lucas wasn't too strong on loyalty, I recollect.'

Stephen shook his head. His handsome mouth curled in a smile, his dark eyes glinted with pleasure. 'No loyalties at all, Sir John,' he said, happily. 'Clever, though. Or – devious, perhaps I should say. His kind are generally devious, don't you think? Birth always shows. Does it not, my dear?' he added, addressing Arbel.

Arbel was smiling too. 'Look, Stephen,' she said, and held up Dowzabel, wrapped like a baby in her own silk shawl. 'Isn't she adorable?'

And Margaret, shivering, closed her eyes.

LUKE took Christie to another of Blaise Lamarque's evenings, partly to annoy Blaise, partly because he had found that Christie acted as an anchor for him, a reminder, perhaps, of a saner world.

Life was cheap in the Borders. But here death was a source of amusement. He had seen a man drown in the Seine in a drunken midnight rowing race, another, soaring high on hashish, tumble from the spire of St-Gervas after pinning the Duc d'Epernon's colours to the apex.

In the course of the months in Paris, Luke had found out as much as possible about Blaise Lamarque. That he was of low birth – not, like Luke, illegitimate, but of peasant stock. That he had risen from the dirt by means of his looks, his intelligence, his inventiveness. That his hand-writing was poor, his reading equally faltering. Yet he had several languages, and had acquired a veneer of culture that enabled him to hide his weaknesses. Sometimes, looking at Blaise, Luke could see a possible future for himself. He knew that was what Blaise intended, and the thought occasionally appalled him. Blaise might know no master, but Blaise's success – the whole, glittering creation that was Blaise Lamarque – was dependent on the whims of others. Just as Luke's own future was now dependent on Blaise Lamarque. Luke had to remind himself of that dependence when he found that he had begun to forget Cherelles, Thomas Phelippes, Sir Francis Walsingham.

The banquet that night was at the Duc d'Epernon's house. A significant step, for it meant that Blaise had succeeded in attaching himself to the Duke's own entourage, reaching, through d'Epernon, the select circle of King Henri's mignons. At some point during the early hours of the morning, Luke found himself seated on the spinet stool next to Christie. She was playing: golden streams of sound faded the clamour of the Duc d'Epernon's withdrawing-room into obscurity. There was a terrible temptation just to rest his head against Christie's blue silk shoulder, and close his eyes. He gave into temptation: he could feel the warmth of her skin through the silk, feel the small movement of her muscles as she played. Events of the evening, the previous day and night, flickered through his head like colourful fish darting in the dark waters. A woman's harsh bleached blonde hair fronded over his pillow ... himself, at Blaise Lamarque's side, hunting in the King's forest in the early hours of the morning ... cards and dice in the afternoon.

The music changed. The 'Fair Flower of Northumberland' blossomed under Christie's fingers. Luke had heard that song a hundred times before, bawled drunkenly by Red Archie in Catcleugh, whistled by the gypsy as they rode across the fells. He thought, briefly, of Arbel and Stephen, and felt sick of rich food and alcohol. He shifted slightly on the seat, resting his cheek and temple against Christie's back. Her hair drifted against his face: it smelled clean, scented only with rosemary. Arbel was the fairest flower of Northumberland, but Christie was much more comfortable ... He had asked everyone, including Blaise, for a woman by the name of Lucrezia, but he had found nothing ... Christie should go home ... if she still had a home ...

He did not know that he had slept, until a hand tapped him on the back, and a familiar voice said, 'You are bored, petit! Don't worry, I have just the thing to cure tedium.'

He opened his eyes.

Blaise said, 'I have lost my handkerchief, Luke. I thought you might retrieve it for me.'

Golden eyes, half-lidded, looked attentively down at him. The wildcat curled around Blaise Lamarque's ankles.

'It's in a hunting-lodge in the Bois de Vincennes. Unfortunately, I seem to have mislaid my key.'

The music had stopped: Luke saw that Christie, beside him, had folded her hands on her lap.

'He's tired,' she said to Blaise. 'Why don't you let him sleep?'

The heavy eyelids drooped, the full mouth twisted into a smile.

'Your concern does you credit, Madame. But my little friend has spent much of the last few days in bed, and will be looking for other entertainment. Or has Paris made him too feeble for such exertions?'

Luke was suddenly very wide awake indeed. You could, he had discovered a long time ago, exist for quite a while without sleep. The danger was that you believed your judgement to be unimpaired.

I have mislaid my key. Which meant, of course, that he would be trespassing in the King's hunting-grounds.

He said to Christie, 'Go home now. And if I'm not back by midday, then you should leave Paris. Blaise will provide you with an escort – won't you, Blaise?'

He looked at Blaise, who nodded. He could see triumph, and reckoning, in the bright tiercel's eyes. Luke thought of England, and, rising, went to the writing-desk and scrawled Sarah Kemp's name and address on a piece of paper. 'Go there, Christie,' he said quietly, 'if you will not, or cannot, go to Adderstone. Mistress Kemp will help you.'

Then he was no longer aware of Christie, at his side, nor of the brilliance of the room around him.

'Jacques will see your lovely wife home,' said Blaise Lamarque, happily. 'You, mon ami, are going hunting.'

AFTER Luke had gone, Blaise Lamarque himself escorted Christie into the nearby ante-room.

It was a small, dark room, with framed charcoal sketches on the walls, polished wooden floorboards, and an escritoire with a bundle of quill pens and a bottle of ink. A manservant had arrived with Christie's cloak.

Blaise said, 'There is an old woman by the name of Lucrezia Quirini living on the Left Bank. I can tell you how to find her, Madame.'

He went to the desk and, taking a piece of paper, began to draw a map. There were no words on the map, but the directions were clear, the tiny roads and buildings unambiguous. Blaise said, his back still to Christie, 'Perhaps you will find what you are looking for, Madame, and then you need stay no longer in Paris.'

She watched him sprinkle fine sand on the paper. He turned, folding the map.

Christie said, 'What do you want of Luke, Monsieur Lamarque?'

His eyes were untouched by the smile on his full lips, and darkened to bronze by the dim light.

'Luke and I have something in common, my dear. We were born with nothing. He is illegitimate, I took my first breath in a mud-floored hut in Chantilly. I lived within a mile of the château. Sometimes I would steal a look at it – the turrets, the towers.'

Blaise picked up Christie's cloak from a nearby chair. 'If I have risen at all, it is by my own efforts. Luke and I could be allies, or rivals. I prefer the former.'

She felt him arrange her cloak about her shoulders, but the heavy material could not take the chill from her heart. 'I don't see how sending him to his death in the Bois de Vincennes will make him an ally,' she said, tightly. 'No. You don't want an ally, Monsieur Lamarque. You don't want an equal. You most certainly don't want a rival. You want a shadow, an echo – a glittering reflection. And I think you have realized that Luke will never be that.'

The smile broadened a little, the eyes filled with delight. 'My dear Madame, you are very perceptive. In different circumstances I would wish you all happiness. But I have what I want almost within the palm of my hand, and no one – however beautiful, however clever – will take it from me.'

LUKE found himself in the Bois de Vincennes for the second time in twenty-four hours. *You, mon ami, are going hunting.* Not quite true: this time, he would be the hunted, not the hunter.

His head had cleared a little by the time he had clambered over the fence to stand inside the wrought-iron gates. He had, simply, to ride to the hunting-lodge on the far side of the wood and retrieve the handkerchief Blaise had left there earlier in the day. Only it would not be simple, for there were men waiting to intercept his journey. The King's men: the archers and swordsmen who guarded the wood and its owner from poachers, brigands and assassins.

The night was fine, lit by the moon and stars, only a little mist curling round the tree-trunks and settling in the hollows. It was, after all, no different from raiding the Borders. Same technique, different quarry. The King's soldiers instead of Armstrongs and Elliots, that was all.

The mist had gathered at the bottom of the valley, winding round the thickets where the deer sheltered, masking the foxes' holes. He had ridden through Vincennes many times now in Blaise Lamarque's glittering company, and he knew the lush woodland and the streams that fragmented it as well as he knew Liddesdale, or the Cheviots themselves. He knew the direction of the hunting-lodge; he knew the easiest exits back into Paris or into the countryside beyond the city. He could almost have imagined himself back in Northumberland, were it not for the fact that he was alone, with no horse, and poorly armed. He had his sword and his knife, and some of the joy that had left him over the months since Hermitage was returning, whistled out of the past by the velvet black sky and the smell of leaf-mould beneath his feet.

He saw the first of the soldiers as he ran up the incline towards the line of beech trees that sheltered the valley. The man was mounted, with steel morion and breastplate, bow and arrows on his back. An archer, one of Henri III's personal guard. Necessary for a king who could trust no one, least of all his own treacherous siblings.

Luke slowed his pace, hidden by the leafless bushes, his boots treading wet leaves and grass, avoiding the betraying dryness beneath the trees. A bow and arrows would be useful. A horse would be even better. The archer was silhouetted against the moon, like a boss on a shield. Appalling positioning: he would have flayed one of his own men for less. He began to climb a huge beech tree, searching for toe and finger-holds in the lichened bark. One of the beech's long branches reached along the rim of the valley: silently, Luke crawled on his stomach along the outstretched branch.

Broadcloth and a leather jack would have been more suitable than quilted black silk. The silk ripped and frayed: he was glad, at least, that he had not worn yellow, like the Duc d'Epernon. Then the moon would have shown him like some great bright caterpillar, slithering along the branch. The desire to laugh that often caught him at the most inopportune moments rose in his throat: he quelled it, and drew three small pebbles from his pocket. One, two, three, their sound half-deadened by the moss below, but enough to make the archer turn, and his horse shift and shake its mane.

He lay flat against the branch, his head, with its betraying fair hair, covered by his arms. Luke waited until the soldier had turned back towards the valley, his face and hands no longer quite as relaxed as they had been, and then he dropped another two stones.

He heard the rider click to his horse, saw the clouds of breath from man and animal, drawing nearer. His own breath was taut and silent, and he kept motionless until the archer was underneath the branch. Then he swung round and dropped, thanking Heaven for the horse's placidity and the archer's stupidity, on to the horse's back.

The horse was broader than the small Northumbrian hobbler Luke was used to, which made things easy. The soldier had not time to use his arrows: drawing his sword he tried to turn in the saddle, but one of Luke's hands grasped his wrist, forcing the fingers apart, and the other arm curled round his throat, leaving him gasping, desperately, for air. The archer swayed in the saddle, his morion rolled, skittering, into a ditch, and then he slithered off the horse, one foot entangled in the stirrups. Luke drew neither his sword nor his knife: he did not kill for entertainment, he had said once, a long time ago. And this was still Blaise Lamarque's entertainment.

He did, however, make sure the soldier was unconscious.

Then, first checking that the noise of the brief struggle had not attracted any of the archer's comrades, he stripped the man of bow and arrows and recovered the horse from the thicket to which it had fled. Mounting the horse, he rode further into the wood.

For a long time he saw no one. The only sounds were the occasional owl's cry, the drip of water as the mist clung and collected on branches, the horse's hooves, soft on earth and ferns. It was a good horse, strong and obedient. He enjoyed the silence, it cleared his head of the disarray of the past weeks. He saw other soldiers as he neared the hunting-lodge. Some were mounted, some on foot. They were easily enough avoided. Once he put up his hand in what he hoped was an archer-like salute, and the other man stared for a fraction of a second, and then saluted back.

When he reached the hunting-lodge, Luke dismounted. They had been there that morning, Blaise and he, and Blaise had made a different, simpler, offer. Luke had rejected it: not because of any moral reservations, or even because he found the idea particularly offensive, but because, tactically he knew he would be making an error. Love, to Blaise Lamarque, was just another sort of power. Give someone like Blaise exactly what they wanted, and he would despise you. And then Luke would be running errands for the rest of his days.

The hunting-lodge was in a small clearing, lit by moonlight, white and neo-classical. You might expect naiads and dryads to appear from behind those graceful marble columns, a greedy Bacchus to recline, wine-cask in hand, on a couch under the portico. The silence had become almost audible: listening, all his senses strained, there was not the sound of a footfall, nor the rustle of a cloak amongst the trees. Yet, just as at the Blink Bonny, there was that certain sense of disaster, a sense that Luke had learned, through the past five years, to trust.

So he dismounted and led the horse to the hunting-lodge, instead of tethering it to a tree on the outskirts of the clearing. He wished he had taken the soldier's morion and breastplate as he walked, the reins loosely in his hand, across the clearing. The grass was dewed, the cobwebs, jewelled like diamonds, slung between blades of glass. He could almost hear the hiss of an arrow through the air, see the moonlight catch and glint on a sword-blade.

From the pillared entrance at the front, he saw the handkerchief lying on a table. White, edged with lace, initials in the corner. Statues guarded the lodge, their plump flesh hard and cold. Nymphs and satyrs were frescoed over the archway: the night deepened the bas-relief, shadowing the figures into life. Luke glanced once more around the clearing, and then, looping his reins around a grinning cupid's upraised arm, he entered the lodge.

He had expected a note, a few well-chosen, mocking words. But no, of course not: the written word was not, he had discovered, Blaise's preferred medium. Placing the handkerchief inside his doublet he heard, at last, a sound, and turned rapidly.

Six of them, circling the lodge, rapiers upraised. Cupid's grin grew a little broader as Luke ran for his horse.

He managed, by a well-calculated jump on to the horse's back, to reach the edge of the clearing, and the shelter of the trees. Birds' wings beat as Luke crashed through the spinney, men's voices shouted. Branches whipped against his face, and his head was pressed against his horse's mane as he galloped for higher land, for the open beech wood. Breaking through the thin fingers of pollarded elms he saw two soldiers, and he reached for the bow and arrows on his back. He had killed them both before they focused on him: he saw each one slip from the saddle. It was not a game now. Putting his heels to the horse's sides, Luke made for the beech trees. The first glimmerings of dawn showed. Easier to see, easier to be seen. One of them was just behind him: he could hear the thundering of horse's hooves. If he could keep up his pace, his pursuer would not have time to fire an arrow. These men were not accustomed to fighting on the move as the Borderer was.

The horse lurched and staggered, a hoof catching on one of the tree roots that broke through the earth. Luke felt the reins slip painfully through his fingers and his feet lose the stirrups as the horse's head plunged downwards. Most of him hit earth, but his elbow struck a tree bole, jarring all sensation from his arm. The horse limped away into the bracken, and Retribution, in the shape of a well-armed archer, smiled triumphantly down at him.

He felt the tip of the man's rapier lash his face before his numb arm could bring up his own sword. First blood: incongruously, Luke recalled Arbel Forster, kissing her scarlet-stained fingers, one by one. He rolled sharply sideways before the sword could strike a second, deadlier time, and, finding his feet, stumbled for the thicket beyond. He had the over-alertness, edged with unreality, that alcohol and exhaustion

267

sometimes gave. The tangle of brambles and nettles pulled and tore at his skin and clothes, his right hand would not work properly.

Crouching in the brake, Luke could see, in the cold first light, three soldiers in the clearing.

The thicket was dense enough to make difficulties for those still on horseback. He wove an irregular path through the thorns and briars, thankful that Vincennes did not have dogs. You needed Randal Lovell when there were dogs. In the centre of the thicket, bisecting the slope of the valley, was a long ditch, cutting through the dead bracken. He paused for breath, hidden by the thick russet fronds, watching. He could hear someone not too far away, pushing his way through bramble and gorse, slashing at the bracken with his sword. Rotten, moss-covered logs, crusted with fungus, were scattered haphazardly in the ditch, brackish water trickled down the incline. The odour of decay reached Luke's nostrils; the footsteps came closer, the sword cut through old bracken and new. He flexed the fingers of his right hand, and they hardly responded, they felt half-dead. He still had his knife and his sword, but he had lost the bow and arrows falling from the horse. The boundary of the forest was, he thought, about half a mile away.

When he could hear the sound of tiny branches breaking and the sibilant noise as the sword sliced through leaves and stem, he rolled, silently, and without disturbing so much as a leaf, into the undergrowth. The dampness of the earth seeped through his clothes, his face was pressed into dead leaves and fern spores, so that he smelled the sweet odour of moss and rotting wood. He knew that the archer stood no more than a few feet away, for he could hear his breathing and the rustle of the bracken as he moved. He made every muscle still and relax, forcing his own tortured breath to silence. I'm good at this, damn you, Blaise Lamarque. I'm good at this, and I enjoy it, and it's what has kept me alive and successful for the past five years. Half Borderer, half gypsy – what better blood for games such as this?'

Still, he was glad that he had thought of Sarah Kemp. Glad,

too, that Christie had understood. He knew what Blaise intended for him: if he were caught, he would rot in the Bastille. And if they hurt him enough, he'd talk, as men with greater beliefs than he had also talked under torture. Christie must not remain in Paris, the wife of an English spy. And Sarah Kemp would, he was sure, shelter her if necessary. Sarah Kemp and Christie Forster were two of a kind.

He waited for what seemed like a decade. His knife was gripped in his left hand, the dampness at the bottom of the ditch began to crawl along his skin. If the sun came up fully, he would be seen, and then, really, his chances were non-existent. He could feel the life beginning to return to his hand, but not quickly enough. He would fight, though, because, if it came to it, he would rather die here, in the open air, than in some foul French prison.

But, miraculously, Luke heard the archer shout, 'Non! Il est parti!' and begin to move away. Then there was the sound of footsteps and horses' hooves. When the woods had returned to silence again, Luke dragged himself out of the ditch, and ran soundlessly for the boundary, and freedom.

HE did not yet return to Blaise Lamarque. Blaise could wait, Blaise could think that he had won. He knew better than to give Blaise the satisfaction of seeing him muddied and bloodied, and besides, by the time he was walking through the city streets, the inevitable reaction had begun to set in.

He had forgotten, as he pushed open the Rue St-Martin door, his parting words to Christie, and how they must have sounded to her. He had forgotten also how he must look. He merely glanced up on hearing bare feet on the floorboards, and saw the expression on her face.

He found what he hoped was a reassuring smile, and pulled Blaise's handkerchief from inside his doublet, and saw her stare, first at the handkerchief, and then at him. He thought for a moment that she was going to cry, but she did not. Instead, she said, in a choked sort of voice, 'I'll get some water,' and ran off to the kitchen.

She returned shortly with a bowl of water and some cloths.

By then Luke had gone to his bedchamber, and he had begun to pull off his doublet. Hers were not the only hands that were shaking as Christie began to dab gently at the cut on his face. He wanted to say something comforting, but he found that he had no words left. He began to struggle with his left hand with the laces of his shirt, but she said, sharply, 'I'll do that,' and unknotted them for him. Her eyes were very dark, shining; he felt her hair brush against his face as she bent to undo the knots. She was wearing a loose robe, with a shawl round her shoulders, but she did not look as though she had slept. He found himself focusing on the skin of her neck, noticing that it was fine and slightly freckled. He was, he thought, still a little drunk.

His elbow was a bruised, swollen mess. He thought again that she was going to cry when she saw it, so he grinned, and said, cheerfully,

'The tree came off worst. Smashed to smithereens.'

Christie did not smile. 'You should see a physician,' she said, when she had finished bandaging it. 'You might have broken something.'

'I doubt it.' The sun was beginning to filter through the kitchen windows. Luke could hear a bird outside, announcing the Parisian spring. He felt intoxicated with success; the past, the future, the present, all seemed, for a moment, perfect. 'We'll go home, Christie,' he said, taking her hand. 'I'll take you home tomorrow.'

Slipping from his grasp, she walked to the window, her face away from his. He rose and followed her. His limbs had already begun to ache; he put his hand on her shoulder, and saw that her eyes were bleak, her face infinitely sad. 'You could go on looking forever, my dear,' he said, gently, 'and it would destroy you.'

She dropped her head, shaking it slightly. He knew what defeat must mean to her; he, too, had recently glimpsed that awful emptiness. The shawl slithered in a rush of silk and colour to the floor, but she did not stoop to pick it up, she remained as still and white as the statues outside the King's hunting-lodge. Luke's hand moved inevitably towards the warm curve of her neck; his head throbbed with exhaustion and alcohol. The golden notes of a spinet echoed in the distance: *Thou shalt be Lady of Castles and Towres, follow my love, come over the strand* . . . and, sliding back the ruffled collar of her nightgown, he bent his head and kissed her bare shoulder. Her skin smelled warm and clean, her hair was as soft as silk. She did not push him away this time; he felt her whole body quiver, and then she turned, deliberately, so that his palms ran up the length of her arms and round her narrow back. He had just enough sense left to hear Emilie stir in the next room, and to kick the bedchamber door shut. Standing by the bed he had not slept in for weeks, Christie's fingers touched Luke's face cautiously, delicately, as though she was afraid she might hurt him. She had upraised her own face, her lips were slightly parted. He felt his heart begin to pound faster as he bent to kiss her. It was like drinking clean spring water after a surfeit of champagne; he was drowning, and it was the most delightful sensation he had ever experienced. His left hand unlooped the laces at the front of her nightgown, and he felt her shiver again as he touched the skin of her belly and slid his hand to cup the full, round breast.

He, who had strung devious ciphers across continents, had not a coherent thought as he laid her on the bed. The sunlight streamed through the unshuttered windows, Emilie sang and spilled flour in the kitchen, the streets of Paris stirred and came to life. But Luke could hear only the rustling of taffeta bedclothes, the small movements of hand and mouth, skin and hair, and Christie's own voice, small and distant, as he caressed her. *Oh, my love, my love.* He could see only her rich, chestnut hair, her gentle dark eyes, and her soft, infinitely generous body. He stayed awake long enough afterwards to be sure that she, too, was content, and then he closed his eyes, and slept immediately.

Chapter Fifteen

*A*N hour later, Mouche at her side, Blaise Lamarque's map clutched in her hand, Christie walked through the rabbit's warren of streets and alleyways that crowded the Left Bank of the Seine.

She had not slept at all: she had left Luke asleep on the bed, drawing the shutters closed before she went, so that the room returned to darkness. She could have stayed there forever, watching him, waiting silently for him to wake, but she knew that she must not. They might leave Paris within a day, and she owed it to Arbel, to Margaret, even to Anne Forster who had brought her up, not to throw away this last, unexpected chance.

Christie did not feel hopeful. She knew now that the trail had grown cold. She and Arbel, living with Anne's increasing irrationality, had fantasized about the past, painting princes and palaces, secrets and revelations. Instead, there was only the commonplace, inevitable truth. Her mother had lain with a man she had loved, and had subsequently born a child out of wedlock. She had sent that child to Protestant England for safety, and she herself had died in the wars of religion.

Today, walking through the cold, shimmering Paris morning, neither the future nor the past bore any fears for Christie. Sunlight glittered on the dark waters of the Seine, there was a haze of green on the river banks and gardens, marking the beginnings of spring. You needed just one person to keep you from being lonely, and she had found that one person.

The spring sunshine echoed her happiness. She recalled Luke's gentleness, and the passion that she had found to match his. She, who had discounted love as improbable, had discovered it in full measure. And it transformed everything, rendering even this last search unimportant. It was all she could do to concentrate on the map she clutched in her hand.

The tall houses, lines of washing from the windows festooning the patch of sky overhead, crowded towards each other, their paint flaked and peeling. Mouche, at her side, kicked stones into the gutter, and cursed the ragged children who ran into their path. Dogs rooted for scraps at the roadsides, mutilated casualties of the civil wars lay against doorways, begging bowls to their sides. But still, it all seemed glazed with a layer of happiness. Christie smiled at the children and found a coin for the soldier's bowl. Mouche had his dagger in his hand. 'We're nearly there,' said Christie, encouragingly, and Mouche scowled. 'We'll be home by midday, and Emilie's making rabbit pie and –'

They had turned the corner, following the last of the tiny arrows on Blaise Lamarque's map. 'Pigs' trotters,' said Christie, breathlessly, and stood absolutely still, just looking.

The alleyway was narrow, hilly, edged with weeds. The first dandelions were already breaking through the compacted earth. Because of the incline of the road, there were steps leading up to the doors of the houses, iron railings to the side of the steps. The windows of the houses were small, some of the hinges of the shutters were broken so that they hung at an angle, the crudely carved hearts, diamonds and fleur-de-lis staring drunkenly at the sky.

She had been here before.

And if it all looked so much smaller, dirtier, less glorious than the image of her memory, then she knew that she must imagine herself eight years old, the height of that uppermost step, with the limited experience and greater wonder of childhood. Slowly, Christie gazed at every house, every tiny, cabbage-filled garden, every inch of the dirt road. She knew that Mouche, beside her, was staring at her, yet she could not speak. She could hardly see, it was all blurred, and yet, when she closed her eyes, all she could hear was the sound of horse's hooves, coming nearer.

Christie took a deep breath, and said, feebly,

'Number fourteen, Mouche. Can you find number fourteen?'

She saw him run off to ask a ragged child making mud pies in the gutter. She had taught him his numbers, and was trying to teach him his alphabet. When the time came, she wanted to leave Mouche with something other than a patched coat and a pair of gloves.

He returned, pointing to a faded green door just ahead of them. If she sat at the top of those steps she would see the past's frozen picture, shockingly brought to life. It was hard even to climb the steps, harder still to fist her hand and knock at the door.

For a long moment she thought that the house was empty. That would have been unbearable; she did not think she could have survived the walk back to the Rue St-Martin. But at last there were sounds of movement from within, and the door opened slowly.

Christie did not recognize the old, lined face that peered at her from under a black shawl. But she saw the unmistakable flicker of recognition in the dark eyes. Hooded eyes, black and Italian, the eyelashes thinned by age to almost nothing, the brows mere pencil sketches.

'Madame Quirini?' said Christie.

'Christiane,' whispered the woman, and embraced her.

CHRISTIE was given a seat by the fire, and a glass of watered wine. She could not drink because the glass shook when she lifted it, so instead she looked around her. Her eyes seemed to jerk, unable to settle on anything. The room was small and dark, the plaster uneven and patchy. There was a crucifix on one wall, with a picture and a posy of primroses beneath it. Once she had arranged flowers in that same chipped pottery flask; violets and bluebells and lilies of the valley. And she had sat at that table, studying the cloth that was still spread over it: phoenixes, wings flaring from a fading fire, prancing griffins and manticores, their vivid colours lightened, their feathered bodies almost threadbare. The past was reality, now, no longer an illusion, and it frightened her.

'You came back,' Lucrezia had sat down opposite Christie. Her eyes, bright and intense, were fixed on Christie's face. 'I knew you would, some day. You are grown into a very fine lady, Christiane. You look so like your mother.'

In Christie's cupped hands the wine in the goblet wavered and slid, as if pulled by miniature tidal forces. She thought that when she spoke, her voice would be as feeble as the old nurse's.

'I wanted to ask you what happened. To my mother. And why I was sent away. And who –'

Her words faded away to silence. The shawl had slipped back from Lucrezia's head; Christie could see the scalp through the fine white strands of hair. Some old ladies grew slow and obese; others seemed to reject the world, their bodies refining and retreating in preparation for death. Life remained only in Lucrezia's eyes.

'It was your mother who told me to send you to England – she could not care for you, my dear, she was too sick. She had never been strong, and the troubles were the end of her. All that hiding in attics and cellars – she was not made for that. I hid you in a chest of old clothes once – do you remember that, Christiane? There were men at the door so I put you in the bottom of a chest, and tucked your mother's gowns over you.'

A musty smell, and cold, cold satin against her face. Hands beating at the door, shouting voices. Outside, smoke clouding the streets, forcing its way into the cracks round doors and windows. Christie closed her eyes very tightly.

'They never found you, though. I am a Catholic, you see, so they left me alone.'

She opened her eyes. The old woman added, proudly,

'It was my job to look after you and your mother. What did it matter that we attended different churches?'

The picture on the wall, a crude black and white woodcut, was of the Virgin Mary.

There was a silence. Outside, Christie could hear a cart rattling up the street, and the scrape of Mouche's knife as he sharpened it against the stone step. If she fixed her eyes on the small fire in the grate, she could still hear the sound of boots on cobbles and men's voices, coming nearer, swords clattering against the steps. But the fear had begun to retreat, to be placed where it belonged, in the past.

'I lived here,' said Christie, uncertainly.

Lucrezia smiled. 'You remember, petite? Yes, you stayed

with me for several months. I used to send you round the corner to Monsieur Jacques for the bread. You liked to run errands.' Her voice grew softer, almost inaudible. 'You went away in the spring. It was very quiet when you were gone . . . not that you were ever a noisy child. You were always a good girl, Christiane . . .'

The old woman's head had drooped a little. 'But my mother?' Christie prompted. 'My mother did not live here?'

'Of course not, petite.' The question seemed to surprise the nurse. 'She went to Geneva, poor lady. She knew she had not long to live. She knew that you would be safe in England, but she found it very hard to leave you behind.'

'So she's dead. My mother is dead.'

She hardly needed to ask the question. She had suffered that same grief a hundred times; surely there must soon be an end to it. The tone of the old woman's voice had told her everything. Christie fumbled blindly inside her pocket for the ring.

Rising from her chair, she knelt by Lucrezia's side.

'Your mother died of the consumption in '73, in Geneva,' said the old woman, gently, touching Christie's chestnut hair.

Christie opened her palm.

The old eyes focused on the ring, the twisted fingers, reduced almost to transparency with age, took it from her.

'Madame's ring. I have other jewels of hers, my dear. I kept them for you.'

Rising slowly, Lucrezia disappeared into the back room. When she returned, she carried a small wooden box in her hands.

'I hid it behind two loose bricks in the fireplace.' The ghost of a grin distorted the translucent skin. 'This is not an honest neighbourhood.'

The lid of the box was carved and powdered with brick dust. When Lucrezia lifted the lid, the dust scattered to the floor like ash.

'There are only a few things left now. I tried to keep everything for you, Christiane, but these have been hard times.'

Christie could see rolled papers, strands of beads, a purse. The old hands feathered air, and then reached hesitantly into the box, as if uncertain what to touch first.

'This necklace matches your ring.' Gold and jet: a tiny seed pearl like a teardrop between each black bead. 'It is Italian. As I am.'

'But my mother was French . . .'

The old woman nodded. 'Oh, yes, your mother was French. But your father was a great traveller. He had been to Italy, to Spain; even, I believe, to the East. These pearls are from the great city of Venice, and this bracelet is made from gold mined by the heathens of the New World. He took me from Venice, to look after your mother. I have never been home since.'

Lucrezia's voice had taken on the unnatural slowness of a dream. Her eyes had half closed, the jewels – coral, lapis lazuli, filigreed silver – were still spread out on her faded black skirts. 'I was waiting for him, Christiane,' she said. 'Is he dead?'

Slowly, Christie's gaze moved from the jewels to the old woman's face. She did not know the answer, she barely understood the question. Her voice was hoarse, painful.

'I don't know. How could I? I am illegitimate –'

The lids stretched open again. The nurse's eyes were dark and angry.

'Illegitimate? Nonsense, my dear. The marriage was hidden, it is true, but look –'

Lucrezia took one of the rolls of paper from the chest, and said, 'This is the certificate of marriage.'

By the time they returned to the Rue St-Martin, Christie knew that the spring had been false.

Winter had returned in rushes and trickles as she had walked out of Lucrezia Quirini's door, and made her way back from the Left Bank to the Right. Winter had found her soul, chilling all the wild happiness of the morning, frosting her hopes for the future before they had time to flower. She had been glad, then, that Mouche, as usual, hardly spoke, glad of the mindless activity of putting one foot in front of the other.

She must leave Paris today, and she must leave without seeing Luke.

She carried the box hidden under her cloak, but she had torn the paper into the smallest pieces and cast them into the

Seine. She had not stayed to watch the white fragments ebb and part, the old ink run into the water so that their secret was lost forever. As she walked, her thoughts were as scattered and disjointed as those tiny snowflakes on dark water. The implications crowded in on her, each one more unbearable than the last. Her horror was unfocused, but she knew where it led. She had no home now.

Most of all, though, she regretted the events of the previous night. A mere hour ago she had not thought that regret was possible; she had believed, as Catherine Ridley had presumably once believed, that the pleasure was worth any pain. Stumbling over cobbles and ruts, Christie learned that belief to be false, and she suspected that, long ago, Catherine had discovered the same.

Because she was married to Luke Ridley, now; legally, and in the eyes of the Church. She bowed her head, and the tears streamed down her face. What had happened last night had bound her and Luke forever. And that could not be, it must not be.

In Northumberland, Arbel told her husband of her forthcoming child.

They were dining at the Warden's house in Alnwick. There were twenty-five to dinner, so Arbel had to shout her glad news almost the entire length of the table. 'I'm as sick as a dog,' she called, scratching her shivering Dowzabel's neck, 'but at least my hair isn't falling out.'

Stephen Ridley took the news with visible pleasure. Congratulations rained upon him. He did not appear to notice – and no-one else commented – on the fact that his young wife had put down her spoon and knife and was feeding her entire meal, a morsel at a time, to her dog. An heir for Black Law, the men said, and the women, looking at Arbel, secretly doubted that she would ever produce a healthy son. But they raised their glasses to Stephen and Arbel and the future child, and warded off the winter and the future in drinking and dancing.

When they had ridden back to Black Law, Stephen took the dog from his wife's arms, and handed her down from the saddle, letting the stable-boy take the horses. Inside, the Great Hall was tidy and free of dust, and the fire was lit, so that its red light picked out all Davey's tapestries and treasures.

'Never,' said Stephen, when he had dismissed the waiting servant, 'will you make yourself ridiculous again. Because when you make yourself ridiculous, Arbel, you make me ridiculous too.'

She did not answer. Dowzabel, her lead still grasped in Stephen's hand, was crouching on one of the Turkey rugs. Arbel was fiddling with the lace of her ruff; her eyes, a dark, luminous grey, darted round the room, resting on each object in turn before, growing bored, they drifted to the next.

'You're not listening, are you, Arbel?'

She did not appear to have heard him. A small smile had begun to play about her lips; she was humming tunelessly. Over the fresh rushes and scented candles that perfumed Black Law's Great Hall, another odour asserted itself, sour and pungent. Stephen turned, and saw the dark stain spreading across the rug from between Dowzabel's legs.

'I'll *make* you listen,' he said. 'Look, Arbel.'

He had the dog by the scruff of the neck in one hand, his knife in the other. When he drew the knife across the creature's throat, a red line could be seen through the patchy fur.

Still, she said nothing.

Stooping, Arbel took the dog from where he had dropped it on to the floor. Holding it to her breast, she closed the dead eyes with infinite care. Then she turned, small and dignified, the front of her yellow satin gown patched with blood, and went up the stairs.

LUKE awoke to an empty bed and the sunlight pouring through the gaps in the shutters.

Opening the shutters, he guessed it past midday. The bed was a crumpled mess, but Christie's robe and slippers were gone from the floor, Christie herself no more than a memory shaped by the hollow in the pillow, the fallen shawl on the polished boards. He knew, instinctively, that he had slept too long.

279

Pulling on his clothes, he found Emilie in the kitchen. She was doing something unspeakable with pigs' trotters: she looked up at Luke and said that she thought Madame had gone out, that morning, and no, she did not know where. Then she sniffed, and wiped her nose with the back of her hand, and returned to the pigs' trotters.

Luke's unease increased when he found Mouche in the courtyard, sitting on an empty barrel, aimlessly throwing his knife across the cobbles. When the knife had stuck in the patch of dirt across the courtyard, he would rise and fetch it and return to the barrel before throwing it again. It occurred to Luke that if Mouche had known how to cry, he would be crying now.

He went silently to the boy's side, and took his arm before he could run away to the warren of alleyways and courtyards beyond Les Halles.

'Madame,' he said, softly. 'Where is she?'

Mouche sniffed. 'Gone away.' He spat on to the cobbles.

'Gone away – where?'

Mouche spat again, and this time the spittle landed on Luke's doublet.

Luke said, 'She's left Paris, hasn't she? Why, Mouche?'

'Dunno.' The boy's head was taut, his eyes narrowed. 'Something that old bitch said.

LUKE found the house easily; indeed, he had ridden past it on his way to Theodore Brune's printing shop. He left Mouche outside with the horse, and knocked at the painted green door. A woman's voice called, 'Go away! I am not well,' and he tried the door and found that it was open.

She was in a small truckle bed in the back room. There was the smell of death and decay and poverty, and the old woman, propped in the bed with pillows and rolled up blankets. He knew immediately who she was, because she had a servant's worn, lined hands, and dark Italian eyes.

'Lucrezia,' he said.

She did not attempt to rise from the bed, but said, her voice surprisingly firm, 'You have the advantage of me, young man.'

'My name is Lucas Ridley.'

He saw her eyes flicker at the name, Ridley.

'Are you Davey's son?' she said.

He had to draw up a stool and sit then, for his own legs suddenly felt as wasted and spindly as hers.

She added, frowning, 'You don't look like him. You haven't his eyes.'

Luke managed to shake his head. 'I have no Ridley blood, madame. Davey Ridley brought me up, but he was not my father. My mother was married at one time to Davey's cousin. That's all.'

Her eyes had closed. He thought he could see the pupils beneath her papery eyelids. 'They are all dead, then,' she said to herself.

It was cold in the room. Luke found that he had recovered the use of his legs, so he bent to light her a fire, breaking a bundle of twigs for kindling, searching through the basket for small, dry pieces of wood.

'Davey died – oh, nine years ago,' he said, his back to the old woman. 'His father had died the year before. And Grace in '77. Black Law belongs to Stephen now.'

His hands fumbled as he tried to strike the tinder.

'Grace? Who was she?' asked the old woman.

'Davey's wife.'

He heard the hiss of breath rapidly expelled from her body. Luke turned, doubting that so frail a frame could survive such a rapid exhalation. But she had raised herself on the pillows, and was glaring at him, her eyes unmistakably angry.

'His *wife*?' she said. 'Nonsense, sir! *Louise* was David Ridley's wife!'

He just managed to keep hold of the tinder. He kept on trying to strike it, because the repetitive action helped him, but there was no flame. He made his voice remain level, unthreatening.

'Davey married Grace in 1572. On All Saints' Day. She died five years later. They had no children.'

He thought for a moment that she was going to spit, like Mouche. The tinder sparked at last, catching the dead leaves and moss. The sudden smoke from the badly draughted chimney was suffocating; it made him want to choke.

'Louise. Louise Girouard,' he said, at last. 'You are saying that Davey Ridley was married to Christie's mother?'

The glaring eyes softened a little.

'Christie is my wife,' Luke added, softly.

She had sunk back on the pillow. He blew on the kindling so that it glowed red, and then flared into flame.

'Christiane was here this morning,' whispered the old woman, exhausted. 'I thought she knew. She is David Ridley's legitimate daughter.'

THE cold air hit Luke full in the face when he walked out into the street.

He had built up the old woman's fire, put a cup of wine and a piece of bread at her bedside, and left money on the mantelpiece. His tongue and limbs had worked like one of Davey's automata: jerkily, with an obvious effort, obeying routine, not thought.

In the street, though, even routine left him. He walked as fast as he could away from the house, seeing neither the people who cleared from his path, nor Mouche behind, leading his horse. He stopped at the banks of the Seine, however, because he was, he thought wearily, going to be sick. Sitting down on the damp grass that edged the river, he let the nausea slowly retreat while the events of the past rattled through his head like a litany.

The nurse had told him that Davey had married Louise Girouard in 1564. Christie had been born a year later. Louise had been French, and a Huguenot; Davey's father an unrepentant Catholic with an unwavering mistrust of all foreigners. So Davey, to avoid disinheritance, had kept the marriage secret, awaiting his father's death. Davey had disliked conflict and criticism: he had enjoyed the approval of almost everyone. Especially women. All women had loved Davey Ridley. Grace, Louise, Margaret, Anne Forster . . .

Luke had picked up a few flat stones; one by one he threw them, watching them bounce on the flat dark water. Facts, not

282

emotions. He had taught himself long ago not to be swayed by anger, or indignity. By putting aside pride, he had made himself almost inviolable. If you did not appear to care about your parentage or your patrimony, then people ceased to use it as a taunt. Except Stephen, of course, things had always been different with Stephen. But he would not think about Stephen. Not yet.

The past. Study it as coldly as you would a cipher. In 1572, after the massacre of St Bartholomew, Davey must have believed his wife and daughter dead. He would have written, inquired, perhaps even searched the chaos of Paris himself, and, maybe, mourned a little. Only a little, for Davey had not liked unhappiness. Finding no-one, he had married Grace Collingwood with his father's approval, so securing his inheritance. And, in his way, Davey had loved Grace, who had been gentle and kind and prepared to turn a blind eye to his flirtations with the kitchen-maids and village girls.

And then, in the spring, Davey had discovered that his wife and daughter were alive. What then? *Think*, Lucas. Yes – bring the daughter to England, well out of harm's way in the South, where no Ridley would know of her existence. To safety with Anne Forster, as a companion for Anne's own wayward daughter, Arbel. And Anne, loving Davey, and having a similarly generous, careless nature, had agreed. Shortly afterwards Louise had died in Geneva, releasing Davey from some of the guilt of a bigamous marriage. Yet he had not then acknowledged Christie, because there was still, after all, Grace. He would have meant to, thought Luke, his eyes fixed, but not focusing on the fishing-boats and barges; he would have meant to, and yet put it off, and off, and off, until eventually a Scottish arrow kept his secret safe forever.

Giving Stephen Black Law. Which should have been Christie's.

Now he must think of Stephen. Black Law, land and house, and all its eccentric contents, were Stephen's, lovingly preserved, jealously guarded. Stephen had rubbed Luke's nose in the reality of that inheritance for as long as Luke could remember. What was Stephen if he was not chief of the name of

Ridley, if he was not master of Black Law? Disinherited, he would be little better than a nameless bastard.

The last of the stones slid from Luke's fingers; he watched his hands begin to shake like quaking-grass. If he had ever wanted vengeance for all the small, terrible tortures of childhood, then now he had that vengeance within his grasp. Stephen's wealth, Stephen's power, Stephen's ability to reduce Luke, if sober, to humiliated silence. He could, if he wished, destroy Stephen, as Stephen had sought, slowly, to destroy him.

As Stephen would destroy anyone who offended or challenged him. Luke had never been a person to Stephen, he had been a living embodiment of promiscuity. His existence had disgusted Stephen. He had lost his innocence when Stephen, ten years older than he, had taken him to the stables and made him peep through the chinks in the stone. A groom and a kitchen-maid, enlivening the long winter months. Stephen's fingers forced against his neck, rough stone grazing his eight-year-old forehead and eight-year-old nose. *That's how you were got, Lucas, that's how you were got.* It had been years later that he had found his only means of defence: to exaggerate the very traits that Stephen loathed. Intemperance, insobriety, carnality. Sins of the flesh: Stephen had no flesh, Stephen's sins were the colder ones of possessiveness and pride. Loss of possession would destroy Stephen.

His hands still shook. He felt his remaining strength drain away, and he thought that if he leaned just the slightest bit forward he would slide beneath the cold dark waters of the Seine. He thought: did Stephen *know*?

Think, Lucas. Was it possible? Stephen had hated Davey; if he had contained that hatred at all it had been for Grace's sake. Stephen, as far as he was able to love anyone, had loved Grace. The only other person Stephen had felt anything for had been his father. God knew how old David Ridley had managed to sire such disparate children as Davey, Margaret and Stephen. David Ridley had terrified Lucas, he had hidden behind furniture to avoid that awful eye. Was Stephen's hatred of Davey anything more than an inevitable clash of personalities, the equally inevitable envy of the younger brother for the elder? Had he known of Davey's ultimate carelessness?

Yes. *Yes*, damn it. Because in Northumberland, someone had tried to kill Christie Forster. At Catcleugh: the Trotters and their extra men, and their pistols, and that one rogue arrow scything through the darkness . . . Someone had followed Christie to Catcleugh, riding back across the hills to gather reinforcements. Someone, paid by Stephen, had intended her to die in the burning house, or with an arrow in her back. Just as, earlier in the summer, again under the cover of a raid, someone had found his way into Adderstone, into her bed-chamber.

But she was no longer Christie Girouard, adopted daughter of Anne Forster. She was Christie Ridley, a Ridley by birth and a Ridley by marriage. By a marriage valid in the eyes of both the Church and the law. Black Law was Christie's.

Black Law was Luke's.

He was only aware that he had sworn aloud, and in English, when the fisherman on the shore turned and stared at him. He rose, shakily, and saw Mouche behind him, still holding the horse's reins. He knew why Christie had run away. Black Law was Arbel's now, as well as Stephen's, and Christie would never, ever deprive Arbel of her home.

Then he was in the saddle and riding hell for leather across Paris.

It was dark by the time he knocked on Blaise Lamarque's door. Cressets hung over the doorway; the tall, half-timbered house swayed like a phantasm over the road. Inside, Blaise was not alone; inside, Blaise surveyed Luke's travel-worn clothes and untidy hair with surprise, and then amusement.

'A bad night, chéri?'

The night had become Christie's: it took an effort of recollection to remember the Bois de Vincennes, the hunting-lodge, the soldiers. Luke took the handkerchief from his pocket, and dropped it in Blaise's lap; the wildcat, stretched on the rug beside the chair, yawned, and showed its teeth.

'A word alone, if you please,' said Luke.

With a single graceful flick of the fingers, Blaise indicated the others in the room. 'I have company, I regret, chéri.'

There was no regret in his smooth voice. Luke took a single piece of paper from the inside of his doublet, and dropped that, too, into Blaise's open hands.

'It was drawn in London. At the French Ambassador's house.'

He spoke softly, so that only Blaise should hear. He watched Lamarque slowly unfold the paper, and then fold it again, and rise. The wildcat reached out a single clawed paw and scratched the ornate wooden chair.

They went to a small ante-room at the back of the house. The fire and candles were lit; on the walls hangings shimmered gently in an unseen draught.

Shutting the door behind him, Luke heard Blaise say, 'You are not a bookseller at all. You have scars on your ribs, and you were searching my bedchamber at the banquet. You, petit, are a spy.'

The drawl had gone from Blaise Lamarque's voice. Luke had no doubt that unless Blaise Lamarque chose to let him, he would not reach the front door alive. But his hand did not move towards his sword, only his muscles tensed in anticipation of struggle.

But Blaise Lamarque had not called for his servants. Seating himself in a carved armchair, he added, curiously, 'And neither do I think you are a Scotsman. I think you are English – from London?'

'Not London.' The most dangerous game of all. Luke found that he had forced back the shock of the afternoon's discovery; he needed all his faculties. 'The north of England. The Borders.'

One of Blaise Lamarque's elegant legs was slung over the other, his hand fingered his beardless chin.

'Bien. London is a dull city. An ageing, virgin queen whose courtiers will either grow fat with waiting, or find their heads on the block if they presume too far. I prefer kings, as you know. I prefer debauched, guilty kings who seek comfort in the arms of their mignons. What do you want of me?'

'Information,' said Luke. He could hear the sound of laughter in the distance. 'I believe we have an acquaintance in common. A Monsieur Cherelles.'

Blaise smiled. 'Monsieur Cherelles is a dullard and a fool. I am sorry to hear that you number him among your acquaintances.'

Luke knew now that he gambled.

'Monsieur Cherelles is not dull at all,' he said. 'Monsieur Cherelles, who is Secretary to the French Ambassador in London, is a fascinating man.'

'Ah.' Lamarque, folding his hands in front of him, assumed an expression of benevolence. 'Information about what, my dear?'

You felt like this just before you laid the brushwood to fire someone's tower. 'About France, about England, about Mary of Scotland,' said Luke. 'I wish to see the correspondence concerned with the relationship between all three. To do that, I need your help, Monsieur Lamarque.'

'There is no relationship.' The room was silent except for the crackling of the fire, the man's calm, cultured voice. 'Mary of Scotland grows old in Sheffield Castle. England and France exist in happy amity.'

'Henri de Valois is weak. There are powerful elements in France who might wish to encourage the Queen of Scots' release – who might, indeed, encourage her claim to the English throne. And there are others – the Spanish, the priests, the English Catholics – who might be happy to join with such Frenchmen.'

'Thus your interest in the tedious Monsieur Cherelles.' Blaise Lamarque shrugged. 'I regret, petit, that I cannot help you.'

Ah, but you can, Luke thought, watching the dark, saturnine face. 'You were Cherelles's lover,' he said, coolly. 'For the beauty of his face – for the pleasure of his company? I don't think so. You left London at the fall of the Sieur d'Aubigny. D'Aubigny was, of course, a creature of the Guises. I think that you acted – for a short space of time, at least – as an agent of the Guises, and with the fall of d'Aubigny you realized that the Guises's ambitious plans for Scotland and England would never succeed. I think that you have since discovered more direct routes to power.'

Blaise's mouth twisted in the smallest of smiles, and his head inclined. 'The Duc d'Epernon? Yes. I will admit that my allegiances have changed a little since I was in England. And I have succeeded, n'est ce pas? You have even helped me a little, chéri.'

Luke said, very softly, 'Then, perhaps you should return the favour.'

'Oh, I don't believe so.' Blaise's eyes were dark and gleeful. 'I do like beautiful things, but I have never been one to lose my head for beauty. I think, in fact, that our friendship has just ceased.'

There was a silence. Blaise Lamarque rose and stood by the fireside, his features drawn only by the orange flames.

Luke said, 'I am going back to England, Monsieur Lamarque. I am following my wife. Whom, if I may hazard a guess, you have recently helped.'

The underlighting of the fire gave Lamarque's face a demonic cast. 'She wished to be free of you, petit. She asked me for an escort.'

Luke made his voice level, his breath even, as he asked the next question.

'Did she say where she was going?'

Blaise turned, slowly.

'If she had, would I tell you?' He paused, considering. 'Yes, I rather think I would. The stifling institution of marriage seems an appropriate punishment for impudence. However, sadly, Madame Ridley did not see fit to tell me her destination. So you will make your journey alone.'

Luke shook his head. 'No. After all, what would the Duc d'Epernon think if he knew that you had worked for his rival, the Duke of Guise?'

The smile had gone from Blaise's face. But the voice was still gentle.

'How should he know? You can have found no evidence.'

'No. You don't indulge much in the written word, do you? However, I have a quantity of sketches such as the one I have shown you already. Drawn by an Englishman who worked as a servant at the Seigneur de la Mauvissière's house. Not enough, perhaps, but enough to make d'Epernon think, don't you agree? Trust is so important in these affairs. It would be a shame to jeopardize such a promising relationship – after all, you've worked so hard, haven't you? And as someone once said to me, evidence can be fabricated, if necessary. I am very good at fabricating evidence, Monsieur Lamarque.'

A second letter had dropped into Blaise Lamarque's hands. He unfolded it, and studied the uneven, ragged handwriting. 'I did not write this,' he said, softly.

'No.' Luke's voice was cheerful. 'I did. But it's good, don't you think?'

There was a silence. Then Blaise said,

'Do you think you will leave this house alive, my friend?'

'If I do not –' and this time it was Luke who smiled '– then the information I have left with the English Embassy will be sent to the Duc d'Epernon. Tomorrow.'

A lie, of course, but Blaise was not to know his own complicated, compromised relationship with the English Secretary of State.

'So clever,' said Blaise, gently. 'I take it that I am instructed to pack my bags?'

'And sail to England. A few interesting letters from the French Embassy in London, Monsieur Lamarque, and you may return to Paris and the patient Duc d'Epernon.'

He held his breath until he saw the Frenchman's dark head incline.

'The letters, I take it, to be forwarded to Sir Francis Walsingham?'

Luke nodded.

He stepped out into the light of the withdrawing-room, sweat on his scalp, his heart beating like a blacksmith's hammer.

CHRISTIE arrived at Gravesend ten days later. An easier journey, in some respects, than that memorable December one. They had had fair weather, so she had not been quite so sick. Though she would never be a good traveller: that was one thing, she thought, wryly, that she had not inherited from her father. But Blaise Lamarque's escort had smoothed away all the tedious problems that might beset a woman travelling alone.

No bandits or whorehouses, this time. She had felt, uncomfortably, on visiting Blaise Lamarque in Paris, that she was making a bargain with the Devil. *I will leave Paris today if you will provide me with money and an escort.* Leaving unsaid the true nature of the bargain: *I make no further claim to Luke Ridley.* Yet she had known by then that Luke could take care of himself. She had seen the joy in him when the Trotters had raided Catcleugh, and she had seen the same joy when he had returned from the Bois de Vincennes, and they had made love. Luke was the equal of Blaise Lamarque in any game, and she believed he would outplay him.

But as soon as she had seen the marriage certificate, Christie had known that what had taken place between herself and Luke must never happen again. Davey Ridley was her father; Davey Ridley was also the man who had taken in the orphaned Luke, had fed him, clothed him, treated him *as his own son.* What if, she had thought, holding that certificate with shaking hands, what if she was not Luke Ridley's distant adopted cousin – but his half-sister? *Le rossignol est mon père, la sirene elle est ma mère.* Catherine Ridley was the mermaid – but what if Davey Ridley had been the nightingale?

Throughout the cold, dull sea voyage, Christie thought of Davey Ridley. It helped to remember that Margaret had loved Davey. Margaret was now truly her aunt; Richie, Rob and Mark her cousins. Stephen Ridley her uncle. And they must never, ever know. She thought of Black Law as well. She mourned the home she had never had, the family she had never known. She did not mourn Luke, because she could not bear to think of Luke. Fragments of the past would come back, though, stiff and immobilized with time like Blaise Lamarque's wall-paintings. Luke at the fair, tucking her precious three sovereigns inside his jack. *It depends whether you like a gamble, Miss Forster* ... Luke at Catcleugh, with that awful cold, barely controlled temper, forcing his ring on to her finger. And then at the Trotter raid, picking her up and carrying her into the pele-house after she had tumbled down the steps. The voyage on board the *Elizabeth*, the brigands in the woods between Dieppe and Rouen. The icy valleys of the Bois de Vincennes, Luke's head against her shoulder as she played the spinet in the Duc d'Epernon's house. His arms around her, his lips on hers when they had made love. No. She must never think of that.

She had money enough to ask the master of the ship to find a reliable man to ride with her to London. All through the long ride to Shoreditch, she held a piece of paper, a single crumpled talisman, in the palm of her gloved hand. Nearing the outskirts of the city, Christie unfolded the paper and saw again, in Luke Ridley's handwriting, the name of Sarah Kemp.

MISTRESS Kemp was used to unexpected visitors. Sometimes they arrived by night, sometimes by day; some were drunk, others were sober. Occasionally they had sword wounds in their ribs.

The visitors were generally men, though. She was not used to unknown young ladies presenting themselves on her doorstep in the late evening. This young lady was soberly dressed, dark-haired and dark-eyed, and looked very tired. Sarah beckoned her in.

'If you're my new neighbour from across the road to complain about the noise, then I apologize and hope all can be repaired with a glass of canary and a spice cake.'

'I'm not from across the road.' The poor thing was shivering. 'I'm from France.'

'The spice cakes aren't that good.' Sarah studied her visitor curiously. 'What is your name, my dear?'

'Christiane –' said the young woman, and stopped. She looked utterly confused.

Sarah said, gently, 'I mean you no harm, Christiane. If you do not wish to give me your name, it really makes no odds.'

The visitor seemed to recover a little. 'It's just that I seem to have had several different names recently, Mistress Kemp. But I suppose that my name is Ridley.'

Sarah went to close the parlour door. Madrigals soared triumphantly through the door, and then fell apart as the alto failed to keep time.

'I know a gentleman of that name,' said Sarah, carefully. 'Lucas Ridley. He stayed here last October.'

Christiane Ridley's face was very pale. Eventually she said, 'Luke is my husband,' and then she began, as Sarah had thought she might, to cry.

Sarah took her visitor into the kitchen, which, in the evening, was always warm and private and comfortable, and sat her down. The kitchen was large, with copper pans and pewter dishes on the walls, and a roaring fire with settles grouped around it. She had dismissed the cook a half-hour before, so Sarah herself made Christie mulled wine and found her something to eat. She was not overtly curious, but the girl seemed to need to talk, and Sarah had always been a good listener. She listened to the description of the handfasting (a heathen custom, if ever she'd heard one), and nodded understandingly at Christie's tangled explanation of her need to discover the past. She thought, privately, that the past was best left alone, and the future, too. The present was generally quite troublesome enough. She listened, and did not show her dismay, to Christie's description of the marriage ceremony in Rouen, her painful search of the streets of Paris. She understood, eventually, the disastrous secret that Christie's search had uncovered. And throughout it all, she recalled Lucas Ridley: fair, blue-eyed Lucas Ridley, who had ornamented her house for almost a month. She had thought of him often, since. Sometimes she had regretted not taking him as her lover. Tonight she did not regret that. She did not believe he would have given this child her address if they had been lovers.

At the end of it all, when even the music of the singers had ceased, Sarah said, gently, 'You may stay here for as long as you wish, my dear. I've plenty of room.'

And then she added, 'Though I think that perhaps you should let him decide. Lucas. It may not be as bad as you fear. Property may be nothing to him. I thought that he had different gods.'

Christie shook her head. There was a bruised look around her eyes, she did not look as though she had slept properly for weeks. 'It's not the property,' she said. 'Luke and Stephen hate each other. I've seen it. Stephen taunts Luke with his birth and his poverty. How could Luke stomach that, knowing that things should be different? I could not ask it of him. It would destroy him.'

Sarah said nothing for a while. The fire was still crackling, but the noise of the city had ebbed away to silence. Then she said,

'If the marriage is one of name only, then you could have it dissolved. It's a tedious business, but it can be done.'

And Christie, covering her eyes with her palms, began to shake her head again. And all Sarah, understanding everything at last, could do was to put her arm round her shoulders, and pity her.

THOMAS Phelippes had not seen his beloved Sarah for a month. Thomas Phelippes had spent a dull, unpleasant few weeks haunting the harbours and seaports of the south east coast of England. Others watched in the north and the east: Sir Francis Walsingham did not want Phelippes too far from London.

He was no longer used to this sort of work. An unrepentant city-dweller, Phelippes wished himself back in Whitehall with his code-books and his ciphers, solving puzzles, sheltered from the bitter winds of reality. Dover was a foul place; it stank of fish and tar and, because of the wind, the girls hid everything worth seeing beneath scarves and shawls. Thomas Phelippes devised new ciphers as he watched the boats arrive in Dover harbour. Wonderful ciphers, impossible ciphers. Trellis ciphers, grilles, ciphers based on John Dee's abstruse esoteric cryptography. Ciphers built on Phelippes' own birthdate, his mother's birthdate, the Great Khan of China's birthdate. The abstruse manipulation of number and word kept him from insanity as he watched ship after dreary ship from the harbour-master's house.

Not that the month had been totally unsuccessful. They had found a priest on board a fishing-cog, had picked up an interesting bundle of letters and money from a French galliasse. But of Phelippes' special quarry, there had been no sign. Phelippes was growing impatient. He had followed that little game from the beginning, and he wished to be there at the end of it. Besides, he needed to show someone his best ciphers.

It was early evening when the *Margarita* put into Dover harbour. By then the light was fading, so Thomas Phelippes, stiff with boredom and inactivity, left the harbour-master's house to stand on the quayside. The wind had dropped a little, but the *Margarita* still scudded nicely into port, her small, fetching silhouette backed by the dying sun. The *Margarita* sailed from Dieppe, the harbour-master had told Thomas Phelippes, which made her particularly worth watching.

He was looking at first for a man and a woman. That had made his task a little easier: women were a rare sight on board ship. Standing on the quayside, his hands dug deep into his pockets, the collar of his doublet pulled up around his ears, Thomas Phelippes forgot the cold and the boredom, and studied the *Margarita*. She was a neat little three-masted galleon, well cared for, flying a French flag. Her sails and pennants twitched rhythmically in the breeze as the pilot called to the harbour-hands, and ropes snaked through the darkening air. Thomas could see the casks of French wine stacked against the gunwale, ready to be unloaded. He pulled his shapeless felt hat over his eyes, and wondered if the *Margarita* traded in any other sorts of cargo.

A woman. He was looking for a woman, who was young, dark-haired and French. And pretty. Thomas smiled a little to himself: of course she would be pretty. Narrowing his eyes, he studied the decks of the *Margarita* for such a woman, but could see only men, shapeless and undistinguished in their layers of shabby clothing. The setting sun drained their faces and clothing of colour; poverty completed the task, reducing them all to greyness. But there was no woman.

He did not yet turn for the solace of a Dover tavern. Thomas Phelippes was good at his job, thorough and conscientious. He continued to watch the ship, knowing that, from the harbour-master's house, other eyes watched him, waiting for a signal. The sun, pink and swollen, flared from behind a cloud, lighting the spars and rigging with scarlet. Men's heads and hands were gilded, as though the entire ship were Midas-touched.

But one of the heads seemed to stay bright a little longer then the others. Thomas Phelippes squinted and frowned, and then he began to whistle tunelessly under his breath. He watched the man for a while, and he found that he recognized him by the way he walked, the easy way he moved. The frown mutated slowly to a smile, and Thomas Phelippes raised his hand to his own watchers. He waited until he saw the harbour-master and his motley militia leave the house, and then he walked to stand at the foot of the *Margarita*'s gangway.

He knew that his quarry had seen him before he left the ship. The fair-haired man did not pause, though, or attempt to run, and Thomas Phelippes respected him for that. A small part of him regretted that this was necessary: a larger part enjoyed the continuation of a fascinating game.

He had taken six soldiers because he knew the man to be as slippery as a snake, and the Kent militia were poorly trained and pitifully armed. The defence of the country might one day rest on ploughboys such as these. When they were positioned, and his quarry had walked the length of the gangway, Thomas smiled, and said, 'Good evening, Mr Ridley. How nice of you to come back to us.'

Chapter Sixteen

ALL Fool's Day. They rode to London on the first of April, the Feast of All Fools, which was, thought Luke, very appropriate. The beginnings of spring were less appropriate: a sprinkling of celandines, pushing through the frosty earth, a linnet, singing paeons of joy for no reason in particular. Having spent an uncomfortable night in a cell in Dover Castle, Luke was not in the mood for spring. There were far too many unknowns, far too many variables, and the pace forced by Phelippes on the small cavalcade allowed no breath for singing. It would have allowed most men no time for thought, but Luke Ridley, who had spent most of his adult years in the saddle, thought unceasingly.

Phelippes had asked no questions; Luke knew that he would be saving the questions for his master. Which gave Luke a short, necessary breathing-space, to think and to plan. Who had betrayed him? How had Walsingham known him to be out of the country?

At midday they stopped at a Rochester tavern to change horses. The soldiers dined in the public room, Phelippes took Luke to a private parlour upstairs. The small window looked down to the courtyard, then beyond to the rolling Kent weald. The thick glass distorted the landscape so that the gentle hills seemed to rise up until they were the height of the Cheviots, white and grey in the dregs of a long winter. Luke blinked and, looking away, began to eat the food in front of him. He felt as though he had a dozen careful threads spun between his fingers, each one dependent on the integrity of the other. He must not lose his concentration.

He watched Thomas Phelippes pour him wine, and he was silent until Phelippes said, 'You are looking a little the worse for wear, Mr Ridley. Was it not a successful journey?'

His arm was more or less recovered; the white scar, fast fading, drew a pale line the length of his face.

'Moderately successful, Mr Phelippes,' he said. 'I am still waiting for the final outcome.'

Phelippes smiled, showing his crooked teeth.

'The final outcome is this, Mr Ridley. And then the Tower.'

Luke did not allow his expression to change. If you concentrated on the devious entanglements of the past, you had no time to consider the future.

'You were waiting for me, Mr Phelippes,' he said. It was a statement, not a question. 'How did you find out that I had left the country?'

Phelippes, running his hand through his sparse pale hair, settled back in his chair. He was looking pleased with himself. 'Can you not guess, sir? And I thought you so well informed.'

Not sufficiently well informed, it seemed. Although there had been circumstances that no one, surely, could have predicted. 'I was in France,' he reminded Phelippes, gently.

'Yes. Since December. You set sail for France on the galleon *Elizabeth* in mid-December. We searched the *Elizabeth* a fortnight past,' said Phelippes, wistfully, 'and found nothing but broadcloth. Does that surprise you, Mr Ridley?'

Luke, innocent-eyed, looked up at Thomas Phelippes. 'Mr Lawson, the master of the *Elizabeth* is a circumspect man. If you feel that he would do better trading in items other than broadcloth, then I'm sure he would be delighted to consider such a suggestion.'

There was a gleam of delight in Thomas Phelippes' pale, colourless eyes. His short, square fingers stopped twisting the frayed fastenings of his doublet. He said, 'We would need a sole trading agreement.'

Luke inclined his head. 'I don't believe that would present any problem. The trading routes are, after all, already set up. It is only a matter of directing the end product.'

Phelippes propped his elbows on the table and made a cat's-cradle of his fingers.

'The trade of the saltpetre man is a foul one, Mr Ridley. England has no natural source, so they have to gather the nitre from dovecotes, pigeon-lofts. I see no harm in easing a man's daily round, do you, sir?'

'None at all.' Insurance, thought Luke, but not enough. His neck depended on Henri Fagot.

He said again, 'How did you know, Mr Phelippes?'

'Through the Warden. We had a letter from Sir John Forster a month past. Forster, it seems, had the information from one of your relatives.'

Luke pushed his plate aside. It did not take a great deal of intellect to guess which relative. If he could not yet see the precise pattern, he knew, with something other than logic, that Stephen had deduced his involvement in espionage. And had used that knowledge for his own purpose.

'You did not travel to France alone.' Thomas Phelippes, rising, picked up his cloak and his battered felt hat from the chair. 'Where is your wife, Mr Ridley?'

The knot tightened a little further. So Stephen had also discovered that he and Christie had taken the same damn ship. And the handfasting? Yes, of course he must know of the handfasting. That was why he, Luke Ridley, was bound for the Tower.

'Your wife?' prompted Thomas Phelippes, opening the door. 'Where is she?'

'I really have no idea,' Luke said, softly. 'No idea at all.'

Sir Francis Walsingham was also interested in Christie.

Phelippes took his prisoner to Whitehall, not to Barnes. The vast brick buildings of Whitehall Palace sprawled over the acres between the Thames and St James's Park: gardens, tennis courts, cellars, banqueting-rooms and tiltyards, and all the busy offices of state. The early evening clatter and bustle of the city streets faded into silence as Thomas Phelippes led Luke through staterooms and ante-rooms. He could no longer hear the apprentice boys scuffling as they ran for the taverns, the street-sellers hawking the last of their wares. Not far away was the French Embassy and the tractable Mr Cherelles. Three hundred impossibly long miles away was Stephen, and Black Law.

Phelippes showed Luke into a small, warmly furnished room. He had thought that they might take him straight to the Tower of London, and he had steeled himself to withstand those confining stone walls, the darkness. But instead, Whitehall. A small reprieve. Looking up, he saw, with no surprise, that Sir Francis Walsingham sat behind the carved oak desk, quill pen in hand.

'I hear that we must congratulate you, Mr Ridley. I hear that you are married to a Frenchwoman.'

There was a slight but unmistakable emphasis on the word, *Frenchwoman*. Walsingham might as well have said viper, or polecat. All three spat venom.

'Christiane is half English,' said Luke, steadily. 'And, I must beg to point out, sir, that her French origins are wholly Huguenot. We were married by a Huguenot priest.'

'You were married,' said Walsingham, coldly, 'in November. A pagan ritual known as handfasting.'

Outside, the sky had begun to dim. Luke could not see the Tower, but he knew its dull, dark outline. He had no doubt now that Stephen knew of the handfasting, that Stephen had also known, for a long time, of the existence of Davey's daughter. He could almost admire the neatness of Stephen's arrangements. Luke to the Tower, and Christie – he must not yet think of what Stephen intended for Christie.

'The ceremony was regularized in December,' he said. 'I have the certificate of marriage, my lord.'

Walsingham did not reply, but his eyes continued to study Luke. He had aged in the few months since they had last met; the skin of his face seemed pinched and refined. There was a sheaf of papers on the table in front of him; more papers, all neatly labelled and categorized, crammed the shelves and bookcases around the room.

'The fact remains, Mr Ridley,' said Walsingham, 'that you left the country when I expressly forbade you to.'

Luke said, carefully, 'You asked me to carry out a task for you. To discover the identity of those behind the "Enterprise of England". In order to do that, I had to go to France.'

Walsingham smiled thinly. 'Your information, then, Mr

Ridley. Names and places, times and dates. Remember?'

Luke remembered. Only he was not ready yet; he had, somehow, to buy a little more time. 'I am not used to working under constraints. The only assurances of good faith that I can offer at present are a quantity of saltpetre and weapons, at present in Dieppe. There could be more if you want them.'

Small arms and saltpetre – necessary for gunpowder – had never been plentiful in England. Luke saw the brief gleam rise and then die again in Walsingham's dark, opaque eyes.

'But a few pistols and a pound of nitre are not enough, Mr Ridley, for an assurance of good faith. How am I to know that, had this meeting not taken place, you would not have sold them to the Catholic Scots – or the Spanish – or even to one of your own rebellious countrymen? Loyalty has, after all, never been your strongest suit.'

In another place, another situation, Luke might even have enjoyed such a conversation. Now, he could only feel the dark, confining walls smothering him, the hangman's rope tightening about his neck. He said, softly,

'What loyalty have I ever been allowed to show, Sir Francis? What sort of loyalty has England ever permitted the Borderer? We both know that when England has had need of the Borderer – at Flodden, at Pinkie – then the skills which you claim to despise have proved invaluable. Our loyalty is to our name, Sir Francis. I have no right to the name I bear. I have had to create my own loyalties.'

The evening's long shadows greyed the papers on the desk, making the small, neat script unreadable. Shadows stripped the remaining colour from Walsingham's face, reducing it to lifeless bones and hollows. Luke knew that this might be all the trial he was permitted.

'War with the Catholic powers is inevitable,' he added. 'All three of us know that. I am neither a particularly religious nor a particularly patriotic man, but, more than most, perhaps, I have seen what war does to people. The Borders have been at war for most of this century, Sir Francis. And because of that, the saltpetre and weapons are for England alone.'

There was a silence.

Then Walsingham, shuffling the papers on the desk in front of him, said, 'You can hardly expect me to place a great deal of value on your word, Mr Ridley. I had expected more of you. Our time is running out, you understand. A few weeks past we talked to Father Holt – you know, of course, that Father Holt is one of the most active of the Catholic priests. We apprehended the good father in Leith. The Scots, unfortunately, later let him escape, but not before we had examined him and copied his letters. Let me read to you from one of them, Mr Ridley.'

Walsingham picked up the paper in front of him. 'Holt confessed that the Pope and various Catholic princes intend – and I quote, Mr Ridley – *To make war on England in the cause of religion and for the benefit of Mary Queen of Scots.* Holt also told us that the Pope has already collected a large sum of money for this enterprise, and that Philip of Spain is strongly involved. He did not, even with considerable persuasion, tell us a great deal more. Which brings us back to our old problem, sir, of names and places, times and dates.'

During the silence that followed, Thomas Phelippes rose to light the candles.

He had woven clever games once, thought Luke, from France, to Scotland, to England. Sometimes he thought that he had overreached himself.

'I have an informant,' Luke said, at last. 'He is a Frenchman. The purpose of my journey to France was to find him.'

'And you took your wife? Really, Mr Ridley, it all seems a little unlikely.'

Luke did not answer, recalling with sudden vividness that last night in Paris. He had acted on impulse, then; he had unwittingly added the final twist to the intrigue that Davey had secretly begun so many years before. He did not want Christie to be a casualty of that intrigue.

He heard Walsingham say, 'And what is the name of your informant, Mr Ridley?'

'His name is Henri Fagot.'

The candles were lit; pools of light in the darkening room. '*Where,*' said Walsingham, softly, 'is your informant, Mr Ridley?'

'In the French Embassy.' And Luke found himself adding a brief, silent prayer that he spoke the truth. Henri Fagot was in the French Embassy, or he was back in Paris as Blaise Lamarque, or he had decided to put his considerable talents to some other, more profitable use. Luke had not seen him since Paris.

Sir Francis rose and walked to the window. The flares in the street corners were bright, the cressets on the barges spattered golden reflections on the black waters of the Thames. 'We are running out of time,' said Walsingham, and turned, his face shadowed, unreadable in the dying light.

'A fortnight, Mr Ridley,' he said. 'I give your Monsieur Fagot a fortnight. After that, I shall have to assume that you have continued your old trade of working for the highest bidder. And when next you talk, it shall be to someone who is a little less courteous.

'Meanwhile, of course, Mr Ridley, you will take up residence in the Tower. I would not wish to lose track of you again.'

IN Northumberland, spring was frequently a reluctant visitor, keeping well out of sight until May or June. At night, men on horseback still crossed the Border, their saddlebows loaded with casks and kirtles, a hundred sheep driven across the frozen moss in front of them. Snow still bleached the hills and fells, snow still lined the crenellations of Black Law's tower, dusting her boundary walls like loaf-sugar.

For Arbel, time had stilled to the minute rotations of the ship clock, the drip of water as the icicles lengthened, long and sharp, like daggers. Barely three months pregnant, the demands of the tiny invader in her belly had stripped the flesh from her bones, taken the strength from her blood. She spent most of her days in the room with the ship clock, her gown spilt around her on the hearth watching the miniature figures gyrate, the entire edifice heave and rock on its non-existent sea. Christie had gone to sea: Arbel remembered waving to her from the quayside. Sometimes she could not remember how long Christie had been gone: a day, a month, years. But she knew that she was alone, because Christie had gone away, and Dowzabel was dead. Stephen had killed Dowzabel: she would punish him for that. Sometimes, when she was very tired, Arbel thought it was Stephen who had taken Christie from her.

She still had her baby though. She loved her baby, even though it made her sick day and night, so sick that she brought up black bile. Sometimes she could not see how it could continue to grow when she was able to eat nothing, but grow it did; Arbel could already see the small swelling of her belly. Between the constant bouts of sickness she was exhausted. She could not recall when she had last walked the quarter mile between Black Law and the village, but it seemed a long time ago. The walls of Black Law castle had become the boundaries of her existence. The hills looked like painted hills, they were so still. Aunt Margaret had fussed and inquired about physicians when she had visited a fortnight ago. There was a physician, of course, Stephen had engaged one, but Arbel had sent him away when he had called. She did not trust physicians, they had killed her mother.

Today she sat on the rug in front of the fire, watching the ship clock. The clock and the fire were the only bright things in Black Law; everything else was dull and faded. The colours of the tapestries and pictures were subdued by the poor light of winter, the furnishings were darkly coloured. Arbel had always liked the sun, bright colours, warmth. Now she fed the fire with small sticks of dried wood, holding them until the flame caught and glowed, orange and amber and scarlet. When the fire became really hot, the centre would gleam pink and blue, and if she dropped rushes in it, or strands of her own long hair, they would blacken and shrivel and turn to nothing in an instant. Fire fascinated Arbel: once she put coals in the ship clock's cannon, so that it would truly shoot. After a great deal of spluttering and choking the tiny ball had shot out half the width of the room, the coals tumbling to the rug. The rug had begun to smoulder, and Arbel had watched it for a while, enjoying the way the fire consumed the whorls and chevrons etched in the faded thread. Eventually, she had stamped out the flames with her own small slippered feet. The soles of her feet had hurt afterwards, and there had been a black hole in the rug, and that wonderful dry warm smell of smoke.

*

THOMAS Phelippes, who had spent a dull month in Dover, and endured a long ride to London, decided to call on his beloved Sarah.

It was pitch-dark by the time he arrived in Shoreditch; horribly near-sighted, he swore as, for the third time, he slipped in the filth that clogged the gutters. It was not hard to find Sarah's house, though; a blind man could have found Sarah's house. The ethereal notes of a spinet filtered through the shutters, overlaid by the more earthy sounds of talk and laughter.

Inside, the manservant showed him to the withdrawing-room. Thomas was not in the least tired: it had been a fascinating day, and the raggle-taggle of musicians, players and poets did not trouble him. Crossing the room to where Sarah was seated in a carved chair, he bowed and kissed her hand.

As always, she did not question him about his absence. Taking the glass of wine the servant offered him, he remembered to compliment her on her gown (crimson silk over petticoats of dove grey, which suited her admirably, but then, thought Thomas, as he drank his wine, anything suited Sarah admirably). Seated at her side, her fingers threaded through his, he let his gaze travel the length of the room.

He knew Mark Faunt: he had spent many fine evenings drinking with Mark Faunt. He knew the players from the Swan rather better than he would have cared to admit to his employer. He knew the man with the bass viol, and the fair-haired woman who, in the daytime, served in a Bankside tavern. He did not, even when he squinted, know the spinet player.

The spinet player had dark hair, a smooth skin, and rather nice eyes.

Thomas Phelippes, who was not, like Sarah Kemp, incurious, said, 'Who is she? The girl at the spinet? Is she Mark's latest?'

Sarah turned, and smiled. 'No, my love. Her name is Christiane Ridley. She is the wife of your decorative associate. Remember?'

'*Christ*,' said Thomas Phelippes, and almost dropped his glass.

*

CHRISTIE was nearing the end of a long, complicated piece called 'The Carman's Whistle' when she realized that Sarah Kemp was standing beside her. When Sarah whispered that someone wished to speak to her, she rose, and followed Mistress Kemp to the small parlour at the back of the house.

Her legs shook slightly, because she could not think who, other than Luke, would wish to talk to her. But, of course, Sarah had promised, and besides, the man seated across the parlour was smaller, thinner, older than Luke.

She curtseyed and the man rose and bowed, and took her hand. 'Christiane Ridley – Thomas Phelippes,' said Sarah, who was looking uneasy. Sarah's lack of ease disturbed Christie: Sarah was the most easy, least shockable person Christie had ever met.

Thomas Phelippes was speaking.

'How long have you been in England, Mistress Ridley?'

'A week,' she said. A week in which she had found time to recover her breath, found time to accept the past, both near and distant, found time to begin to think about the future.

'You are French?'

'Half-French. My father was English.'

My father was Northumbrian. My father never acknowledged me, never gave me his name. Christie did not think that would ever cease to hurt.

'But you are a Protestant?'

She began, for the first time, to consider the profession of Mr Thomas Phelippes. His clothes, though worn and untidy, were made of good quality material; his fingers, she noticed, were stained with ink.

'My mother was a Huguenot. And besides, I have lived for the last ten years in England. And I attend church regularly, Mr Phelippes.'

Christie sat down on a stool by the fire, and watched Mr Phelippes warily. She saw that Sarah's expression had altered to impatience, and she heard her say, '*Thomas,*' and saw Thomas Phelippes wave his hand, and answer, 'One moment, my dear. One moment.'

Then he directed his gaze to Christie, and said, 'Are you

married to Lucas Ridley, of Catcleugh in Northumberland?'

She knew now that this inoffensive-looking man was every bit as dangerous as Blaise Lamarque; more so, perhaps. Her eyes met Sarah's, and Sarah said, stiffly, 'I will not have it, Thomas. Mistress Ridley is a guest in my house, and I will not have you question her here.'

Thomas Phelippes did not even look up. 'Better I question Mistress Ridley here than somewhere less comfortable,' he said, and Sarah, her eyes bright with anger, subsided.

Christie's heart was pounding rather rapidly. Mr Phelippes said, 'Well, Mistress Ridley?'

She nodded, and answered as calmly as she could, 'Luke and I were married in December. In France. In Rouen.'

For some reason, her answer seemed to please Mr Phelippes. He said, 'Do you know what trade your husband follows, Mistress Ridley?', and the beating of her heart became painful, her throat dry and constricted.

'He has a bastle-house on the Borders,' she answered, eventually. 'He follows the trade of most Borderers.'

'Yes, yes. Horse-theft and cattle-rustling,' said Phelippes impatiently. 'It has been the Borderer's way of life for nigh on a century. No doubt it will continue to be so for a few years yet. But I am not speaking of horse-theft, Mistress Ridley. Your husband has other, more unusual, talents.'

Despite the seat by the fire, Christie felt cold, as though the raw April weather had seeped through the snug timber and plaster of Sarah Kemp's home.

She looked up at Sarah, and Sarah, anger snapping in her grey eyes, said, 'Mr Phelippes works for Sir Francis Walsingham, my dear. The Queen's Secretary of State.'

Utter confusion replaced the fear. She glanced rapidly from Sarah to Phelippes. Mr Phelippes' small, pale eyes gleamed. Sarah looked furious. 'But so does Luke work for Sir Francis Walsingham,' said Christie, weakly. 'He told me.'

Thomas Phelippes leaned back in his chair, pressed his finger-tips together, and smiled. Sarah still looked cross.

Phelippes said, 'Then tell me why Mr Ridley went to Paris, my dear.'

So she told him, as simply as she was able, about Blaise Lamarque. And then, at his request, an edited version of her own search, and of the discovery that had made her leave France.

Phelippes' eyes had narrowed, but his voice had become more gentle. 'So what will you do now, mistress?'

Christie had had a week to find an answer to that question.

'I have a little money of my own, now – the sale of jewels from my mother. I must find somewhere to live, and some sort of employment. But first I must know whether my sister has married. And that she is safe and well.'

Mr Phelippes frowned and ruffled his hand through his lank yellow hair. His voice was slightly apologetic. 'I can help you, if you wish, with your sister. Someone can deliver a letter or make a few discreet inquiries, if you prefer. We have the facilities for that sort of thing.'

Thanking him, Christie accepted.

Phelippes added, curiously, 'You don't intend to live with your husband, then?'

Christie stared at the folds of her gown. 'I can't, Mr Phelippes,' she said, very quietly. 'Not ever.'

'Would you wish him to know where you are now?'

The pleats of silk seemed to have blurred a little. She shook her head. She could not lie to Luke Ridley, neither could she tell him that she was the daughter of the man who had brought him up. She was utterly trapped, and for a moment, despair threatened to overwhelm her. Then, as the implications of Mr Phelippes' last question began to sink in, she looked up, and saw that he no longer smiled, that there was even a little pity in those red-rimmed pale eyes.

It was hard to speak. 'Do you know where he is?'

The answer was distant.

'I'm afraid so,' said Thomas Phelippes. 'Lucas Ridley is in the Tower of London.'

HE was in the Salt Tower, where they often put traitors. Unfaithful consorts in the Queen's House, pretenders to the throne in the Beauchamp Tower, less ambitious traitors in the

Martin Tower or the Salt Tower. Unless you were a nobleman, you could look forward to the coyly termed 'question ordinary and extraordinary', involving such niceties as shackles, iron gloves, or manacles. Or the 'Scavenger's Daughter', a cage whose loving iron embrace squeezed the life out of you. Luke was not a nobleman.

If you were a nobleman, you had a comfortable bed and a table and decent food and wine. Luke's cell had a window, very high up, bare walls and a straw pallet. He could tell whether it was night or day, but little more. He could hear the wind and the rain, and the clanking and calling of the Warders on their rounds, but he could not see them. He could smell the stench of the Tower's dubious drains, but he had not seen the outside world since Thomas Phelippes had taken his leave of him at Traitors Gate. He had a few bruises as a legacy of that journey, from an utterly futile attempt at escape. He had a cell seven foot square to walk, and walk he did, a hundred circuits twice a day, trying not to lose count. He had food and wine because he had bribed the gaoler, but its appearance was irregular, and its quality poor.

Not that he felt like eating. He had no Dand's Jock with him, this time, no cards, no company. He did not mind solitariness – God knew, there was no more solitary place than Catcleugh – but he did not like walls, or bars. The prospect of torture and eventual death was unpleasant, but it was the confinement itself he found hardest to bear. Until Hermitage, he had been lucky; he had not even sampled the hospitality of Haddock's Hole in Berwick. Luck had recently become a scarce commodity: luck depended on the complex cobweb he had himself set up, and on that most unpredictable spider, Blaise Lamarque.

Someone – Thomas Phelippes, he thought – had left him pens and paper. The paper had remained unwritten on. Any letter to Margaret, for instance, telling her about Stephen, would have involved explaining Davey's secret marriage. He had some idea what Christie's visit to Blaise Lamarque, what her abrupt departure from Paris, must have cost her. If she wished the past to remain a secret, then he must respect her wishes. He did not, in any case, think her returned to Northumberland. She, unlike Davey, had not the easy charm, the natural amorality, to sustain a deception of that magnitude for any length of time. And she had not gone to Sarah Kemp: he had asked Thomas Phelippes that. He hoped she had gone back to Salisbury.

He had even thought, briefly, of writing to Stephen, to use his own knowledge in an attempt to constrain him. But, no: Stephen would simply have to threaten Arbel in order to control Christie. More innocent lives at risk. And besides, there was his own reluctance to confront Stephen. You are cousins, Davey had said, a long time ago. And though it had been a lie, and though most of Davey's life had been a lie, those words had lingered. Sitting curled up on the rank straw, Luke doubted if he would ever be able to walk through Black Law's gates and put a sword to Stephen's throat.

If he closed his eyes and shut out the poor light and the walls and the filth on the floor, he could see Catcleugh. He could feel the cold air, and hear the kestrel, and see his own land, green and purple and black, all around him.

A fortnight, thought Luke. A fortnight.

GREY days, the promise of spring lost in bitter winds, constant rain. Any ability that Christie had once possessed to plan her life, to try to erase the chaos of her early years, had gone, destroyed like the daffodils and snowdrops that lay battered at the roadsides. With Thomas Phelippes' words, life seemed to have frozen, locked into dreadful immobility. Minutes, hours, days passed: she helped Sarah in the kitchens, but her bread did not rise and her cakes sank in the middle. Letting herself be measured by Sarah's dressmaker for a new gown to replace the ones she had left behind in Paris, Christie held swatches of material and stared blankly at them, unable even to attempt to choose. Silk, satin, velvet; light colours, bright colours, dark colours, they were all the same. Sarah, eventually, took a jade green silk, and said, 'This will suit you very well, my dear,' and Christie had to walk to the window and dig her nails into her palms and think of anything but Blaise Lamarque's banquet, and the Bois de Vincennes, and herself and Luke looking down to the ice-covered valley.

The green silk gown had arrived that morning. Sarah had made her try it on, had then dressed her hair, and found her a pair of eardrops to wear. Steered to the long silver mirror, Christie had stared dully at the elegant reflection, the neat curls of chestnut hair, the dark eyes brightened by the pearls hanging from her ears. 'There is nothing like a new gown to lift the spirits,' Sarah had said, giving her a hug. Adding, 'And you shouldn't worry so much about him, my dear. I thought your husband a man most extraordinarily capable of looking after himself.'

She had then sent Christie out for a walk, ordering her to get some fresh air. The skies had finally cleared, but Christie still had to lift the skirts of the green gown in order to avoid the mud and dirt of the streets. London was crowded, reminding her of Paris. Often she found that she longed for the empty hills and pure air of Northumbria. Patches of blue smudged the grey sky, and the street-sellers called of bluebells and primroses, gillyflowers and violets. Violets, sweet violets, a voice sang, and on the horizon the Tower of London loomed, squat and ugly, its stone still wet with the departing rain. She thought of thumbscrews, chains and hot irons. Someone thrust a bunch of violets into her hands, and her fumbling fingers dropped them so that the tiny blossoms dropped to the gutter, bruised and broken. She stooped, but could not save them: they were borne away on a small, rushing yellow river. Finding a coin for the hawker, Christie almost ran back to Sarah Kemp's house.

Inside, Sarah sat Christie down in front of the parlour fire, and handed her a letter. It was signed by Thomas Phelippes, the handwriting neat and regular. Mr Phelippes was, he explained, too busy to visit. One of his men had made enquiries of Mistress Ridley's sister through a friend of her aunt, Margaret Forster. Mistress Forster's friend, a Mistress Grey, had talked to Phelippes' agent at great length.

The smile that the last sentence brought to Christie's face died as she read the next words.

'I regret that the news of your sister is not good. She is married, as you thought, to Stephen Ridley of Black Law, in the Middle Marches. She is with child, and her health is delicate. The marriage is not thought to be happy.'

There was a brief postscript after the signature.

'Of our other mutual acquaintance, I can assure you that he is well, and not mistreated. I will do what I can for him.'

THE information that Thomas Phelippes wanted arrived two days later. He took the letter first to Sir Francis Walsingham, laying the single misspelt piece of paper in front of him, while his face, refusing to obey him, continued to sport the most ridiculous grin.

But Walsingham, for once, answered his smile.

And when Phelippes, sitting down beside him, had found pen and paper, Walsingham began to dictate a note for the Lieutenant of the Tower of London.

HE had made marks in the stone wall with his ring, because he knew how easy it would be to lose track of time.

There were eleven scratches there already: Luke put the twelfth in carefully, the same height as the others, a measured distance apart. Hearing the footstep in the corridor outside, his stomach performed its accustomed gyration, and then he straightened, and stood beneath the window, watching the small square of light that illuminated the door.

There was the grating of a key in the lock, and then the door swung open.

Thomas Phelippes.

Too early, thought Luke, but managed to keep his breathing steady, his voice calm.

'Mr Phelippes. How delightful. I have been in need of company.'

Phelippes let the door close behind him. His doublet was half unlaced, his hair more than usually untidy. He held out a piece of paper.

'Ah, not pleasure,' said Luke, cheerfully. 'Business. Instructions for the Lieutenant of the Tower?'

Phelippes nodded. He seemed to have been running. Cracked thumbs and a sudden lengthening of the spine, thought Luke. A traitor's death. Stephen would be overjoyed.

'Your Pardon,' said Phelippes, recovering his breath. 'I brought it as soon as I could. This place –' and he glanced, wheezing, round the cell ' – is vile.'

Luke felt no joy, only a deep, drowning relief.

Sir Francis Walsingham's secretary grinned. 'We received a letter from a certain Henri Fagot, of the French Embassy. Misspelt and badly written, but it told us the names of the Englishmen who frequent the Seigneur de la Mauvissière's house. It also –' and for a moment Luke thought that Phelippes was going to embrace him '– tells us the names of those who are in correspondence with the Queen of Scots.'

He followed Phelippes out of the cell and to the Lieutenant, and then into the sunlight, beyond walls and bars, turrets and cannon. The sun pasted light on the crowded, crooked houses and shops, washed with light the broad meandering Thames.

They took a wherry from the Tower, and in the boat, Phelippes asked, 'What will you do now? We have work for you, should you wish it. And it would be well paid.'

An offer, not a demand. He might almost have accepted. 'A generous offer, Mr Phelippes – I thank you. But I have to find Christie first. My wife.'

Odd how easy those words had become. *My wife.* He heard Phelippes say, curiously, 'I thought your marriage to be one of convenience, Mr Ridley.'

'I wasn't as well informed as I should have been, Mr Phelippes. The marriage has put my wife into a position of danger, though she does not yet know it herself. I need to warn her.'

The wherry drew in at the wharf; Phelippes took a coin from his pocket.

Standing on the wharf, enjoying the wind against his face, Luke realized that Thomas Phelippes was looking at him. 'Christie Ridley is staying with Sarah Kemp,' said Phelippes bluntly.

Then, at last, he felt joy.

*

SARAH Kemp's heart, which had begun to beat a little erratically when Joseph had announced Lucas Ridley, stilled and resumed its accustomed calm. Putting aside her sewing, she rose from her chair.

She went to Luke, taking his hands in hers. He had lost weight; imprisonment had given him a greyness about the eyes, had aged him.

She would have loved him, though, white-haired and in sackcloth. 'I am glad to see you safely returned,' she said, and kissed him on the cheek. 'But Christie has gone – she rode from here two days past.'

Luke's fingers gripped hers until they began to hurt. Sarah saw the fear in his face, and knew that her own eyes had begun to mirror that fear. 'Where has she gone?' he said, hoarsely.

'She had a letter – about her sister –' said Sarah Kemp. And she felt her hands slide from his as she heard herself say,

'My dear – Christie has gone to her sister's house.'

Chapter Seventeen

FROM her bedchamber at Black Law, Arbel could see the Cheviots, white and featureless, rolling endlessly away into the distance. The hills were white, the sky was white: they seemed to circle over her, trapping her, small and insignificant, beneath them.

She had propped herself up with pillows so that she could see Black Law's courtyard and the wall with its single stout gate. She had given up going to the room with the ship clock, because she was too tired. Her hands and feet had swollen up, so that she could no longer wear her rings or squeeze her feet into her slippers. Arbel thought, looking dreamily down at herself, that pregnancy had made her grotesque: narrow stick-like arms topped with those disproportionately puffy hands. Her hands and feet and belly continued to grow while the rest of her was burned away. Aunt Margaret had thought she might be expecting twins. Arbel knew that Aunt Margaret had been here sometime because she had woken to find her sitting on the edge of her bed, but she could not remember when Aunt Margaret had been or gone, or why she had looked so worried. It made Arbel too tired to try and remember things like that.

She did not care that she had lost her looks, because she had never, as some might have thought, been vain. She had never considered her beauty; it made men behave in a particular way, which was useful sometimes, that was all. She had no need of men now, because she had her baby. Or babies. If she had a son and a daughter, she would never have to be so ill again. She would never have to sleep with her husband again, and that would delight both him and her. She had never forgiven Stephen that look of disgust, just as she would never forgive him for killing Dowzabel. There would be other men, Arbel knew, if she felt cold or lonely.

Propped on her pillows, she stared out of the window. There was a tray with food at her side, and she had forced herself to eat a few mouthfuls for the baby's sake. She herself, she thought, no longer needed food. Crumbling the rest of the bread and cheese, she opened the window-latch and scattered the food on the sill for the birds. Once a jay had come to her window-sill, a flash of blue feathers and bright black eyes, dancing and bobbing on the cold stone.

It was while the window was still open that Arbel saw the riders enter the gates. A man and a woman, their saddle-cloths bright against the dirty snow, the horses' breath making clouds in the frosty air. She did not recognize the man, and at first she thought that she did not know the woman. She could see dark hair folded neatly under a wide hood, and a jade green gown trailing elegantly over the horse's flanks. Then, Arbel, leaning further out of the window, focused on the rider's face. She began to smile, and found, to her surprise, that she was also crying. 'Christie!' called Arbel, waving the first thing that came to hand. A flounced silk petticoat unfurled from Black Law's tower window. *'Christie!'*

CHRISTIE could not, no matter how hard she tried, disguise the horror she felt on first seeing Arbel. They both sobbed together, and Christie hugged her sister tenderly, afraid that her embrace might snap the fragile bones, squeeze the remaining life out of that wasted figure. *Her health is delicate*, Thomas Phelippes' agent had written, but nothing had prepared Christie for those hollowed, haunted eyes, that distorted body.

Arbel insisted on dressing to celebrate Christie's return. The two halves of her buckrammed bodice would not meet: 'It's twins, Arbel said, gaily, and Christie's heart sank even further.

'You should rest,' she said, gently.

Arbel began to pull a comb through her loose, tangled hair. 'I've been resting all day. All week, I think. I feel so much better now you're back, Christie.'

Christie took the comb from Arbel's swollen fingers. 'I've come to look after you.' She began to carefully unloosen the tangles.

'Stephen says that you are married. To Luke Ridley.'

Christie's fingers did not pause in their task. Only her eyes began to ache a little. It seemed a betrayal to ride away from London, leaving Luke in the Tower. She could do nothing for him, she must not even see him, but it had still seemed a betrayal. She began to plait Arbel's hair.

'I want to hear about you, Arbel. Is Stephen happy about the baby?'

'He wants a son. I'd rather have a daughter.' Arbel turned, and grasped Christie's hands. 'I could call her Christiane, after you. Would you like that, Christie?'

She heard the sound of horse's hooves on the cobbled courtyard. Glancing out of the window, Christie saw Stephen Ridley, his hair bright Scots gold against the pallid landscape, his scarlet cloak a violent splash of colour in a land reduced to monochrome. Christie took one steadying indrawn breath, and then kissed Arbel's thin cheek.

'I would like that very much, my dear,' she said.

CHRISTIE had had a three-day start.

She had left London accompanied by a friend of Sarah Kemp's; she had, presumably, been sufficiently anxious about Arbel to hurry. Luke, too, hurried, changing horses frequently, barely pausing to eat, cursing himself when, in the early hours of the morning, his eyes began to close, and the reins to slip through his fingers.

His only grain of comfort was the thought that Stephen might not think it necessary to hurry. If Christie managed to keep up a sufficiently convincing pretence, if Stephen believed his unloved cousin to be conveniently incarcerated in the Tower of London, then Christie might be safe for a while. Stephen would choose his time, choose his method, overseeing it himself, presumably, in view of the botched attempts of the past. Luke knew how easy it was to make murder look like accident on the Borders.

So he spurred his horse through fields and valleys, along all the pot-holed tracks and paths that brought him back to the country of his birth. He did not see the villages and hamlets, churches and cottages: they were nothing more than a blur, irrelevant and fading. Luke saw only Black Law, the home that he had not returned to for more than five years, whose gates he had intended never to recross. He saw only Christie, and in Christie's face a sharp fleeting image of Davey, whom he, like too many others, had loved.

It was easy enough to avoid Stephen, because he, too, avoided her. Christie took most of her meals in Arbel's bedchamber, read to Arbel, talked to her about Paris and the past, tried to make her eat a little. The brief febrile energy that Christie's return had provoked had disappeared: Arbel had returned to her bed, her skin much the same colour as her pillow, her swollen fingers threaded through Christie's. She reminded Christie of Anne.

When she had seen Stephen, he had been courteous and considerate, inquiring after her health, expressing his own concern about Arbel. But his eyes still told Christie the same story: dark blue and cold, they studied her as though she was unclean, tainted with the supposed irregularity of her birth. Christie could not meet those eyes, she thought their own dreadful alchemy would inevitably uncover the truth.

On the third day of her stay at Black Law, Christie breakfasted early on her own in the withdrawing-room. Outside, it was a clear, bright day, but already the mullioned windows showed minute flakes of snow twisting down from the sky. The parlour was warm, though: the linenfold panelling kept out the dampness of the stone, and the large fire cast a warm light over the dark wooden table and chairs. Hearing the door open, she looked up and saw Stephen. Stephen had ridden out already that day: snow encrusted the soles of his boots, and his golden hair was feathered by the wind.

Greeting Christie, Stephen sat down opposite her. 'A long winter this year,' he said, smiling. 'Was it so in Paris?'

He never, Christie noticed, addressed her by her name. Neither Christie, nor Christiane, nor Miss Forster, nor Mistress Ridley. She managed to return the smile.

'It was growing warmer. The spring had begun before I left.'

And died again, she thought, but did not say.

Stephen said, slowly, 'Arbel told me that you went to Paris to look for your family. Did you find anything – anyone?'

Christie shook her head. She could not speak; carefully, she placed her spoon on the plate.

Stephen was silent for a moment, watching her. Then, 'How unfortunate,' he said, and rose. 'The wasted journey, I mean.'

He walked to the window. The sun had pushed through the thin clouds. 'I don't believe this weather will last,' said Stephen. 'So I propose another journey.'

He swung round. His dark eyes were bright, attentive; one hand gripped the bevelled sill. 'I'm concerned about my wife,' he added, softly. 'About Arbel. About my heir. I intend to ride to Adderstone today, to consult my sister, Margaret. These are women's matters – I know nothing of such things – so I would like you to come with me.'

Christie's mouth was dry. 'Arbel –' she said, uncertainly.

'The housekeeper will care for Arbel.' His voice was sharp, clipped. He added in gentler tones, 'We can return tonight, if you wish.'

She nodded again, and Stephen said, 'I will await you, then,' and left the room. Christie rose from the table, her knees shaking, her palms sweating. Yet she had no need to fear – if the prospect of returning to Adderstone unnerved her, if the prospect of a morning's ride with Stephen unnerved her even more, then those fears dissolved into unimportance when she thought of Arbel. And Luke. If he could endure the Tower of London, then she could endure Adderstone, and Stephen Ridley.

Christie ran to her room to fetch her cloak.

LUKE arrived at Black Law at midday, having spent most of four days and three nights in the saddle.

There were too many memories associated with the final, familiar, ride up the hill. Black Law, midway between castle and house, was backed by the dense might of the Cheviots, row upon row of rolling, white-crested hills. Luke recalled himself and Rob Forster, twelve years old, perhaps, discussing how they would take Black Law. Fifty riders and the biggest fire you ever saw. Black Law had been Ridley land for generations.

He rode through the gates as though he had left Black Law only yesterday, nodding to the old man sweeping snow in the courtyard, swinging from the saddle to loop his reins to the hitching-post. The house was quiet; the windows stared back at him, blank, black, dead. He made himself walk to the great doorway, made himself beat upon the door.

He recognized the woman who opened the door as Stephen's – and Davey's – housekeeper. She recognized him too, of course. He saw her eyes widen and take in his face, his clothes, the sword he wore at his side.

Luke said, 'I wish to speak to Christie Forster. Or to Stephen.'

The woman still stared at him. Then she opened the door a little further, and beckoned him in. 'I'll fetch Mistress, Master Lucas,' she said, and disappeared upstairs.

At first, he did not want to look round the room he had once known so well, but his eyes grew accustomed quickly to the dim light, and he could not help but see that it was all unchanged. Stephen had done nothing to alter the Great Hall since Davey and Grace's time. The same tapestries, the same furniture: he almost thought the burning logs in the fire untouched, faery wood, frozen in time. A little of the tension began to relax from Luke's shoulders, a little of the nightmare of the past fortnight to recede.

But it was not Christie who greeted him, but Arbel. Luke heard the movement from the top of the stairs, and his eyes jerked upwards to the small, pale figure slowly descending the staircase. The rush of emotion was almost uncontainable: fear, regret, pity. Then he was halfway up the stairs, and had taken her arm to help her halting progress.

He did not think, as he drew up a chair for her, that she recognized him. Arbel smiled vaguely as though he was anybody. She seemed to have no recollection of that night in the Blink Bonny Inn. Luke knew that Arbel was with child: her bright yellow gown was unlaced, and her tiny frame was not one to disguise pregnancy easily. He knew also that she was very ill.

'Arbel.' Luke knelt in front of her, waiting until she finally focused on him. 'Is Christie here?'

He waited, unbearably, for her answer. Arbel smiled, a little life returning to the great grey eyes. 'She *was* here,' she said. 'She came back.'

The smile altered to a frown, and Arbel moved restlessly in the chair. 'She's gone again, though. She went this morning. With Stephen.'

He felt his heart pause, and then, unwillingly, begin to beat again. He made his voice stay gentle. 'Where have they gone, Arbel?'

She shook her head. Strands of blonde hair fell over her confused eyes. 'I can't remember. Christie told me, but I can't remember. I'm too tired.'

Luke took her hands in his. Her skin was hot and puffy, he could not feel the fragile bones. It angered him to think that Stephen had taken a bare four months to crush the life from this exquisite, doomed creature. She had seemed wholly made of light, once.

'Try to remember, Arbel,' he said, patiently. 'It's very important.' And then, when she did not reply, he used his final card.

'Christie may be in danger,' he said. 'I believe that Stephen means her harm.'

He saw no surprise in the shadowed, hungry eyes. Only, with a growing respect, he recognized the dark candle-flame of hatred. 'He killed Dowzabel!' Arbel hissed, her swollen fingers knotting together. 'You mustn't let him hurt Christie.'

'I won't. But you must tell me where they've gone, Arbel.'

Her brow creased, and her head bowed a little. 'Adderstone,' she said, at last. 'They've gone to see Aunt Margaret.'

Luke saw that Arbel's eyes had half-closed, that she seemed exhausted with the effort of speech. Draping her shawl back over her thin shoulders, he rose and ran to the stairs, and called the housekeeper's name, his voice echoing through all the vast dark rooms of Black Law.

EITHER they travelled a quicker way, or Christie, who had

rarely made the journey, had misremembered the route from Black Law to Adderstone.

She had followed Stephen up into the hills, to where the ponies' hooves made deep pits in the smooth snow. A kestrel flew overhead, a soaring black arc in a featureless sky; ravens huddled together beneath the crags. Black Law itself was no longer visible, curtained by the rise and fall of the hills. The sky, steel-grey and ominous, closed in, welding to the horizon.

The worsening weather, and the constant effort involved in riding such country, failed to take Christie's mind off other, darker matters. There was, she had found, no comfortable place for her thoughts when the safety of the two people she loved most in the world was threatened. Christie's mind jerked anxiously from Arbel to Luke, Luke to Arbel, finding little solace. Aunt Margaret would surely do what she could for Arbel, but what could anyone do for Luke? Thoughts of Luke were a constant ache for which there was no remedy. Her mind sought for solutions constantly, whirling around like a trapped bird in a cage. She thought of him all the time, but every thought was unprofitable, terrifying, a beating of wings against immovable bars. Only Christie's concern for Arbel had provided some distraction from that other unbearable misery. Sarah Kemp had promised to write and tell her any news, but there had, of course, been no letter yet. There might be no letter for weeks.

They were still climbing, heading deeper into the hills. Christie's reins oozed water, and where the folds of her skirts showed beneath her cloak, dampness had darkened the bright colour. The snow, contrary to Stephen's expectations, was still falling. Mist veiled the hills like gauze, but Christie could still see Stephen ahead, his scarlet cloak spread over his horse's rump. Every now and then he glanced back at her, yet he had not spoken to her since they had left Black Law. He had taken no servants, which had surprised Christie, but she had not questioned him. She could never have imagined questioning Stephen Ridley about anything.

Christie knew, with disquiet, that they were not travelling in the right direction. She knew now that she had inherited her sense of direction from her father, that it was Davey, the Borderer, who had given her the ability to tell north from south, to find her way through the hills and marshes of the Cheviots. And it did not seem to Christie now that Stephen Ridley was leading her to Adderstone. They were heading north-west, not north-east; into the hills, not towards the coast.

Yet she shrank from speaking to that cold, daunting figure ahead of her. Bowing her head against the vile weather, it seemed to Christie that the only colour in the entire landscape was the square of trailing scarlet that she was bound to follow. She told herself that Stephen, like every one of his neighbours, knew the hills and valleys of the Middle Marches; that he, too, would have followed hot trod and cold, fetching cattle and horses back from across the Border. That surely she must be mistaken.

Yet she knew, in her heart, that she was not. A new fear began to gather inside her, a fear that had first flickered coldly to life in Hexham, when she had looked up to see the naked hatred in Stephen Ridley's eyes. What if, thought Christie, beginning to shiver with a different sort of chill. What if –

She did not know that she had reined in her horse until Stephen turned, no longer hearing her horse's hooves in the silence. He rode back to her side, and took her reins in his hand, and she knew then that she had no need to speak, that her face said everything for her.

'Why do you stop, *niece*?' said Stephen Ridley, softly. 'We are not yet there.'

'*Where?*' She could hardly speak; she could read his intention in his eyes.

'Catcleugh. You are riding to visit your husband. But the weather is poor, and you are in a strange country and will lose your way. Don't you think?'

Stephen was staring at her: Christie could see the triumph beginning to etch itself on that smooth, handsome face. She shook her head.

'I never lose my way. And Luke is in the Tower of London.'

'Alas, that is no longer true. The fools saw fit to release him. He was seen in Hexham early this morning. Thus the urgency of our little trip.'

Still holding Christie's reins, Stephen spurred his horse forward. The hills and the snow had become a cage, sealing off the rest of the world. 'You should have been a better liar, my dear,' called Stephen Ridley through the patter of hooves and the soft whisper of the snow. 'Like your father.'

ANOTHER desperate journey, another threshold he had never expected to cross again.

It took Luke just over an hour to ride the twenty miles from Black Law to Adderstone, just over an hour to find no trace of Christie or Stephen. At first, Adderstone's courtyard seemed to be empty, but then he heard, through the silence of the snow, the clacking of geese, and a woman's voice. Margaret's voice.

One of the geese, hissing like a holed barrel, made a bid for liberty as Luke pushed open the gate. White feathers, almost indistinguishable from the snowflakes, clouded the courtyard. Children slithered on the cobbles, seizing handfuls of goose feathers and stuffing them into sacks. Margaret, her brow creased in a frown of irritation, pointed Tom Dodd in the direction of the gate.

Her hand, though, outstretched, froze in mid-air, and then dropped slowly down. Luke, clicking his teeth gently to his horse, rode across the courtyard towards her.

He did not dismount. Margaret's head, hair crammed severely under a cap, was roughly level with the top of Luke's boots. The shock in her eyes chilled to aversion.

He had not ridden to Adderstone, though, to make amends for past errors, supposed or deliberate. 'I'm looking for Christie and Stephen,' he said. 'Are they here?'

He saw, his heart thudding, that bewilderment had replaced some of the hostility.

'Stephen is at Black Law,' said Margaret. Adding pointedly, 'I thought Christie was with you, Lucas.'

'She was.' His hands tightened on the reins. 'She returned to Black Law a few days ago, to look after Arbel. Neither of them are there now – Arbel told me that they had ridden here, to see you.'

A single white feather, jaunty and curling, danced on the

edge of Margaret's head-dress. 'Then they are delayed, perhaps.' Margaret's voice was as cold as the snow that drifted alongside Adderstone Tower. 'Stephen will look after Christie. He means her no harm.'

'He means her every harm!' The words were out before Luke could stop them; he had already wheeled his horse around to ride from Adderstone. 'If Christie comes to you, then keep her here, Margaret, by your side. Do that for Davey's sake, not mine.'

He left Margaret standing in the courtyard, feathers fluttering from her loose hands.

Rob was standing behind her.

LUKE was alive, Luke was free, Luke was no longer under sentence of a traitor's death. Husband or half-brother, he was alive. Ridiculously, Christie felt happy.

She and Stephen travelled towards Catcleugh, their pace doubled, Christie holding on to the saddlebow for support, the horses lurching and bouncing on the rough ground. It was hard to breathe: the great gulps of cold air that Christie did manage to take in seemed to give her no strength. Once, on a former ride to Catcleugh, she had found the hills themselves threatening, but now that threat had a focus, a point of origin, in the tall, golden-haired man riding by her side. Indeed, the hills offered sanctuary, perhaps, a place of hiding. Improbable ideas of escape flickered rapidly through Christie's mind, unlikely butterflies that died as soon as they left the chrysalis. Stephen's gauntleted hand gripped her reins like a hangman's noose, Stephen's expression was fixed with all the fervour of half a lifetime's obsession.

Knife, pistol or sword. Which would he use? All would leave their mark, all would lead to questions, investigations. The murder of a young girl alone in the hills was not so commonplace a thing as cattle-rustling or horse-theft. Stephen did not appear to carry a pistol, but Christie could see the sword gleaming wickedly at his side, and she recalled the knife that he always carried in his belt. She, too, had a knife, tucked into the capacious sleeve of her gown. Arbel had given her that knife, to defend herself against pirates. Arbel's husband had proved a greater enemy than any marauding pirate. Carefully, Christie slid the tiny penknife out of her sleeve, and clutched it inside the palm of her glove.

Yet she saw, when finally the sickening pace slowed, that Stephen would have no need of weapons. They were nearing a precipice: black, jagged spears of rock reared out of the snow. Stephen turned and spoke.

'You were visiting your husband, and you lost your way. Such treacherous hills in the winter, don't you think?'

Christie's mind cast about frantically, clutching at useless, fragile straws.

'Arbel knows that we left Black Law together.'

She knew his answer before he made it. 'Who will believe Arbel?' said Stephen Ridley, coolly. 'She is mad, and she is a liar. You, more than most, will know that.'

One of Christie's hands clutched the penknife, the other still gripped the saddlebow. Her eyes focused on the dreadful blackness ahead.

She found her voice at last. 'How did you know?'

'Davey.' said Stephen. 'He told me himself a few weeks before he died. He said that he had married a Frenchwoman, by whom he had had a legitimate heir – a daughter – who was safely out of the way, where no one but he could find her. He had lost his temper, you see. I guessed who you were as soon as Rob Forster told me Anne had adopted a daughter. Davey was a fool, as well as a liar and a libertine. I believe he had actually considered bringing you to Black Law, but even he saw that was impossible. So we were forced to endure the gypsy's get instead. As a salve to what was left of Davey's conscience.'

'Perhaps Davey pitied Luke,' whispered Christie. 'Perhaps he loved him.'

'Love?' Stephen laughed, drawing up his mouth around his teeth, flinging his head back. 'What has love to do with any of this? Lust and property, my dear, those are the forces that drive people like Davey.'

'And you?' Even in the silence of the hills, her voice was hardly audible. 'You are worse than any of them. You destroy anything that you touch. You intend to destroy me now, and you are destroying Arbel. No doubt you tried to destroy Luke, but he was too strong for you. Did you –' a new thought crossed Christie's mind '– did you kill Davey?'

Stephen shook his head. The snow had darkened his hair; for the first time Christie saw the beginnings of age loosening his fair, opaque skin.

'The Laidlaws did the job for me. Although – I was, sadly, delayed somewhat in going to his defence.'

Christie hated Stephen Ridley with a hatred that burned pure and cold. Inside the palm of her glove, the hilt of the knife slipped and slithered against her damp skin. 'But you loved Grace,' she said, flatly.

'Grace was everything a woman should be.' Stephen's brow creased, his eyes darkened. 'She was too good. She was taken in by Davey – and the bastard.'

Again, that rush of almost uncontrollable hatred.

'Davey was your brother,' said Christie, coldly. 'And Lucas has a *name*.'

The ghost of a smile travelled fleetingly across Stephen Ridley's pale face. 'Not his own, my dear Mistress Ridley. Not his own.'

Under the cover of her cloak, Christie had pulled off her glove. The knife was balanced in her hand; a short blade, but deep enough to kill. The mist had closed in, almost blocking that dreadful precipice from view, snowflakes floating like tiny spectres in the greyness. In one clumsy, achingly slow movement, Christie slithered from the saddle to the ground.

She began to run away from the precipice, but it was as though she was in a dream. The cold, the snow, her own voluminous skirts, hampered her. She stumbled once, the knife in her bare hand digging into the snow and rough grass, her ankle twisting painfully as she slipped. 'Bitch!' called Stephen, from somewhere close behind her, following it with a different, coarser word.

She pulled herself to her feet, gathering up her gown in her free hand. Something held her back: she saw that Stephen's fingers, ringed with gold, clutched at the hem of her gown. Not

326

letting herself think, Christie drove the knife downwards, puncturing the back of his hand. She heard his scream, but she was free, and running down the hillside. She thought she could see ghosts coming towards her out of the mist, but they were rocks, surely, jutting like teeth out of the hazy ground. Stephen was still behind her, taller, stronger, with a man's advantages of breeches and boots . . .

Her breath came in great, painful sobs, and her chest felt as though it would burst. The thin sole of her shoe slipped on an icy stone, and Christie felt the knife fly from her hand, and herself falling, just as Stephen had intended. Then she felt his body against hers, and his hands grasping her, forcing her to her knees. 'Whore,' hissed Stephen Ridley, and struck her with the flat of his unwounded hand across her face. Pulling Christie to her feet, he began to drag her up the hillside.

Stephen's fingers clutched her, his breath was hot against her neck. The blow had stunned her, the fall had knocked the remaining breath from her body. The grey ghosts seemed to have come closer. The greyness had become patterned with black stars. She recognized a familiar sound: the whistle of an arrow.

LUKE had ridden to Catcleugh in the hope of finding the gypsy.

He knew that he was being followed as he rode up Yeavering Bell, and across White Law. He knew also who followed him, and that Rob must wait. Christie was all that mattered now. Bent over the mane, Luke galloped his mare for Catcleugh.

The horse was tiring, though. He had ridden from Hexham to Black Law to Adderstone. He heard the hooves behind him drawing ever closer, and he spurred his own horse through the mist and snow towards the low black outline of Catcleugh.

But with increasing certainty Luke realized that this was one race he would not win. Glancing back over his shoulder, he could clearly see Rob, bloody vengeance written on his face and carried in his hand, choosing, as always, the most inconvenient time to pick up the lingering traces of the family feud. Rob rode a bay that seemed equal to the Trotters' chestnut, or

Rob's own lamented black. Sometimes Luke regretted having taken the black gelding: that horse's price seemed to have magnified over the months.

He saw Rob pass him, a flicker of black against a blanched sky, and he knew what Rob intended to do. He would cut him off at the mouth of the valley, the single opening that allowed easy access to Catcleugh. Catcleugh's strength, soon to be his own downfall. Luke reined in his horse, and he saw that Rob, ahead, had done likewise, and that he was darkly framed against the bleached landscape, his sword already in his hand.

A snow-covered chessboard of clammy moss and scrub spanned the distance between them. Luke's hand did not yet touch his sword. Rob's bay was stepping delicately through the moss, avoiding the acid-green swatches of treacherous ground, and the brackish pools of water, crusted with ice, that showed through the snow. Tiny flakes of snow settled on Rob's dark hair.

In what sometimes seemed like a lifetime of artifice, it was an effort to be plain-spoken, placatory. But Luke tried.

'It's damned cold out here, Rob. If you've something to say to me, you'd better say it at Catcleugh, in comfort.'

Propitiation failed. Rob edged a little closer. 'I'm not here for your comfort, Luke. I'm here to settle a few outstanding debts. And don't think of reaching Catcleugh, either. No doubt you've half a dozen Lovells hidden there, all nice and eager to come to their brother's aid.'

He was within a couple of yards of Luke now, the moss and streams behind him. The fitful breeze caught and pulled at Rob's hair, his horse moved nervously. 'Draw your sword, Luke,' said Rob Forster.

'Let me through, Rob.' One of Luke's hands held the reins, the other, loosely fisted, waited. He kept his voice and eyes steady. They had shared something once, he and Rob: family, horses, and hills, but now Luke could feel all the avenues and byways of the last months – years – channelling inevitably to this.

'But you will fight me.' The white afternoon light increased the pallor of Rob's skin, emphasizing the blueness of his eyes. 'You're not afraid of me, like you are of Stephen.'

Stephen. My God. 'I'll fight you any time you wish, Rob. But not here, not now. Name the time and the place, and I'll give you my word that I'll be there.'

'Your word? An unreliable commodity, don't you think, Luke?'

Luke's eyes measured the distance between himself and Rob, assessed the steep rise of the valley to either side.

'You'll fight me *now*,' added Rob, coldly. 'Not tomorrow, not in a week's time. Because of Christie. She was in our care, and you raped her.'

An ugly word, as cold and cruel as the landscape. Again, that awful squeezing of the heart as he recalled Paris, the silk shawl baring Christie's rounded, freckled shoulders as it slithered to the floor.

'Let me through, Rob.'

Rob let his breath out in a hiss. 'It's all so easy for you, isn't it, Luke? You entice a girl to your house, force her through some travesty of a marriage ceremony, and then return the damaged goods to her home the following day. Then you decide you'd like a little company on your trip abroad. Have you tired of Christie, now, Luke? Did you leave her in France?'

'Christie is here,' said Luke. 'Christie returned to Black Law to be with Arbel. I'm trying to find her.'

'Are you cold at night?' Rob's sword danced a little, then stilled. 'Why not leave the poor girl at Black Law, if Stephen's good enough to take her in?'

The gathering wind picked up Rob's words, whirling them in twists and eddies, and returning them, unimproved, to Luke's ears. He could feel time slipping through his fingers like sand. He could hear desperation in his own voice.

'Christie isn't safe with Stephen.'

He heard Rob's curse. There was a flare of dull metal, and Rob's sword jabbed at the quilted broadcloth of Luke's doublet. Something began to stain the cloth, darkening the frayed, faded black. Luke's own sword had already slid from the scabbard: he wheeled his horse round to the side. The swords met, high in the cold air, the clash of steel against steel breaking the silence of the valley, making yet another battleground of the familiar battleground of the Borders. Luke slit through the ties of his saddlebags with his knife. If he could unhorse Rob, then he might still get through to Catcleugh, and be free of this fatal fiasco. *If* he could unhorse Rob. For Rob was good, damn him. And as at Berwick, Rob wanted to win.

The scree, the moss, the stubborn angle of the hillside, were all potential snares. Rob's darting sword pushed Luke back against the flurry of stones and snow that pasted the hillside, where a horse might lose its footing, sending its rider swordless to the grass below. Rob's right arm moved like a scythe through the icy air, and he guided his horse as though it were part of him. Luke parried the sword over and over again, spurring his horse along the thin line between the silver blade and the hill's edge, aware that the stones were wet with snow and the ground turned to glass with cold. He needed time, he needed breath enough to tell Rob Forster the unbelievable truth.

Rob had swung back his sword: Luke ducked, expecting to hear the swinging whirr of the blade through the frosty air. But there was nothing: only a sudden jerk as his horse's head was pulled round.

Rob's sword had dropped, his hand held Luke's bridle.

'*Fight*,' said Rob Forster, softly. 'I told you to *fight*. If you baulk at drawing blood, cousin, then I would recommend you start absolving yourself of your sins now. Though that might take a while, mightn't it, Luke?'

'Christie.' It was difficult to speak, the words were taut and painful. 'Christie is Davey's legitimate daughter. She found that out in Paris. Black Law is Christie's, and because of that Stephen means to kill her. For God's sake, let me through, Rob.'

There was no understanding, only another flare of anger. Rob had a Ridley's looks and a Forster's temperament. 'Damn you,' said Rob Forster. 'Damn you and your lies to hell, and *listen*. I intend to kill you, whether or not you defend yourself, whether or not you aim one good swordthrust in my direction. Here, let me show you.'

Rob's sword clattered back into his scabbard, and his hands

lunged for Luke's collar. Luke felt his balance go, and heard his sword fall to the scree as he was dragged from the saddle by Rob's weight. Then they were rolling down the last few feet of hillside to the bottom of the valley, and Rob's fists were pummelling Luke's face, over and over again, just as he had at Berwick.

Or almost. For when he opened his eyes, Luke saw that it was not quite as at Berwick Fair, but that Rob held a dagger in his hand, and the dagger was plunging downwards to his chest. He had time only to twist sideways, to see the tip of the dagger scrape and skate in the stony earth, and then his own sword was in his hand again, and he had found his feet. There were no rules, suddenly, and no more holding back: too much depended on the outcome of this dogfight. He did not wish to die, here and now, on a cold Northumbrian hillside, within sight of the Border he had so lovingly violated, within earshot of the land he learned to call home. If he died, so did Christie. If she were not already dead . . .

The horses had ambled over to the far side of the valley, avoiding the follies of their masters. Rob swung his sword up in a wide arc: there was no sun to touch the blade with light, only the fast deadly path of the blade, the necessity to evade, to parry, to capitalize on any small errors. But Rob was making no mistakes: his face was a grinning, distorted mask, his hair damp with sweat and snow, his features blurred by the same mist that dewed Luke's own lashes, that ran from his own forehead.

'Nice Luke – clever Luke –' Rob's words made white clouds in the chill air '– you're fighting now, aren't you, you bastard? There. *Bastard.* Never could get used to that, could you? That's why you hate Stephen – that's why you slander him. Can't fight Stephen, can you, Luke? I saw you at Wark – remember? Couldn't even speak to Stephen. Because he's stronger than you.' Rob's sword jabbed at Luke's ribs, ripping through layers of doublet and jack. 'Better than you. Compared to Stephen, you're nothing.'

Bow, wow, wow. Whose dog art thou? . . . If only he was not so damned tired. Christie's best hope, his own best hope, was to

331

disable Rob as quickly as possible. Luke's sword sliced through the air, meeting resistance, flesh, blood, bone. Rob glanced rapidly down at his shoulder, his features registering surprise for a moment, then pleasure.

'Now you *are* fighting, cousin. Only a scratch, but it shows you'll dance when I call. Think of Black Law, Luke. Think of all those acres of good land, and think of yourself, living like any broken man or outlaw. Think that Stephen will be able to give his son his own name. He's married now – you did know that, didn't you, Luke? To Arbel.' Rob's mouth twisted in a grin, blood stained his sleeve. 'You had your tawdry eyes on her as well, didn't you? But Arbel would have nothing to do with filth like you –'

I've come to seek the former vows you granted me before . . . Rob's blade almost found him, and Luke stumbled backwards in the snow, his feet sliding beneath him, his muscles jarred and his fingers dead with the impetus of sword on sword. Arbel and Stephen . . . a marriage made in hell . . .

The ground was a fatal combination of snow, marsh and stone, but he had found his feet again. Luke knew that cold and exhaustion would soon begin to dull the muscles in his legs and shoulders, worse, to take the edge from his concentration. Oh God, let Rob fall, let him slip and lie long enough for me to reach my horse and Catcleugh and Christie –

Rob was forcing him backwards towards the stream that threaded the centre of the valley, towards the treacherous sand and rocks, away from the comparative security of grass and snow. Rob used his sword like a lance, flicking, prodding, forcing Luke into a corner he did not wish to occupy. He'd trip, fall, and Rob would have him, a knife through his back or his heart, sprawled on the cold earth. Like Davey. He'd seen Davey, at the foot of Black Law's tower, dying fingers scrabbling at the pebbles, something scarlet running from the arrow wound in his neck . . .

Luke felt his heel begin to slip on the edge of the bank. The bank was less than a foot high, the stream only a few inches deep, but then he was not likely to die of drowning. His limbs felt like lead, as though he were already moving through water; his mind, usually so clear, had become a chaotic jumble of images past and present. In the flick of an eyelid, he lost Rob, and misreading his intention, let his guard fall. Luke saw the blow coming from his left, the movement unnaturally slowed, like a dumbshow, and he knew he could do nothing to stop it. He could only throw his body aside, using what remaining strength he had, and wait, his mind, if nothing else, prepared for the agony.

But it was the sensation of falling that he felt first. Slipping, sliding, over the rim of the bank, his body twisting like a fish. Then: coldness, the coldness of the icy water on his face, his hands, his side, and a much greater, intolerable coldness in his thigh as Rob's sword found its mark.

He knew that he screamed; the sound seemed to echo all round the hillsides.

When Luke opened his eyes, he saw that the blade of Rob's sword was scarlet, and that his own leg, from thigh to ankle, was scarlet too. Rob's sword had dropped, there were two trails of red in the water. Rob was not looking at him; his eyes focused, dazed, were on the hills.

Luke's leg did not hurt, it simply did not belong to him. He heard Rob say stupidly, 'Luke –' and he saw him raise his right arm.

But though he waited, free of fear or pain, for the final blow, the sword did not fall. Instead, Rob Forster's father's sword spun high in the air, a grey, hypnotic succession of arcs and whorls, until it fell, noiselessly, on the heathered slopes of the Cheviots.

'No,' said Rob Forster, dully, as he turned away. 'You're not worth it, are you, Luke?'

Christie, he wanted to say, *Christie*. At first, he could not speak, and when he finally pronounced the name it was like a lament. Hatred simmered on the Borders like rich, fermenting wine, hatred of English for Scots, Scots for English, Elliot for Armstrong, Forster for Ridley. The Forsters and the Ridleys had fought for years, stealing each other's sheep and cattle, burning towers and bastle-houses, cutting down fathers and sons. A blood feud was an inexhaustible chain of love and hate, reeled in over months, years, generations. Davey Ridley, a man of magnificent gifts and equally magnificent faults, had broken the chain, severing the links by the marriage of his sister to Richard Forster.

But peace had been precarious, embattled with history and old resentments. When Luke opened his eyes, he saw that the snow on the river-bank was pink, not white, and that blurred shapes moved towards him from out of the thinning mist. It was cold, so cold. He had not meant it to be cold. He had not meant any of this.

The blurred forms shapeshifted into Randal Lovell and his brothers. 'You daft bugger, you should have seen that last one,' said Randal, kindly, as he crouched by Luke's side.

ROB, at first, did not know where he was riding. He had mounted his horse and cantered away through the snow, registering, yet hardly seeing, the gypsy. Luke's dark twin, Luke's brother. Rob tried not to be sick. He had killed often enough before, but to kill someone whom he had, in spite of everything, always regarded as family . . . his hands, gripping the reins, shook, and his scalp crawled with sweat.

For he knew that Luke might die. He had seen the light fade in those blue familiar eyes. Catherine's eyes. And he had heard the voice mutter that one word, and then fall silent again.

Christie. There had been fear in that single word, but not, Rob thought, fear of his own sword. Luke had been beyond that sort of fear. And, try as he might to convince himself otherwise, Rob had recognized another, unexpected emotion.

Love. He had not thought his cousin prey to love. *Christie is Davey's legitimate daughter*, Luke had said, and the story had been so preposterous, Rob had not even paused to consider it. And yet –

If Luke had been going to lie, then surely he would have lied better than that. Luke was inventive enough, ordinarily. Was it possible that he had spoken the truth?

And Rob remembered, as the ice in his soul cracked and splintered, what Luke had said next.

Stephen means to kill her.

Rob Forster spurred his horse for Black Law.

ARBEL was alone at Black Law. The housekeeper was dealing with some tedious tradesman, the other servants were busy in the kitchens. Dowzabel was buried in a corner of the garden – Arbel remembered digging up the hard earth with a stick – and Stephen had taken Christie away. She was alone now, and she had never liked to be alone. The walls and ceilings of the Ridleys' castle seemed to bear down on Arbel, so that she could hardly breathe. Sitting at the window in her bedchamber, her hands, knotting at her loose hair, had grown white with the cold. She hated to be cold, and she hated to be alone.

Most of all, Arbel hated Stephen. Stephen had taken Christie away, and Lucas had said that he meant her harm. She believed Lucas, they had once enjoyed themselves together. And she had seen what Stephen had done to Dowzabel. Arbel bit her nails and thought of Stephen's knife drawing a red line across Christie's throat.

She knew then what she must do. It was hard even to stand, and she had to ignore the flashing lights that increasingly obstructed her vision, but she rose from the seat and went over to the bed. Stephen would pay for hurting Dowzabel, and he would pay for hurting Christie, whom Arbel loved most in the world. Things made no sense without Christie. Arbel began to drag the sheets and coverlet off the bed.

By the time she had finished she was terribly tired, and her hands and feet were so swollen she could hardly move. In the room with the ship clock, Arbel knelt in front of the fire. Quilts, hangings, sheets and rugs were piled around her. She had gathered all the books that Black Law possessed, and torn the pages out and scattered them around the room. Arbel felt no sorrow as she took the tongs and lifted the first burning coal from the fire. She only felt terribly tired, and glad that Stephen would see his house burned to the ground.

She had meant to go outside, and watch it from the gardens. But she did not have the strength even to walk to the door, and besides, it was very cold outside. Huddled in the window-seat, Arbel watched the fire take hold.

At first, the dry fabrics and paper merely scorched. Then the flames began to crackle, and then to devour everything that was Stephen's, turning all the rich, beautiful silks and satins to ash. The rising flames glowed the most glorious colours: scarlet, carmine, gold and amethyst, outdoing the shades of the silk. Even the smoke was beautiful: winding wraiths climbed to the painted ceiling, turning and twisting like dancers. Arbel felt warm at last, and her shawl slipped to the floor. Then her eyes slowly closed, and her head lolled against the stone, and she slept.

EVEN though he had ridden like a fury from Catcleugh to Black Law, Rob Forster, looking down the valley, knew that he was too late. He still galloped forward, though, pushing his lathered, exhausted horse to its limits, his eyes fixed on that beacon of awful light.

When he reached Black Law, he fought through the mêlée of servants in the courtyard to reach the great front door. There was no fair, exquisite head in the courtyard, and he heard the same name on every despairing tongue. His own voice called her name: not once, as Lucas had called for Christie, but over and over again. Arbel's name resounded against the Tower, against the great dying heap of Black Law Castle. Rob's fingers pulled at tumbling burning wood, and the tears that streamed down his face blinded him. But the fire had gripped the entire edifice, and as he choked and retched in the smoke, he saw through the haze the initials, Davey's and Grace's, carved above the doorway.

Chapter Eighteen

WHEN Christie opened her eyes, she found herself not at the foot of the precipice, but lying on the thin snow blanketing the edge.

She was only a few feet from the drop. The dreadful grey abyss floated before her, falling endlessly into the mist: Christie choked, and tried to sit up.

She heard a voice say, 'Miss Forster?', and she turned, fear catching again at her throat, half expecting to see Stephen's smooth blond face. But instead it was a stranger whom she saw crouching beside her: dark-skinned, his knotted hair dewed with mist, his clothing ragged layers of once gaudy doublet, shirt and jacket.

'Mr Lovell?' said Christie, uncertainly.

'Johnnie Lovell.' The gypsy gave her his hand, and she scrambled unsteadily to her feet. 'Randal's over there.'

She turned, and saw Randal Lovell, kneeling in the snow. The dizziness threatened to overwhelm her again when she saw what Randal knelt beside: Stephen Ridley, an arrow protruding from his back, his body cast like some vast, limp starfish on a whitened strand.

'Leave the arrow,' called Johnnie, handing Christie a small flask. 'There's no mark.'

Randal nodded, and Christie, her hands shaking, unstoppered the bottle.

The aqua vitae eased the shivering, and she managed to say, 'Luke. Have you seen him?'

Johnnie shook his dark, tangled head.

Randall Lovell, rising, said, 'Luke'll like as not make for Catcleugh. But let Johnnie take you back to your auntie now, mistress.'

Another gypsy was leading her pony up the incline. She was

337

bundled into the saddle: the mist had begun to thin to the east, the hills to pleat themselves against a steel-grey sky. Randal Lovell had already ridden away.

She wanted to say, as they rode down the hillside, that they should go to Black Law, not Adderstone, to Arbel, not to Margaret. But she could not speak. Christie shut her eyes tightly, but the tears ran down her face, and all she could see was Stephen Ridley, her father's brother, sprawled in the bloodied snow.

By the time they reached Adderstone, the light had died, and there was only the moon to pick out the uncompromising lines of the Tower.

Richie Forster and an assortment of servants spilled out of Adderstone Tower into the courtyard as Johnnie Lovell helped Christie dismount from her horse. Then the doorway of the manor house opened, and Christie saw Margaret.

Margaret's gaze flicked rapidly from Christie to the gypsy. 'Christie . . . Lucas said –'

She did not finish the sentence. Margaret walked a little way out of the doorway, but Christie did not go to meet her, did not attempt to cross the threshold. Stephen had been Margaret Forster's brother.

'Stephen is dead,' said Christie.

Richie's sword was in his hand. She heard him say, softly, 'Luke –', and she shook her head.

'Not Luke. I haven't seen Luke. One of the gypsies killed Stephen because he was going to kill me.'

Oddly, there was little surprise on Margaret's face. Christie found that her hands were clenched into fists, and that she could not keep the anger from her voice.

'Luke. Where is he? Is he here?' Christie glanced desperately, foolishly, back to the gate, and then towards Adderstone's door and the blank, cold windows. Margaret walked a little further into the courtyard.

'He was here. He was looking for you.' Margaret's voice was dazed, unsteady. She sounded old. The light from the candle deepened the lines on her face, and picked out the bands of grey in her hair.

'He told the truth, then.' Margaret was staring at Christie. 'Lucas said that Stephen meant you harm. *Why*, Christie?'

'Because I am Davey's legitimate daughter. I found that out in Paris. He married my mother secretly in France. He was never truly wed to Grace Collingwood.'

She did not soften her words, because she meant, perhaps, to hurt. Margaret's beloved Davey had begun all this, had led her to that cold, lonely hillside, had branded her a bastard and deprived her of her inheritance.

She heard Richie's muttered profanity, and saw, clear in the pale light, Margaret's tortured face. There was a grating noise as Richie's sword was returned to its scabbard.

Rob arrived back at Adderstone halfway through the night. By then Richie had left the house to ride first for Catcleugh, and then for Black Law. Christie slept, having been given something strong and soporific by Margaret.

Margaret, though, did not even attempt to sleep. In the parlour she waited, sewing in hand, her needle idle. She thought without cease of Davey and Stephen, her brothers. Stephen, child of her mother's old age had, knowing his own claim to Black Law to be invalid, tried to kill Davey's daughter. Margaret knew, had always known, what Black Law meant to Stephen, but that he should kill for it –

But why not? she thought, dully. The needle was lost in the rushes, the thread was a tangled, dirty ball. Every Borderer killed for his land, because land and name were security, the difference between an empty plate and a full one. Stephen had simply tried to kill to ensure his own survival. To kill an innocent, yes, but innocence died often here. It was Davey's duplicity, she found, that hurt her most. Davey, her beloved Davey, had lied, even to her. She had given herself to a stranger, an adversary, at Davey's bidding, and yet Davey himself had not made that sacrifice. Davey had married Grace Collingwood for her money, Louise Girouard for love. She did not think she could bear that betrayal.

She heard horse's hooves in the courtyard, and waited, expecting Richie. But it was not Richie who pushed open the parlour door on seeing the candlelight, but Rob.

Margaret hardly recognized him at first. Soot blackened his skin and his hair, his clothes were ripped and scorched. Rob's eyes, swollen and bloodshot, did not focus on his mother, but she recognized death in that blank, dark indigo blue.

'What is it?' She rose from the chair, cloth and thread falling unnoticed to the floor. Her voice was hoarse, the words scratching against her throat. 'Where have you been?'

Rob did not reply. He had let his cloak slip from his shoulders, and Margaret noticed that he no longer wore a sword.

'Arbel is dead,' said Rob.

Margaret stared at him. What nonsense: Arbel was not dead, it was Stephen who had died. Arbel, fragile, unpredictable Arbel, was safe at Black Law. But then, looking at Rob, she began to believe. Rob had loved Arbel Forster once. She found, with only a limited sense of shock, that her first thought was that Stephen had killed Arbel. But no: Lucas had seen Arbel alone at Black Law, and had then ridden hell for leather to Adderstone. And then she noticed anew Rob's blackened clothing, the charred fringes of his sleeves.

Tracking her gaze, Rob said dully, 'There was a fire. Black Law is razed to the ground, mother. Arbel did not get out in time. They said she was sick –'

'She was.' Margaret said, without any calculated effort to offer comfort, 'I saw her a fortnight ago – I did not think she would survive the birth of the baby.'

She moved towards him, feeling her age in the aching of her bones, the disobedience of her muscles. 'Arbel was not strong, Rob. She was like Anne . . .'

She saw his eyes shut tightly, pain hidden behind the acrid, singed brows and lashes. There had been something else in that familiar dark blue – an evasion, perhaps.

But Rob, whatever his other faults, had never lacked courage. She heard him say, 'Christie – Stephen – I don't know –'

Margaret's own heart was battering against her chest. Lucas, she thought, Lucas. Her affection for Lucas had, she supposed, been planted by Davey. Davey had loved the boy, had given him a home. She did not think she could bear any more, but she knew she must speak.

'Christie is here,' said Margaret, and Rob's lids jerked open. 'One of the Lovells killed Stephen to protect Christie. Lucas,' she added, with an effort. 'Where is Lucas? What have you done?'

Rob did not look away, did not flinch from his mother's eyes. 'Luke is lying in the valley below Catcleugh. Unless the gypsies have taken him away.'

She would have thought his voice callous if she had not known him so well. For the first time Margaret noticed the blood that streaked Rob's charred layers of clothing, the unmistakable rip of a swordcut across his shoulder. Mechanically, needful of the solace of action, Margaret went to the kitchen and found a bowl of water and cloths for bandages. In the parlour, she made Rob sit, and she helped him out of his shirt and jack. She seemed to have spent a large part of her life doing these same dreary, repetitive tasks. For her husband, her sons, her brother . . . Looking down at Rob, her favourite son, Margaret's eyes were weary, devoid of feeling.

'So you killed Lucas, Rob?'

He did not answer at first. The swordcut was superficial, the burns that blistered his hands and arms were not. 'No,' he said, eventually, and did not even wince as Margaret began to bathe the burns. 'I didn't. I don't know why. The gypsies came.'

'But you hurt him.' Margaret ripped the cloth and smeared salve on Rob's arms.

'Yes. It was – bad.'

Their eyes met again, mother's and son's. She saw the pain behind those opaque dark blue Ridley eyes. She thought: they are all that is left now, my sons. Davey, Stephen, Lucas and poor Anne's daughter Arbel, all are gone. Her hands still knew what to do even as her eyesight blurred and the tears began to trickle down her face. But still, even as she mourned, she knew in her heart that her sorrow was not only for Lucas, for Arbel. You could not lose the habit of love so easily. It was Davey whom Margaret grieved for, always Davey, for one final, most painful time.

*

NEWS filtered slowly down to London.

In Whitehall, Thomas Phelippes, bearer of both good and bad news, stood, framed by blue skies and the scent of roses, in Sir Francis Walsingham's study. He held a letter in his hand, and repeated slowly, a perceptible gleam in his eye, one sentence of that letter.

'*The chief agents of the Queen of Scots are Mr Throckmorton and Lord Henry Howard.* So writes our good Monsieur Fagot.'

The letter was placed on the desk in front of Sir Francis Walsingham.

'They are both Catholics, of course, sir. Francis Throckmorton is a foolish youth.'

'Kings have died at the hands of fools before now.' It was midday: the window was open a little, letting in the lazy birdsong and the slow early afternoon buzz of the streets. Sir Francis studied the letter in silence, squinting, as Phelippes had, at the crabbed, ugly writing.

'We will wait a while. This looks – hopeful, Thomas. Set men to watch Mr Throckmorton.'

'Sir.' The letter was returned to a drawer, and Walsingham found paper and pen, but Thomas Phelippes did not yet leave the room. 'Mr Ridley –' said Thomas, running a hand through his pale, tangled hair, and Sir Francis looked up.

'I had a letter from Sir John Forster,' said Thomas, uneasily. 'It appears that Lucas Ridley is dead. Killed in some family feud.'

For a brief moment there was silence. Then Sir Francis Walsingham said, 'A wasteful place, the Borders,' and returned to his letter, the pen scratching through the quiet of the afternoon.

THERE was a tunnel, and he was at the end of it. There was no pain in the tunnel, but if he tried to move towards the speck of light at the far end, then the black walls constricted and hurt him. It was better to stay where he was.

Only they would not leave him alone. There was Stephen, of course: Stephen's hand encircling his neck, pushing him up against the black stone wall until he could feel the sharp granite cutting his face, until he could see the chink of light between the tumbled stones. Stephen made him see things he did not want to see. Sometimes Luke saw Arbel Forster, with only her own spun silver hair for a covering, her lovely eyes sunk into her skull. Sometimes he saw Christie, her eyes closed and her skin as white as the snow that covered Catcleugh, a single thin line of red across her throat.

There was another face, one he had not seen for a very long time. He could not see her features clearly, but she had a scarf round her head like the gypsy woman, and her eyes were an intense, light blue. When eventually his eyes focused, Luke found that she had altered. There was still the scarf – a torn, tarnished, green – but her hair and eyes had changed colour, her smooth skin aged grotesquely. He tried to turn away then, twisting aside, putting his arm over his face, but they would not let him hide. Someone held his arms, someone else put a cup to his lips. *Death wine*, he heard a voice say, and he saw a witch pull a mandrake root screaming from the ground and boil it to a pulp. He tried to clench his jaw, and the voice said, *Panni, Lucas, panni.* He knew that she lied, that it was not water, but still he drank.

After he had emptied the cup, the faces went for a while. There was still the black tunnel and the white light. He knew that he could sleep now if only they left him alone. He drifted for a long while somewhere dark and dreamless, and then they began to call again. Numbers, at first, accompanied, he thought, by the distant music of a spinet. Walsingham's number codes: three for the imprisoned Scots Queen, thirty for her son, six for the Countess of Shrewsbury, her gaoler . . . What number for Davey's daughter, what for her murderer? Now there were voices, too, hands grabbing him. The weight on his leg as they dragged him along the tunnel was terrible, crushing. Two figures were waiting for him, their arms outstretched, their faces shadowed and hazy. The figures resolved themselves into Stephen and Christie: Stephen held a sword in his hand, and Christie looked like a ghost, her face white and pleading. Luke tried to run back down the tunnel, but his leg hurt too much, and his limbs moved uselessly. Someone called to him in a language he did not understand, and then another voice said his name, over and over again.

Opening his eyes, he saw Randal Lovell and old Ashena. Ashena, muttering to herself, was doing something to his leg. She wore a dirty green scarf tied round her head, and her face was seamed and lined like oak-bark.

The wagon he was lying in was covered with dark folds of cloth and branch. The light at the open end of the tunnel was the sky, blue and bright. His skin burned unbearably.

He heard Randal Lovell speak to Ashena, and the old woman answer him sharply. Usually he understood most of their language, but now it made little sense. Randal said, 'Just water, then,' and the cup was held to Luke's mouth again. He drank long and hard, and this time it was just water, nothing else. He could hear sounds from outside the wagon: horses' hooves, children crying, the rustle of the wind, all unnaturally loud. His heart hammered as though he had just run up the Cheviot, his hands had not the strength to take the cup from Lovell.

He could not form his tangled thoughts into coherent sentences. *How long* . . . he thought, and, *Why does it hurt so much* . . . and *Christie, oh God, Christie.* He began to shake, cold suddenly overlaying the heat. You couldn't feel hot and cold at the same time, that was impossible. The sky and hills began to turn a hazy pink, and then blood red. The old woman snapped at Randal again, and Randal said, 'You must keep your leg still, Luke. You're quite safe.'

Two consecutive sentences from Randal Lovell – my God, he must be sick. Luke tried to smile, but his lips were too dry and cracked. He realized that he had a fever, just as he had had at Hermitage, which was why his eyes, his bones, even his hair seemed to ache. He had no Dand's Jock and no cards to distract him this time. Randal would have cards, but Randal's cards were tarots, and Luke had no wish to see tarots. The Empress, the Fool, the Hanged Man . . . They had hanged Dand's Jock at Hermitage, and Christie had died on some silent hilltop in the Cheviots. Luke knew that it would be better to go back into the tunnel again, to hide there and never come out.

344

Ashena had finished dressing his leg. Luke closed his eyes and shut out the sky and the light.

In the end, though, he began to feel better. The past no longer dictated his dreams: instead he became increasingly aware of the sounds of the gypsy encampment – the cries of the children, the muffled tread of horses' hooves on the grass. Opening his eyes, Luke saw that it was evening, and that he was alone in the wagon.

He hauled himself into a sitting position by means of his elbows. It took him a good five minutes to recover from that, for the shaking to stop and the sweat to cool on his skin. The semi-circle of sky framed by the opening of the wagon was bronze fading to green, the hills were like burnished metal. Cautiously, Luke touched and moved his injured leg. There was a large bandage around the thigh, but, thank God, everything still seemed to work. Hearing soft footsteps, he saw Randal Lovell, silhouetted black against the dying light.

'She says you're to eat this.'

Randal held a bowl of broth in his hands. 'She', Luke knew, was old Ashena, and even Randal was afraid of Ashena.

Eating the broth was a messy, humiliating affair, dribbles of soup on the coverlet and his shirt, a rising anger at being unable to hold a spoon. He said, forcing the words out, 'Did they find Christie?'

'On Haggs Edge.' Randal put the bowl and spoon aside.

Luke, his eyes continuing to focus on the evening sky, saw nothing.

'She's at Adderstone, now. With your cousin Margaret.'

The sweat began to run from his brow and palms; his shirt was sticking to his back.

'Christie's *alive*?'

'Of course. No thanks to you. You should have kept that fool of a Forster for another time.'

'He didn't leave me much choice . . .' Luke made an effort to sit more upright: Randal had already turned away, and was scraping the mud off his boots with his knife. 'Randal. For God's sake –'

Briefly, Randal looked back at him. 'We followed them from Black Law. Stephen was going to push her over the Edge.'

'He always was an unoriginal bastard . . . You *followed* them.' The effort of thinking, Luke found, exhausted him. 'Why?'

'The archer,' said Randal, sheathing his knife. 'At Catcleugh. Remember?'

A whistle of an arrow in the darkness, Christie tumbling down stone steps to lie in a heap on the grass . . . Luke nodded.

'Our over-enthusiastic Trotter. You found out his name, then?'

Randal shook his tangled head. 'No. But I found out who he worked for.'

'Stephen –' The name was no more than a whisper.

'Johnnie killed him. It was hard to get close enough with the mist. We almost wished we'd let him live, though. Black Law is burned. His wife, poor bitch, died in it.'

He could not control the shaking, then. Images of the past, of an unseen present, forced themselves to the forefront of his mind.

'Elliots –' said Luke. 'Armstrongs –?'

Randal, climbing out of the wagon, grimaced. 'Neither. Rumour is, the poor lassie set fire to the place herself.'

JANET's baby was born on a bright June afternoon. It was a boy, another Forster to hold a sword, to carry a lance. Like all newborn babies, his face was crumpled and wise, his cry tearless and inhuman. Carefully, they called him Richard, avoiding other, more painful, family names. He had the Ridley eyes, a cool, dark blue, and a scattering of Janet's reddish hair. His tiny hands clawed at nothing, but his mouth already knew where to find comfort. Christie cradled the baby, aware of the incredible softness of his cheek against hers and the small, suckling lips that instinctively searched for food.

They had buried Stephen, and had said their prayers for Arbel. Stephen's death was generally believed to be just another casualty of the brittle politics of the Border – the Scots, perhaps, or some long-forgotten English enemy. Only the Forsters and the gypsies knew otherwise. Black Law's land would go to

Margaret, but Margaret had already drawn up the papers to make it over to Christie.

As for Luke, no one had seen or heard of Lucas Ridley since Rob had left him wounded in the valley below Catcleugh.

To everyone at Adderstone, Christie had given a carefully edited version of her stay in France. Luke's ring lay at the bottom of her chest. If she ever saw him again she would return it to him. If, by some miracle, he lived, she knew that they owed each other nothing. She might never marry again – she would not repeat Davey's mistake – but now, unusually for a woman, she had land of her own, and land meant independence. She need no longer fear the coldness of charity.

Sitting by Janet's bedside, rocking the carved wooden cradle with her foot, Christie thought of Arbel. Arbel's ghost was here sometimes: a whirl of bright fair hair, a peal of laughter. Neither Anne nor Arbel had ever been wholly of this world, they had both needed Christie to remind them to eat, to sleep, to clothe themselves. Arbel's tragedy had been inevitable the day she had married Stephen Ridley, the day she had met Luke, the day, perhaps, she had travelled to Northumberland. But Luke's death Christie did not think she could ever accept. Luke belonged to the Borders, and Christie found that it outraged her that Catcleugh should go untenanted, that she should never again hear that drawling, insulting voice on the restless wind, never again see him on horseback, clad in a reiver's garb of leather jack and steel bonnet.

It was a fortnight before Luke began to walk again, more than a month before he could ride. Even then, he tired easily: a mile, and he felt as though he had ridden twelve. News filtered intermittently back from Adderstone, from Black Law, but it all seemed irrelevant to Luke. Only the long, slow struggle to health seemed real, only the taking up and pitching of tents, the wandering through hills and valleys, following the wagons. Even the events of the past year began to fade: Hermitage, Sir Francis Walsingham, Paris, Blaise Lamarque . . .

At the beginning of June, he returned to Catcleugh. Alone, he began to repair the damage inflicted by the Trotters and six months of neglect, sweeping the old, charred straw from the byre, making good the doors and their bolts. He worked steadily, not giving in to the ache in his leg, envisaging new horses in the byre, and perhaps a few sheep on the hilltop. But there was an emptiness about Catcleugh that he had never noticed before. He had enjoyed the silence, the solitude of it all, . but now the quiet seemed to mock him, as though, for a while, he had known something better.

In the middle of June, he had a visitor. Red Archie, gangling and sandy browed, whom he had not seen since he had first married Christie Forster, rode up the valley towards Catcleugh.

'Jamie Trotter,' called Red Archie, sliding off his horse, 'is saying that you're dead.'

Luke put down the shovel he was working with, and crossed the grass to meet Archie. If he concentrated the limp hardly showed. 'Then Jamie Trotter hasn't the wit to tell the quick from the dead. Do I look like an apparition, Archie? A wraith, perhaps?'

Archie's broad face split into a grin. He looked at Luke consideringly.

'You should keep away from these foreign countries. They're bad for the health. I saw Long Martin,' went on Archie, his eyes not leaving Luke, 'in the Angel. With Willie Graham.'

Luke did not answer.

Archie said, 'Willie lost a lot of gold at the races. He never had much of an eye for a horse. He's a mite short of funds.'

'I suspect,' said Luke, thoughtfully, 'that one of Willie Graham's sources of income has recently dried up. Yes. And you, Archie?'

Archie's pony searched for clumps of grass between the heather. It was a good horse, a dark, shining red. Luke ran a hand along its neck.

'Oh, I'm well enough, Luke,' said Archie, cheerfully. 'I rode for the Greys a while back. That's how I found this mare. They lost the sheep, though.'

Luke grinned, and moved round to the horse's head. 'I'm keeping the mare,' said Archie, his gaze sliding over the grey silhouette of the pele-house. 'After all, we'll be riding again soon.'

'I'm thinking of taking up a new vocation.' Luke stooped to pull some grass. 'Something quiet, like lion-taming, or bear-baiting. Besides, it's summer.'

'So the Trotters will be off their guard.' Archie's pale eyes were bright with laughter. 'You owe them, man. And they've still got the chestnut, and Rob Forster's black –'

'Ah.' Archie's mare sucked sweet grass from Luke's flattened hand; Luke's light eyes were narrowed.

'Long Martin's fine with horses,' said Archie, persuasively. 'And Willie was always a good man in a fight. I could find the others within a week.'

The wind had picked up, rippling the heather, furling the horse's dark red mane. Luke's face was shadowed, but Archie could see the beginnings of a smile about his mouth.

'Midsummer's night, then, Archie,' he said. 'I need that black gelding.'

THEY were back across the Tweed just after midnight on Midsummer's Night, with two fine horses in tow. A crowbar to a rotting byre door, a ladder to an unglazed upper window of the appalling Trotter pele-house, and it had all been pre-dictably simple. Archie cherished the recollection of Jamie Trotter, stark naked and armed only with a candlestick, staring open-mouthed as Luke Ridley, for the second time within a year, balanced the tip of his sword upon his throat. Jamie had been in bed with his wife; they had, thought Archie happily, interrupted the Trotters' midsummer celebrations.

Even in the middle of summer, the waters of the Tweed were still cold. It was a fine, warm night, and the moon, like the finest goose quill, drew every blade of grass, every ripple of the river. Safe on the English bank of the Tweed, Archie squeezed the excess water from his breeches, and tightened the leading rein of the chestnut he led at his side. Silently, he drew a flask of aqua vitae from inside his jack, and passed it round.

When they had finished drinking, Archie said, 'Do we take

them straight to Catcleugh, or hide them at Stob's Edge for a while?'

Luke restoppered the bottle. 'The chestnut and the others go to Catcleugh. Lovell and I will take the black to Adderstone.'

Archie frowned. '*Adderstone*,' he said, but softly. Even if they were back in England, there was still the Warden, still the possibility that the Trotters might follow. 'You're not thinking of stealing the Forsters' horses? I know you owe Rob Forster one, but still –'

Luke, handing the bottle back to Archie, had already gathered his reins. 'I'm not *taking* their horses,' he said, happily. 'I'm giving one back.'

THE following morning Christie was woken by voices in the courtyard. Wrapping a shawl around her shoulders, she went to the window and looked down. She could see Rob, Richie and Mark, a lot of servants, and a black horse. Everyone was staring at the horse: Rob was fondling its pointed black ears. Still in her nightgown, Christie left her bedchamber and ran downstairs.

At first, she could not understand the fuss about a horse. She had never understood the Borderer's preoccupation with horses, but when Mark gave her an apple and a piece of loaf-sugar, she, like the others, fed the creature and patted its mane.

Mark, grinning hugely, said, 'It's Rob's gelding. The one he lost to Red Archie.'

Even then, she did not understand. 'He stole it back?' she said, stupidly.

Mark, who was now taller than Christie, found another piece of sugar for the horse. 'No. Someone brought it back last night.'

Turning away from the horse, Christie stared at Mark. His voice was a man's now, but there was still something of the boy in his blue eyes. Margaret said that he had begun to look like Davey.

'Someone brought it back . . .' she repeated, slowly.

Her heart, she found, had begun to beat very fast. Rob and Richie had come to stand beside her.

'Someone quietened the dogs,' said Richie, 'opened the gates, led in the horse and tethered it to the post. And then rebolted the gates, and left.'

She didn't need to ask who would do such a ridiculous thing. She saw the laughter, the appreciation of a good joke, in Rob's eyes.

Mark added, 'The gypsies are supposed to be good with dogs.'

And Rob said, 'Aye. He's been with his own kind, then. The Lovells will have looked after him.' He grinned. 'Cousin Luke will be filling the stables at Catcleugh again, no doubt.'

But there was no resentment in his voice. Christie, walking back to the house, began to remember what happiness felt like.

SHE rode to Catcleugh at the end of the week. Christie travelled alone, as she had done once before, but this time she felt no fear. She could smell the summer in the honey-scented heather, see it in the small puffy white clouds that trailed raggedly across the horizon. She had written her letters, packed her saddlebags, waited, as before, for the Forsters to be fully occupied before setting out, yet again, on a journey.

She did not hurry as she had a long way to go, and she must not tire her horse. She guided the mare easily along the valleys and ridges, dismounting to lead it up the steeper slopes. At the two jutting hands of rock that guarded Catcleugh, she paused, and looked.

He was outside, raking straw from the byre into a heap.

She had known that her heart would leap and dance, she had known too what his first glance would do to her. She had never thought that anything would have changed, she was not fool enough for that.

She saw Luke put aside the rake, and begin to walk across the grass towards her. The dancing of her heart stilled to a slow ache as she noticed the slight limp, carefully disguised.

'That was better,' he said. 'Quietly, and in the shadow of the hills. You'll be raiding Liddesdale next.'

She had not even meant to dismount, but she did.

Hot, Christie untied her cloak and threw it over her horse's back, where it slithered unnoticed to the ground. Luke's hand touched her elbow to steady her, and she felt the strength go from her limbs, the words dissolve to silence on her tongue.

'Rob found the horse?' he said, gently.

She could see the marks of illness that shadowed his eyes, thinned his face. 'I thought –' she began, and then stopped.

I thought you were Davey's son, she had intended to say. But she knew better now: *He's been with his own kind*, Rob had said. And Luke was not a Ridley, had never been a Ridley. The gypsies would not have cared for one who was not of their own kin.

She said, 'A little – extrovert, don't you think?'

He grinned. 'It was either that or lose at cards to him, and I was damned if I was going to do that.' He nodded towards the pele-house. 'You'll come in?'

Christie shook her head. She felt stiff with the struggle to keep control of herself. 'I'm not staying.'

The words sounded cruel. 'Ah,' he said, and let his hand slip from her elbow.

'I just came to give you back – this.' The ring, clutched in her hand the length of the journey, gleamed in the morning sun.

Luke did not take it. 'It's yours,' he said. 'Twice given. You may wear it or not, as you please.'

There was a silence.

Christie, staring at the ground, bit her lip. She heard Luke say, 'I'm sorry about Arbel.'

The ring slid from her palm to the grass, a golden circle in the shining green stems.

Christie said, jerkily, 'It was no one's fault. And Margaret said that she would not have survived the baby.'

'It was no one's fault.' She could hear the bitterness in his voice. 'It was everyone's fault. Mine, Anne's, Stephen's – even Margaret's for not keeping a closer eye on her.'

'And mine for leaving her.'

'No.' Luke glanced at Christie sharply. 'Thank God you did not stay with Arbel.'

She had not been sure until then that he had known. A little of her reason for leaving crumbled, blown away like dust.

He said, patiently, 'I went to see Lucrezia – Mouche told me where to find her. Eventually.'

The pony had moved away to crop at the grass. 'I made Blaise Lamarque promise to take Mouche as a kitchen-boy after you'd gone,' said Christie.

'Poor Blaise. A fitting punishment.' Luke's face hardly altered as he added,

'So I know that you are Davey's daughter.'

'And you don't – mind?'

'Mind?' She saw him study the thought as though for the first time. 'That you are legitimate, and I am not – that you are the child of the man who brought me up?' He shrugged. 'I've found that it doesn't much matter. No, Christie, I don't mind.'

'I do.' It was her turn to sound bitter, to turn away from him and let her gaze study the vast, beautiful land that should have been hers since birth. 'I mind very much.'

He had taken her hand in his. For comfort, she thought, nothing else. 'Davey meant no one harm,' he said, gently. 'He thought he could please everyone.'

His fingers were threaded with hers, she could feel the warmth of his body through her thin gown. 'What will you do?' she said.

'Find myself some horses. Maybe I'll become a sheep farmer –'

She had to smile at that. Luke Ridley carrying a shepherd's crook and with a straw in his mouth. 'What of your other – occupation?' she asked, delicately.

He grimaced. 'That had better remain quiescent for a while, at least. Blaise Lamarque obligingly provided the key to release me from the Tower, but I feel it would be inadvisable to return to France in the near future. Though there's always work to be had in England and Scotland.'

'Walsingham's work?' They had moved towards the edge of the hilltop: the clouds cast dark moving patches on the slopes.

He nodded. 'I find also that I am forced to choose sides. There will be war eventually, Christie, and I do not wish it to be here. We've seen enough.'

She did not know whether he referred to the Borders, or to themselves. She stood in silence for a while, watching the shifting patchwork of the hills. The Border was there, somewhere, but she could not see it. The fragile line, fought over for so many years, was indistinguishable in the bright summer's sun.

'And you?' he said, softly.

She did not look up at him. Their hands were still linked, their bodies still touched. 'Oh, I'm packed and ready to go,' she said. 'I've left a note for Margaret.'

'Another sea voyage?' he asked, mockingly.

'I don't believe I would survive it. No – I shall go to Sarah Kemp. She was a good friend. And then I shall decide what to do next.'

She managed to look at him at last. The wind, never absent at Catcleugh, ruffled his fair hair, flicking at his shirt and sleeveless doublet. 'You belong here,' he said. 'You're a Ridley.'

She shook her head. 'An unacknowledged, unclaimed Ridley. Margaret Forster and I are agreed that we must never make public Davey's marriage to my mother. I could not do it, Luke. It would inevitably raise questions about Stephen's death. And it would make a mockery of Arbel's marriage. I find that still matters.'

'You have another right to the name.'

She knew what he meant, of course. The overheated parlour in Rouen, with the Huguenot minister and the stuffed popinjays.

'Twice over,' added Luke. 'The Lovells considered the handfasting to be valid. That was why they kept an eye on you when you returned to Northumberland. They consider you to be their good-sister.'

She closed her eyes. 'It was a marriage of convenience, Luke Ridley. You said so yourself.'

'It was a marriage. It is – it is a chance to reclaim what should have been yours. Look, Christie.'

Her eyes opened; his hand steadied her shoulder. To the north lay Scotland, to the west the turbulent marches of Liddesdale and Teviotdale, to the east Adderstone and the sea. And behind them, Catcleugh. They had stood like this once before, but that had been in France, gazing down to the icy valleys of Vincennes. But now the summer's sun picked out the harebells and ragwort, and powdered the hills with purple heather.

'You don't hate it now, do you?' he said. 'You have begun to love it, as I do. Davey gave you that, just as he gave you the ability to find your way through the moss and streams. He did not leave you with nothing, Christie. And the name is yours, should you choose to use it.'

She knew that Luke was right, that she no longer hated the country she had come to only a brief year before. And yet –

'I want to choose,' she said. 'Not to be blown this way and that like some damned boat. I have money, now, and land, and I have a past. You are somewhere in that past – and in the future, perhaps – but I'm not sure yet, and I want to be sure.'

'I am sure. I love you, Christie, and I want you to stay.'

She heard the words she had never expected to hear, and she moved away from him, hugging her arms round her shoulders. An unexpected difficulty, making her pause in her resolution.

'A marriage of convenience,' she said, faintly. 'I would not hold you to it.'

She began to walk back to her horse. She noticed, for the first time, what he had done to Catcleugh, that all the signs of the Trotters' despoiling had gone. She made herself mount the horse, and it felt like an act of betrayal. He had made a home for her, and yet she did not know whether she should share it.

She did not look back as she rode away down the valley. She let the horse take her where it would, because she could not see for tears.

CATCLEUGH was empty again.

He knew now what the place lacked, and he knew that he would fill that absence. He had always got what he wanted, one way or another.

He found the ring, a circle of bright gold, knotted in a tussock of grass. And her cloak, caught on a gorse bush, flapping aimlessly in the breeze. He had tracked horses, sheep and men before: now, he had a different quarry in mind.

On horseback, pausing for a moment at the mouth of the valley, he saw her, a splash of light blue against all those quiet shades. She was not even going the right way: her sense of direction had failed her for once. She was halfway down White Law, and her horse, a sensible Forster horse, was stepping its way carefully through the mire, pausing now and then to chew the green grass.

He knew their future as well as he knew the Borders, sweet and troublesome, ranging before him. Luke Ridley clicked to his horse and started down the hillside.

Historical Epilogue

THE Guise-inspired Throckmorton Plot ended with the arrest of Francis Throckmorton in November 1583. Under torture, Throckmorton made a full confession. The plot involved the invasion of England by Spain, and the release of Mary Stuart.

The subsequent Babington Plot, nursed and abetted by Sir Francis Walsingham and Thomas Phelippes, led to the trial of Mary Stuart. In February 1587, Mary Stuart was beheaded in the Great Hall of Fotheringay Castle.

Sir Francis Walsingham died in 1590, having witnessed his country resist Spanish invasion. Sir John Forster lived on into the next century, dying, aged over a hundred, in 1602, a year before Queen Elizabeth herself died.

The death of Elizabeth I, and the succession of Mary Stuart's son James, joined the crowns of England and Scotland, and ultimately ended, after years of bloodshed, the warfare of the Borders.

Of Henri Fagot, Sir Francis Walsingham's semi-literate informer inside the French Embassy, nothing more seems to have been heard.

J. L-S 1990